Nina Milne has always ... Mills & Boon—ever sin... her mother's stacks of M... a child. On her way to this dream Nina acquired an English degree, a hero of her own, three gorgeous children and—somehow!—an accountancy qualification. She lives in Brighton and has filled her house with books—her very own *real* library.

Elle Brown is a creative polyglot. She is a romance writer, painter, digital communicator, web designer, speaker, costume maker, camp director, and pied piper. Regardless of title, the common denominator in every endeavour is that Elle is a storyteller. A Pittsburgh native and Carnegie Mellon graduate, her greatest joy is hosting epic meals in which her husband cooks, she designs fantastical tablescapes, and their dog blisses out on leftovers. With all her heart, she believes that everyone deserves a happily-ever-after. Find her at ellebrownauthor.com.

Also by Nina Milne

Royal Sarala Weddings miniseries

His Princess on Paper
Bound by Their Royal Baby

Winter Escapes collection

Cinderella's Moroccan Midnight Kiss

Summer Escapes collection

Their Mauritius Wedding Ruse

Princesses of Palosia collection

Secret Royal's Napoli Reunion

Bridesmaid's Fast-Track Fling
is **Elle Brown**'s debut title.

Look out for more books from Elle Brown.
Coming soon!

Discover more at millsandboon.co.uk.

RINGS AND RUSES

NINA MILNE

ELLE BROWN

MILLS & BOON

First published in Great Britain 2026
by Mills & Boon, an imprint of HarperCollins*Publishers* Ltd,
1 London Bridge Street, London, SE1 9GF

www.harpercollins.co.uk

HarperCollins*Publishers*, Macken House, 39/40 Mayor Street Upper, Dublin 1, D01 C9W8, Ireland

Rings and Ruses © 2026 Harlequin Enterprises ULC

The Bride Wore His Convenient Ring © 2026 Nina Milne

Bridesmaid's Fast-Track Fling © 2026 Lisa Brown

ISBN: 978-0-263-41934-4

01/26

This book contains FSC™ certified paper and other controlled sources to ensure responsible forest management.

For more information visit www.harpercollins.co.uk/green.

Printed and Bound in the UK using 100% Renewable Electricity at CPI Group (UK) Ltd, Croydon, CR0 4YY

THE BRIDE WORE HIS CONVENIENT RING

NINA MILNE

MILLS & BOON

To my Mum for her courage
and her positive outlook on life

PROLOGUE

AMARA ROSSI HAD no idea that her world was about to upend as she walked towards the crenelated, turreted castle with its rugged stone walls, set in the rolling Tuscan hills. Castle Alavario, surrounded by the glorious Rossi vineyards, was the place she had called home for all her twenty-seven years, a place where the Rossi family had lived for centuries.

The word *family* panged pain through her as it always did, the linger of a bone-deep grief. A sense of loss that she'd learnt to live with thanks to her grandfather, Vittorio Rossi, the man who had essentially brought her up. He had been her rock, supported and loved her, been there. In addition, he had imbued her with a sense of her heritage, ensured she'd grown up with a love of the Rossi estate, the vast tumbling sweep of the vineyards, the smell of the grapes at harvest, rich and redolent on the Tuscan air. All of it was a part of her. As the Rossi heir she was determined to ensure that Rossi wines went from strength to strength. The idea that one day it would all be down to her never daunted her, perhaps because it wasn't possible for her to envisage a world without Vittorio in it. The idea one she refused to contemplate, even though she knew no better how foolish that was.

Her steps imperceptibly quickened with a need to see him, to be reassured by his presence, at their daily catch-up in his study.

Minutes later she pushed the heavy arched door open and smiled as her grandfather rose to his feet from behind his leather-topped desk, moved towards her for the customary embrace. As always, he was dressed in a pale crisp shirt, discreetly branded and tucked into a pair of light grey checked trousers with a slim belt demarcating the two; the whole epitomising the fact that Vittorio Rossi was still in his prime, despite the fact he was approaching eighty. That fact backed up by the still thick iron-grey hair and the brightness of the chocolate-brown eyes that characterised the Rossi family.

An eye colour that Amara didn't share; she had inherited her mother's green eyes and a mane of red hair to go with it.

'I've opened a bottle of our favourite Chianti,' he said. 'I thought tonight we could talk over a glass before we eat.'

Amara stepped back and studied her grandfather's face, caught a touch of reserve in his voice, saw something in the brown eyes. A suppressed excitement alongside a touch of anxiety.

'That sounds good,' she said carefully. 'What's the occasion?'

'I have some news,' Vittorio said.

A sudden sense of foreboding trickled through Amara even as she told herself not to catastrophise. It could be good news after all. Whatever it was she knew it must be significant to warrant a bottle from one of their best years, the wine made from her favourite Sangiovese grape. She accepted the carefully poured glass with a smile of thanks and for a precious second they both sipped the deep ruby red liquid, savoured the intense taste of ripe red berries that lingered on the palate. Both of them recalling the harvest from a year that had produced such a good crop.

Then Vittorio walked towards the fireplace, placed his glass on the mantelpiece and turned.

'I am not sure of the best way to put this Amara. So, I'll just say it. It turns out that you have a half-brother and half-sister.' He hesitated. 'Twins.'

The world seemed to spin and for a second, she thought the heavy crystal glass was about to drop from her hand. Summoning every ounce of control, she forced herself to remain completely still, then she instructed her feet to move, one step at a time towards the polished teak sideboard where she oh, so carefully placed the glass down.

'I don't understand,' she said, amazed that her voice could sound so calm, her brain telling her that this wasn't possible, it didn't make sense. That this was all some sort of hallucination, a dream, a joke.

'It was a shock to me as well,' Vittorio said. 'A few weeks ago, I received a letter from a Lorenzo Cavendish. He said he had found documentation that suggested we could be related. It was plausible enough that I agreed to DNA testing. It is the truth Amara. Lorenzo and you are siblings.'

'But…how? When?' It didn't make sense, couldn't make sense.

'Lorenzo and Daisy are two years older than you. They have grown up not knowing their true father.'

'But…did my father know about them?' Amara's brain was spinning now, and with each spin it felt as though her carefully constructed world was shattering. Ever since the accident it had been her and her grandfather, a safe dependable unit, a format she had based her life on. And her memories of her parents, or at least the idea she had constructed, had been based on a devoted couple, childhood sweethearts. Now her brain started to do the math. Her parents had been married for three years before she had been born. That meant her father had been unfaithful. Now hysteria threatened—she had twin siblings. The irony pierced her soul, poked at the jagged wound left from the loss of her own twin brother, who had perished along with her parents in the tragic helicopter accident that had changed the course of her life, and ended Luca's just days after their fourth birthday.

'Yes. It appears that Roberto did know about the pregnancy.' Vittorio's voice was sad now and instinctively Amara put her own thoughts aside, realised what a shock this must have been for her grandfather. 'But he made a decision to walk away. It looks as though he cut off all contact with Lorenzo and Daisy's mother when she told him she was pregnant.' Vittorio raised his hands. 'I know this is hard Amara but I think we should focus on the positive.'

'What positives?'

Right now, she couldn't see any, didn't want to believe that her father had behaved so dishonourably, certainly had no wish to have new siblings. She'd lost her twin. It was a loss that she knew would sear her forever; she didn't want a replacement brother or a sister. She certainly didn't want both. For an instant she tried to picture it, tried to imagine a brother and a sister sitting in this very study. Everyone smiling, laughing, discussing the year's harvest. The type of family scene that she had pictured so many times with a sense of yearning and what might have beens. Only in her imagination it had been herself and Luca sat on the leather armchairs, her parents stood with Vittorio at the mantelpiece. An alternative timeline where the accident hadn't happened, where she had grown up with a family.

But it wasn't like that. For twenty-three years it had been herself and Vittorio and that was how she liked it. The idea of a new, larger family made panic rise and swirl inside her. She and Vittorio were a unit that she understood, relied on, felt secure with. Another thought crept in, she was the Rossi heir, she loved every vine, every acre, every furrow of Rossi land. It was her inheritance. She shook her head, knew that at least was unworthy. Lorenzo and Daisy hadn't had a chance to know about the estate, had been robbed of that chance by her father. *Their* father. The thought sent a tremor of rejection through her, the idea repugnant, unacceptable. Impossible.

No. It was possible. More than that, it was fact.

Vittorio Rossi was nobody's fool; he would not be telling her this unless it was truth.

'They are family,' Vittorio said. 'Rossi blood runs through their veins. They could be a *good* addition to our lives. I am getting older. And as I do one of my biggest worries is leaving you alone.'

Hearing the emotion in her grandfather's voice, she pushed her own feelings to one side, as she moved towards him. 'It is all right, Nonno. You will be around for a lot longer yet and you need not be concerned for me. You have taught me so much that there is no need for you to worry about what will happen in the future. I swear to you that I will look after the Rossi estate, it will continue to thrive and flourish. I love this land—it is in my blood.'

'I know that, Amara. But…' Her grandfather hesitated. 'I trust you. But it may feel…lonely. And what about after that? Future generations? I would never pressure you into a marriage or ask that you have children simply to provide an heir but…'

But—that one syllable somehow said so much and further emotions piled in as her grandfather skirted a topic they had always studiously avoided ever since Amara's first relationship had fizzled out. Then her second. Amara had tried, she really had. But she couldn't do it, could not navigate a relationship. It was as though there was a switch inside her that was permanently switched to off. Her two brief forays had not been successful; letting anyone in was too hard, made her too uncomfortable, too panicked.

Not for the first time she wondered where that left her. She knew love was not for her, not when she knew how easily it could be lost in a blink of an eye, how fragile the threads that bound people were. Tragedy could strike completely unannounced, or events that were out of your control could tornado in and destroy what had been built up. Better to walk alone, to make sure you and only you were in control of as much as it was possible to control.

Which meant of course there was a question mark over the future. The Rossi vineyards had been tended by Rossis for centuries; what would happen after Amara?

'Do they, Lorenzo and Daisy, have children?' she asked, a sudden sense of displacement hitting her; so strong that she realised she was clenching her hand around the back of a brocaded chair, the beaded material cutting into her fingers.

'Not that I am aware.'

But they might, or they might be in happy relationships. Perhaps her newly found siblings understood how to navigate all the pitfalls and minefields that relationships seemed to bring. Rendering the whole shebang pointless. Why engage in something perilous, in something that could bring hurt and pain and profound loss in a blink of an eye? Looking at Vittorio now, though, she knew the answer. A relationship would bring children, heirs to continue the Rossi dynasty. How could her grandfather not welcome that possibility?

'This is very early days,' Vittorio continued. 'I know very little about them, except that Lorenzo is a very successful businessman in his own right. But I would like to invite them to come to visit the estate, to meet us. Roberto was my son and I loved him, but what he did was wrong. Lorenzo and Daisy are his children and they were his responsibility. They are Rossis even if they bear a different name. I believe we have a moral duty to welcome them. But also would it be so bad to have a larger family circle? We lost so much. These people—they are family.'

Amara gathered herself together; she would not hurt this man, a man she loved with all her heart. This was important to him and how could she blame him for that? Tragedy had taken so much from him, his wife as well as his son, daughter-in-law and grandson. He'd then had the responsibility of bringing up a four-year-old on his own. This was his chance to have more family, a chance to make the future of the Rossi heritage safer. She had to respect that—she owed him that and so much more.

Moving across to him she gave him a hug. 'I understand. Of course, I do. And of course, I will welcome them. But…' Not yet. She needed time to get her head round the sheer enormity of what had happened. 'It has been a lot to take in. I think I need a little time to reflect. To think.' To work out a strategy that would enable her to put a good face on this, even as she felt an inner determination to hold these newcomers at bay. They may be predators; whatever they were they could not replace her real family.

'Of course you do.' Her grandfather's voice full of understanding. 'Why don't you go away for a week? Have a break. A holiday. I will contact Lorenzo and see what his feelings are about a meet up.'

CHAPTER ONE

GIOVANNI ROMANO ENTERED the busy hotel restaurant with an impatient stride. A day on the ski slopes, nestled in the grandeur of the Bavarian Alps, should have improved his mood. But the adrenalin from his curving, swooping descents had done nothing to satisfactorily distract him from his thoughts. His subsequent stint in the pool, lap after rhythmic lap followed by the heat of a sauna, hadn't bolstered his thought process or brought him any closer to a conclusion as to what to do.

No closer to an answer to a life-changing decision. Did he want to become part of a family firm when his family, with the exception of his grandparents, couldn't stand him? If he did want to, how would he fulfil the conditions that were part of the deal?

He didn't need to do this; he was a multimillionaire in his own right, had his own company to run. More pertinently, he'd spent his entire childhood with one clear ambition—to sever his family ties and live his own life unfettered by family bonds. Any bonds.

But now his grandparents had asked for his help. Asked him to enter the Romano business empire. A supreme irony, seeing that Gio had been excluded from the family company from his birth. He had been given the Romano name but nothing that went with it except a childhood where he'd spent months of every year in forced proximity with his father, stepmother and two half-brothers, a proximity rendered horrific by their treatment of him. Inclusion in the echelons of Romano Confectionery—that was for real family. Whilst Gio was simply a second-class Romano, evidence of a deeply regretted, extremely brief marriage between his father, Salvatore Romano, and his mother, wild child, rock star Luna Rocca.

But all that had changed now. Now his grandparents *wanted* to bring Gio in. The idea still seemed fantastical, filled him with disbelief and elation that he, Gio Romano, could be admitted, invited to the hallowed boardroom of Romano Confectionery.

Gio ran through the facts in his head. Or at least the facts his grandparents had shared. Unease nudged him; he had the feeling they had been holding something back, but he didn't know what.

Fact: now in their eighties Aurelio and Ava Romano had decided to step back from the company. Fact: they had handed over some of their shares to Salvatore. Fact: unsurprisingly, in Gio's opinion, now they regretted that decision because Salvatore was doing things his way, according to *his* vision. A vision that did not accord with his grandparents'. Or with Gio's come to that.

Gio knew exactly how low his father would go, believed implicitly that Salvatore would have no qualms in inflicting a cost-cutting regime, would sacrifice quality for profit and in so doing would ruin Romano Confectionery's reputation for high standards, would undermine the ethos the company had been built on. And in so doing he could well ruin it. Breaking Aurelio and Ava Romano's hearts. Gio couldn't let that happen.

But…next fact: he still didn't really understand why his grandparents needed Gio, they still retained enough shares to outvote Salvatore.

Instead they wanted to bring Gio in, give him a controlling number of shares and appoint him to the board as a 'counterbalance'. They *said* the company needed new blood, *said* they didn't want the scandal and bad publicity associated with sacking their son, *said* that it would be difficult given the number of shares he owned and the fact he had the support of the rest of the board.'

It made a certain sense, but Gio couldn't help feeling he was still being manoeuvred, was still a Romano pawn, being moved across the Romano chess board.

Which brought on the next problem. Because the articles of Romano Confectionery, written by its founders Max and Elisabetta Romano stipulated that family board members had to be married. His great-grandparents had had a clear vision for the company's future, which stated that, 'we want this to be a family business that continues for generations. Therefore, we stipulate that any family member admitted to the board must be married. This will ensure a commitment to producing a future generation and also ensure they have a settled, responsible lifestyle allowing them to fully commit to the business.'

So Gio would need to get married, a state he had avoided for years. Commitment was not for him. He believed in keeping a distance because that way you didn't get sucked in, you retained control of your own life.

Yet he was considering it because he owed his grandparents, cared about them; their relationship a complex one, that even now Gio didn't fully understand. But he did know that his grandparents had intervened to end the bullying, the humiliations inflicted on him by his father, his stepmother and his brothers. Had made his childhood more bearable. Once they had discovered the bullying, they had even taken an interest in his life and over the years he had become close to them. Or as close as it was possible for him to be with anyone. He didn't believe Aurelio and Ava loved him, but they at least had the decency, the morality, to take some responsibility for him, which was more than either of his parents had done.

His mind still whirring, his eyes scanned the restaurant. The spacious room was full of diners, tables arranged to maximise table space but yet ensure privacy. The décor combined a sense of splendour with a surprising intimacy, the walls a deep red, the dark wooden tables lit by artfully placed wall and overhead copper-coloured lights and separated by impressive pillars and swathes of russet and shimmering gold fabrics.

There were couples who'd headed to the Bavarian Alps for a post-Christmas winter vacation, interspersed with larger groups of business convention delegates gathered to discuss the new year ahead. His eye fell on the only table set for one. His table, he assumed, as a staff member walked up.

'Good evening, Matteo.' The same waiter from the previous night who he'd engaged in conversation.

'Mr Romano. Come this way.' Gio followed him to the table, sat down and picked up the menu.

'I'll be back in a few minutes,' Matteo said. But in fact, Gio had barely glanced at the menu before Matteo returned, a slightly worried look on his face, accompanied by a woman.

Gio blinked; the woman had a glorious cascade of red hair that shimmered with tones of auburn, russet and a glimmer of copper and fell in waves to below her shoulders, framing a delicate face with luminous green eyes, a straight nose and glossy lips that he had to force himself not to focus on. Dressed in an elegant grey cashmere dress, made slightly different by a knotted side that emphasised her slender waist before falling into a skirt that fell to mid-calf, she took his breath away. He knew he should stop staring, but he was captivated and as his eyes met hers, he saw a spark in the emerald hue, an answering arrest as if she too were caught in the sudden iridescent mesh of attraction. *Whoa.* Enough. Now was not the time to become enmeshed in any sort of attraction, mutual or not. At the exact same instant, they both broke eye contact.

Matteo turned to the woman. 'I am so sorry. I really can't apologise enough. There has been a mix-up. Both of you ordered a table for one and somehow…'

'We've both been given the same table?' the woman enquired; her tone neutral rather than censorious.

'Exactly.'

She looked round the crowded room. 'It's okay. Mistakes happen. Perhaps I could be given a different table.'

Matteo now looked harried. 'I am not sure… we are very busy today. There is a concert being held later and I don't believe there will be a table free for a couple more hours. I could try but…' His voice trailed off.

'Or,' Gio heard his voice say. 'I am happy to share

the table.' Told himself it was common sense, common courtesy. Nothing more.

The waiter looked hopeful. 'If that would suit, of course that would be no problem for us, Mr Romano.'

The woman hesitated, glanced around the crowded dining room as if searching for a different table, any table, then back at Gio and he could see a reluctance that he'd swear was personal. Then the expression passed, her green eyes took in Matteo's worried, hopeful expression and her lips turned upwards in a polite smile with a hint of rue.

'Thank you for the offer, Mr Romano. If you're sure it's not a problem, I accept.'

'No problem at all,' Gio said aware of a misplaced sense of anticipation as she sat down opposite him and smiled her thanks as Matteo set her place and then left them with a promise to return for their order.

He watched as she studied the menu, noted the expression of concentration as she read it. As if sensing his gaze she looked up. 'Sorry. I take my food seriously. This may take some time.'

'That's fine with me.' Gio took the chance to study her face properly, in an attempt to work out what it was about her that was continuing to poleaxe him. He watched as she turned her attention to the wine menu and then glanced back up at him and he hurriedly perused his menu, just as Matteo returned.

Gio waited as she ordered and then Matteo turned to him. 'And for you?'

'I'll have...' he stared at the menu and then back up. 'Actually, that sounds so good I'll have the same.'

Once Matteo had gone, Gio looked across at his dinner companion. 'I'm sorry about the mix-up with the table, especially as I get the feeling you'd rather have had dinner alone.'

'It's not your fault,' she said. 'I was planning on eating alone with a book for company, so I didn't want to share a table with anyone, and esp—' she broke off, consternation on her face.

'Especially not me?' he finished for her.

'I'm sorry. I didn't mean to say that. I'm just not used to having dinner with someone like you, with your reputation.'

Her voice was even and he sensed the apology was sincere, but the words still caught him on the raw, even as he told himself there was no need for him to explain or justify his reputation. That was the beauty of his life—he answered to no one, could live his life as he wished. Had no dependants, was responsible for no one's happiness. That allowed him to live the lifestyle he lived, one where he worked hard and partied hard.

Just like his mother did but with a crucial difference. Gio had a clear remit to hurt no one. Luna hadn't cared who got hurt in the process, not the various men she pursued and discarded and not her son either. Luna Rocco had never let the minor matter of parenthood cramp her style at all.

She'd never been actively unkind to him; she was even carelessly fond of him, but it would never have occurred to her to curtail her excesses or change the way she lived or put herself out in the slightest for her son. At any age or time. Gio had grown up cast into the care of various staff members of Luna Rocco's entourage, many of whom definitely had no child care qualifications. Interspersed with this had been the even worse sojourns with his father. So, his whole childhood he'd looked forward to the day he would be in control of his own life, no longer reliant on the whims of others. And that's where he was now, so he had no intention of explaining anything to this woman. That he was not like his mother, someone who pursued what she wanted without much, if any, thought for the impact it had on others.

That was his business. So maybe he should call this now, suggest he leave this woman to the solitary meal she clearly wanted and was entitled to.

But before he could speak, he realised she was studying his face, her expression intent and then to his surprise she gave a small rueful smile and raised a hand, contrition in her green eyes and in her voice. 'I shouldn't have said that. I'm really sorry. I don't know you and I shouldn't judge you on a few articles I read in my dentist's waiting room. Can we start again?'

There was a silence as brown eyes met green.

Amara took a deep breath, held his gaze as she waited for his answer, wondered why she'd even asked the question. Wondered what the hell was going on. Ever since she'd set eyes on Giovanni Romano something had happened to her. A sudden, instant, ridiculous reaction to him. One look and she'd been bowled over, her body on high alert, a funny dipping sensation in her stomach and she didn't like it. Liked it even less when she'd realised his identity.

Because it was galling to admit that she'd succumbed to his charms just like the string of women he'd dated, according to the articles she'd read. They identified Gio

Romano, son of rock star Luna Rocco, as a Lothario who went through women at speed. A man with a reputation for being a serial dater of celebrities.

A few days ago, his reputation probably wouldn't have resonated with her so much. But tonight, it did. Who knew how many women he'd hurt, or betrayed. Like her father had betrayed her mother. Had her father loved Lorenzo and Daisy's mother? Or just slept with her? Once, numerous times... Come to that, for all she knew her father had had a string of affaires. The only reason she knew about this one was there had been a consequence. Two babies.

The idea, the knowledge, had shattered her world. So right now, Amara had no tolerance for men who played the field. Men like the man she was now sat opposite. The man who her errant body had identified as the bee's knees.

But then she'd seen his expression, seen something she'd swear was anger and hurt touch his brown eyes, and she'd known that she'd struck a nerve and had a sudden strong, albeit irrational, sense that she was somehow in the wrong. A feeling that grew as their gazes locked, the moment stretching.

Without thinking, she reached out and touched his hand, and as she did so something fizzed through her, the jolt of awareness, the sense of connection so intense she snatched her hand back and just stared at his. Focused on its shape, its strength, and imagined the imprint of his fingers on her.

Her gaze jerked up and she met his eyes, saw a mirrored shock in their brown depths, and a flash of desire so strong she felt her body heat up in response.

She had to get a grip; she must have imagined her reaction. She must have.

Gio blinked, gave his head a small shake, and she'd swear his brain was scrambling to recall the question she'd asked. Then he visibly pulled himself together.

'Yes,' he said. 'Let's start again.' He held his hand out. 'Hi. I am Gio Romano and you are?'

Amara glanced down at his hand and then back at him, was met with a wide-eyed look of innocence with a hint of a challenge. Fine. Maybe he wanted to test whether or not that earlier reaction was a blip. Well, so did she, to prove that whatever had happened earlier was some sort of strange one-off reaction. Not to be repeated.

Yet as she continued to look at the outstretched hand, once again she could feel something bubble up inside her, and in an almost abrupt movement she grasped his hand and bit back an expletive.

Holy moly. She had no idea what was going on but the earlier reaction had not been an isolated one. The feel of his hand round hers was causing her pulse rate to pound and was certainly enough for her to tell herself she had to make sure there were absolutely no more touches, even as she realised her hand still rested in his, his grasp firm and welcome and…

Right now, she couldn't even remember why she was holding his hand; all she knew was she didn't want to let go.

The sound of a throat clearing brought her to her senses and she dropped his hand, looked up at Matteo's carefully expressionless face.

'Your food,' he said.

Amara realised for once in her life she had no idea

what she'd even ordered, studied the plate Matteo carefully placed in front of her, her brain scrambling to even identify its contents. Her only consolation that Gio looked as shell-shocked as she did.

'This looks… incredible,' she finally managed.

'And smells as good as it looks,' Gio said and credit to him that he sounded so together. 'My compliments to the chef and all the kitchen staff.'

Once Matteo had gone, Amara focused on the smells that wafted up from her plate, on the light colour of the Grüner Veltliner she'd ordered to go with the food. This was what she knew, what she understood. Tastes, flavours, blends, smells, scents, wine…this was her forte, her world, a place where she was confident. A place where physical desire, the force of attraction had no place, a lexicon outside her comprehension. It was important not to give this attraction any power; just because it existed there was no need to overreact to it. One dinner and they'd go their separate ways.

A deep breath and she looked across at him.

'I still don't even know your name,' he said.

'Um, right. Sorry. I'm Amara. Amara Rossi. Pleased to meet you.' Possibly.

CHAPTER TWO

GIO WONDERED WHAT the hell was going on. If shaking hands could cause that level of reaction what would happen if he kissed her? He closed his eyes. He was *not* going to kiss her. For a start this was not a date. He was in the Bavarian Alps to consider his future; come to that, if he agreed to his grandparents' proposal, soon enough he'd be getting married. Possibly to one of the suitable women his grandparents apparently had lined up for him. Again, the sensation of being expertly guided across a board crossed his mind.

'I am pleased to meet you, too,' he said. 'And please note that if at any point you would prefer to read your book please go ahead.'

She shook her head. 'Thanks, but I'm good. It wouldn't feel right when this food deserves all my attention.' She sighed. 'Anyway, I'm not sure it would work. I love the author, but somehow, for once, reading isn't really working as a distraction. I read the same page ten times on the plane and it didn't go in.'

The idea that she was looking for a distraction triggered a strange sense of connection, highlighted the feeling of warmth that she had revised her original opinion of him, that she had genuinely seemed to get his philosophy. 'Tell me about it.' He gestured to his laptop. 'I was planning on a working dinner. Because earlier I read the same page of a report ten times and I can't remember a word of it. And seeing that I wrote it, that's a bit worrying.'

'If you would rather work that's fine.'

He shook his head. 'I think I'd far rather be distracted by you.'

Amara looked as though she wasn't quite sure how to take that and settled for, 'Well let's hope we both manage to enjoy the food. It looks incredible.'

'It does,' he said. 'Even though I have to admit I'm not sure what it actually is. I was already a bit distracted when we ordered.'

'By what?' she asked, her eyes narrowed in suspicion.

'You,' he said simply and truthfully, as a sense of recklessness emerged. Of course, he wasn't going to act on attraction, but surely a little bit of banter was allowable. It sounded as though it could be a welcome distraction for them both.

'Oh.' She looked down and then back up at him, as if she too had made a decision, putting her hand up in mock defence. 'Is this some of the famed Romano charm?' Now her lips upturned into a delightfully impish smile.

'Absolutely not. That was the unvarnished truth. The Romano charm only comes into play on a date. This is a chance meeting.' The words, though said lightly, seemed to resonate, and for some reason a little tingle ran over his skin. As if he was being touched by the hand of fate. He blinked the fanciful thought away.

'So, what comes into play on chance encounters?'

'I have no idea. I'm making this up as we go. Feel free to say what *you* want from this.'

There was a silence, and as their eyes met there it was again, the zip and zing, the pull and push of attraction.

'Nothing complicated,' she said softly and there was a husk to her voice. 'A simple, friendly dinner.'

'Hmm. How friendly would you like to be?' he asked, exaggerating his tone into a drawl, adding an eyebrow wiggle for extra effect.

Her green eyes widened and then she laughed, a genuine ring of laughter and a disproportionate sense of satisfaction warmed him.

'Friendly enough to enjoy the food and the company,' she said. 'In that order,' she added. 'This is delicious. And so you know, we're having truffle tagliolini with a Prosecco foam to start with. Followed by sea bass cooked with a special caper sauce and lemon and chard with fondant potatoes.'

'Simple but not the sort of thing you'd usually have at home,' he said.

'Exactly. Though it is Italian, so maybe I am feeling a little homesick. But definitely not your normal fare. Did you know that truffles grow underground as compared to mushrooms that grow overground, and there are truffle hunters who use trained dogs to find the truffles?'

He gave a sudden smile. 'I didn't know that.'

'I am a mine of trivial food information,' she said lightly. 'And I have always wanted to try Prosecco foam, though I have to admit I have no idea how to make it.'

She tipped her head to one side, as she took a small first mouthful and he could see her actually savour the taste and flavours. 'Mmm. The pasta really works—it's like spaghetti but flatter so the texture is great. And the truffle is amazing.'

Gio took a bite and nodded. She was right, though right now he was more focused on watching Amara, seeing the focus, the concentration on her face, the way her forehead creased slightly, the slight jut to her chin.

'Kind of nutty, oaky. It reminds me of woods or forests.' She broke off. 'It's a good thing this *isn't* a date.'

'Why's that?'

'Because I can focus on eating and savouring every mouthful. My ex used to get annoyed because I took so long to eat and drink. Plus the running commentary.'

'Feel free to take your time. Personally, I'm in agreement with you. Food is far too important to rush. I believe in taking my time over pleasurable things.'

One part of his mind wondered what the hell he was doing. The other didn't care, revelled in the tinge of colour that touched her cheeks, even as he wondered if he'd gone too far. He didn't want to spook her or actually make her uncomfortable. But as he was about to apologise, she smiled right back.

'That's always good to know,' she said, each word slow and drawn out, her voice low. Her eyes met his and he could see his own desire mirrored in the green depths of her eyes. A desire that was swiftly superseded by shock and she blinked rapidly, picked up her wine glass and sipped carefully. He could almost see her ground herself. 'It's important to appreciate good food and wine,' she said, her voice commendably even.

'Yes.' Hell, was that strangled voice really his? He couldn't take his eyes off her, and dammit, he wasn't thinking about the pleasure of food or wine and he was sure that neither was she.

But she was at least trying to steer the conversation to smoother, safer waters. The least he could do was attempt the same. Think. Conversation.

'What brings you to the Bavarian Alps? Are you here on pleasure…' Really Gio? 'Or business?' It was abrupt, but it truly was all he could think of. Other than kissing her. Tasting the wine via her lips.

Her gaze skimmed his lips and he knew she was struggling as much as he was. 'Um… It's a few days' break,' she said. 'Though I may try and include some business and make a trip to a winery over here. My grandfather owns a vineyard in Tuscany. I live and work there.'

'That sounds fascinating,' he said. 'It must be incredible watching it all from start to finish.'

'It is. I've been living, breathing and drinking wine since I was born.' There was an emphasis in her voice he couldn't quite identify. 'I can't imagine working anywhere else. And whilst obviously I think Italian wine, or at least our Italian wine, is the best in the world, I am open to learning from and enjoying produce from other countries. So, I'd be interested to visit a Bavarian winery.'

'Even though you're on holiday?'

'It's not exactly a holiday. I came here…to…think,' she said quietly. 'I thought a change of scene and solitude would help. Usually walking round the estate works, but this time it seemed important to be away.' She shook her head as if regretting the words. 'What about you?'

'Oddly enough I am here for the same reasons you are. I wanted to clear my head and think. I'm at a crossroad in my life. I have a choice I need to make and for the first time in a long time I am conflicted. I can't make a decision and that's a novelty for me.'

He'd mapped out his path in life from the moment he'd realised the importance of being in control. As a child he'd been at the mercy of his parents' whims, shunted from chaos at his mother's to misery at his father's. All he'd wanted to do was be in charge of his own life. To live it on his own terms.

Amara sipped her wine, smiled up at Matteo as he brought their next course, waited until he'd placed their plates in front of them. 'At least you are in control of your decision. It's something you *can* make a choice about. You are in charge of your own destiny.'

'Aren't you in control of yours?'

'It doesn't feel like that right now. But then again, I'm not sure anyone is in complete control of their own destiny. Fate has a habit of intruding.'

Like today, he wondered. 'Sure. But you can still call the shots to a degree. Some decisions are just harder than others to make.'

'I know.' She sighed. 'Right now, for me it's not so much about making a choice. It's more about coming to terms. Acceptance. But the more I think about it the more I'm struggling.'

'I get that. The more I think the more I can't decide.'

She gestured to the tables around them. 'Maybe that's the point of commitment. All these couples. When there's a decision to be made you've at least got someone to talk it over with.'

'But then you've also got their welfare to think about. And you may disagree, which makes it all even harder. At least I'm only arguing with myself.' He couldn't miss

the opportunity. 'Then you're not married. Or in a relationship?'

'Absolutely not.' She sounded as though the concept
was a difficult one to grasp, but there was a hint of sadness there too. 'I'm not interested in any length of commitment.'

A shadow crossed her eyes and he could see too that
her face held signs of tiredness, sensed that whatever
situation she was facing it matched his own. Curiosity
was superseded by something else—a desire to help, to
smooth away the strain.

'So, your plan for the next few days is to think over
your situation on your own? Whilst reading your book
as a distraction.'

She nodded. 'That about sums it up.'

'Then I've got an idea.' The words seemed to be
stringing together almost without his brain's involvement. 'I am planning to go on a hike tomorrow. See if
the beauty of the Alps, the fresh air, the snow underfoot
will help me get some perspective. Would you like to
join me? Maybe company will work better than a book
or a work report as a distraction.'

There was a silence and then to his surprise and
perhaps her own she gave a small mischievous smile.
'You're asking me to come along to distract you?'

Gio gulped. Her smile, which made her green eyes sparkle and this time revealed an enchanting dimple in her right
cheek that completely captivated him, took his breath away.

'Yup. But I'll return the favour. It'll be a mutual distraction pact. What do you think?'

There was a pause and her smile widened. 'Sounds
like a plan.'

* * *

The next morning Amara opened her eyes, looked around the unfamiliar room as memories of where she was filtered in. Leaning back on the luxurious pillows she took in the terracotta and cream décor, the clean lines of the room, with its gleaming wooden floor and light-coloured furniture. The neutral colours enlivened and brightened by the luxurious handmade wool rugs, a hue of red she'd never seen before and the thick brocade of the russet curtains, behind which she knew were nearly floor-to-ceiling windows that provided a glorious panoramic view of snow-dusted terrain. Blinking away the aftermath of her dreams, she was aware of a bubble of anticipation that had lightened the sense of weightiness that she'd carried since that conversation with her grandfather. A bubble that expanded as she got ready, aware that she was taking extra care as she brushed her hair, applied a touch of mascara to emphasise her eyes. Stopped there. Gio Romano was a distraction. Nothing more.

That was why she'd agreed to this hike. They were both here because life had thrown them a curveball. The attraction was irrelevant. In fact, maybe it wasn't Gio per se she was attracted to—it was the distraction he provided.

Amara had the feeling there was a flaw in her logic, knew she had to tread warily. Whatever the reason for it, she would not give into this attraction, would not give it power.

Yet it was hard to remember that as, half an hour later, she headed across the opulent hotel lobby. She tried to focus on the sense of space, the parquet floor with its dark red inlays, the wide sweeping pillars, the wall enclosures containing vases and statues from different corners of the globe, delicate blue and white china and fluting Venetian glass. But her eyes kept honing in on Gio, and, as she approached, her heartbeat accelerated as she took in his height, his breadth, the muscular whole. He was dressed for the weather in a dark blue down jacket, his dark brown eyes looking at her with a warmth that sent her heart even faster. He looked… Utterly scrummy. Scrummy? *Really, Amara?* She must be in a bad way—scrummy was not in her usual vocabulary.

Forcing herself to keep her steps even and a polite smile on her face, she approached.

'Good morning,' he said and handed her a steaming cup. 'Hot chocolate. Proper hot chocolate.'

She accepted the cup as they exited the lobby and stepped out into the magnificence of the hotel grounds. Stopping, she turned to look at the sprawl of the building with its hipped pyramid roof, turrets and Art Deco–styled architecture. Took in the utter beauty of the landscape. The building was nestled at the foot of a sloping valley of forests, the trees peeking dark green through layers of snow on one side whilst in the distance majestic jagged ice-peaked mountains loomed and spiked grandly up to the clear cold blue sky.

Turning, she saw Gio indicating a path headed towards a sloping hill. 'I thought we'd go that way,' he suggested. 'It's about an hour's walk to a restaurant which apparently does an amazing fondue.'

'Sounds good to me.'

As they started to walk, the snow crisp and crunchy

under their booted feet, she inhaled the aroma of the hot chocolate appreciatively. 'This smells gorgeous,' she said. 'Rich and dark and I can smell cocoa with a hint of vanilla.' She broke off, remembered how much her tendency to analyse everything she ate and drank had annoyed both Stefan and Silvio. Better to continue to walk in silence and take in the beauty of the scenery around her, the scattered snow-coated pine trees that sent a scent of evergreen to mingle with the tang of un-shed snow in the air.

But the memory of her failed relationships had trig-gered a reminder of her own shortcomings, her inability to let anyone close, a failing that was a deep disappoint-ment to her grandfather, the person she loved most in the world, the person she owed everything to.

No wonder Lorenzo and Daisy had given Vittorio hope for the future. A hope for heirs. No wonder her grandfather wanted to welcome them into the family. Of course Amara would be by his side.

Though how long for? Because somehow, she felt dis-placed; felt outnumbered. She *was* outnumbered by Lo-renzo and Daisy; twins who would share the same bond that she and Luca had once shared. A bond she still felt. So how could she welcome Lorenzo and Daisy? How could she possibly allow herself to get close to new siblings, even if she could figure out how to. Even if she wanted to.

And now she winced as an image flashed in front of her eyes. A memory of running through the vineyards with her twin. They had been so close; in games of hide-and-seek they had always been able to find the other, sensed where the other was hiding.

But Luca was gone now, had barely had a taste of life.

Instead, there were two adults, two newly minted Rossis, a unit. And there was Amara… Alone. And that was how it would stay. How could she betray Luca's memory when the pain of his loss was still so raw? And any sort of real connection to Lorenzo and Daisy *would be* a betrayal, as if it were possible to replace Luca, forget him. It would somehow devalue his memory, dilute it, reduce him. The very idea jarred through her.

'You okay?'

Amara blinked, turned her head to meet Gio's brown eyes.

'You're marching like a woman on a mission and I'm pretty sure I can see steam coming out of your ears. Any second now the snow will melt.'

To her surprise she realised he was right. She slowed down and took a deep breath.

'Sorry. Yes, I am angry.'

'Believe me, I get it.' He gave her a rueful smile and her anger almost started to recede, almost pushed away by the sheer wattage, the way little lines crinkled around his brown eyes, the crease in his cheeks, the set of his jaw, the shape of his mouth. Almost.

'You can't get it,' she said, the anger holding strong and now directed against if not him, then herself, for almost believing him.

'Try me,' he said and paused as the meaning of his words blurred. And suddenly, somehow in that pause anger and frustration morphed into something else, different emotions colliding and bouncing—push and pulling an urge to throw caution to the wind, to try his lips, try to see what kissing him would be like. And the pause stretched.

Their gazes locked and silence reigned; a silence that seemed to blanket the moment, the air cold and crisp, and as if of their own volition her feet took a step towards him and as if in answer, he too closed the gap between them and Amara knew exactly what would help. Damn it, she wanted to take that final step, grab him by his jacket, pull him down and lock her lips against his. The desire so intense, the image so clear, the anticipation so head spinning that for one mad, glorious instant she nearly translated words to action.

What *was* happening to her? This heady sense of anticipation, this churn of desire was so alien to her. But she knew it was to do with Gio Romano's presence, something in the air that was turning her into someone intent on flirting with danger.

Because this was dangerous—it was something she didn't understand, another unexpected twist and she didn't like it. Or perhaps the problem was she did like it, this head-whirling distraction. But surely the fact that he was good-looking, try utterly drop-dead gorgeous, should not be playing riot with her hormones like this.

Shouldn't be turning her insides to mush, her legs to jelly and worse, urging her to take one more step forward. This wasn't what Amara Rossi did. Not her style. This man had a reputation, most likely a merited one, even if she'd decided it was none of her business.

In a movement so abrupt she almost fell over she leapt awkwardly backwards and he reached out a hand to steady her. Amara forced herself not to react, reminded herself that her coat was insulated dammit, so she couldn't possibly be feeling anything. Carefully now, she took another step backwards.

'Try you,' she repeated.

He nodded now, took a deep breath and a step backwards as if he too needed distance. 'I think I do get it. From what you said yesterday, I think you have found yourself in a situation you feel you can't control, a situation that has come about through no fault or action of your own. Yet it impacts you and that is making you feel mad because you have limited options and you don't like any of them. That would make me feel pretty mad too, because it makes you feel like a chess piece being moved across the board at the whim of someone else, playing a strategy where you count for nothing.'

Amara stared at him and realised virtual stranger or not, playboy or not, he did get it; knew that his insight could only come from empathy. 'You do get it.'

He gave a small smile, one that invited trust. 'If you want to talk to me, tell me more, maybe I can help. Or maybe just sharing will help.'

Amara studied Gio's expression, saw seriousness there and sincerity. Could she trust the instinct telling her that, or was that instinct coloured by the tug of attraction, his sheer proximity?

Did it matter? Gio was a stranger, a man she'd never see again; in some ways maybe he was the perfect person to confide in. Perhaps he could help see through the tangle of her thoughts, have a clarity of perspective.

CHAPTER THREE

GIO WATCHED AMARA as she considered his offer, an offer he had meant. He did want to help. With an intensity he didn't quite understand, any more than he understood the sense of connection. But he wanted to do something to push back the shadows under her eyes, the strain of tiredness, the trudge of her feet in the snow before they'd progressed to a stamp.

He watched as she came to a decision. 'Perhaps it will,' she said. She paused for a moment as if marshalling her thoughts 'I told you that I was brought up on the Rossi estate. The estate has belonged to the Rossi family since the twelfth century, and we've been producing wine for hundreds of years. We aren't the largest estate in Italy or the best-known but we are successful and I am proud of the wine we produce.' He could hear that pride in her voice, wondered what that must feel like, to be an accepted member of the family. Amara was a real Rossi and he could tell. A sudden qualm hit him—what if his father was right, what if he wasn't a real Romano? He shook the thought away, focused instead on Amara, saw her expression tauten. 'My grandfather brought me up. I lost my parents when I was four.' Her voice was even, didn't stumble or pause or break and he instinctively knew she didn't want to discuss it further. 'Since then, it has been him and me. Until now. Now it turns out that I have two half-siblings. Twins.' Now her voice did stutter slightly and he moved closer to her in the hope she would take comfort from his presence. 'They are two years older than me and they had no idea about their real paternity until recently. But when they found out they contacted my grandfather and testing has proved conclusively that they are…definitely family.' Her voice held a bewilderment that was almost tangible and he got that. Tried to imagine how it must feel. At least he and his half-brothers grew up knowing of each other's existence. Their relationship had been warped from the start and they now had no contact but at least that was through his own choice. He stopped, took both of her hands in his.

'That is a massive amount to take on.'

'My grandfather sees it as a positive—he feels we have a moral duty to welcome them to the family. Which I agree with,' she added hastily.

'But you aren't feeling as positive as he is?' he said, picking his words carefully, keeping her hands firmly clasped in his when he sensed her about to pull back. 'It's okay. It's completely understandable if you have some reservations. You must be feeling…displaced.'

Surprise sparked in her eyes. 'That is it exactly. I feel pushed aside, unnecessary, outnumbered.'

'And angry.'

'Yes. You do get it,' she said softly. 'I feel as though I should go out, do something to fight back. When there isn't even a fight. That's hardly welcoming. And of course my grandfather wants to welcome his grandchildren, his flesh and blood, into the family. It's not a duty to him, he is looking forward to it, and I should feel the same way, should be happy for him. Because this solves everything really.'

'How so?'

'They may already be married or in long-term relationships, hell for all I know they may already have children. Ready-made heirs for the Rossi estate. I should be pleased—it takes the pressure off me.' She sighed. 'That's not fair. My grandfather has never pressured me to marry or have children. Ever. But of course, he is worried about the future of the Rossi estate. But I have always been happy to avoid the issue, avoid the topic. All this time it must have been bothering him—of course it must. I just wanted to pretend it was all okay.'

'Maybe it was okay. Maybe it is okay. There is still plenty of time for you to find a relationship.'

'No.' Her voice was quiet but absolute. 'I don't want that, I don't want a relationship, or to get married. It wouldn't work and I can't fake it. I don't want love. I like being on my own.' Gio heard the sincerity in her voice, an echo of his own sentiments on love and autonomy, wondered why Amara was so adamant. 'That's why I should be happy with the idea of these new people. But I'm not, because I know what I may have to do.' Now her voice was weighted with sadness and without thinking he stepped closer, so they were oh, so close.

'What?' he asked.

'I haven't admitted it until now, until saying it all out loud. My grandfather will make my siblings heirs, will want them to be involved in the estate. Assuming Lorenzo or Daisy or both of them grow to love the estate, I'll have to step aside. For the sake of the estate, for the sake of its future. There are two of them. If they are married there would be four of them. The decisions would be theirs to make. The estate will become their children's future, their legacy. They won't need me.'

And she wouldn't need them, the inference clear. 'I cannot believe your grandfather would want you to step aside.' Not from everything she had said about their relationship. Plus, it would clearly break Amara's heart to relinquish her place in the Rossi dynasty, to step aside from an estate she clearly loved. Yet she would do it. And Gio wasn't sure that made sense, wondered if there was something deeper going on.

'Of course he won't and as long as he is alive and wants me to, I will stay. But…the future has changed now. And I need to accept that and try to embrace it. For my grandfather's sake, for the estate's sake. That is what is most important.'

There was no doubting her sincerity and his heart twisted as he heard her attempt at positivity, at acceptance. 'Don't jump the gun too quickly. Your half-siblings may not be how you picture them. They may not even want to be involved with the Rossi estate. They may not consider themselves to be Rossis.'

'I cannot believe or wish for something like that. If that was the case, I would encourage them to be true Rossis to love the land and their new heritage as I do. For my grandfather's sake.'

A sense of admiration touched him and without thinking he reached out, and gently cupped her face in his hands. 'I don't know you very well, Amara, but from what you have said I can see how much you love your grandfather and your heritage. I believe you will do what is right and I hope that there is a way that means you don't lose what you love.'

He looked down at her upturned face, struck once again by how beautiful she was, though he couldn't quite pinpoint what it was about her that called so emphatically to him. Made him want to drown in the green depths of her eyes. But he wanted more than that. He wanted to help, to make the sadness in her eyes go away, to find a solution. He wanted to kiss her, distract her in a way he knew would chase her troubles away. Albeit temporarily. And he was almost sure that was what she wanted. *Almost.* Or perhaps Amara felt exactly what he felt; an overmastering attraction that she didn't want to feel.

He inhaled the fresh crisp cold air, relieved that it cleared his brain at least a little, as she gently pulled away from his grasp.

'Thank you, Gio.'

'You're welcome,' he said and now he did know what to do. A better solution to a kiss. 'And now I think it is time for some distraction.' From the gravity of her situation and from the attraction that threatened to overcome common sense.

'Agreed. Any ideas?'

'I do have an idea. Let's make a snowman.' He shrugged. 'Or a snowwoman.' For a moment he thought she'd scoff at the idea and then her face broke into a smile. 'It will use up some of our energy and it may even be therapeutic.'

'I like it,' she said. 'Let's do it.' Warmth touched him as her luminous green eyes lit with a sparkle. She scanned the landscape and Gio watched her, absorbed by the glint of sunlight on the waves of her reddish gold hair visible under her dark green woolly hat, on the slant of her brow faintly creased in contemplation. 'How about we make him over there.' She pointed. 'And we can find things for his face and body in that wooded bit over there.'

'Sounds perfect. I will follow your instructions. In fact—' and now his smile deepened '—your wish is my command.' There was a silence and they both stilled, their gazes locked, and he could see his own desire mirrored on her face. 'You just have to tell me what you want me to do.'

Her green eyes held his and what he saw in them ratcheted his pulse rate and it seemed to him the simmering attraction should be melting the snow around his boots.

'I'm not sure that's such a good idea,' she said softly, and then blinked and shook her head. 'I mean… I mean… I'm not really a snowman-making expert. But I'll give it a try.' Looking away from him she started to walk towards a flat bit of snow.

Gio knew he should feel relief that she'd broken the spell, severed the shimmering spark of connection, but he didn't. 'Let's get started,' he said.

Twenty minutes later they studied the sum of their efforts.

Gio had rolled a massive snowball for the bulk of the body and Amara had assembled two smaller ones.

'Right,' she said. 'Let's get them on top of each other.'

They both lifted the medium-sized snowball up and placed it carefully on top of the larger one, and Gio caught his breath. She was so close now, looking at him over the top, her face flushed pink with exertion, her eyes alight—and now tension strummed anew, and all he wanted to do was lean over and kiss her. But instead, he focused on picking up the head and placing it on top and then she walked round so they were next to each other, side by side, and he could feel the tautness of her body next to his, knew she was reining herself in the same way he was bracing himself, in case they should so much as accidentally brush hands. She leaned down and picked up the pine cones they'd found. Handed one to him.

Ten minutes later they stepped back and surveyed the finished product. Amara gave a spontaneous peal of laughter. 'He looks quite…'

He tipped his head to one side and looked at the arrangement of stones, twigs and cones that they had used to make his face.

'Frustrated,' he said without thinking.

Amara moved closer to him to see the snowman from the same angle. 'Oh,' she said. 'You're right.'

Gio couldn't help it, he gave a sudden crack of laughter and then Amara joined in and somehow, without him even knowing it they had turned to face each other and as the laughter died down, they were close, so close, her face upturned to his and…

This time he couldn't help himself. Couldn't stop something that felt so right, so inevitable. Without thinking he leant down, meant to simply brush her lips with his, no more. But as their lips met, the gentle fleeting gesture he'd intended ignited the spark that had been simmering since they'd laid eyes on each other.

Now she stepped forward into his arms and he tasted the lingering vanilla tones. Her lips parted and he deepened the kiss, and sheer pleasure flooded his veins, sent him to dizzying heights of sheer exhilaration. The taste of her, the exquisite passion of her response, the feel of her arms looped round his neck, the press of her body against his all combined to create a heady glorious tornado of sensation.

One that was too short-lived, even though it took at least a minute to identify the noise that was trying to penetrate the sheer density of the bubble of need and desire. Eventually his brain told him that it was a phone, his phone, the ringtone identifying the caller.

Amara must have heard the insistence of the noise because at the same time as he oh, so reluctantly broke the kiss she too stepped back, and even then, they stood staring at each other, until finally he reached into his pocket, tried to even his ragged breath. 'I—I have to take this.'

She nodded and he could see shock in her eyes as he moved away, his legs leaden as he exhorted his brain into gear, sought to shut out the rippling after-effects of a kiss that had blown his mind.

But he had to focus; his grandparents would not be calling him without good reason. They had understood he needed time and it wasn't Aurelio or Ava's style to pressurise him now. They'd agreed a week.

One more deep breath and he answered, looked down at the screen and his brain kicked in, showed him they had video called. He turned to angle the screen away from the glint of the sun and now he focused, saw the expression on his grandparents' faces.

'What's wrong?' he asked.

'Gio?' He could hear anxiety in Ava's voice. 'I…'

'It's okay,' Gio said and now foreboding touched him. 'Take your time. Is there a problem?'

Ava took a deep breath. 'Yes. There is. There is something we didn't tell you Gio.' She took a deep breath. 'I have been diagnosed with Alzheimer's.' Gio's chest contracted, the thought of the future caught at his heart. 'It is early days but…that is why we are standing back from the company. We want to spend the next years together, travelling, making the most of our time.'

'We told the family about your grandmother's condition,' Aurelio said, and Gio could hear the anger in his grandfather's voice. 'Salvatore said he knew something was wrong, that now he understood what it was, that he is ready to take over the reins. When we questioned his plans, he at first refused to discuss them, said that was no longer our concern. I said until we actually stood back it was very much our concern. I am afraid things went downhill from there.' Aurelio's voice held both anger and sadness and it hurt Gio to also hear a soupçon of doubt. Never before had he heard doubt in his grandfather's voice. 'His plans will ruin the company. Worse, he has threatened legal action, will question our capacity if we don't comply with what he wants.'

Gio tried to think of something comforting to say, but he couldn't, because to him this sounded like a typical bully's tactics. And his father was a bully. But what was worst of all was that for the first time ever Aurelio Romano looked vulnerable. And Gio understood why. The one person who Aurelio loved more than his company was his wife. Ava Romano was her husband's world and Ava Romano was ill and their only son was taking advantage of that. Threatening their world.

There was no way Gio was letting that happen. He

would not allow his grandmother's final years to be further blighted. By Salvatore.

Memories flooded his brain. The silky tones of his father's voice as he explained why actually it was allowable, permissible for Max and Antonio to punish their brother for perceived wrongdoings. 'This is their house, Giovanni. They are my real family and you are merely a mistake. Therefore, if they ask you not to touch their toys you shouldn't.' Gio had tried to explain that he hadn't, that in fact, they had offered to let him play with one and only afterwards had they told him he should have refused. Salvatore had shaken his head. 'It is simply a lesson you must learn, Giovanni.' And so whatever punishment it was had been meted out. Perhaps he was asked to sit at a separate table during dinner, facing the wall. Or his brothers had made him do pointless exercises, push-ups or running on the spot. Or worst of all when he was small, the simplest thing, force him to sleep without a night light. And all the while his father had looked on. Until one day, his grandfather had stepped in. Had made the bullying stop.

But now Salvatore would turn those silky explanations onto Aurelio and Ava. Gio could imagine it. Would use the Alzheimer's as justification and threat. To wrest control under the guise of being 'real family'. *You have Alzheimer's, therefore if I ask you not to interfere you shouldn't. It is simply a lesson you must learn.'* Or accept the punishment, the scandal, the legal wrangling, to wrest control.

Once Aurelio had saved him from Salvatore, now Gio would return the favour. Because it was the right thing to do. Ava Romano had been sentenced to such a heart-wrenching future; his grandmother deserved to enjoy every minute left to her, deserved for it to be as stress-free as possible, deserved to be able to stand back and spend the next years with her husband knowing that their company was safe. But it was more than that—if Gio was honest with himself he would enjoy taking his father down, showing Salvatore that Gio was a real Romano, showing him that finally Aurelio and Ava had decided he was 'real family' after all. Because however much he genuinely cared for his grandparents he'd never been that to them. Until now.

'It's okay,' he said. 'I've got this. I will sort this out.'

After he disconnected, he inhaled the crisp cold air and it was as if each breath crystalised the sharp, ice-cold edges of his determination.

He headed back to Amara, saw that she had moved away from the snowman towards the wooded area where they had found the decorations for their creation. She was stood by a tree, her gloriously red hair a stark contrast to the snow-laden branches and the wood of the tree trunks. As he approached, she turned, and he saw concern in her green eyes, along with a lingering knowledge, a memory of the kiss they had shared.

'Is everything okay?' she asked. She studied his expression. 'Now *you* look angry.'

'I am,' he admitted.

'Can I help? You helped me earlier. I'd like to return the favour.'

'Actually, you can help.' Gio wondered if he should think this through more, decided he shouldn't. 'You could marry me.'

CHAPTER FOUR

AMARA STARED AT HIM, wondered if she'd heard right, knew she had and a shaft of hurt pierced her—was he mocking her offer of help? Was he in some way she didn't understand mocking the kiss they'd shared? A kiss that for her had been...sublime. She had never been kissed like that, equally she'd never kissed anyone like that. It had been as though her life depended on it, as though she and Gio were the only people in the universe. Every nanosecond had increased the scale of pleasure until she hadn't been able to think of anything except never wanting it to end. Had wanted to escalate and prolong every feeling. Surely that couldn't have been one-sided. But if he wasn't mocking her, what could he mean? Was he joking?

Then she studied his expression, saw the shadows in his eyes and the pallor of his face and the now-grim set to his lips. Realised he was deadly serious.

'I don't understand.'

He glanced around, but she had the feeling he wasn't seeing the snowman they had been laughing over just moments before.

'I need a wife,' he said. 'And I'd like you to consider my proposal.' He raised a hand. 'I haven't lost my marbles or the plot. I told you I came here to make a decision. That was part of it.' No doubt seeing she didn't look any the wiser, he gave a small rueful smile. 'Okay. My grandparents are Aurelio and Ava Romano and they own and run Romano Confectionery.'

'Oh.' Amara stared at him, cast her mind back to the articles she'd read about Gio Romano. Most of them had been about Gio's romantic exploits, alongside his relationship to Luna Rocco; she did have a vague memory of the connection, but she had had no idea that he was a direct descendant.

'For various personal and business reasons my grandparents need me to join the board of the company. However, the articles of Romano Confectionery cite that all family board members must be married.'

'But that's…' Amara tried to find a word for it and settled for, 'Gothic. And surely that can be questioned in a court of law? Or can't your grandparents change the articles?'

'Perhaps, but that would all take time and we don't have time.' There was sadness and determination in his voice. 'This is the quickest, least complicated way.'

Amara felt her jaw drop. 'It may be quick, but getting married is hardly uncomplicated. Plus…' She was really struggling with this. 'You can't get married just because some articles demand it.'

'I can if it gets me what I want.'

'But why is it so important?' Questions were churning around her brain. Why did his grandparents need him to join the board now? Where was his father in all this?

'Because I want my grandparents to be happy, to live out their final years in peace, knowing their company is safe.' His voice was even, but it held steel and a sadness that touched her. 'My grandmother isn't well, is getting frailer.' His voice caught and she saw the pain in his eyes. 'My grandfather...for him the most important thing in the world is his wife, even more than the company they both love. But neither of them wants to see their company go under, or be absorbed by a huge conglomerate. Romano Confectionery is incredibly important to them.'

'And that is what will happen if you don't join the board?'

'Yes.' He hesitated and now his face hardened, the lips that an hour ago had wreaked such magic, formed a thin line. 'I believe so. When my grandparents decided to stand back, they handed over some shares and some control to my father. It turns out that he has made decisions that they fundamentally disagree with, is determined to do things his way, regardless of their wishes.' Amara heard cold anger in each syllable. 'My grandparents want me to stop him. They will give me enough shares to enable me to outvote him, but to do that I need to be on the board. So yes, I can get married just because the board demands it. So back to where we started. Will you marry me?'

Amara stared at him, and now she did understand. If Lorenzo and Daisy tried to destroy the Rossi estate she would do anything to stop them. Including marriage. But the idea was impossible. And even if it wasn't...

'Why me?' She shook her head. 'You don't even know me.'

Now Gio smiled. 'I get it sounds a little off the wall,' he admitted. 'But I think we can maybe help each other out. This is a deal, an arrangement that can benefit us both.'

'I do not need or want to be paid to marry you.'

'Good. Because that is not what I mean. I am not offering you money or love.'

She shook her head. 'There is nothing you can offer me. I'm not interested in marriage.'

'Aren't you?' Gio leant forward slightly, his brown eyes intent. 'If it was a marriage without love, a partnership, wouldn't that be a good thing? You'd have support when your half-siblings come on board, and it would make your grandfather happy.'

His voice trailed off, presumably because he'd seen her reaction as her mind explored the idea. Hypothetically of course; not as a serious proposition. Because it wasn't off the wall—it was so far out there, aliens were probably listening in.

But the thought crept in that there was a certain symmetry to this. Gio was getting married because he cared about his grandparents and his family company. Why shouldn't Amara do the same thing? She pictured Vittorio Rossi's face, could see the width of his smile, his happiness that she was settling down, that she wouldn't be on her own after his death. The hope for the future it would give him. It would also give Vittorio someone else he could welcome to the family and if for any reason Lorenzo and Daisy didn't work out there would be backup.

Vittorio wouldn't need Lorenzo and Daisy so much and it would put less pressure on Amara to welcome them, bond with them. In a way she knew she couldn't do. The very idea weighted her stomach. She remembered having a family. Remembered running through the castle with Luca, playing a game of make-believe. Her father reading them a story, her mother brushing her hair. And two days later coming home from the hospital, to a castle empty and bereft of her twin, her parents, her grandmother. The only noise the echoes of her own memories, the patter of feet, the laughter, the games. Only her grandfather and Amara left.

Because that was what could happen. Life could implode in a flash. Fate could wreak tragedy. Amara wouldn't put herself in fate's path again. There was no point forming bonds, forging relationships, letting people in.

But despite herself, another scenario snuck in, herself showing these unknown siblings round the castle, getting to know them, laughter, banter, a shared bond. An image she pushed down and out. She would go through the motions; she would do what she had to do for Vittorio's sake.

But now she thought about doing it with someone by her side. With Gio by her side. A person *on* her side in the formation of the new Rossi family dynamic. It would give her a sense of security.

A warning bell clanged in her mind. What happened to the idea of it was best to be alone? But that was the beauty of this. Gio would be by her side as a business partner. He would be an ally rather than a romantic partner. She wouldn't have to worry about whether she was doing things right, wouldn't have to worry she was letting someone too close. She would make the rules. She wouldn't have to change or compromise her life. She could remain on the Rossi estate, Gio could live…wherever he lived.

They could spend as much or as little time together as they wanted. She wouldn't have to worry about hurting him, analyse how she was feeling. Most importantly, this would be an alliance that would reassure her grandfather, make Vittorio feel he wasn't leaving her alone.

Surely this would have all the advantages of a relationship and none of the downsides? No real commitment, nothing confusing or complicated.

Whoa… This was Gio Romano. She shook her head. 'What about your lifestyle?' she asked. No way could she even consider this. She couldn't face being humiliated by infidelity even if there was no love involved. The question flashed through her mind—had her mother known of her father's infidelity? Had he been perennially unfaithful or had it been a one-off, one mistake? How could she not have known? Perhaps she had been like Amara, unable to sift through the nitty gritty, the unspoken nuances and rules of relationships.

For a moment he looked confused and then understanding dawned and a flash of anger sparked his brown eyes.

Her eyes narrowed. 'It's a fair point,' she said. 'Because if I married you, even if it's an arrangement your reputation is now my business. And whilst I accept I am basing this on a few celebrity gossip articles, those articles have you down as a playboy.'

Now the anger left his eyes and he nodded. 'You're right. I owe you an explanation.'

He thought and then, 'First I accept that I am seen with a lot of women. But they are mostly first and often also last dates.'

Amara thought about this and frowned. 'So you reject them after one date and move on to the next?'

'In actual fact, they tend to reject me, or I suppose you could say it is usually a mutual decision to not take things further. Because I never promise anything that I can't fulfil. For me the point of the first date is honesty, to lay down parameters, set out intentions.' His voice was clear, guilt-free.

'And what are your intentions? Or lack of?'

'That depends,' he replied. 'I make it clear that I have no intention of long-term commitment or marriage. But that my short-term commitment would be genuine.' He shrugged. 'Some of my dates have been happy with that, others have been less happy. Which is fair enough. I understand that for a lot of people a first date should at least have the potential to lead to the long term one day. Or what's the point?'

'What is the point?' Amara asked, aware that she was genuinely interested in his philosophy, even if she didn't see how it squared with his idea of getting married to her. Or getting married to anyone.

Now he smiled, a smile so full of promise that she had to force herself not to react, as her toes curled. 'A good time for both people where no one gets hurt,' he said simply. 'Companionship, great sex, a bit of a laugh and when you part no hard feelings.'

'And then on to the next woman?'

'Not straightaway,' he said. 'In the past two years I have probably had relationships with three women. I just happen to have dated a lot more. Hence my reputation.'

'So you're saying on *every* first date you go on you tell your date that you are only up for the short term? If they are good with that you proceed. If not then you don't.'

'Yup. I think it is fair to make it plain I don't want long-term commitment.'

Amara stared at him. 'I hate to point this out but marriage is a long-term commitment.'

This pulled a smile from him. 'I get that. But the reason I am averse to long-term commitment or a long-term relationship is because I don't want love. I don't want to run my life around an emotion that isn't predictable. I don't want to be ruled by an emotion. Unfortunately, most people believe that love is a prerequisite for marriage. If I do meet any women who don't, they seem to want to marry me for my money. I got the idea that you aren't interested in love or money. If I'm wrong then I take back my proposal.'

'You're not wrong. I meant what I said earlier. Love is not something I want. I don't want any commitment at all. And I certainly wouldn't marry you for money.'

'Then consider this marriage. I have no problem giving up my lifestyle, my string of first dates. I am not a heartless two-timing Lothario leaving a string of broken hearts in my wake. I have no wish to hurt anyone, or make any promises I cannot fulfil. I will only promise you what I can fulfil. Not love. But I can offer fidelity. Friendship.' His eyes met hers full on. 'Amongst other things.'

A shiver ran over her skin as the atmosphere morphed into something else and she tried hard to focus on the reality of this conversation. Yet she could hear the husk in her voice as she asked, 'What other things?' She gulped. 'Just to reiterate I am not interested in how much wealth you have.'

Gio waved a hand. 'That's not what I am talking

about,' he said, and his voice deepened, held a promise that caught her breath. 'An attraction we know is off the Richter scale. The one kiss we shared was utterly mind-blowing so I am pretty sure we are…compatible.'

He drew out the syllables in a long drawl and she could feel her skin heat up under the deep rumble of his voice.

'One kiss doesn't mean we are necessarily compatible,' she managed to say.

'We could try another,' he offered and God help her she nearly leapt forward into his arms. Forced herself to remain still.

'Not a good idea,' she said firmly. 'We can't let attraction affect our decision-making here.'

'But it is a factor,' he said. 'If we are serious about this then the chemistry between us is crucial.'

'Then the question is, are we serious about this?' she asked as the sheer surrealness hit her. Was she truly contemplating marrying a stranger? 'I mean surely you must know women better suited for this than me.'

Gio shook his head, and his face was deadly serious now. 'No,' he said simply. 'This sounds a little off base, but it almost feels like fate sent us here at the same time. Two people mulling over two different problems, with the same solution. Marriage helps both of us. Two people who have similar views on relationships, two people who don't want love. That feels like fate to me.'

Fate. The idea made her feel edgy. After all, it had been fate that decreed that she had been the sole survivor of the helicopter accident that killed the rest of her family. It had been fate that decreed a last-minute crisis at the vineyard meant Vittorio hadn't been aboard. Now fate had brought her to the Bavarian Alps. All because one night over thirty years ago her father had been unfaithful to her mother.

'A set of random circumstances that meant we both meet at this point.'

'Yes,' he said and the syllable seemed to thrill through her. 'So yes, I am serious.'

She looked at him. 'How serious? I mean is this marriage something you need for a limited amount of time? I won't lead my grandfather up the garden path, sell him a marriage story only for it to fizzle out, end in divorce once you have your place on the board.'

'As far as I am aware no board member has ever got divorced. I have no intention of testing the principle, won't give anyone any ammunition to get me removed. Plus, I wouldn't do that to you. I will keep my part of the bargain—our marriage arrangement will remain in place until we make a mutual decision to end it.' He took both her hands in his. 'So, Amara Rossi. Will you do me the honour of marrying me?'

There were so many questions buzzing in her head, but in the end, this was the fundamental question and a sudden exhilaration gripped her.

'Yes. I will,' she said. And as she said the words, she felt a sudden surge of optimism, a sense that perhaps this could work. Because she would be in control, they could live by actual rules, terms, a contract. Things she did understand. 'What happens next?'

'We go back to the hotel and work out a plan.'

CHAPTER FIVE

GIO HEARD THE knock on the door of his hotel suite, strode across to open it and felt a mixture of relief, disbelief and a strange warmth as he pulled the door open and saw Amara.

'I wasn't sure you'd come,' he admitted. She'd gone back to her room to change out of her hiking clothes and they'd agreed to meet and plan over lunch. 'I thought you may have changed your mind.'

'Nope. I do keep wondering if I am caught up in a dream or that perhaps this is some sort of prank, but I'm here.' Exhilaration raced through him and he could see that she felt the same way. Her green eyes held an element of shock but no doubts. That in itself buzzed through him. The idea that this could work. For both of them.

'I'm glad.' He stepped back and she entered, looked round the suite and her mouth opened. 'Wow,' she said.

He glanced round and grinned. 'You like it?'

'What's not to like? I take it this is step one in our plan.'

'Yup. We need privacy to plan, but we also need to start to be noticed. So, I requested a romantic lunch for two and the staff have really delivered.'

'They really have,' Amara agreed. She took in the roaring fire in the fireplace, flower petals spread across the table, the champagne in the wine cooler, the beautifully laid table and the elegantly presented food.

'I promised you fondue, so fondue you shall have.' They both surveyed the large pot of molten bubbling cheese. Flanked by plates with cubes of different bread, ready to be picked up with the gleaming silver fondue forks and dunked straight in. 'There's rye bread, pretzel bread, sour dough and good old-fashioned crusty white. I asked.' Because he knew she'd be interested.

'I'm betting the pretzel is amazing with the extra saltiness and the rye bread will give a real contrast.' She looked round. 'They've really thought about it. There are vegetable crudités which add the healthy touch and pickled vegetables, as well. I'm guessing the tartness of the pickle will give a bite against the creaminess of the cheese.' She gave a sudden laugh. 'Sorry. I have no idea why I am discussing food when we are here to discuss getting married.'

'Maybe because it seems a little surreal?' he suggested. 'And at least the food is real.'

'And will make a very memorable meal.' She pulled out her phone. 'If this is the start of our relationship, I think we should take some pictures for social media.'

'Bright and beautiful,' he said.

'What do you mean?'

'I mean you got it straight away.' She'd taken one look at the setting and figured out what he'd done and she was running with it.

'I guess I am a natural at faking it,' she said.

'I'll bear that in mind,' he said.

She closed her eyes and he grinned as her cheeks tinged pink. 'I didn't mean it like that…'

'You sure?' he asked.

Amara narrowed her eyes. 'This is *not* a conversation we should be having,' she said. 'We're here to plan what happens next.' She took a deep breath. 'Though…to be clear that doesn't include sleeping together. We need to make sure this is a good idea for other reasons than attraction. Sleeping together would complicate things and they are already complicated enough.'

'Agreed.' He met her gaze, wanted to reassure Amara that he got it. 'There's no rush. I don't want you to feel any pressure about that side of things.' There was also the sneaking suspicion that the attraction would be too all-consuming, too overwhelming and right now he needed to be focused on the big picture. On pulling off this marriage. He was pretty sure that his father wasn't going to go down without a fight and he needed to make sure he didn't win. 'We need to focus on getting this right and I know it's early days.'

'Exactly. It is early days. But we need to move fast, because you need to be appointed to the board as quickly as possible.' She paused. 'That means a quick marriage, which doesn't give us time to be absolutely sure this is a good idea. We both need to be able to change our minds, or change the terms and I think that will be more difficult if we are sleeping together.'

'Agreed.'

'Good. Now I'll take some photos then let's eat. I'm ravenous and this looks incredible.' Once she'd finished taking pictures of the table she glanced at him. 'I guess we'd better take a picture of us together. Our first selfie…'

He nodded. 'Hang on. I'll open the champagne.'

A few minutes later they were holding crystal glasses full of the pale sparkling wine. Amara held it up to the light that flooded in from the floor-to-ceiling window, and then took a tiny sip, before nodding in appreciation. 'Lovely. I wasn't sure about champagne and fondue but this will go really well. It's got a crisp floral tone that should complement the food beautifully.' Seeing that he was watching her, she bit her lip. 'Sorry. I think it's either a bad habit or a nervous habit.'

'Don't apologise. I really don't mind.' Truth be told he already liked it, the small frown of concentration that creased her forehead, the way she crinkled her nose slightly as she tasted the wine. The thought that went into her verdict.

She gave a small smile, but he was pretty sure she thought he was just being polite. 'Let's get the photo.' She edged towards him and stopped. 'Actually, I feel a little silly. I mean it's a bit awkward. Are we supposed to look all lovey-dovey? That's not really my style, plus this is meant to be the start of our relationship, so perhaps we need to look more...dazed? I really have no idea how to do this.'

He put his glass down on the table and gestured to the window. 'Let's stand there so we've got all the snow and scenery behind us and then I guess we try to look relaxed and happy.'

One photograph later they looked at the result and Amara grimaced. 'We look like we're desperately trying *not* to touch each other or get too close.'

'That's because we are desperately trying not to touch each other.' By so much as a brush of the hands. 'And that's not going to work. We have to look as though we are comfortable together or none of our social media pictures will work. Or any subsequent publicity.' Gio wasn't a huge celebrity, but as Luna Rocco's son and as someone who had dated his fair share of celebrities, he was still worthy of some coverage. 'My idea is that anyone checking our social media will be sure to see a real credible timeline of our romance. And if we can get pictured tonight at some celebrity hangout then all the better. The more publicity we garner, the more open we are, the more authentic it will look.'

'So we need this photo to work,' Amara said.

'I've got an idea.' Gio wasn't sure if it was a good idea or not but what the hell. 'Whilst we're taking the photo think about the kiss we shared. Remember how it felt and maybe that will help.'

Doubt floated across her eyes and then she gave a small shrug. 'Okay. Right, here goes.' She held her phone up and Gio thought back to earlier, remembered the feel of Amara in his arms, the taste of her lips, his hands pulling her closer, the press of her body against his.

'Done,' she said and her voice sounded as breathless as he felt.

They surveyed the photo. 'I guess that did it,' she said. 'We look…'

'Dazed,' he completed. 'And happy.' And he couldn't help thinking how happy they would actually both be if they repeated the kiss in reality. Bad idea. Because that would distract them from what they were supposed to be doing. 'Now that's done we'd better start figuring out exactly how this is all going to work.'

They sat down and picked up their fondue forks. He couldn't help smiling as he saw how carefully she chose which bread to sample first, the way she made sure the cube was perfectly coated in the fondue before tasting it. 'Good?' he asked.

'Incredible. Creamy with a kick of something. I reckon it may be mustard.' She chose the next cube and said, 'Right. Okay. After eating all of this, what happens next?'

He took a moment to appreciate the food himself before answering. 'After our social media blitz to set the scene for a whirlwind romance, we'll announce the engagement as quickly as possible. Followed by a marriage as fast as possible.' He was damned sure his father would keep him off the board until the marriage was watertight and would be plotting in the background. Assuming his father even considered the idea that Aurelio and Ava would bring Gio on board. There was a good chance he wouldn't even contemplate so fantastical a notion. Gio was finding it hard to get his head round the idea himself. Knew the only reason was the fact Aurelio Romano couldn't think of another play, had decided this was the only move that would save his wife and their company. Whatever the reason, it gave Gio a chance to repay the debt he owed his grandparents and show his father that he was a real Romano after all. And he had every intention of taking that chance. 'There will be nothing hole and corner about it. Love at first sight is the theme and it's a story we'll stick to. The whole thing should look like a fairy tale.' Because once his father did cotton on to events, he would look for any reason to challenge the marriage.

Amara thought for a while. 'The key is to make this believable so we need to show this is different from your usual relationships. But we need glamour too. I agree we need a bit of external publicity, not just generated by us.'

He sipped his champagne. 'I propose we head to Munich tonight, go to a celebrity-studded restaurant, get our photo taken, stay in a fancy hotel. Then we change it up. We'll go and spend a few days in a romantic chalet in the Alps. Maybe make it a bit of a road trip, stay in different places.'

'That makes sense. We could take it in turns to pick where we stay. If you book tonight's hotel I'll book tomorrow's chalet and so on.'

Gio nodded; he appreciated Amara's practical viewpoint and the fact she clearly saw this as an equal partnership.

She prodded a potato and carefully coated it in cheese. 'I will talk to my grandfather this afternoon.' There was a hint of worry in her voice. 'I think he will be happy and I hope he will believe the story. He and my grandmother had a whirlwind romance. He always describes it as a love tornado and they were happy for decades.'

He thought he saw wistfulness on her face and a qualm struck him. 'Are you sure about this? About marrying me. I know you said that you have no interest in relationships, but are you sure? Are you sure you don't want to hold out for love, a real happy ever after, something you can tell your grandfather is genuine?'

'I'm sure.'

'I need to know more than that. I need to understand so that I can be absolutely sure before we start the charade for real. I get you had a relationship that didn't work out, but that is hardly grounds for believing love isn't possible or that you don't want it.'

'It's more than that. I had two relationships that didn't work out. *You* don't want love because it's an emotion you can't control. I don't want it because I don't get it. And I can't. I can't see the point of it.'

'What happened with your exes?'

'I met Stefan at a wine-makers convention. We fell into conversation. It was the first time I'd gone without my grandfather and Stefan was very knowledgeable about wine and I suppose I was flattered when he asked me out. We started seeing each other. But it wasn't fun. It felt like hard work. I'd feel like I had to prepare all the time, plan, think about good topics of conversation, look right, say the right things.'

'But surely you could just be yourself?'

'That's exactly it. I couldn't. I couldn't work out how. Everything I said sounded silly. Stefan didn't like it if I overanalysed food or drink, he didn't like it if I spoke too much about wine. It felt as though he didn't like lots of things about me. But I'm not sure I was actually ever being me. The whole thing made me edgy, nervous. Stefan said I was too cold and he was right—I was. I couldn't relax.'

'Maybe Stefan wasn't right for you.' Gio couldn't help thinking the man sounded like a bit of a pretentious arse, but hey, what did he know. 'People shouldn't try to change other people in a negative way.'

'That's what I thought. Especially when he left me for someone else. But two years after, I met Silvio. He was really different from Stefan, nicer, kinder, but the same problems were there. I couldn't relax, I couldn't figure out how to behave. And he ended up frustrated because he really was a nice guy, but I couldn't seem to let him in. I was still always on edge. I never felt at ease. The whole thing made me… Anxious. And the harder I tried the worse it became. In the end I ended it because he deserved someone who could actually appreciate him. The whole thing made me realise that I'm not cut out for a relationship.'

'But however nice Silvio was he still may not have been right for you.'

'I don't want to meet someone who is right for me. That would make it even worse, even more scary. Make me even more worried if I'm doing the right thing. If I really cared about them, if I loved them, I'd be a wreck. I am way happier on my own, in my own space and solitude. I'm not interested in investing my emotions, my time, in all the anxiety love seems to require. So this arrangement works for me.' She tipped her head to one side. 'Come to that, how do *you* know you don't want love? And are you sure this works for you?'

They were fair questions and he took some time to marshal his thoughts, didn't want to give Amara a flip or glib answer. But he was sure. He'd spent his whole childhood reliant on other people's whims. People who didn't want him or love him. After his grandfather discovered the bullying, Gio spent one weekend a month with his grandparents and those had been his most treasured times, shared with people who chose his company. And during those visits, over the years they had forged a bond, had built a relationship, a mutual respect and a liking for each other's company. But Aurelio and Ava had never wavered in their belief that he shouldn't be treated as a true family member, shouldn't be allowed into the echelons of the company. Fundamentally, even his grandparents didn't truly want him, or accept him. But they at least made the best of him, the Romano they too saw as a 'mistake', a blip in the respectable traditions of the family, the child who should never have been born, from a marriage that should never have been made. A Vegas joke.

But now he would be having the last laugh. He was the one his grandparents had turned to, to take down the 'real' Romano, the pillar of respectability. And he would do it because he cared about them, because it was right, but there was no point denying that a part of him felt vindicated. Vindicated but still not loved. The knowledge sent a swirl of emotion through him, a sense of anger, but most of all a sadness.

Enough. He'd long ago accepted love wasn't coming his way, had spent his childhood wishing that someone wanted him, cared about him. He wasn't opening himself up to that again. And he wasn't allowing anyone else to control his life either, wouldn't act on someone else's whims.

So now he met Amara's gaze full on. 'I am sure this works for me and I am sure I don't want love. I like to live my life the way I want to live it. I don't want to answer to anyone else.'

'Is that how you see love, as answering to someone else?'

'Yes,' he said. 'Or at least it should be. It's a responsibility.' He'd never understood why his mother didn't feel responsible for him, didn't feel any maternal obligation to be there for him. 'If you love someone you should think about them, take their desires into consideration. I don't want to do that. I want to make my own choices.'

'That works for me. I don't want you to feel responsible for me and I am quite happy for you to make your own choices. Plus, if this does go all wrong neither of us can get hurt—that's the beauty of it.'

She raised her glass, and Gio followed suit, but as he did so, a sudden, small doubt that he couldn't pinpoint pinged at the back of his brain. A doubt he squashed. Amara was right—this was foolproof. They were both on the same page about love. This would work.

'To us,' he said.

'To us,' she echoed.

Amara pushed her hotel room door open and put her purchases on the bed. Thank goodness the hotel had a boutique. She glanced at her watch; she didn't have much time to get ready before they left for Munich. They'd decided to head straight to the restaurant for dinner and check into the hotel in Munich after their meal. Which had at least given her some time; time to get into character, time to do some shopping before they announced their relationship. Started the social media campaign.

She surveyed the clothes and hoped she'd made the right choices. She hadn't packed in the expectation of wining and dining with Gio Romano as his soon to be fiancée. The whole idea was still hard to wrap her head around, especially when she contemplated the glare of publicity she was about to step into.

Yet, truth be told, that hadn't been at the forefront of her mind when she'd been stood in front of the clothing racks. She'd been thinking about Gio, about the reaction she wanted to evoke; had pictured his brown eyes darkening with desire, gleaming with appreciation when he saw her.

And that was all wrong. It was the camera she was

playing to, not Gio. This was a contract marriage and for all she knew it wouldn't actually work out. She liked the synergy, the idea that she was helping not just her own grandfather but also Gio's. But she still didn't fully understand the Romano family dynamics.

There were still so many questions, so much they didn't know about each other, and Amara knew she had to tread carefully, had to make sure the attraction didn't affect her ability to assess the situation. She, *they*, both needed clear heads. And she needed to remember that if the Romano dynamic changed Gio might change his mind. Come to that, he might change his mind full stop. He might spend a few days with her and decide it couldn't work. Stefan and Silvio had found her lacking. There was every chance Gio would too. Equally Gio might not be the man *she* believed him to be. After all, she barely knew him. It could be that the attraction was colouring her vision of the man; her hormones could be jamming her brain signals. That was why they had both agreed not to act on the attraction.

So maybe the dress she'd chosen for tonight wasn't a good idea.

Her phone rang just as she was contemplating a mad dash back to the shop.

Her grandfather.

Swiftly she picked up.

'Amara! I am returning your call. How are you? How is Bavaria?'

'It's all good, Nonno. Really good. Something…unexpected has happened.'

'Are you okay?' She could almost see him frowning. 'You sound different.'

'I'm going out for dinner with someone,' Amara said.

'You didn't need to call to tell me that.'

'I do. Because the man I am having dinner with is Gio Romano. He's not a celebrity or anything, but he is in the public eye a bit so there may be some publicity.' She knew her grandfather would go away and do some research, so she continued. 'I promise you, Nonno, he is not like the papers say, he is…' She paused, wanted to lie as little as possible. 'He is a good man, I know it. I…feel something I have never felt before. And he does too.' Neither of them had ever contemplated marriage before, that was for sure.

'I trust your instincts, Amara. I always have. But be careful.'

'I will, I promise. It's only dinner—it may lead to more or it may not. I just didn't want you to be surprised by the publicity.' Amara decided she had done enough for now. Sown the seeds for a potential engagement announcement as best she could. 'How is everything at home?'

They discussed work and then Amara asked the question she'd been dreading, hoped that her voice was civil, interested, positive.

'Is there any news on Lorenzo and Daisy?'

'Yes. I am hoping to set up a meeting with Lorenzo for when you are back. I assume you will wish to be here.'

'Of course. I am planning on flying back in five days. Is…is he coming to Tuscany?'

'Yes. He will be on his own. We decided that was best. I believe he is quite protective of his sister.'

Amara realised her hand had clenched into a fist. Would Luca have been protective of her? What would life have been like if fate hadn't stepped in and doled out tragedy?

'That's wonderful,' she heard herself gush. 'Let me know the final arrangements. I'll be there.' Even if the very thought weighted her with dread.

Putting her phone down she turned back to the clothes laid out on the bed and suddenly all her earlier qualms seemed irrelevant. It was a dress. In the scheme of things it didn't matter if she wore it. After all, life could change within moments in ways it was impossible to fathom. In a few days' time she was going to meet a half-brother she could never have imagined existed. Just as Lorenzo Cavendish could never have imagined that he had a different father than he'd believed all his life. Then a little later she was planning to marry a man she barely knew. As part of a contract that would benefit them both.

So, she needed to play her part. Honour the deal she'd made. And the dress she had chosen would do exactly that. As for the reaction she hoped to provoke—well why not? As she got ready, wriggled into the dress, brushed her hair, swiped on what she hoped was the right amount of make-up, Amara had a sudden urge to seize the moment, to let Gio distract her from thoughts of Lorenzo and the forthcoming meeting. Why not play the part to the hilt? Make sure this whole fake relationship looked real.

Only it wasn't a fake relationship.

She was really going to marry him.

The thought sent a swirl of panic-laced anticipation through her as she heard the knock on the door. Knew it was Gio.

CHAPTER SIX

GIO OPENED HIS mouth to say hello and realised no sound was coming out.

Amara looked… Utterly sensational. The dress was a gorgeous concoction of cascading sequins, that shimmered with the reddish-gold hues of a sunset, and fell in a glittering swirl to her calves. The tank-styled neckline showed the column of her throat encircled by a topaz necklace and her hair fell in silken waves past her shoulders, crying out to be touched. Hell, all he wanted to do was touch. To pull her into his arms and kiss the glossy lips, to inhale her scent.

Somehow, he managed to get his brain and vocal chords to connect. 'You look…breathtaking,' he settled for, and somehow, he knew he would never forget this vision of her.

'You look pretty good yourself,' she said, her voice low and shy and her eyes bright with desire.

'Thank you.' Dammit, desire was literally rendering him tongue-tied. 'The car's waiting downstairs.'

By common consent they walked down the stairs to the lobby; the idea of being confined in a lift simply too risky at this point. Gio wondered if there were sparks flying around them visible for all to see, and noticed they garnered a few looks as they walked across the marble floor.

Telling himself he was using the moment, he took her hand in his, felt a shock wave course through his body, saw her step falter slightly. Turning, she looked up at him, her eyes flecked with desire, her lips slightly parted.

Once outside they both inhaled sharply as if in hope the cold night air could shock them. Then he opened the door to the chauffeured car he'd organised to take them to Munich.

'You're definitely making a statement,' she said, as they waited for their luggage to be collected and put in the boot.

'I'm aiming to get us noticed. The restaurant should get us some publicity, as well. There are usually photographers lurking to get some celebrity pictures. Will that be okay?'

She thought for a while as the car started its journey. 'I think I'll be fine. Over the years I have been the face of Rossi wines. I manage our PR and I've done some talks. It's terrifying, but I'm good at pretending. I imagine a wall between me and other people. It's a wall that protects me—it keeps me safe. It's like a knowledge that no matter what happens it's not a worst-case scenario.' She frowned. 'I'm not explaining myself very well. I always think what is the worst thing that can happen? I can make a mistake. People could laugh at me. I could drop a bottle of a wine. I could taste a Bordeaux and say it's a merlot.' She gave a quick smile. 'But I can come back from all those things. What's the worst that can happen tonight? They get an unflattering picture of me? That wouldn't end the world. The worst I can lose is a bit of pride or dignity.' She smiled at him and he saw a wealth of sadness in her green eyes and his chest twisted. He guessed nothing could be worse than losing your family in one fell swoop. If you'd lived the worst-case scenario you would be able to not get too involved in the angst of social situations.

He shifted slightly closer, hoped he was conveying some comfort or reassurance and they completed the journey in a silence that felt comfortable, both of them lost in thought until the car glided to a halt.

'We're up,' he said. 'You ready?'

'I'm ready. The wall is up.'

A wall that held the world at bay and kept her safe. Safe from caring about the things so many people cared about. He got that. And that created a sense of connection along with a reassurance that this marriage idea really could work. Because Amara was safe behind her wall and he was equally safe behind his.

As they emerged from the car, he took her hand in his, again felt that zing and jolt of sheer electricity, enough to light the way towards the renowned restaurant, the haunt of the rich and famous.

He saw the flash of cameras, sensed the buzz, felt her slow down ever so slightly, not enough to call it an invite for attention but enough to allow them to be seen. Then she turned and looked up at him with a smile that lit her face and he leant down and brushed her lips with his, a clear signal to the onlookers that they were a bona fide couple.

He felt the shiver run through her and it was only the knowledge that they were in public that stopped him from deepening the kiss, and as they walked in it was increasingly hard to focus on saying the right thing to the staff who met them, to keep a smile on his face, to try and look suave and charming when all he wanted to do was tug her hand and race out of the restaurant and on to the hotel. Where they were sharing a two-bedroom suite he reminded himself.

As they sat down opposite each other she smiled at him, reached over and covered his hand. 'So far so good,' she said softly and turned her attention to the menu.

She was still looking when the waiter returned. 'I've brought some complimentary hors d'oeuvres and a glass of champagne.'

'Thank you. Could I have a little more time to look at the menu?'

'Of course.'

'Hmmm…' He heard the small sigh she gave as she looked back down, the crease of concentration on her forehead. 'How on earth can I choose?' she said. 'This is all…amazing.'

'There's no rush,' he said. 'I'm quite happy sitting here watching you choose.'

She shook her head. 'No way. You can't order whatever I do again.'

'Why not?'

'Because we have to choose different things. That way I get to taste more things. But no way am I doing that cringy couple thing where you feed each other bits of food.'

'Cringy?' He raised an eyebrow.

'There is nothing good about two people feeding each other in a cutesy way.'

'It's supposed to be quite enjoyable,' he said.

'Are you speaking from experience?'

'No. I have never fed anyone anything. But…we've got the perfect food to give it a try.' He gestured to the beautifully presented plate of appetisers.

She glanced at the selection. 'It almost seems a shame to eat them,' she said. 'They look incredible, I mean they are even colour-coordinated. Each one is a work of art.'

'All the more reason to use them for the camera. It's what couples do.'

She looked at him suspiciously and he grinned, won an answering smile. 'Go on. I reckon it may be… Interesting. Close your eyes.'

'I'm not sure. I don't really like surprises. I like my food in a certain order. Plus, not knowing what I'm about to eat is a bit unnerving.'

'Trust me.' There was a pause and he realised in some ways the words had a deeper meaning. Because all this was about trust. They were trusting each other. He was trusting her not to go to the press with the whole fake marriage idea; she was trusting him to sustain an illusion of love for the sake of her grandfather. 'I'll make good choices. And if I don't, you can tell me.' Honesty was the basis of their deal, after all, and without love, without that constant worry of losing it that would be easy.

Her gaze met his, then she gave a small nod and closed her eyes. He looked down at the food, picked a caviar-topped blini.

'So first up I am going to choose something light and delicate. A creamy, slightly briny flavour that brushes over you gently, and leaves you wanting more.'

He saw her gulp slightly, saw the rise and fall of her

chest, wondered how wise this was. But he couldn't help himself. Carefully he put it into her mouth, just let the tip of his finger brush against her lip and desire twisted his gut as he saw the shiver run over her skin.

'It's lovely, the topping is slightly nutty as well, the whole thing is nuanced. It feels like I'm floating.'

'Now try this.'

This time when he put the morsel of smoked salmon canapé in her mouth, he'd swear she oh, so lightly nipped his finger, leaned towards him slightly. And his breath hitched, caught in his chest.

'This one has a smokiness and a tang of spiciness. A jolt to the senses.'

'Like this?' he asked.

And now he ran a finger over the palm of her hand, his thumb making small circles as she caught her breath.

Her eyes flew open, dark and dreamy with desire. 'My turn. Close your eyes.' Her voice was low and slow; it seemed to slide over his skin heating it up.

He closed his eyes and he felt her gently rub his lips, tasted the fizz and bubble of champagne.

'Taste the bubbles, how they fizz over you with a vanilla overtone and let the taste linger. Savour the unique blend that makes it explode in your mouth.'

Now he opened his eyes and their gazes locked and it truly felt like there was no one in the room except them, the hustle and bustle seemed to have faded to mere background noise and all he could see was Amara.

Until awareness trickled in and he realised the waiter was now stood by the table. He blinked, knew he had to get things back in focus, saw Amara visibly pull herself together as she picked up the menu, smiled up at the waiter and made a choice. Gio followed suit, made a random choice, his interest in food minimal, his whole being still swirling with desire.

Once the waiter had gone they simply stared at each other.

'Um… I'm not really sure what to talk about,' she said.

'That's because it's quite hard to actually string a sentence together.' He ran a hand through his hair and tried to think. 'Tell me about wine,' he said. 'Maybe it will refocus us on conversation.'

'It's worth a try,' she said. 'Unless I bore you to death.'

'You won't do that.'

Though he did expect her to launch forth into a blitz of technical information or how grapes ferment, but instead she said, 'I think what I love best about wine is its history, how people were drinking wine millennia ago, not centuries but millennia.'

Her voice held awe. 'And I suppose I love that I am a cog in the whole history of wine. Did you know that it is probable that wine was first made in China in 7000 B.C.? I mean, that is mind-blowing. I am not sure how it was done, but I think honey and fruit were fermented to make alcohol. The idea spread to Georgia and then Persia, over the next two thousand years. And it was then that grapes were first used.'

'That is pretty amazing.' Gio thought for a minute. 'I mean, I can't even picture what people looked like back then, what they were wearing, but they were drinking wine.'

'All over the world. The ancient Egyptians even "bottled" theirs in jugs by labelling them with the year the wine was made and who made it.'

'And when did wine come to Italy?'

'In about 4000 B.C., most likely to Sicily. But it was all a bit haphazard until around 800 B.C. when the Greeks arrived. They brought vines with them and more importantly, they had a system—they organised things and brought their techniques and equipment and that's when it all really started.'

She broke off as the food arrived, waited for the dishes to be carefully placed and the wine poured and then glanced at him. 'Sorry I *have* been wittering on. You should have stopped me.'

'I didn't want to.' He knew the words to be utterly true. His interest in the topic was genuine, but he'd also been absorbed by her sheer seriousness, her passion for what she was talking about. The way her hands moved, her eyes sparkled, the way she leant forward to emphasise her point, the sound of her voice.

'And the Rossis have made wine for hundreds of years,' he recalled.

Amara nodded, a fleeting look of something he thought may be surprise on her face. As though she was surprised he remembered. Then she smiled, a smile that lit her face. 'I guess that's why I feel so involved. We are part of the Italian wine heritage and history. I've been part of it since I took my first breath. I was even born on the estate. It's in my blood and I love it. When you see it, I think you'll know what I mean.'

'Tell me about it.'

And as they ate, she did and he could almost see the rolling landscape, meadows scattered with wildflowers, a rugged, turreted stone castle with an ancient steepled chapel in the background. Cypress trees, olive groves and of course the stretch of vineyards, the vines going through the seasons from the unfurling buds of spring, the growth and ripening of summer and then autumnal harvesting when the vines change colour and the grapes were picked and then the winter where the vines re-grouped and rested. And as Amara spoke, he could see that she was at one with the estate she'd grown up on, would cultivate and nurture each vine as though it had a personality, an individuality.

'But enough of me,' she said, breaking off with a self-conscious smile. 'What about you. Where do you live?'

'I move around a lot for business but I'm based in Milan. I've got an apartment there and I've also got a place in LA where quite a lot of my business is.'

'Tell me about your company. I know you are phe-nomenally successful and I know you are a med-tech entrepreneur, but I don't really know the details.'

'I designed an app that allows home health monitor-ing, so it can help patients with existing issues keep an eye on their health and allows everyday people to moni-tor various things. So people who are worried because they know they are at high risk of say heart disease, can monitor some of their risk factors.'

Amara tipped her head to one side. 'What inspired you to do that?' she asked.

He shrugged. 'I always had a bent for technology and engineering and I was interested in health. My grand-father had a heart attack when I was in my teens.' Gio could remember the shock he'd felt. To him, his grand-father had been invincible. And underlying the shock and the worry had been a craven fear that without the protection of his grandfather, his brothers, his father, would once again have power over him. Along with a sense of exclusion—he'd only found out about the heart attack weeks after the event. Hadn't been involved, was on the fringe of events.

He'd suppressed the thoughts, hated himself for his own cowardice and selfishness and perhaps from that had come the seed of an idea.

'I think that spurred me on and I came up with the concept and then I managed to get proper backing and it took off.'

'You make it sound easy.'

'It wasn't easy, but…' He hesitated. 'But I was so driven that somehow even when I got knockbacks, even when things went wrong, it never occurred to me that I wouldn't succeed.' Failure hadn't been a possibility. Because he'd had too much to prove. To himself and every single Romano, whether he loved or loathed them. That he could make it on his own, forge his own success.

He realised that he'd put way too much emotion into his voice, saw her green eyes looking at him with scrutiny and an understanding that made him edgy because he sensed a connection he wasn't sure he wanted.

'You definitely succeeded and I am guessing that you love your company, just as your grandparents love theirs.'

'Yes, I do. And I'm proud of the product we supply. I've got plans to branch out into other med-tech areas. There is so much out there now, so many things worth investing in, putting money into that can truly make a massive difference to people's lives. AI tech, robotics. Our R&D department is huge, and I also try to help out as many startups as I can. I also want to help places and communities that don't usually benefit from this type of technology, make it more accessible and affordable.' He broke off. 'Now I *really* am wittering on.'

'You really aren't. I can hear how much this means to you and how important it is. It sounds incredible and a pretty full-on job. It's also a very different industry to chocolate. Also…' She hesitated and he gestured with his hand.

'It's okay. You can say what you think.'

'I was curious. What made you set up your own company? And why an industry so different from chocolate? I mean you must have always known you'd end up at Romano Confectionery?'

Gio shook his head, knew that it was another fair question and that Amara deserved a fair answer.

'My parents' marriage was incredibly brief. It wasn't even real apart from in a legal sense. They got married in Vegas on some sort of drunken dare. Their whole relationship only lasted a matter of weeks, a brief aberration in both their lives. They annulled the marriage a few days after the Vegas ceremony. My father quickly remarried and my stepmother, Bianca, was already pregnant when my mother announced her own pregnancy. To my grandparents, I was the equivalent of illegitimate and they are old-fashioned enough for that to count. Respectability is important to them. They were moral enough to believe my father must acknowledge me and spend time with me. My mother insisted I took the Romano name.' Gio suspected she had done that quite simply to annoy the strait-laced disapproving Romano clan, had done it to emphasize her insistence on joint custody. Financial support hadn't been a consideration for either party, his

mother was a multimillionaire in her own right and the
Romano wealth was immense. But his mother had not
wanted to be lumbered with a child full-time and his
father hadn't wanted to be lumbered with a child at all.
So, the fight had been over who could care for him the
least. 'But although I would bear the Romano name,
spend time with my father, I wouldn't be part of the
Romano business. That would go to my father and then
my half-brothers.'

'They excluded you? From the company that means
so much to them?' Gio heard the shock, the outrage in
her voice. 'So, you had to grow up watching your brothers being welcomed into the family business that you
were barred from.'

'Yes. But…'

Amara shook her head. 'I know it is none of my business and I'm sorry if I'm overstepping, but what they
did wasn't fair. And it isn't fair now for them to ask you
to put aside your own business, your own global success to… To bail them out. Maybe you should think
twice before joining the Romano board. Before getting
married. I am doing this because the Rossi estate, my
grandfather—they have been there for me all my life. I
do owe my grandfather something, a marriage, a comfort and reassurance that I won't be alone. But from what
you've told me I am not sure why you owe your grandparents anything.' He could hear a suppressed anger in
her voice. 'What they did wasn't fair.' Another breath.
'You don't have to do this.'

Surprise slammed into him as he realised that Amara
was actually incensed on his behalf. The knowledge
twisted something in his chest and sent a warmth over

him—after all, for most of his life no one had taken up the cudgels on his behalf.

Except, he reminded himself, except for his grandparents. But he couldn't tell Amara about the bullying. There was nothing to be gained by explaining or reliving past humiliations. Admitting weakness and guilt. Because sometimes in the recesses of his soul Gio wondered if it was his fault. After all, Salvatore appeared to care about his wife and his other sons. Maybe it was all just him.

But he knew he owed his grandparents. Not only for ending the torment, but for continuing to see him, for making him feel wanted, however briefly. But also, because Gio was the catalyst that had brought out and exposed Salvatore's worse traits. And that must have hurt Aurelio and Ava, to believe ill of their only son, their pride and joy. Their heir. And somehow, Gio had felt it was all his fault and he'd never once told another soul about what had happened.

Yet, as he studied Amara's face, he was almost tempted to tell her. Almost. Abruptly he shook the feeling off.

'I want to do this, Amara. Even though I was excluded from it I do love Romano Confectionery and I do care for my grandparents. I want to help them. They did what they thought was right and they showed me affection. And now, when they are old and frail, I won't turn my back on them. I want to do this.' He hesitated, and then honesty compelled him. 'And I want to show them that I can do this, that I am a real Romano.' He regretted the words as soon as he said them; knew he'd given away too much. Gave a shrug that he hoped would lighten his tone, hurried on. 'I suppose I'd like to make a point. But any which way, I want to do this. I want to marry you.'

There was a short silence and then she smiled. 'Then let's keep this show on the road.' She hesitated. 'I told my grandfather earlier that you are a good person. And you are.' And with that she leaned across the table, and with the lightest of touches she brushed her lips across his. And he knew that it was an affirmation that they were going forward; it felt different to the kiss before. This was sweeter and lighter and there was a shimmering strange sense of connection.

It engendered a warmth that set a warning bell off in the back of his head. One he sensed that she could hear, or perhaps her own thoughts followed his. Her green eyes stared at him as she sat back and she lifted a hand to her lips. Then, as if she was allowing the clatter and clink and surrounding conversation in, she blinked and she smiled but it was a smile that still left her eyes holding a hint of confusion.

Reaching out he raised his glass. 'To us,' he said softly. 'Our joint venture may not be easy but we are going to succeed.'

'To us,' she echoed, and somehow as their glasses clinked, the ring of crystal hitting crystal seemed to reverberate through the air, and the words took on a significance that echoed around them.

They placed their glasses down almost in perfect synchronicity. Their gazes met and he wondered if it was possible to drown in the green depths of her eyes. Knew he had to break the spell before he lost perspective. 'Dessert?' he asked, aware his voice was almost a croak.

She shook her head and he saw her hand clench round

the edge of the table. 'I'm not hungry.' She took a deep breath. 'But maybe we should have something. Stay a bit longer. We mustn't forget we're being watched, putting on a show.'

The reminder exactly what he needed; right now, the most important thing was pulling this off.

Making it look real. Not making it actually real.

CHAPTER SEVEN

AMARA COULDN'T REALLY even remember what dessert they had eventually chosen; somehow the kiss, though it had been so brief, had evoked a slow burn of desire and now that the driver had dropped them off and they were stood in front of the hotel, she tried to clear her brain. Gio had clearly chosen the place for its opulence and she forced herself to focus on the building itself, the sprawling edifice in the centre of Munich a mixture of historic and modern architecture with its neoclassical exterior. As she stared at the arched windows, she hoped it would ground her, reduce her pulse rate, force her to remember that all of this was an act. Only it wasn't, was it? The attraction was definitely extremely real and it felt as if everything was moving at warp speed.

She'd given Gio a chance to opt out and maybe she'd really believed that he would take the option. Until now, there had been a bit of her sure that the momentum would stop, but now… Now she knew Gio was serious. The momentum was going to keep on keeping on.

Which made it even more important to at least slow something down; to ensure they didn't act on the attraction.

'Are you okay?' he asked.

'I'm good. Ready to check in and play my part.' That

was the key. This was a part. There was no actual whirl-wind romance, the dinner had been for the cameras. It was important to keep reality and fiction separate.

They entered the sweeping high-ceilinged marble lobby and approached the stretch of the sleek reception desk.

'Mr Romano, Ms Rossi. We have assigned you the deluxe suite on the top floor.' Amara smiled, still oh, so aware of Gio, aware too of the interested glances and she could only hope she was carrying this off. She felt Gio's hand encircle hers and a sudden reassurance touched her, one that lasted all the way up the elevator and as they entered the suite.

Once inside she took in the expanse of the room, the walls adorned with canvas pictures of Munich, the grained wooden floors dotted with bright rugs and co-lourful leather sofas. A sleek chrome desk ideal for business was placed under a large window and a state-of-the-art television covered another wall. The whole room exuded luxury. A sudden reminder of how much money Gio actually had.

But that wasn't what was making her feel awkward; the awkwardness came from the idea that the suite was made up of an opulent lounge and a no doubt equally opulent bedroom.

'Um…about sleeping arrangements,' she said.

'There are two bedrooms,' he said. 'There's an adjoin-ing room through there.' He gestured towards a door.

Relief swathed her. A short-lived relief as it happened. Because…

'That's great and I really appreciate that. But…' Amara took a deep breath. 'I'm not sure separate bedrooms will work. Not because I don't want separate bed-rooms,' she added hurriedly. 'But…'

For a second he looked puzzled and then the penny dropped. 'Of course. The hotel staff will clean the rooms and they'll realise we aren't sharing a room.' He thought for a moment. 'It's fine. I'll sleep on the sofa. I can take a pillow and duvet from the bedroom and that will be fine.'

Amara opened her mouth to agree and then reluctantly shook her head. 'We could do that. But…it's still risky. Someone may knock on the door and we'd have to scramble to hide everything. Plus, the staff will notice the pillow and blanket have been used. I am pretty sure I've read about reporters paying hotel staff to check celebrities' rooms really carefully. I know that's probably unlikely but we have to make sure we look legit.'

'How?' he asked.

The million-dollar question. Gritting her teeth Amara said, 'We could share the bed. I'm betting it's king-size so there's plenty of space. That way if anyone knocks on the door or there is an emergency it will all look…authentic.'

'Are you sure it's a good idea?'

'No. In fact, I know it's a terrible idea. But if we're going to do this, we need to do it properly and let's face it, realistically there are going to be lots of occasions over the next weeks where we will be expected to share a bed.'

He nodded, though she could see the tension in his jaw. 'You're right. You go ahead then. I'll do some work and creep in later.'

Amara opened her eyes and stifled a gasp. Last night, sheer exhaustion had finally sent her to sleep before Gio had come in. She'd been tempted to pile cushions down the middle of the bed but had resisted the idea as unworthy. At best it was juvenile, at worst it would imply a lack of trust in Gio or worse a lack of trust in herself. She was an adult and quite capable of respecting Gio's space, as she trusted him to respect hers.

After all, she'd always believed that it was the person that mattered more than the attraction and yet with Gio the attraction threatened to overcome that belief. Overcome everything but the urgent need to give into the desire.

To lose control.

She did believe he was a good man, but she wasn't willing to do that. Instead, she dropped into slumber, clutching the edge of the bed to prevent herself from falling out.

But now…she held her breath as her brain took in what had happened. Somewhere in the night she'd stopped clutching the edge of the bed, burrowed across the king-size space she was supposed to be *respecting* and now she seemed to be clutching Gio. *Somehow*, she was right next to him, one arm slung over his chest, *oh God*, his *bare* chest. And now she was thinking in italics and praying he wouldn't wake up. But her treacherous mind was also wondering exactly what Gio was wearing. Her body was on high alert, was oh, so aware of the hard muscle under her arm, the rise and fall of his chest, all too aware of an urge to run her hand downwards, to explore, to shift even closer to him.

Instead, with excruciating care, she shifted infinitesimally away and instantly Gio's eyes opened, looked directly at her, though sleep still clouded the brown depths.

Then he smiled, it was a sleepy smile that held sweetness and the remnants of dreams. Dreams that Amara suspected had run along the same lines as her own, dreams where touching was allowed, *welcomed*. Then his smile widened and in one automatic move he had somehow scooped her up so she was straddling him and she caught her breath as white-hot desire swooshed through her and then she saw sleep blink from his eyes and he swore.

Then 'I'm sorry. Hell, Amara, I didn't mean…'

Hurriedly she scrambled off him. 'It's okay. It's not your fault. It's not anyone's fault. I knew I should have used pillows!' Finding a pillow, she grabbed it and hugged it to her, surveyed Gio over the top and suddenly his face creased into a grin and without even thinking she chucked the pillow at him.

'It's not funny,' she said, even as a chuckle escaped her and then he caught the pillow and threw it straight back at her and they both began to laugh.

Eventually they subsided and Gio smiled and it took every single bit of willpower not to throw herself at him. And as their gazes met, she saw the warmth of his smile deepen into a heat, a desire and they were so very close and…from somewhere, she managed to move away.

'Right,' she said. 'We'd better get up.' And she hoped there wasn't even a hint of question in her voice, knew that now if he reached out and tumbled her over, she wouldn't even try to resist. But instead, she saw him tense.

'Sure.' He swung himself out of bed and Amara gulped, shoved her hand under her thighs in a reminder she couldn't, *mustn't* touch. He was wearing pyjama bottoms, but his chest was definitely a hundred percent bare and in full view. She watched as he reached down and tugged on a T-shirt, watched the stretch and movement and ripple of muscles and hoped, really hoped, she wasn't making little mewling noises.

'You can use the bathroom first,' he offered and she nodded, not trusting her voice. Not trusting herself. All she could hope was that a shower would bring her to her senses.

Half an hour later she emerged, feeling at least marginally more in control now that she was dressed in dark blue jeans and a dark terracotta knitted jumper.

Gio was sat at the table, his laptop open. 'We've made a good splash,' he said indicating the screen and she was relieved at his matter-of-fact tone, aware of a tacit consent to put the morning behind them. 'We're dotted over social media and there's plenty of curiosity as to your exact identity. Only a couple of particularly enterprising reporters seem to have worked it out for sure.' He rose. 'Have a read. I'll use the bathroom then I have a breakfast plan for our campaign trail.'

'Perfect.' As Gio headed to the bathroom her phone pinged and she saw it was a message from her grandfather. Sitting at the table, she looked to see what he had said, kept the screen open in front of her so she could see what Vittorio may have seen.

Dear Amara, I am glad you warned me about the incipient publicity—it was lovely to see you enjoying yourself and I hope good things come of this holiday. I look forward to seeing you in a few days. We will show Lorenzo the Rossi estate in all its winter glory. Nonno

Amara felt her tummy clench and instinctively she turned her screen off, sat for a few minutes staring sightlessly out of the window, oblivious to the hustle and bustle of the Munich street below.

'Amara?' She heard Gio's voice and blinked, pulled herself into reality, a reality that felt suddenly bleaker. 'You okay?'

'Sure. Ready to go.' She knew her voice sounded overbright and she looked away from him as they made their way to the door, then down into the lobby. On automatic, she managed to smile as they checked out, and then headed down to the car park to the car, climbed in and clicked her seat belt on.

Forced herself to focus on the job at hand; there was no point thinking about what was happening in four days' time when there was so much happening right now. But it was hard not to let the images seep into her brain and for a while she watched the blur of the snowy landscape, the splashes and colours of other vehicles, listened to the almost imperceptible hum of the car engine.

'Here we are.' Once they were stood in the parking area, he looked around. 'This way,' and he gestured towards a horse and carriage stood a few yards away. 'Your carriage awaits,' he said. 'We're going to have breakfast at a castle,' he added as she climbed up into the open-air carriage and a gentle whirl of snowflakes flurried down from the sky in a magical cascade. Amara was content to remain silent as they clip-clopped along the road, surrounded by snow-laden trees and the sound of the horse's hooves, muffled by the blanket of snow, the jingle of the reins a musical accompaniment until twenty minutes later they arrived at their destination.

'You alight here and there is a viewing platform, then it's a ten-minute walk to the actual castle,' the driver told them.

They headed to the platform and Amara gasped. Multiple turrets and spire-topped towers soared to the sky, the whole building a romantic, magical, almost exaggerated fairy tale image, a mix of Gothic and Byzantine style that brought images of chivalry, dragons and sunsets to mind.

'It's like a fairy tale brought to life. Not that I believe in fairy tales,' she added quickly. The last thing she wanted was for Gio to think she had even a shred of romance in her.

He shrugged and the movement distracted her. Her eyes watched the lift of muscle; the breadth and strength and heat warmed her body. 'I don't believe in falling in love, but I do intend to live happily ever after.' His voice sounded deep and sincere and now he took her hand in his. 'That's the point of this marriage just as much as in a more conventional one. For us to live happily ever after.'

'But not together,' she said. 'Because we will both be individually happy, but our happiness won't depend on the other person. Our marriage is a…framework, an arrangement where we will spend some time together at the start, but as time goes on, we will naturally evolve to more separate lives.' Which was ideal for her, would allow her to retain her solitude, keep her safe from the anxieties and risks that came with a fairy tale happy ever after. You couldn't lose what you didn't have.

'Exactly.' His voice held satisfaction, one she shared wholeheartedly and yet as she looked back up at the castle Amara felt a strange sense of wistfulness, wondered what it would feel like to be the type of person who could actually feel love, the sort of person who could cope with that heady wave of emotion, could believe in fairy tales where the happy ever after was all about love and romance.

But that wasn't possible. She wasn't that person and she knew now she never could be. She'd tried—with both Stefan and Silvio, she'd tried. Hoped that somehow, she'd be able to do it, to experience closeness, love, a family. All the things she'd lost. But after the experience of those relationships, she knew it wasn't within her to get close to anyone or let anyone close to her. The wall was there, built of impregnable bricks of sorrow and knowledge and pain. She'd seen that happy ever afters could be crushed, wiped out, seen and experienced the sear of loss and grief. Could still remember her four-year-old self witnessing her grandfather's sorrow, a sorrow that she knew he still carried in him.

She turned to look at Gio, told herself that this arrangement was something she was capable of and dammit she would be happy. Without love. Behind her wall.

'Shall we walk up?' Gio suggested. 'I've booked a private tour and breakfast for us before the castle officially opens to tourists.'

Ten minutes later they arrived at the entrance, where a woman approached them, a smile on her face. 'Welcome,' she said. 'I'm Claudette. As we arranged, breakfast has been prepared for the two of you.' She smiled at Amara. 'We don't normally do this but Mr Romano was very persuasive. There are no working kitchens in the castle, but we have done our best. First, I'll show you some of the inside of the castle and then all we ask is that you finish in an hour so we can clear away and be ready for when the castle opens.'

'Of course.'

They followed Claudette and for the next half an hour Amara lost herself in the sheer magic of the castle's interior. Exquisitely detailed frescoes depicted ancient mythological tales, stained glass windows glinted and refracted shades of red and blue and delicately ornate chandeliers hung from numerous ceilings.

Until they ended up in the feasting hall, where an enormous fire crackled in the grate and a table was set for two by the leaping flames. Either side of the fireplace were tapestries and another wall was painted with a fabulous medieval mural.

'This is beautiful,' Amara said.

'It is. We really appreciate the effort you have put in,' Gio said.

'Then I will leave you both to it,' Claudette said.

Amara stood and took in the breakfast, different types of bread, cold meats, cheese, massive pretzels, honey and jam, along with a large steaming cafetière of coffee. 'This is amazing,' she said. And for a moment, a stupid moment, she wanted it to be real; that Gio had arranged this magical breakfast in a magical castle because magic existed. But it didn't and she mustn't forget that. This was a marriage of convenience. 'An excellent campaign stop,' she said lightly as she sat down. 'I'll take a photo.' As she pulled out her phone it pinged and instinctively, she looked down, saw the message and froze.

Hello, Amara. Lorenzo has sent a photograph of himself. I am sure you have already searched for him on social media, but just in case here it is. Nonno.

'Amara?' She heard Gio's concerned voice. 'Are you okay?'

'Yes.' She pushed down the wave of panic; right now, she didn't want to face reality. Wanted to lose herself in the illusion of the castle. Quickly she took a photo and then sat down. 'We'd better get started.'

On automatic she reached out and picked up a piece of rye bread, a piece of cheese, a heart-shaped pretzel. Took a bite. Sipped the coffee.

'Amara? What's wrong?'

'Nothing. Why should anything be wrong?' Now she'd gone from over bright to over breezy. 'I'm fine.'

'Is this all a bit over the top? Fairy tale castle, romantic breakfast? I'm sorry I should have warned you.'

'No! This is lovely. And it's a great idea.' She managed to force her lips upwards. 'Sorry. I know I should be looking a bit more loved up in case someone comes in.'

'No!' Gio shook his head. 'That doesn't matter. What matters to me is that clearly something has upset you. I know it must have because you haven't said a single thing about the food.'

She glanced down at her plate and back up at him, suddenly absurdly touched that he'd even noticed, that he cared enough to ask. Neither Stefan nor Silvio had been so attuned to her moods, would have been relieved she'd not offered a running commentary.

'If you want to talk about it maybe I can help, but if you prefer to have a bit of space to think you definitely don't need to act any part.'

She looked across at him, saw nothing but concern in his brown eyes and suddenly she did want to talk to him, all the feelings so raw, swirling round her brain.

Maybe he could give her some perspective. After all he knew about Lorenzo and Daisy already.

'My grandfather has messaged me. About Lorenzo. My half-brother.' The words sounded wrong, alien, surreal and a sudden image of Luca flashed across her brain. Her real brother. Her twin. 'Lorenzo is planning to visit the Rossi estate in four days' time. He sent my grandfather a photograph.' Her voice caught and she gave an impatient shake of her head. 'I don't know why it hit me so badly. I mean I've known about Lorenzo for days now. I knew he was going to meet my grandfather.'

'But now it's real,' he said quietly.

'Exactly. I hadn't looked him up, or Daisy. Maybe because I don't want it to be real. And seeing him…it's set me in a spin. He looks like my father. Dark-haired, dark blue eyes. Same as my grandfather, as well. A true Rossi. Whereas I…'

'You are beautiful,' Gio said firmly. 'And you are a true Rossi.'

'Yes, but so is Lorenzo and…' She broke off. 'Just like you are a true Romano.' She stared at him, suddenly stricken, realising how terrible she must sound, as if she were doing to her half-brother what was done to Gio. Excluding him. 'I'm sorry. I shouldn't even be talking to you about this.'

'No. It's fine.' His voice was low and reassuring as he rose and moved round the table, shifted his chair closer to her. 'It's not comparable. Lorenzo has turned up out of the blue. You said he didn't even know who his father was until now. If your grandfather had known of his existence before, or if your father had acknowledged him, then everything may have been different. You would have grown up forming a bond. Now your feelings are natural. You're scared; you feel like your whole destiny is being threatened.' A shadow crossed his eyes and she wondered what he was thinking, wondered if he was thinking about his own half-brothers and how they would react to his arrival on the board.

'It is,' she said softly.

'Perhaps your destiny is being changed rather than threatened.'

'What's the difference?'

He thought for a moment. 'Your whole life you've known that you will run a vineyard. Haven't you ever wondered what you would have done if that wasn't your destiny? If you had a choice. If your destiny wasn't to continue your family's heritage?'

'No, I haven't. I always knew that was my life.' And that knowledge had been comforting, safe, secure. It defined her.

'Then perhaps you should think about it now,' he said gently. 'Face your biggest fear. You said yesterday that you may have to walk away from the estate for the sake of the estate. If that happened, what would you do?'

Her first instinct was to lash out, to tell him he didn't understand, couldn't understand and then she looked into his eyes, saw a seriousness there, a sympathy, but more than that she saw empathy and now she thought, really thought, about his apparent acceptance of what his family had done. They had given him acknowledge-ment without acceptance, he'd been forced to grow up in sight of the 'holy grail' of entry into the family busi-ness, but always knowing it was a prize that would be withheld. Had to endure being a second-class Romano;

Gio had had to face that. 'Is that what you did?' she asked now.

'Yes.' His voice quiet now as if he were looking back into his past. 'When I was young, all I wanted was to be part of Romano Confectionery. I did everything I could think of to prove myself worthy.' And now she could picture the dark-haired young boy, desperate to please, trying to show his family that he deserved acceptance, was worthy of it and her heart twisted in sympathy. 'But in the end, I had to face it wasn't going to happen. That I was chasing an impossible dream and it was stopping me from finding anything else. I had to find my own path.'

'I'm sorry.'

He shook his head. 'I'm not. Because it gave me a chance to go and do something else, be myself, make my own destiny. I would never have discovered that I have a technological bent. I'd never have got the thrill and the satisfaction of founding my own company if I'd already had a future mapped out for me. And I do truly love my company. What I've achieved, what I hope to achieve. So maybe you should think about the possibility that good can come of forging your own path. An opportunity. To do something that is yours. As Amara not as a Rossi.'

And when she thought of all he'd achieved, thought about the real difference he'd made and was making, a small flicker of excitement ignited at the thought of the unknown. A flicker that flared and then died as she tried to think. 'I can't think of anything.'

'Don't sound so sad.' He reached out, took her hand in his and she felt the familiar jolt, but alongside something else. A warmth, a reassurance, a sense of being listened to, thought about. And she couldn't remember anyone other than Vittorio making her feel like that. And even with her grandfather, there was so much they didn't talk about, both of them intent on protecting the other. 'It's completely normal not to instantly think of another career path. And there's no rush.' He gave a sudden smile, and his brown eyes held a warmth that felt like a caress. 'I get that Lorenzo is coming in a few days, but he won't arrive in an armoured tank planning to take over the estate.'

The words held such understanding and Amara felt lighter, the bleak panic receding and she laid a hand on his forearm, revelled in the lithe muscle, the texture under her fingers. 'Thank you, Gio. For listening and giving me some perspective.' True perspective because to give it he'd had to share something of himself, of a childhood she sensed he didn't visit often and she valued that.

'That's okay. And I will be with you,' he said.

'What do you mean?'

'When Lorenzo comes to meet you, I will be there.'

A happiness touched her, along with a relief that she knew she had to clamp down on. Yet the idea of having support felt novel and beautiful and for a minute she wondered if it should alarm her. She shook the thought away. This was the beauty of this type of marriage. He wasn't coming out of duty or love because that wasn't what this was about. He was coming as part of their deal, to bolster the show. To demonstrate to her grandfather that she wouldn't be alone. That she could lead the Rossi estate. And that was a good, positive thing. She'd wanted support, a person, an extra body, and if she was glad on her own behalf, glad that it was *Gio* who would be there, she refused to acknowledge it.

'Thank you.' Reaching out she picked up the pretzel, layered on the cheese, and took a bite. 'This *is* lovely,' she said. 'I can taste the crunch of salt crystals and the cheese is incredibly nutty.'

She stopped as he laughed. 'Now I know you are feeling better,' he said. 'Because you're thinking about what you're eating. In fact…that's something else you could do. You could be a food critic; come to that, you could be a wine critic. You could research and write books, travel the world.'

Amara looked at him, imagined a completely different life, a life where she travelled, wrote about wine, about food, experimented with cooking, did a Cordon Bleu course. She and Gio could go to… She stopped the thought. She and Gio—there was no Amara and Gio. They were going to live separate lives. Do their own thing. The last thing Gio would want to do was accompany her everywhere, be at her beck and call. They were going to walk alone, coming together sometimes when circumstances demanded it. And that was what she wanted. Her space and solitude, control. Not being close to anyone. Because that's when things got complicated. 'I'll bear it in mind,' she said. 'And I'll start by trying this pastry right here.'

'Good plan. And when we're finished, we can look round the castle and then head for our next destination.'

CHAPTER EIGHT

Two hours later, Gio pulled into a parking space. 'I thought we'd break the journey here. It's meant to be a truly picturesque little Bavarian village.'

And as they walked through the cobbled streets of the old town he couldn't help but agree with the reviews. The houses and shops, which dated back to the fourteenth century, had kept all their medieval charm. In addition, the pastel façades were made unique by the paintings that adorned them, biblical references as well as scenes of everyday life in such detail that they kept stopping to study them. The whole made all the more awe-inspiring by the backdrop of the Alps that loomed up and overlooked the town.

'Another magical place,' Amara said. 'Another fairy tale setting. Good thing I know fairy tales are just a story,' she said. 'There are no glass slippers or hundred-year sleeps. And kisses do not turn frogs into handsome princes.'

'No,' he agreed. 'But let's not rule kisses out completely. I think they have a part to play in marriage. And kisses can be pretty magical in any setting.'

Pink tinged her cheeks and he wondered if she was remembering the kisses they'd shared, or waking up that morning accidentally entwined in each other arms. The memory caused a sudden rush; her nearness, the soft welcoming warmth of her, her hand on his chest, her fingers over the beat of his heart, her hair tickling his chest.

Gio took a deep breath, decided it would be a good idea to change the subject, before he offered to demonstrate how magical a kiss could be right here and now. 'There's apparently an amazing Baroque church that's worth a visit—if you'd like to see it.'

'Sounds good.' As they walked down the cobbled street, lined with small stores and cafés, she glanced up at him. 'Have you been to Bavaria before?' she asked. 'You seem to know your way around.'

He shook his head. 'No. This plan is all down to some internet searches and trying to come up with a few places that fit our story.' Even as he said the words he knew they weren't strictly true; he'd been looking for places that Amara might enjoy, as well. He'd known that it must have been exhausting playing to the audience the previous night in a celebrity-studded place under scrutiny, and had wanted today to be more laid-back. 'I wanted to at least try to make this a bit of a holiday. Have *you* been to Bavaria before?' he asked. 'Is that why you chose to come here to think?'

She shook her head. 'It was a fairly random selection. I thought the cold might clear my brain.'

They arrived at the church and halted, stood and absorbed its beauty, the soaring rise of the bell tower, the painted frescoes of St Peter and St Paul.

'It's incredible really to think of how many people have stood here, how many people over the centuries have gone inside to worship or pray or perhaps simply for a sense of peace,' she said softly.

'Shall we go in?'

She nodded and they stepped forward into the incredible interior, the whole place surprisingly light thanks to the massive arched windows. Amara craned her neck to study the ceiling painting and he followed suit, took in the story of the saints, then turned his attention to the red marble of the altar, the numerous Baroque paintings, the statues and gilded, golden pieces and the overall sense of awe and majesty.

'So full of so much beauty,' she said softly

He nodded and took her hand in his, wanted her to know he shared her sense of awe and appreciation until a few minutes later, by tacit consent, they left and headed back into the crisp, cold air.

'Café?' he suggested and they moved towards one of the many picturesque eateries that lined the cobbled streets. Once inside they sat at one of the wooden tables, covered in a red-patterned cloth and ordered coffee.

'So, you came somewhere cold to think? Where would you usually go on holiday?'

'I don't really travel much or if I do, it's work-related. The vineyard is hard work and neither my grandfather nor I are very good at delegation. Growing up we didn't really go on holiday much—I think my grandfather felt awkward taking me on holiday on my own. He is pretty fit for his age, but he couldn't run around after me. And child-friendly holidays weren't really his thing. He would sometimes go away with one of his… relationships, but he didn't take me. He didn't really like involving any of his girlfriends in my upbringing. He said it wasn't fair. For either party to get attached.' She shook her head. 'Some of them tried though, but I wasn't having any of it. I was happy with it just being my grandfather and me.'

Gio studied her face, tried to imagine her childhood, wondered how old she'd been when she'd lost her parents. He could have tried to find out, though he wasn't sure how easy it would be with the information he had, but he had elected to not even try. If Amara wanted to share her past she would.

Her expression turned sad. 'I thought he was happy too. But now I wonder if he always wished for a larger family, if maybe he didn't remarry because of me. And I also wonder if he wants great-grandchildren so he can enjoy them without the responsibility of being a surrogate parent.' She stilled, her hand hovering over her plate. 'Actually, that's something we haven't even spoken about. Children.'

For an instant an image flashed through Gio's mind, himself and Amara and next to them were two children, a boy and a girl. He blinked fiercely to dispel the images. The idea too much, too enormous to contemplate as a reality. An idea that wouldn't work, couldn't work within this arrangement. And that was fine with him. Of course it was.

'You're right,' he said. 'We haven't and we should.'

'You go first,' she said and he saw a wariness in her tone, in her green eyes.

'I've always believed I wouldn't have children. I never intended to have a long-term relationship so it wasn't something I ever considered as a possibility.' And that had been a relief. Because he wasn't sure he could be a good parent. Maybe never experiencing good parenting meant you couldn't be a good parent yourself. Couldn't

manage the responsibility even if he was pretty damn
sure he knew what that responsibility entailed—it meant
making your child your priority, being present, spending time with them. Making sure they knew they were
loved and *wanted*.

'And now?'

'Now…given the type of arrangement we have agreed
on, I still don't think it is possible. But I'd like to hear
your thoughts.' Now wariness touched him; from everything Amara had said the future of the Rossi estate was
of paramount importance to her. Vittorio Rossi wanted
heirs. Amara was faced with watching her half-siblings
provide heirs, with the possibility of being pushed out
from the future of the estate. 'What about you?'

She picked up the coffee, put it down again. 'I used
to think I would have children. But after Stefan, after
Silvio, I knew I wouldn't. But when I think about it, it
makes me feel guilty because I know how happy it would
make my grandfather but…'

'Would it make you happy?' he asked. 'You shouldn't
have a child to make someone else happy.'

'We're getting married to make other people happy.'

'And that's our decision to make. It impacts us. And
I wouldn't do it if it was going to make either of us unhappy. But either way it is our choice. Children don't ask
to be born.' He could hear the edge to his tone, he knew
what it felt like not to be wanted. His mother was at best
ambivalent and his father would have happily erased him
from the timeline. 'And I should make something very
clear. I won't be used to provide the Rossi heir. If I have
a child, I want to be part of that child's life. Properly. I
won't be a part-time dad.'

Now anger flashed from her eyes as she pushed her cup aside in a jerky gesture. 'If you think I would ever stoop so low as to use you for a child then I suggest we call this whole marriage off. Right here, right now. Do you believe I'd do that to you? Do that to a child. To a baby. Bring them into the world if I didn't want them, just to make my grandfather happy?'

He closed his eyes at the sheer outrage in her voice. 'No, I don't think that,' he said quietly. 'But that's not enough. I have to be sure. How can I not be? That would be wrong. I know what it's like to be a child who isn't wanted, to be shunted around at other people's whims. I won't let that or any echo of that happen to my child.' He paused for breath, wondered how this situation had got so out of hand. He couldn't remember the last time he'd had such a heated discussion with anyone, the last time he'd cared enough about something to argue. Now in the heat of the moment he'd shared something he hadn't meant to. But it had needed to be said. He wanted Amara to understand that he meant what he said, that it was important. And he didn't regret it.

There was a silence and then, to his surprise, she reached out, touched his arm, left it there. 'I'm sorry. You're right. You can't know for sure my motivations on a few days' notice. But I agree with you. I don't want to bring children into our marriage. I know children aren't for me and our arrangement doesn't change that. But for what it's worth, in an alternate universe if I were ever to be a mum I would want my child, and I would love that child and do my best to give my child a happy childhood.' And there was that image again. Of Amara holding a baby, *their* baby, with him by her side. But she was right;

that was a different universe, another timeline. He heard sincerity in her voice but he heard sadness too. Then she reached out, covered his hand with hers. 'And I'm sorry that your childhood wasn't how I imagined it to be.'

'How did you imagine it?' Perhaps he should close the conversation down, but he didn't want to. He wanted Amara to understand that what he'd said had come from his heart, that he hadn't been trying to shoot her down or accuse her.

'I suppose I assumed you had quite a laid-back privileged rock 'n' roll childhood with your mum. I know you aren't close with your dad, but I assumed that meant you didn't see him very often.' She shook her head. 'That's a lot of assuming. I'm sorry.'

'You don't have to apologise.'

'So how was it in reality?'

'My mum and I—we get on okay now, but when I was young she wasn't very present. She was never cruel to me, or deliberately unkind, she just didn't really have any interest in me. She never wanted children—she's always been honest about that. So somehow, she felt that excused her from having to be at all maternal. It was more as though I was a stray dog who she had taken in during a moment of charity and now wasn't quite sure what to do with. So, she handed me over to her entourage and got on with living her life exactly as if she didn't have a child. It was a bit like sending the dog to a kennel I suppose.'

He tried to keep his voice amused, light, but he had the feeling he wasn't fooling Amara, and tried to hide it with facts.

'The problem was that her entourage weren't interested

in me or babysitting me. They were there because they adored my mother. I mean I do understand I probably wasn't much of a draw compared to a rock 'n' roll life-style, so I was definitely the short straw. It was great for building self-reliance and I became a dab hand at making sure they didn't misplace me, but it wasn't the sort of upbringing I would want for my child. I would want to be there, present, part of my child's life.' He shrugged. 'That's why I got so heated. I didn't mean to accuse you.'

'I understand that.' Her voice was soft, all her previous anger gone. 'Thank you for telling me and I am sorry that your mum was like that. Sorry for you, but I am also sorry for her.' He saw the anger in her eyes, an anger he knew was directed at his mother, but he saw no hint of the pity he dreaded so much.

'I don't think many people feel sorry for my mother,' he said, still trying to keep it light.

But Amara was having none of it. 'Well, I do,' she said roundly. 'Because she missed out on you, watching you grow, spending time with you, seeing you become the kind, caring, successful man you have become. She could have been part of that journey and she missed out. Big time. And no amount of hit songs or concerts or wild parties can make up for that. She missed out and that is not your fault. You are not a short straw and it is on her if she believed that.'

He forced his expression to remain still, touched by her words but aware that Amara didn't know the whole of it. It wasn't only his mother who had seen him as a short straw, it had been his father, as well. And Gio knew that was personal, knew his father loathed the sight of him. Salvatore Romano was a family man, with a wife, and two other sons he had always treated well. Gio could excuse his mother, she'd never wanted a child full stop. But his father as well? It seemed to him the common denominator was Gio himself.

The passion in Amara's voice, the caring, warmed him but made him feel edgy at the same time. Conversations like this brought closeness and sharing and those were all things to be wary of. 'Thank you,' he said. 'Truly. But now how about we try a piece of cake?'

'Works for me,' she said and he was grateful that she seemed to instinctively understand the need to back off, the abrupt change of subject. 'I'd love to try the *Prinzregententorte* if they have any. I read about it somewhere. It's really thin layers of sponge filled with buttercream and then covered in chocolate.'

'Sounds good.' He eyed her. 'Is there anything else you'd like to try? I'm happy to let you choose for me.'

She grinned at him. 'How well you know me!' There was a sudden silence as if they were each realising both the truth of the statement and its absurdity. After all, he'd only met Amara two days before. 'I'd love to try the apple torte if that's okay with you.'

'No problem at all.'

And as they shared the two cakes, discussed the merits of different fruit fillings, how it was possible to make such a light sponge, the texture of different creams, Gio was aware of a sense of contentment, told himself it was okay to enjoy it. This period of time with Amara was important, crucial to setting up this whole marriage. It had to look real and they had to spend time together. Soon enough they would announce the engagement and then the proverbial would hit the fan when his father found out what was going down. But there wouldn't be a damn thing he could do about it. And that was what was most important. And that was what this marriage was about. Once the actual wedding took place, once he was safely on the board, it would be different. Everything would change. Amara would be caught up with the Rossi estate and forging a relationship with her siblings and he would be caught up in all the flak and difficulties of combatting his father. This was a period of respite for them both. Nothing more.

It was dark when they reached the chalet they were staying in for the night. 'Here we are,' she said and they both peered out. Amara gave a sigh of mingled relief and satisfaction; she'd chosen the chalet based on the fairy tale whirlwind romance theme and it looked like she'd made a good choice.

'How lovely. They've put the lights on for us. I'm guessing they're on a timer.'

The chalet glowed like a beacon, illuminating the wooden building in a yellow gold aura; swirls of snow fell on the twinkling lights that adorned the snow-dusted sloping gables of the roof.

'It's perfect,' he said. 'So now I suggest we grab our bags and make a run for it.'

They did exactly that, through the swirls of snow that flurried down from the starry skies, each flake landing with a sizzle on her face as she put the code into the key safe and retrieved the key.

The interior was beautiful, yet another fairy tale image and she was beginning to think she should just cave in and live in the fairy tale for a few days. Allow herself to believe all of this was real whilst knowing it was fake.

The idea whirled through her mind and she tried to imagine what they would do if they were a real couple. Imagined walking hand in hand through the property, imagined… Enough.

'Shall we look round?' he asked and she nodded. As they walked through the rooms she took in the rustic cosiness of the décor, the warm lighting shining from lamps ensconced in the wood-panelled wall enclosures, comfortable, brightly coloured sofas and armchairs arranged round a massive fireplace, loaded with the sweet-smelling scent of freshly cut logs.

The kitchen housed a range cooker and a polished wooden table. Amara checked her phone. 'I asked them to leave us a dinner we could heat up, unless you'd rather eat out. I thought if we stay in, we can take photos and big up the "romance" of a cosy night in by the fireplace.' She gave a sudden gurgle of laughter. 'Unless you think that's a bit over the top and completely out of character for Gio Romano.'

'But remember I am a reformed, new Gio Romano, caught up in a whirlwind romance. I am pretty sure I can come up with some believable moves in my new persona.'

Amara couldn't help herself. 'What sort of moves?' she asked softly.

'Well,' he said and now he moved a little closer to her. 'I'd put dinner onto a slow heat and then whilst it was cooking, I'd suggest…various ways we could work up an appetite.'

Amara gulped, managed a smile. She wasn't going

to let this attraction take over, even as she realised she had taken a step closer to him. 'Good idea,' she said. 'We could…go for a brisk run in the snow.'

'We could. Followed by a slow session in the sauna.' For an instant Amara imagined Gio, chest bare, sat in the sauna, herself next to him, both of them warm and glowing and close and… She blinked, took a determined step away from him and headed to the fridge, tempted to stick her head in it in an attempt to cool her thoughts down. Carefully she took the casserole dish out and lifted the lid, looked at the contents, relieved to have a new topic of conversation.

'It says here this is Flädlesuppe, which is a pancake soup to start with. Sliced pancakes which look a bit like noodles in a clear broth. Followed by another more filling soup called Brotsuppe.'

'Bread soup?' he asked.

'Yup.' She opened the second dish. 'But I think it's a posh, luxury version.' She inhaled. 'There are definitely some aromatic spices in there and I'm pretty sure I can smell caraway and nutmeg. And after the soup they've put together a picnic dinner. I'll start heating the soups up.' Somehow it seemed important to keep talking, to try and forget the idea of steamy saunas and Gio's moves. Keep focused.

Once the food was heating, Amara scrolled down her phone. 'I thought I'd check to see how we're doing publicity wise,' she said. 'And it looks good. I guess we should think about what we do next. How we escalate to make the engagement believable. To the public but also to my grandfather.' As she said the words, anxiety emerged as she tried to imagine telling Vittorio that she was engaged, that she and Gio were in love. Realised the enormity of the lie, the enormity of what they were doing.

'You're worried about telling him?' The words half question, half statement. 'Do you think he'll disapprove of us getting married so fast? Or will he disapprove of me because of my dating history?'

'Some or all of the above. But mostly I'm worried because I want him to believe it's real, that I've found love. But I don't think I've ever lied to him about something important. And love is important to him. He wouldn't want me to marry without it. I don't think your reputation or the timing will matter to him as long as he believes we love each other. So half of me is scared we won't be able to pull it off and the other half hates lying to him.'

'I get that.' He turned to face her, his back against the worktop so she could see his expression. 'I don't like lying either, but I am not sure what we will achieve by telling him the truth. He wants you to be happy. I hope our marriage will make you happy.'

'I think it will,' she said. 'I really do.' And stood there right now she was sure of it, mesmerised by his sheer presence, by the sincerity of his intent. And she had an urge to reach out to gently cradle his face in her hands, to move closer to him. *Whoa, Amara.* That was attraction speaking. She wasn't marrying him just so she could go to bed with him. She was marrying him because it made sense. Would make her grandfather happy. 'I guess the only option is to lie.' Because there was no love in this marriage and for an insensible fleeting moment that made her feel sad. A sadness she pushed away. Love begat sadness. She looked at him, willed him to understand as they carried the soup over to the table.

'But I don't think he'd understand our arrangement and he would hate the idea I was marrying without love. Or doing this for him in any way.' They sat and started to eat, and she took a few minutes to savour the taste. 'So somehow, I have to pull this off when I tell him. All these years he's been there for me, changed his entire life for me. It took Lorenzo and Daisy's arrival to show me how hard it has been for him. How hard I have made it for him.' She bit her lip, turned her head away as she felt tears coming.

'No. Amara, I don't think it was like that. I think your grandfather loves you and he wants you to be happy. I think you have both been through so much that I don't know about, but he stepped up for you and that was the right thing to do. I am sure you brought him so much joy over the years.'

'Not enough. Without him...' Her voice caught and something twisted in his chest. 'I couldn't have survived without him. Quite literally really. He brought me up.' She looked across the table at him. 'After the accident.'

'You don't have to talk about it if you don't want to,' he said softly. 'I don't know what happened and I haven't tried to find out.'

The fact that he hadn't checked up, hadn't tried to work out what had happened, had decided to let her share her past if and when she was ready, warmed her and she knew that she wanted him to understand, to really know why this was so important to her. 'I'd like to tell you.'

'Why don't we move into the lounge? We can eat the next course later?' She nodded. 'I'll light a fire and we can talk.'

CHAPTER NINE

ONCE AGAIN AMARA appreciated what Gio was doing; giving her a chance to make sure she really did want to do this. Wanted to discuss something painful and personal. But he also wanted her to be able to do it in a place where she would feel comfortable, and his thoughtfulness touched her. Curled up on an oversized sofa, she watched him prepare the fire, saw the sparks light and flare into crackling reddish-orange flames and she knew she did want to tell him. Wanted him to understand the depth of her motivation, her love for her grandfather. Wanted to share a little of her life just as he had shared a little of his earlier in the day. She marshalled her thoughts.

'My family died in a helicopter accident. I was the only survivor. If I had been sitting in a different seat, I guess I would have died too. Instead, somehow, I got thrown clear of the wreckage—I broke my arm and a rib but otherwise I was fine. I woke up in the hospital and for a few minutes I thought it was all going to be okay and then I knew inside me that it wasn't. Something told me that I'd lost a connection I'd had all my life. With my brother, my twin.' Gio stilled. 'He died too. Luca. My twin brother.'

'Oh, Amara.' In one seamless move he shifted toward her and then she was in his arms, held close, the warmth of his body so full of comfort that she could feel tears start to form and she blinked fiercely.

'Hey. It's okay to cry. I wish I knew what to say, but all I can say is that I am truly sorry. How old were you both?'

'Four,' she said softly and felt his arms tighten around her.

'I can't imagine how it must have felt having that bond severed.'

'It was like I had lost a part of me. A part of my soul. A part of my being that can't ever be replaced. I remember opening my eyes and feeling a void. Then I was looking round for my parents and they weren't there. Then my grandfather came in and he looked… Broken. Like a ghost. He told me that my parents were gone and my grandmother. And Luca. It felt as if my world shattered. My world did shatter. It was all gone. And I felt alone in a way I never had before.'

'Tell me about Luca.' Gio's voice was soft.

'We were very, very close. I knew what he was thinking and he knew the same for me. We fought sometimes, of course we did, but we truly were best friends. Luca was naughtier than me—he'd always come up with some plan. To sneak an extra cookie or stay awake a little longer. And he'd always persuade me to go along with it. To help.'

She could hear the smile in Gio's voice. 'I bet even at that age you improved the plan.'

'I did! I've always thought that if he'd lived, he and I would have made a perfect team. I can imagine him coming up with the idea to make a wine that would be really out there and me working out a way to actually do it and the wine being amazing. Even when we were kids, we kind of sparked off each other, we were a team. After the accident, I knew nothing could ever be the same again—I'd never have that kind of bond again. Losing it was like severing something vital in me. It changed me somehow.' It had numbed her, deadened something inside her. Had killed off her ability to love anyone new. She still loved her grandfather because she'd already loved him. She still loved her family even though they didn't walk this earth any more. But she knew there was something broken inside her, which was why she couldn't have a loving relationship, couldn't risk having children, couldn't risk new bonds when she knew the pain of losing them. But she was good with that, because her inability to love kept her safe. Instinctively she shifted a little closer to Gio, and a sudden qualm struck her, one she pushed away. After all she *was* safe, protected, behind her wall, her barriers that didn't really let anyone close. Not in ways it counted.

'When you compound that with the loss of your parents as well, that must have been earth-shattering,' he said slowly. 'I am so sorry. And now the fact these new siblings are twins must be wrenching you.'

Amara nodded. 'What are the chances of two half-siblings you had no knowledge of suddenly turning up out of the blue and upending everything you believed? It's not just the fact they are twins that is wrenching. Their sheer existence overturns everything I believed to be true. They've rewritten my past.'

'Shattered your world all over again,' he said and she

paused, arrested by the sheer understanding embodied, encapsuled, in those words.

'Yes. My favourite photo has always been a picture of my parents and Luca and me. Taken on the vineyard— a happy family. It was taken a month or so before the accident. But now that photo…it feels fake, false. The story I've always believed, that my parents loved each other—it turns out that it *is* a story, a *fictional* fairy tale.' Another reason, if she needed one, why she and Gio could never have children. Because it would be fake— what would she tell them? *Your mama and papa got married as part of an arrangement. We live separate lives but we both love you. We just don't believe in loving each other.* Or would they lie? Create another fictional fairy tale. She couldn't do that. 'None of what I believed is true. My father was married when he slept with Lorenzo and Daisy's mother. And then he walked away.' Had he loved her? Presumably not. 'That means nothing is how I thought it was and I'll never know the answers. I'll never know the truth and I can no longer take comfort from the past.'

'It must seem as though you have lost them all over again.'

Gio really got it and she moved closer to him, felt the reassurance of his bulk next to her.

'I get that,' he said softly. 'I do. And I understand that you must be wishing Lorenzo and Daisy had never shown up. That you could keep the story, that it was true.'

His arm was around her now and she was nestled close, the sensation unfamiliar and yet strangely comfortable, as his words further demonstrated his understanding of how she felt.

'But…' He hesitated and she gestured with her hand.

'It's okay. Please share your thoughts. I value them.'

'Okay.' He thought for a moment, clearly wanting to choose his words carefully. 'You're right, you may never know the full truth of this, all of this, but none of it is Lorenzo and Daisy's fault.'

'I know that. But I also know they are gaining so much—a wonderful grandfather and a heritage that…'

'That maybe they don't want.' His voice was gentle. 'I understand all that you have lost and the pain it must be causing you. But they have lost something too. They have spent their whole lives believing they have a different father, believed that they shared blood and genetics and a heritage with the man who brought them up.'

Amara gave a small gasp as the knowledge slammed into her. 'You're right,' she said, heard the smallness of her voice. 'All I've been thinking of is myself and my feelings and that's not fair or right. It's selfish.'

Instinctively she tried to move away from him, but he still held her close. 'No. It's not. That's not what I meant at all. It's completely normal for you to feel exactly how you are feeling. And…it could be that Lorenzo and Daisy are terrible people. I am not advocating that you fall on them with happiness, I mean…'

'That maybe they are struggling too.'

'Maybe,' he said. 'But that doesn't take away from how you are feeling or make those feelings any less valid. But don't be too hard on them or yourself. Or your father.'

'What he did was wrong. I have always believed he was perfect.'

'Of course you have. You lost him when you were so young. What he did was wrong—I can't try and excuse that. But although what he did was inexcusable it doesn't mean that he was all bad. It doesn't define the whole of him. It doesn't mean that the photo that you love doesn't hold truth. I believe it does. What he did doesn't mean he didn't love you and Luca. Doesn't mean your mother didn't love you both. Think back to your memories of them. With you. What are they like?'

Amara thought back, felt her face break into a smile. 'I remember laughter, and I remember my dad throwing us up in the air, telling me I could reach the sky and I remember stretching my fingers up to the clouds. I remember my mum brushing my hair and telling me stories. I remember my dad baking with me, all of us making a birthday cake. And he got me to smell all the different things, the cinnamon and the vanilla and the sugar, even the milk. My mum playing hide-and-seek with us.'

'Then no matter what *their* relationship was, they both loved you and that is incredibly precious. Don't let what has happened tarnish or taint your memories of that. That photo is the truth—that was a real happy moment and you should treasure it.'

The intensity, the gravity of his words, was palpable and she knew they came from a place of truth. Knew too that Gio didn't have any of those memories; his mother hadn't played with him, or held his hand, hadn't been there for him. His father had acknowledged him, but that seemed to be pretty much it.

'Thank you,' she said softly. 'Truly. Everything you

have said has made a massive difference to me.' She
turned to face him.

And he was so close, so close she could see the length
of his eyelashes, the glint of firelight dappling his skin.
She could see the compassion and the intentness in his
brown eyes and she could see that intent morph from
compassion to a different type of intent.

Saw latent desire spark into reality, saw his pupils
darken, his jaw clench and felt him start to move away.

And she knew that she didn't want him to. Didn't
want to move away either. Didn't want to do anything
but this and so she moved forward and brushed her lips
against his, an invitation and a question.

Then he was kissing her, really kissing her and this
kiss was off the scale, completely different from their
previous kisses. There was no doubt now and sensing
that, Amara too surrendered to desire, freely and willingly, not even a vestige of reservation in her mind.
She wanted this, wanted him, her whole body crying
out in need.

Then she stopped thinking, lost herself completely in
a kiss so sensual, so overpowering, so glorious. Desire
swirled as he deepened the kiss and now she was pressed
so close to him, so very close, but it wasn't close enough.
She needed to feel his body against hers and now she
was fumbling with his shirt, pulling at the buttons and
for one awful second he broke the kiss.

But the loss was only fleeting as he rose and gathered
her up to lay her down on the sheepskin rug in front of
the flicker and flare of the fire. And then he was un-
zipping her dress, his fingers lingering on her skin, on
her body, teasing, tantalising. She pulled his shirt off,

revelling in the feel of his shoulders under her fingers, watching the glow of the flames dapple the muscle and breadth of him and then he was lying next to her, kissing her, touching her and she relished touching and being touched, lost in a vortex of pleasure.

Gio half opened his eyes, instantly aware that something was missing. Not something. Someone. Amara. In the moment between sleep and waking he felt a smile curve his lips as he recalled the previous night, let the memories wash over him. The sheer joy, elation, pleasure given and received. The soft sound of her laughter, the intensity of her reactions, her generosity and her passion. The taste of her, the tickle of her hair, the flecks of emerald pleasure in the depth of her eyes. Recalled picking her up and carrying her to the bedroom, the renewed passion, the wonder and the awe as they continued to learn and explore each other, until finally sated they'd fallen asleep, still entwined.

But now he frowned slightly. Where was she? He reached out, felt the warmth of the bedsheets and now he opened his eyes fully and turned, saw Amara perched on the end of the bed, carefully edging away.

'Morning,' he said softly and she jumped slightly, before turning to look at him, her glorious red hair tumbling past her bare shoulders, the edge of the duvet pulled up.

'Morning,' she said and he saw a wariness in her eyes. 'I was going to go and sort out breakfast and tidy up. I'm sorry I didn't want to wake you up...' the words were coming out in a breathless tumble and she was continuing to edge away.

Carefully he held on to the duvet, his mind racing. Last night Amara had shared so much, given so much. Spoken about her family, her twin, the raw pain of loss and grief, she'd revisited memories, shared something precious with him. And then attraction had overwhelmed them. They'd slept together without discussion, or planning or thought. So right now, she must be feeling vulnerable and all he wanted to do was reassure her. Even as a small warning bell tolled at the back of his own brain, telling him that perhaps Amara was right to be wary.

But now the most important thing was to reassure her. 'Amara?'

'Yes.'

'Why don't you come back to bed?' He smiled at her. 'Unless this is a cunning plan to pull the duvet off me. You don't need a plan. You just need to ask.'

Now she blushed and he saw a small smile begin to upturn her lips.

He patted the space next to him.

'Come on—come back to bed. Talk to me.'

She hesitated and then scooted back so she was sat next to him, both of them propped against the headboard, though he noticed the tension in her body, the scrupulous care she took not to let their bodies touch.

'What's wrong?' he asked. 'Are you regretting last night?' He glanced at her and decided that the direct approach was best. 'Because I'm not. I'm glad. I'm honoured you told me about Luca, about your parents.'

Amara turned to him. 'Truly?' she asked. 'You see, I never talk about Luca or my family. It's too raw, too painful, something I hold close to myself.'

'It's also something precious and I feel privileged that you shared your memories with me.'

'Thank you, Gio.'

Her smile was small but genuine, and admiration surged inside him at the inner strength she must have to negotiate so much pain and loss. Well, she no longer had to navigate that alone. The thought stopped him in his tracks. *Whoa. Hold your horses, Gio.* Their whole marriage was about wanting to be alone. About not living in each other's pockets. About not being answerable to each other or responsible for the other's happiness.

He pushed the thought away, told himself there was nothing wrong with being supportive, nothing wrong with caring.

'And as for what happened later, it's not possible for me to regret that.' They were on safer ground here and he risked a smile. 'Turns out we are super compatible, Richter scale compatible.' Now sudden uncharacteristic doubt touched him. 'Or at least that's how I see it. If I've got it wrong then…'

'Well actually… Given that we are faking a whole whirlwind romance I thought it would be best to…' Then seeing his expression her impish smile broke out. 'You haven't got it wrong,' she said softly. 'Last night was… I haven't really got words. It was magical, the kind of thing you do read about but don't believe really exists.' She broke off. 'It was definitely great sex.'

Gio recalled their words of the previous days, the idea that they would be compatible. Well that was a definite—Amara was right—they had definitely shared great sex. Yet the thoughts that streamed through his brain were of holding her, the way she'd nestled into his body, a desire to keep his arm around her to keep her safe. Enough. That was just the aftermath of great sex. A chemistry, a physical connection that they had already known they had. A physical connection that had nothing to do with emotion. Physics, chemistry, great sex. 'It was,' he said. 'I know we were planning on waiting, but I'm good with what happened. I hope you are too.'

'I'm good with it too,' she said, but he heard a soupçon of doubt in her voice and as if to echo that she shifted a little away from him before turning. 'Right. I'm ravenous. Breakfast and then we should make a plan for the day.' Now she moved further away and he sensed the conversation was over. 'Maybe we could have the picnic supper as a picnic breakfast?'

'Great plan.'

Twenty minutes later they reconvened and he noticed she'd set the table in the kitchen, clearly had no wish to return to the lounge and he wasn't sure he could blame her. Knew it was important for them both to remember, in the here and now, that the most important thing was the campaign trail.

'This all looks great,' he said as she laid out bread and cold meats and cheese.

As they started to eat, she looked across at him. 'So what's today's plan?'

'I thought we could go and visit a vineyard. You said you wanted to do that at our first dinner so why not today? I don't want you to miss out on one of the reasons you came here.' And maybe it would ground Amara, give her back some normality when everything felt overwhelming and when he could sense her vulnerability. From the emotions of the night before, from shared intimacy. 'Maybe even stay somewhere nearby so you can maximise your time there.'

Now he was rewarded by a massive smile. 'Really? Are you sure? I mean, won't it be boring for you?'

'Absolutely not. In fact, I've been doing some research and I'm genuinely interested—I hadn't realised there was so much cutting-edge technology associated with wine. It's fascinating, especially the AI tech.'

'It's a difficult balance.' She spread butter on a piece of bread and then added cheese and salami. 'Between tradition and new ways, I don't think I could ever completely back AI over human instinct, knowledge and experience, but I know technology cannot be ignored. Not if you want to continue to thrive in today's world. But I would hate it to become that any grape could be controlled to grow anywhere, until there are uniform vineyards throughout the globe.'

He nodded. 'I don't think AI can replace your love for the wine you are creating. Or your human instinct.'

'I'm guessing the same goes for chocolate,' she said thoughtfully. 'Though nowadays there is so much mass-produced stuff.'

'That is what my grandparents don't agree with. I mean, they accept that products have to be produced in bulk, but it is really important to them to keep it as close to the original handmade chocolate as possible.'

'How did it all start?' Amara asked.

'It all started out small,' he said. 'I suppose like once upon a time the Rossi estate only grew a few vines and produced a few bottles of wine. Romano's started out as a small bakery run by my great-grandfather. He and my great-grandmother expanded into larger premises and then opened up a number of bakeries in neighbour-ing towns and villages. All family run. My grandfather was at the counter at the main store one day when my grandmother came in.' It was a story Aurelio was fond of telling, a story that Gio could somehow picture as he told it to Amara. His grandmother dressed in a chic tai-lored skirt and blouse, perfectly groomed. His grandfa-ther a young man, dressed for work in an apron. 'She'd brought some of her homemade chocolate and wanted to know if the bakery would sell it on her behalf. My grandfather said he fell in love with her and her choc-olate at the same moment. And that's where it started. Soon the bakery became known for the chocolate. My grandmother said love made her improve her recipe— that love was the magic ingredient.'

He glanced at Amara, wondered if she'd scoff but she didn't. Her face was intent as she listened and he re-membered that she'd said that Vittorio Rossi had loved his wife, as well. And for a moment, Gio wished that somehow love was possible for him even as he knew it wasn't. Knew he wasn't capable of loving or being loved. Knew he wouldn't be enough, that there was something flawed inside him. That something that his grandparents had taken for granted was something that he couldn't understand. Like some people understood equations and others didn't.

'Go on,' she said.

'Well after they got married, Aurelio and Ava de-cided to branch out, to set up a separate confectioner's and then as time went on, they slowly expanded, grew the business. A business based on the premise of quality. That is their guiding principle. Romano chocolate is the real thing, not processed rubbish that shouldn't even be allowed to be marketed as chocolate. They want to preserve the ethos behind what they started. Chocolate that is a treat, something to be savoured and enjoyed. They would never produce or align themselves with a company that markets massive bars of cheap, badly made chocolate.'

'And that's what your father wants to do?'

'Yes. He claims that it isn't possible to retain my grandfather's principles and survive.'

Gio heard his voice harden. 'I disagree. My grandparents have managed the company with incredible success for the past fifty years and I respect their principles and I believe they are right. Romano Confectionery is known for its quality. Its chocolate is the real thing. I understand that the profit margins matter, but not at the expense of quality. I believe in moving forward, in research and development, in trying to find ways to keep quality without sacrificing price. As a private company it should be possible to have profit margins that are acceptable to us personally rather than being accountable to the stock market.'

'You do really care,' Amara said softly.

'Yes, I do,' he said. He couldn't help it. 'Maybe it is in my blood. Or maybe it is because I know how much my grandparents have put into the company, how hard they have worked, how important it is.' Or maybe it was the fact that admission to the family business had always been the prize he thought he could never have, would never be good enough, worthy enough to win. Maybe he cared because this ultimate prize was finally within his grasp. Now his grandparents did see him as a true

Romano. But did they? Or was this simply a move they had made of necessity? A temporary solution. A means to bring his father to heel and then they'd let Gio go. The thoughts caused a swirl of emotion and for a minute he questioned his decision to walk back into the family fold. Back into the conflicting complexities of a relationship he didn't really understand. Gio shook his head. 'My grandparents built the company up—they deserve to have their vision followed.' That was what was at stake.

'My grandfather says the earth, the land, the grapes belong to all the generations, but it is the responsibility of each generation to respect those gone past and those to come. I guess it's the same idea.'

Gio nodded. 'Those are very wise words,' he said. 'And if I can I intend to make sure that principle is honoured.' It was a good principle and he felt determination retrigger inside him. He would make this happen, would make sure Romano Confectionery thrived. And to do that he needed to be married. A plan began to form in his head, a plan that caused a flutter of anticipation in his gut, a thrill that he told himself was simple satisfaction at the idea of progress. Was nothing to do with Amara at all.

'We'd better get up and get going. I just need to make some calls.'

A few hours later they arrived at the vineyard and Gio turned to Amara, kept his voice casual. 'Looking forward to this?' he asked.

'Absolutely. I spoke to Erika Merz, her family have owned the vineyard for the past three generations and she sounds wonderful. In fact, from what she said the whole family sounds wonderful and we have so much to talk about. They've recently started making a red wine, having only made white wines, and we're starting with a tour of the vineyard.' She hesitated. 'Are you going to come for that?'

'I wish I could, but I've got some work calls and meetings I have to take.' This was true, but he had other plans as well, needed some time to implement them.

Yet he was aware of a wish to stay with Amara. To watch her in her element, see her discuss the subject she loved so much with likeminded people. And for an instant he thought he saw a quickly concealed flash of disappointment in her eyes. Reminded himself that his plan would hopefully chase disappointment from her face and replace it with the smile that lit her whole face, released the dimple that captivated him.

'Of course,' she said easily. 'It's worked out really well that they have a guest chalet here so you can work.' She glanced out of the window and unclicked her seat belt. 'Oh look. This must be Erika and Peter now.'

Minutes later introductions were made. 'It is lovely to meet you. We are so looking forward to talking to you and showing you round. We are sorry you can't make it, Gio. I will ask Carl, our son, to show you the chalet. There is Wi-Fi and everything you should need to work.'

'Thank you.' He approached Amara, leaned down and brushed her lips with his, felt the tremor run through her body and his own. 'See you later.'

CHAPTER TEN

AMARA GAVE A final smile to Erika who had driven her to the guest chalet in a small buggy used to drive across the vineyard. 'Thank you so much. I've had a wonderful time and I've learnt a lot. And this is beautiful,' she added, gesturing to the chalet nestled within sight of the vineyard. Another fairy tale place, a vineyard muffled in snow, resting and preparing for the following year's harvest, a place of potential and hope.

'You and Gio are welcome back any time, and if you wanted to bring your grandfather we'd be honoured to meet him.'

Amara felt her smile falter a little, recalled that it wouldn't be herself and Gio. Because once they were married, they would be living separate lives, pursuing their own goals. That was what she wanted, she reminded herself, what she could cope with. Separate lives meant they wouldn't be dependent on each other for happiness, no angst and worry over if she was doing the right thing. No trying to dismantle her protective wall, or flip a switch that was already flipped and locked on permanently off. Instead, they could live separate lives, but the time they did spend together could be carefree and easy and fun. No responsibilities or obligations.

Even so as she waved goodbye to Erika, she felt a sudden fillip of anxiety. Had today been about Gio needing space form her? Was she grating on his nerves? Or had she encroached too far? Was she getting this wrong?

A memory of the morning shivered over her, the feeling of waking up nestled next to him, the warmth and the closeness that felt somehow magnified by everything she'd shared, emotionally and physically.

Remembered panic regenerated. What had happened to her wall? Because despite the comfort and the help he'd given, the idea that she'd shared such a personal part of herself, her memories of Luca, was terrifying. She didn't let people close, wouldn't risk more hurt and loss. That idea reinforced by the knowledge that her parents' seemingly idyllic marriage had been anything but. Love brought nothing but complications and she mustn't forget it. What she needed now was distance, not proximity. And maybe Gio had felt the same. He'd spent a couple of hours with Amara and the Merz family but had then returned to the chalet to work. And she understood that, but now she wondered if it had simply been an excuse to give them both space. If so she respected that.

But despite all the thoughts, she was aware of a bubble of happiness as she approached the front door, a sense of anticipation, a desire to see him.

She quickened her pace as a flurry of snowflakes swirled down and she pushed the door open. Stood in the hallway for a second just as Gio emerged from a room on the left and closed the door behind him.

'Perfect timing,' he said as she hung her coat up on the hook, aware of a sudden sense of awkwardness. Should she step forward and kiss him or was that not appropriate? She was pretty sure throwing herself into his arms when it was just the two of them would send the wrong signal. In the end, she settled for a smile and a raised eyebrow in question. 'I'm getting dinner ready,' he explained. 'And you have time for a relaxing bath.' He stepped forward and pulled her into a quick kiss, a kiss that dizzied her, distracted her. 'The bathroom is down the hall on the left,' he said and she nodded, her heart still beating extra fast as she headed to the bathroom.

Warmth doused her as she saw Gio had laid out a fluffy towel and by the bath was a bottle of luxurious bubble bath, scented with her favourite vanilla scent. She frowned. How had he even known that?

After her bath, she headed into the bedroom, a bedroom they would share, the idea sending a thrill through her as she thought about what to wear. Wanted to make sure it was something that would distract Gio as much as his kiss had distracted her, would make it clear that she was more than up for a repeat of the night before.

In the end, she settled for one of her new purchases. A red flower–printed dress, with a lace underlay, long-sleeved and high-necked but falling to mid-thigh, it combined demure and sexy, especially when paired with open-toed, black high heels.

As she surveyed her reflection, she barely recognised herself as the woman who'd packed to escape to the Bavarian Alps mere days before.

Now she looked radiant, her eyes held a sparkle, a brightness, and her whole body seemed to move with more confidence, more awareness. A body that now knew so much more, knew the pleasures and joy that

Gio's touch had evoked. Great sex, she reminded herself. Nothing more. A bonus factor.

But right now, those words of common sense didn't matter anymore. All she wanted was to be with Gio, enjoy his company, enjoy bantering, flirting, talking, sharing—and that was all right. Soon enough they would embark on their separate lives and until then there was no harm in revelling in these new-found sensations, the chemistry...

She walked down the corridor to find him standing near the front door, facing her, waiting for her, she realised, and now she did a double take. He looked gorgeous; his dark hair shower damp with a hint of errant curl. He'd changed into dark denim slim-cut jeans, with a black V-neck shirt under a deep grey charcoal blazer.

And now Amara didn't care about rules or appearances. All that mattered was that she was allowed to look, allowed to touch, allowed to get close. The thought seemed to occur to them both at the same time and she stepped forward just as he did, almost wonderingly. Then they were so close, so very close. 'You look stunning,' he said softly.

'And you look gorgeous,' she responded, taking one more step, let his sheer warmth, his heat, the tantalising woodsy scent of him dizzy her senses.

Then he said, 'Close your eyes. No peeking.'

She complied, and he moved behind her and she caught her breath as he gently placed his hands round her waist to guide her forward. The sound of a door opening and then she stepped forward and stopped, inhaled, aware of a glorious floral scent, the sweet scent of violets underlaid with perhaps a hint of vanilla.

'You can open them now,' he said, and she'd swear that there was a hint of nerves in his voice.

She opened her eyes and felt her mouth drop open in a small 'O' of surprise. The room had been transformed. Flowers were strategically placed around the room, the vivid purple of violets, bright red amaryllises interspersed with blooms she didn't even recognise, a riot of colour. Pillared candles of various heights were strategically placed around, adding a golden aura of illumination. The furniture had been pushed back against the walls to allow a small wooden table, liberally scattered with petals, to be the centrepiece, led to by an arched trellis. Music played in the background; music she recognised as her favourite classical composer.

Gio took her hand in his and led her to the table where a bottle of deep red wine stood and her eyes widened in further surprise as she saw the label. It was from the Rossi estate; a bottle from one of their very best yields from years before. Her absolute favourite. Already open, and Gio stepped forward and poured them both a glass and smiled at her, a smile that lit his whole face and sent a shiver through her whole body.

'This is beautiful.' For some reason she felt tears blink her eyes as she realised the thought that must have gone into this. 'How…?'

'Well, I did have to make some calls, but they weren't work-related. I called a florist, I visited a few shops, got a few things delivered and…here we are.'

'But those are my favourite flowers,' she said. 'And it must have taken ages to decorate the room like this and…' Amara made herself stop, reminded herself of their arrangement as she pulled her phone out of her pocket. 'I know this is for show, but it is really lovely of you to have gone to so much trouble to make it so...real.'

He took a step forward now. 'This *is* real.' The words made her heart give a funny little jump and she willed her expression not to change. 'This isn't for the cameras. This is for you. To show you my thanks for agreeing to this venture, to mark another step on our way. To show you that I value you, and I admire your strength.'

He took a deep breath.

'It's also for another reason.' He took a deep breath. 'So here goes.'

Amara watched him, aware of a sudden tingle of nerves, as he moved towards the table, saw that his hand was shaking slightly as he reached out and picked up a cardboard box from the petal-strewn surface.

He stepped back towards her and she saw that the box bore the Romano Confectionery label. He opened the lid and she looked inside.

There were three Romano truffles and in the space where the fourth one should be a ring nestled.

Amara reached in with trembling fingers and took it out. 'It's beautiful,' she breathed. And it was. Double banded, one band was rose gold the other was embedded with diamonds and the sparkle of a square ruby gemstone. Amara blinked back tears at the sheer thoughtfulness. The wine, the chocolates symbolising their marriage, the choice of gemstone, her favourite colour and the colour of the wine she loved so much.

'Will you, Amara Rossi, do me the honour of becoming my lawfully wedded wife?' he asked and his voice was husky and she knew he was genuinely asking, that in a way this was her chance to back out, that he meant this as a proposal not a fait accompli.

A mixture of emotion swirled through her. A happiness she knew to be out of proportion, a sudden dangerous sadness that this *was* all about the law. Gio needed a lawfully wedded wife. *Enough.* Amara refused to even acknowledge the sadness, refused to allow such a pointless, irrational emotion any headspace. This marriage was what she wanted, what she had agreed to willingly.

This partnership.

And dammit they were going to be happy. And so, in this moment she would only allow happiness in, would believe in their happy ever after.

'Yes. I will marry you.'

'Thank you.' His smile crinkled and lit his brown eyes. 'I know this isn't a conventional proposal and I won't insult you by saying words that neither of us wants or means or needs, but please believe all of this is not for show or the cameras. I have no intention of taking a single photo—this is truly for you. For us. This is the only proposal I propose to make in my life and I hope it is the only one you will ever receive because I truly want to make this work.'

'So do I.' She lifted her glass of wine. 'The perfect choice.'

'For the perfect bride.' He reached out and picked up the ring and she held her hand out, and as he slipped the ring onto her finger, she felt something she couldn't quite identify jolt through her and quickly she turned away from him slightly, under the pretext of holding her hand up so the gemstones caught the light.

'Does it fit?' he asked. 'I had to guess your ring size.'

'It's slightly loose but only slightly. And I love it, the design… Everything. I love all of this. But how on earth could you know that this is my favourite wine, that this is my favourite music…?'

He smiled at her. 'I have a source,' he said. 'I spoke with your grandfather.'

Amara stared at him.

'I asked his permission to ask for your hand in marriage. Old-fashioned, I know, but I thought… Well, I thought it would make it easier for you if I paved the way. I know how worried you are about lying to him.'

Now Amara didn't even bother to try to blink back the tears. 'You did that?'

'Yes. It was very nerve-wracking, but I'm glad I spoke with him. He is a real gentleman. We had a good chat. I like him very much and I think, I hope, he approved of me. He did say that he would never stand in the way of your decisions, or interfere, but he did also give us his blessing and he is looking forward to us going there in a few days.'

Relief washed over Amara, along with a sudden fuzzy feeling that everything really was going to be all right.

'Thank you,' she said softly. 'I truly mean that. It makes all of this even more special and precious than it already was.' And she didn't care if her words could be misinterpreted. This was precious. It did mark the start of their marriage. And it was a good, auspicious start.

'You're very welcome.' Now he grinned; the type of grin that sent a warmth of a different sort over her skin. 'And if you're looking of ways to show your appreciation, I can think of a few.'

She grinned at him. 'Well please feel free to share. Or

better yet, why don't you show me.' Reaching out she took his hand, 'Let's go to bed. I wouldn't want you to lose the thread of your thoughts. And for the record, I am feeling very grateful indeed.'

An hour later and Gio watched as Amara stretched luxuriously, gloriously unselfconscious and oh, so very beautiful. A beauty that seemed to pierce his heart as he studied her, so relaxed, a smile on her face that he knew was mirrored on his. A smile of satiation, contentment and sheer awe at the sensations experienced over the past minutes, passion, joy, yearning, sheer voluptuous pleasure. He saw the glint of the ring on her finger, his ring, a symbol of commitment and felt a fierce pride that this woman had agreed to marry him. No matter what the motivation, no matter that it was a ring of convenience, it bound them together. She was his.

She smiled lazily at him and he grinned back. 'How about we stay right here and eat dinner in bed?'

'That works for me,' she said

'I'll be right back.' His grin widened as she gave an admiring whistle as he climbed out of bed and another when he returned ten minutes later carefully balancing a tray.

'Perfect. I'm guessing my grandfather told you my favourite food too.'

'Well, he gave me a choice and I went for the one I thought I could manage to cook most easily,' he admitted.

'This looks incredible. I love Spaghettini Verdi.' She twirled up a forkful and sighed happily. 'Exactly the right proportions of parsley and Parmesan,' she said. 'And this is proper Parmesan, as well.'

Once they had eaten, they sat propped up against the headboard, their legs pressed together, her hair tickling his shoulder and she sipped her wine, then made an exclamation of annoyance. 'The ring. It must have fallen off whilst I was eating.' Quickly she rummaged around in the bed and found it, put it on the bedside table, suddenly scared that she would lose it. 'So, what now?' she asked. 'Now we are officially engaged.'

'We'll announce our engagement. I'll get that sorted in the morning and we can put it on social media. Then we're meeting your grandfather in a few days and I'd like you to meet my grandparents, as well.'

He felt her stiffen a little bit beside him and he took her hand.

'Don't worry. They aren't scary.'

'I know. I'm just worried I'll mess this up. I know how important this is to you. How much you care about them. I don't want to say the wrong thing or let them see how angry I am that they excluded you from your birthright. And I'm worried in case your father or brothers are there. I know how important it is to make this believable to them. What if I let you down?'

The very fact that she had asked the question twisted his chest, brought home the knowledge of what he was asking her to do. Yes, he had to put on a show, but his show was for the benefit of Vittorio Rossi, a gentleman who had behaved with honour, a man who truly loved his granddaughter and would welcome Gio Rossi into the family. *Gio* was expecting Amara to put on a show for his grandparents, who were essentially happy for her to be used as a pawn on the Romano chessboard. He was going to expose her to the manipulation and scrutiny of his father, a man he knew to be an unscrupulous bully. Even though Gio *knew* he would protect her, would never let his father even whisper the hint of an insult… *knew* his grandparents would treat Amara with respect and civility at a minimum, *knew* she would be living her own life, the idea still jarred.

He took a deep breath. 'Perhaps it would be better if you didn't get too involved with my family. Maybe you don't have to actually meet my grandparents and…'

'Okay.' Her voice was small and he felt her body flinch, saw her face take on a sudden shuttered look. 'Maybe you're right. It's better that way. To keep a distance. Make sure we don't get too involved in each other's lives.'

Gio blinked, considered her words. Was she right? The idea of this marriage was that they lived independently, didn't have any of the complications that went with emotional entanglement. Yes, they needed the marriage to look real, but his grandparents were aware that it wasn't. So did she need to meet them right now? At some point she would need to meet his father, but not instantly. Another thought hit him. Was this her way of saying that she didn't *want* him to come with her to meet Lorenzo? Accepted the *necessity* that it was *needed* to keep Vittorio happy, but it wasn't what she wanted. That she didn't want him to be part of her world? That idea also jarred, it hurt because he wanted to be there, by her side.

But was that too much—was that infringing on the rules, the underlying principle of their agreement? A principle that perhaps she wanted him to honour; a principle that meant of course Amara didn't want him to be an intrinsic part of *her* life.

Gio glanced at her, saw the shadows, the questions in her eyes and alongside that he also saw hurt. Maybe *she* was hurt, maybe she thought he didn't *want* her to meet his grandparents.

Too many questions.

'Amara…' he began.

Just as she said, 'It's okay, Gio. You don't have to explain. I understand if you don't want to take the risk of me meeting them. I may mess it up…'

Huh? Now all thoughts of independent lives flew out of the window, even as a fleeting alarm bell told him to stop, to think, to at least file the thoughts away for later. But all that mattered now was clearing up the misunderstanding.

'That's not what I meant,' he said. 'I don't think you'll mess up.'

'Then why?'

'Because if things get difficult, get nasty, it's not fair on you.'

'So, you're protecting me?'

'I'm being fair. Why should I expect you to embroil yourself in my family dramas?'

'Because you'd be a fool not to embroil me. Me meeting your grandparents, your family, bolsters our whole pretence—that this marriage is real. You do need your father to believe it or he will have ammunition to try to keep you off the board. So right now, I don't need protecting. I don't want protecting. I want to keep my side of our marriage deal.'

Amara was right, but it still felt wrong. Not when she didn't know what she was letting herself in for.

'Okay,' he nodded. 'But if you are going to do this then you need to know the truth. About my family.'

She laid a hand on his arm. 'You don't have to tell me, Gio.'

'Yes, I do.' That at least did feel right.

Amara turned to face him, her face serious now, still flushed, but her eyes were soft, focused on him and he knew she would really hear him. He took a moment to think about what he wanted to say, oh, so aware that he had never shared this with anyone; that he was revisiting memories that he had held at bay for years.

'Okay. Here goes.'

CHAPTER ELEVEN

AMARA WAITED, knew that what Gio was about to share was intensely personal, could see shadows crowd his brown eyes, the rigidity of his jaw, the tension in his body, oh, so close to her own.

'I told you that I felt I owed my grandparents. For being there for me, for acknowledging me. But I owe them for more than that. My grandparents stepped in when no one else did, when I thought no one else would.'

She didn't push him, waited for him to be ready to explain further.

'I told you about my parents' wedding. It was a marriage my father deeply regretted mostly because it brought about my existence. Otherwise he could have written it off as youthful folly. As it was it lumbered him with me. Literally. Thanks to my mother insisting on joint custody, my father and his family were stuck with a physical reminder of my existence on an ongoing basis.'

'They were also your family,' she said quietly. 'Your father's sons were your half-siblings.' Just like Lorenzo and Daisy were hers. The knowledge a sudden pinprick of guilt, but also of a shift in feeling.

'They didn't see it that way.' She could hear the underlying bitterness in his voice, saw him try to smile, to soften his tone. 'It was difficult for my father and step-mother and it was difficult for me, because…they made it obvious how they felt about me.'

'Obvious how?' Her voice was neutral, neither judge-mental nor pitying.

'They allowed my brothers to bully me, at first it was letting them get away with what they called "rough and tumble", but it wasn't play fighting. It was more one of them pinning me down and the other one putting the boot in. And my dad and my stepmother, Bianca, would look the other way. Then it slowly escalated. Ignoring it evolved into active encouragement. Every visit things got a little bit worse, almost as if my stepbrothers were pushing the boundaries of what they could do. I will say though that my father and stepmother were never physi-cally abusive themselves. It was more what they said, how they treated me. Mind games, ways of making me feel different. Inferior. Taunts. My brothers would play a game of consequences where basically they could choose what forfeit I had to pay if I did anything "wrong". If I smiled it was a smirk—if I didn't smile, I was sulk-ing. It all cost a forfeit. My father and stepmother would think it was all hilarious. They'd do everything they could to make it clear that I was different.' Amara lis-tened in growing disbelief that anyone could behave to a child that way, to any child let alone your own flesh and blood. How could Salvatore Romano have let it hap-pen? And what must it have done to Gio, the constant humiliations, the sense of inferiority, of being second-class? She could almost see the small dark-haired boy stoic and hurt, refusing to cry, perhaps even thinking it was true, that he deserved the treatment meted out to him. 'It all sounds daft really,' he added.

'No, it doesn't.' Amara tried to control her voice, but she couldn't, could hear the choke of anger, the outrage. 'It sounds vindictive and mean and bullying and downright wrong.' Her hands clenched into fists. 'You did not deserve to be treated like that, Gio.'

'I know.' But he didn't; she could see it in his eyes, the doubt, the questions. His head might tell him she was right but somewhere deep inside him that small boy still lived on.

'Good. Because you deserved love and if they couldn't give you that then there is something wrong with them. You are his son. But if for some reason he couldn't love you he could at least have shown you respect and kindness and civility.' The words had an echo to them, resonated, and she blinked, realised that that was what they were basing their marriage on. The idea sent a sudden discomfort through her and she pushed it away. This was about Gio, not about them.

'I think that's what my grandfather thought, too,' he said. 'He arrived at the house unexpectedly one day and came in. He saw what was happening and he…well, he made it all stop. I don't know how. He asked me to leave the room and wait by the front door. Half an hour later he came to the door and took me back to his house.'

'Did your father talk to you about it?'

'Nope. Nobody did, not even my grandfather. I have no idea what my father said to my grandfather. I assume he played it down. I assumed he blamed it on me somehow. But whatever they said, from then on things changed. My grandparents would invite me to stay with them sometimes.'

Amara could hear the surprise in his voice and it tugged at her heart that all these years later the idea that someone could actually want his company could cause Gio surprise. No wonder he saw relationships as deals, things to be controlled and negotiated.

'And the visits to my father were different.' He shrugged. 'We were all marking time until I was old enough for the visits to stop. They pretty much ignored me. I mean there were still sighs, and dirty looks, but on the whole, they left me alone.'

Amara took his hand. 'I'm guessing in some ways that hurt too.'

He nodded and she thought he'd withdraw his hand and she increased the pressure of her hold, wanted him to know that she was there, wasn't going anywhere.

'I guess at first, I hoped that somehow my grandfather had worked a miracle, somehow made everything change, make them if not love me at least like me. But that's not possible—you can't make people like you and you certainly can't make them love you.'

'No. You can't. But it sounds as though your grandparents loved you.'

There was a silence and she could see the confusion in his eyes. 'I think they… Care about me. I think they always felt they had some sort of moral duty towards me. And I admire them for calling my father out when no one else did. I tried to tell my mother, but she didn't want to believe me, didn't want to rock the boat. Because it might have meant she would have been required to have me with her more.'

Amara placed her hand on his, wondered how Luna Rocca could have justified being so caught up in her own life that she had ignored the pleas of her own son.

'My grandparents did do something, but I know that was hard for them. My father is their only son, their pride and joy, their blood. To believe ill of him wouldn't have come easy. It would have been easy to ignore. They didn't. But…' He hesitated.

'But you believe they somehow blame you?' Her voice was gentle now, her heart twisting further as she followed the logic the young Gio had followed.

'Yes. After all, my father cared for his second wife, cared for my brothers. He certainly never mistreated them. They were a unit, a family. I brought out the worst in him. I created the problem. Or at least, I was the catalyst.'

'No.' Amara's voice was firm. 'Your father and stepmother created the problem. They had no right to treat you like that. None at all.' But she could see how easy it was for Gio to blame himself. A distant mother and a father who despised him; he'd concluded he was the problem. 'It wasn't you,' she said again. 'You did nothing wrong. You didn't turn your father into a bully—his actions are on him. You say they were a family unit and maybe they were, but what he and your stepmother did was wrong on so many fronts. They brought your half-brothers up to be bullies, encouraged them to inflict pain and hurt—that in itself is a travesty of parenting, shows no understanding of what family means.'

He glanced at her and she could see that this hadn't occurred to him. That for him, his father's house had simply been a place of torment, a place where he was the one outside the 'true' family unit. The one who deserved to be treated badly.

'It is not on you,' she repeated. Hoped she'd got through.

'Either way I won't let my grandparents suffer from his bullying tactics.'

'I agree with that.' Whatever their faults, and she couldn't absolve them fully, they had been the best people in Gio's childhood. 'And I want to help. I will not let you down and I will be by your side.'

The words echoed around the room and for a few moments they sat, hands clasped and as she looked down at their joined hands a sudden sense of strength, of togetherness, of connection seemed to shimmer and solidify.

Then he squeezed her hand and said, 'Come on.'

'Where to?'

'A starlit walk. You can show me the vineyard and we can think about the future. Our future. Because we're going to make this work, and I want our engagement night to be full of a whole plethora of memories, of great sex, confidences, sharing the past and looking forward to the future.'

'I love that idea.' And she did. Suddenly wondered if she would have loved any plan that involved being with Gio. Decided it didn't matter. She didn't care. She wanted to walk by starlight hand in hand and think about the future, their future. Yes, she knew medium-term they would have individual separate paths, but for now she could see that for a while there was a good reason for them to be together. For a while they *needed* to be together. *Needed* to make sure the wool was pulled over Salvatore Romano's eyes. The idea filled her with a disproportionate happiness and a danger signal clanged.

But there was no danger. There was no choice; they needed to do this. The fact that she wanted to do it was a bonus, surely. Once Gio was established, once Salvatore accepted their marriage as real, they would both back off. By then they would both want to. Sorted. So in the meantime, why not focus on the moment, the job in hand. She of all people knew there was little point dwelling on the future.

Half an hour later they were outside and she gathered her thoughts, tried to sound brisk and professional.

'I think the best plan is to make sure that we look the part for at least a few months. That way your father shouldn't suspect anything whilst you establish yourself. From a practical viewpoint I am happy to spend time with you, getting to know your grandparents better.'

'I'd appreciate that, but I also want to be at the vineyard. I know you are needed there.'

She shrugged and for the first time she said the words without minding. 'Yes, but my grandfather will be there and I suppose that Lorenzo and Daisy will be spending time there too. So I will need to be at the vineyard for some of the time, but...'

'*We* will need to be there,' he corrected gently. 'I have no intention of leaving you to face Lorenzo and Daisy on your own. Not until we have figured them out.'

Amara looked up at the glitter and gleam of the stars. And despite the knowledge that it was all part of the deal, happiness welled up inside her and she wondered if indeed the stars had aligned to bring her and Gio together.

'That sounds like a plan,' she said and as he bent to kiss her, she knew she would always remember this starlit night and the feel of his lips on hers.

* * *

Amara woke up, opened her eyes, intensely aware that the space beside her was empty. Panic touched her and she told herself not to be foolish. Gio had probably gone to the bathroom or to start breakfast or maybe he wanted some space.

Memories of the previous night washed over her, the way they had held each other, had fallen asleep in each other's arms, and she knew her dreams had been happy. Images of walks around the vineyard with Gio, cooking dinner with Gio, meal planning, choosing restaurants, standing side by side. Gio and Amara. Amara and Gio. And now, still half asleep, other images streamed her mind, herself holding a baby. A tiny, perfect scrap of humanity with Gio's dark hair, cradled in her arms and Gio standing next to her, looking down at the infant with love and pride.

Now she sat up; that was taking things way too far. Yet why? Why couldn't all those dreams become reality? The question, the fact she'd even thought it, poleaxed her and she stilled, one hand clenched around the sheet. But somehow the sense of happiness, contentment, the sense of possibilities and potential remained. Other people experienced real happy ever afters, maybe she actually could? Because she'd never felt like this before, never been so comfortable with anyone, never felt so close, so connected. Why should it go wrong? If fate had brought them together, perhaps fate could keep them together.

The idea was too big, too enormous, too much to contemplate and she swung her legs out of bed. Headed for the bathroom where she showered quickly, dressed and headed to the kitchen. Despite herself anticipation showed in the goofy smile she felt upturn her lips, as somehow the idea of being a couple, of being Amara and Gio, Gio and Amara still permeated her brain. But as she approached there was no noise, no waft of coffee or toast coming from the kitchen and she told herself she shouldn't expect breakfast to be prepared for her. Yet a small worry surfaced as she listened, was suddenly very sure she was alone in the house.

A belated glance at her watch showed her that it was ridiculously late; she couldn't recall the last time she had slept so deeply and now a vague memory surfaced, a sense of Gio stood over her, a fleeting gentle kiss that had sent a flutter of happiness through her without fully waking her. A dream or reality?

She pushed the kitchen door open, saw that it was indeed empty, though a rinsed-out mug showed that Gio had had coffee before leaving. He'd also taken the trouble to clean the kitchen from the night before.

And now she spotted a note on the kitchen table, moved over to read it.

Amara, I have headed into Munich to have your ring altered for you. I was going to wake you up to see if you wanted to come, but you looked so asleep I thought I would leave you. I will bring back some extra breakfast (breakfast in bed?) I shouldn't be back late, I am aiming to be there when the shops open. Gio

So, he must have set off pretty early and he should be back any minute now. But as the minutes began to stretch she became aware of a sense of worry, an edginess that she tried to alleviate with a cup of tea, another cup of tea, recleaning the already clean kitchen, and eventually she messaged him. Tried not to sound clingy or needy.

Looked up as she heard the ting of a message being received and then she spotted it. Gio had left his phone behind, he must have been charging it and forgotten to pick it up. The idea should have made her feel better. He'd just been held up and couldn't let her know. Yet somehow panic was beginning to churn inside her, and she checked the local news, stared down at what she saw and now panic crystallised and surged into a tsunami.

There'd been a pile-up; she saw the images of firefighters, ambulances, police, tried to make head or tail of it all, desperately Google translating, checking maps and all the while panic getting worse and worse.

There had been a crash, there were fatalities, it was the road that Gio would have been on at some point in his journey. She made frantic calculations as she paced up and down, forced herself to try and work out timelines, tried to tell herself he was caught in traffic, couldn't contact her. That he was all right. He had to be all right.

But she knew how fate could work, how a series of random events, a ring that was a size too big, a ring that had slipped off her finger, a man who had woken up early, perhaps motivated by a sense of edginess after a night of spilling his soul. A man who happened to be located on a Bavarian vineyard because he happened to be engaged to a wine heiress. Domino after domino. Because the dominoes of fate had fallen for some people; there were people who had died.

She tried to think, she had to work out how to get

to him. Up and down, trying to block out images that filled her with pain and horror. Perhaps she could call the hospital, call a helpline call…call who? There was nothing she could do, but wait and pace and pray and try to block out memories, memories of loss and pain and grief. Of finding her grandfather, his face streaked with tears. Her grandfather, a man who never showed emotion, didn't cry. He'd held his grief to himself but she'd seen it. Seen what losing a loved one did. Even now she hadn't healed from all the loss. Losing Luca. Now what if she'd lost Gio?

He might be lying somewhere dead, caught in a wreckage, his body twisted and splayed. He may be gone. The thought tore at her insides, hollowed her out with pain. How could fate have done this? Further pain ratcheted as she realised her own involvement, how fate had used her. Because she was part of the domino effect. If she hadn't agreed to marry him then Gio wouldn't have bought the ring in the first place. Hell, if she'd only thought to give him her ring size. If, if, if… That's how fate worked, worked to use events and people and cause accidents that wrenched happiness from people. That's why she understood it was better to walk alone, to remain safe behind a wall. Because she knew now it didn't just protect her. It protected others, kept her from becoming a domino in fate's hands. She should never have agreed to this arrangement. Never have done this, and then Gio would be alive and well. This had all been a mistake, she'd let Gio close, allowed herself to dream.

Now how bitterly she regretted those dreams, those illusions of happiness. How bitterly she regretted letting him so close, allowing a connection, allowing herself to care. And as she paced, Amara knew she couldn't do this; made a deal with herself. If Gio lived, if Gio was all right, Amara would release him from this. Would release herself from what commitment brought. Release them both. Would walk away before she actually married him, brought them even closer, spent more time together.

Her vision of earlier came back to mock her. Herself and Gio as parents. She couldn't be a mother, because she wouldn't be able to protect her baby from the unpredictability of fate. Would coddle them, wouldn't know how to parent without wrapping them in cotton wool, making their lives miserable with her anxieties. As for herself and Gio, Amara and Gio, Gio and Amara, the words took on a taunting rhythm.

Up and down she paced, the horrific images unfiltered now. Nothing was worth this risk, the risk of this type of loss. But first, please God let him be all right.

And then finally, finally she saw the front door swing open and she leapt to her feet.

Gio pushed the front door open, knew that Amara must be wondering where he'd gone. It had been daft to leave his phone behind but when he'd left, he hadn't really been thinking practically. The previous night had blown him away, made sleep difficult. He'd felt so much lighter sharing his past, and it was as though the connection between them was fizzing and sparking, becoming more solid, more visible, more real. And that had made him feel…energised.

A bit fizzy himself, full of energy, a need to keep going forward, without thinking too hard. But when he'd seen how asleep Amara looked a protective sense had prevailed, a desire to keep her cocooned and safe and so he had decided to get up, and then he'd figured he might as well do something proactive. And also, he wanted his ring to be on her finger. It might be a convenient ring, but it proclaimed to the world that she was his fiancée and it felt…right that it should sit on her finger securely.

And so, he'd set off.

The trip to Munich had been fine; it had been the trip back that had taken a long time.

'I'm sorry…' he started and then stood back as she moved towards him, stood and stared at him as though she couldn't believe her eyes. She reached out and placed a tentative hand on his chest, then his cheek and then she heaved a great sigh and he saw the shudder run through her.

'I heard the news, that there had been an accident. I thought…'

Oh hell. She'd thought it might have been him.

'Oh, Amara, I am sorry. My phone… I should have stopped somewhere. I didn't realise why they'd closed the road. But I should have called.' He should have found a payphone, paid someone to use their mobile… Anything. Instead, he'd just wanted to get back.

'It's okay. The important thing is that you are all right. That you aren't one of those poor souls who died.' Her voice broke and he stepped forward to take her into his arms, shared her sadness at the tragedy that had plucked people's lives away with no notice, all because they were in the wrong place at the wrong time. Knew his sadness was nothing compared to Amara's. Knew all the memories it must have brought back to her. No wonder she looked so dazed.

But as he approached her, she stepped back, held one hand out and he saw something almost akin to revulsion on her face, her green eyes glittered now with something he couldn't identify. Sadness, anger and a steely determination and yes, a rejection, a clear *do not come near me*.

Gio felt a sudden wrench of panic twist his chest, told himself to keep calm. It was completely understandable for Amara to be having all sort of reactions and emotions.

'We need to talk,' she said and now her voice was weighted, with anger and sadness.

'Okay.'

They headed into the kitchen, sat at the small table and looked out at the vineyards in the distance and he recalled their starlit conversation of the night before.

For some reason every detail of the room seemed to be etching itself on his memory as if by focusing on the detail he could put off whatever Amara was going to say. The gleam of the fridge, the jut of the marble counter, the smooth wood of the floor.

'I can't go through with this marriage.' Her voice was jerky.

'Why not?' His voice harder than he had meant it to be, but as she said each word it felt as though each one was a bullet that shattered each precious image of the future he'd been building up. Building up without even realising it.

'This morning… When I thought I'd lost you I realised exactly why I can't deal with commitment of any sort. It's too big a risk. I can't do it. I won't do it.'

The words cut into him with unexpected ferocity. Of course she couldn't commit to him. He wasn't worth committing to, worth taking a risk on. That's what his parents had both believed. Why should Amara be any different? He should have known this couldn't work. But he hadn't expected this hurt, this pain, this bleak sadness. But his own pain didn't matter now. All he could see was Amara, her ravaged face, and from somewhere he tried to draw some reserve of strength. Because she was hurting.

'I am so sorry, Gio. I should never have agreed to this and now… Now I have wrecked things for you.' Her green eyes held panic, and he could see the clench and unclench of her hands and it killed him not to step forward and hold her, reassure her. But he couldn't, because she didn't want him to. His touch would only make things worse for her and that was another gut punch of pain. 'Maybe, maybe we can get married,' she said and his heart leapt with joy, at the hope of reprieve.

The idea he could fight back, show Amara that they could make this work. That he was worth the risk. That really nothing had changed since last night, when they'd made their plans. Wanted to face the next months side by side.

'Just on paper,' she said. 'We could go through a ceremony, then legally you'd be okay. We could come up with a story, that I'm ill or was called away for work…' Anything so that she didn't have to be near him; shades of his parents. Shades of his life. Amara didn't want to be by his side, wanted out of their arrangement. She didn't want to take the risk of commitment to him. And that was her right. He saw sadness on her face, but he also saw determination. She had made that decision, a decision to walk completely alone, to live her own life, to answer to no one but herself.

It seemed so clear to him now; somewhere down the line the rules and boundaries of their deal had blurred. Amara was right, they couldn't walk side by side and remain uninvolved, uninvested in the other. He was involved, was invested, wanted nothing more right now than her happiness. And that meant letting go. However much he didn't want to, however much he wanted to try to persuade her that it would be all right. That the risk was worth it. Because it wasn't. He wasn't. Amara had gone through so much. He wouldn't add to it, wouldn't try to force her to do something she didn't want to do.

'No,' he said. 'You don't need to do that and you haven't wrecked anything.' It all seemed so clear to him now. 'I should never have embroiled you in this. I should never have embroiled anyone. I should have worked out a different way in the first place. This whole idea was misguided from the start.' Completely misguided. He should never have asked her to do this. After all what had he done? He'd made her and himself into pawns on the Romano chessboard once again. Perhaps his motivations had been good, but his actions had been wrong. A continuation of the past. He would fight his father and he would support his grandparents, but he would find a different way. A better way.

It was time for them both to get off the chessboard. Time for him to do the right thing and let her go.

'Truly, Amara. It is all right. It's time to do this properly. Above board. So we can dissolve our arrangement. We didn't announce the engagement—the publicity will die down soon enough. This will be written off as another of my affairs.' The words so hollow he could almost feel them scoop out his insides. Logically surely, they should be true; he had only known Amara a few days, but logic seemed to have flown out of the window. Logically he shouldn't be feeling this soul-shrivelling pain, a pain that was bleak and desolate and personal.

'I will sort this out Amara. I will find a way, do what I should have done in the first place. But now what would you like to do? You are welcome to stay here, or I can drive you to the airport or...'

She shook her head. 'I'll get a taxi from here once I've sorted out a flight. I'm going home. I'll tell my grand-father the truth.' She took a deep breath, her green eyes large and stricken. 'Goodbye, Gio. I hope with all my heart that this works out for you. You are a good man and I know you will find a way.'

'Goodbye, Amara. I wish you all the luck in the world and I know you have the inner strength and courage to navigate everything, to do the best for yourself and the Rossi estate.' He managed a smile. 'I'll buy a bottle of next year's harvest.'

She stepped towards him and lifted a hand to his cheek, the touch, so brief, so fleeting but he knew it would be imprinted on him forever.

CHAPTER TWELVE

Two days later
Castle Alavario, Tuscany

AMARA SAT OPPOSITE Vittorio Rossi in the study that she knew so well, looked round at the dark green curtains tied back with tassels of gold, at the leather-topped desk, the teak sideboard, the worn leather sofa and the patterned rug, the portraits of Rossis gone by on the walls.

Yet the items, all so familiar, gave her no comfort, seemed somehow faded and grey, like everything felt. Exactly as everything had felt since she turned her back on Gio and walked away. How could she miss anyone this much, so much that it was a dull physical ache, a constant reminder of what she'd lost? She tried not to think about him, tried to take solace from the castle, the estate. Her grandfather had taken one look at her face and simply told her to rest, take her time, talk to him when and if she was ready. Hadn't asked her where Gio was, hadn't asked her anything.

And so, she'd spent two days trying and trying to erase the memories, trying to tell herself she'd made the right decision. After all, if it hurt this much now, how much more would it have hurt later down the line?

She didn't even understand why it hurt so much. Her relationships with Stefan and Silvio had lasted over a year and she'd tried to get close, wanted to let them in. But when those relationships had ended, she'd been disappointed in herself, made sad by her own shortcomings. She hadn't missed them at all. They had barely scratched the surface. Whereas Gio, in a scant few days, had got under her skin. No, he'd done way more than that—he'd got into her heart, her soul…he'd somehow connected to her. A connection she could feel, would swear still shimmered and simmered between her and him, wherever he was at this moment. She closed her eyes, told herself that it would fade, and eventually surely it would dissipate, dissolve, disappear. It would just take time… And then somehow, one day she'd be alone and happy in her solitude.

'Amara?' Vittorio's voice was gentle. 'You said you wanted to talk.'

Amara nodded, knew she owed her grandfather an explanation.

'I assume the marriage isn't happening?' he asked, his voice devoid of judgement or censure and yet guilt swirled an extra layer into the fog of misery that engulfed her. She'd raised her grandfather's hopes, deceived him and now she couldn't follow through. She'd let him down, let Gio down.

She shook her head. 'I'm sorry, Nonno. I know you must be disappointed in me. I should have gone through with it. Or I should never have agreed to marry Gio.' But looking back, even knowing what she knew now, even when every heartbeat seemed to hurt, when everything, every scent, every taste reminded her of him, even now she couldn't regret the past few days.

Remembered how he'd held her, his smile, the deep brown of his eyes, how he looked when he was asleep, his laugh, his touch. Every second of her time with him etched into a treasure trove of bittersweet memories.

'Why did you agree?'

'It was a business arrangement. He needed a wife for business reasons. I wanted to make you happy, provide you with reassurance that I wouldn't be alone when you died. I wanted support so that I wouldn't be outnumbered by Lorenzo and Daisy.' She gave a small helpless shrug. 'It seemed like a good idea at the time. I'm sorry. Sorry I lied to you, sorry I raised your hopes.'

'Amara you have no need to apologise to me. Not now, not ever. I do love the estate and of course I hope that there will always be a Rossi at the helm. But I know too that the world does not hinge on it. I would give up the whole Rossi estate in a heartbeat if it could bring our family back. I would give it up just to spend one more day with your grandmother, to have had a chance to tell her how much she meant to me. But that tragedy, the only good thing from it was, *is* you Amara. You were spared and I thank God every day for that. You have brought my life joy. I wouldn't change anything about you. It is enough for me that you are here. If you wish to do something different with your life that is okay with me—if you marry, if you have children that is up to you. I simply want your happiness.' Amara blinked back tears, reached out and touched her grandfather's arm.

'Thank you, Nonno. You have always been my rock, my anchor. I couldn't have survived without you.'

'As for Lorenzo and Daisy, I do want to welcome them to our family. I do hope to build a relationship with them, but not at the cost of your happiness. Forgive me Amara, I did not realise how much their arrival would affect you.' He hesitated. 'Is that why you are so unhappy?'

'No.' Amara answered without thinking. 'They aren't the reason why.' The words the truth. Her time with Gio, hearing how his half-siblings had treated him. Hearing how his family had treated him because they resented him, feared him, regretted his existence…somehow without her even realising it it had caused her own resentment against her siblings to fade away. 'I want to give them a chance.'

'I am glad. But then, Amara, what is causing your unhappiness? If you feel guilty about me, I hope I have made you see that there is no need.'

'You have, Nonno. It's not that either.' Her unhappiness was caused by missing Gio. She had to assume that one day work, her grandfather, perhaps even her siblings would give her purpose. That one day she'd smile again, but right now the idea that she would never see Gio again was a sheer, bleak knowledge of a future that seemed desolate.

'Then what is wrong?'

The kindness, the concern, the love in his voice undid her resolve to say nothing. 'I… I miss Gio,' she blurted out. 'It's foolish, ridiculous and I know it will pass.' She gulped, blinked hard and then forced a smile to her face. 'I think it was all a bit much. Truly, I will be fine.'

'I am sure you will, but… I don't understand. Why did you decide not to marry Gio? You said you couldn't go through with it. I thought that meant you decided you couldn't enter a loveless business marriage.'

Amara shook her head. 'I couldn't marry him, because I couldn't take the risk of losing him.' Couldn't risk losing the man she loved. *Loved.* The word resonated round her brain, ricocheted and echoed as she tried to encompass the meaning.

There was a silence before Vittorio spoke and when he did his voice was gentle but none the less fervent for all that. 'But you have lost him already.'

Amara shook her head. 'I know, but time will heal the pain and I will be okay on my own again.'

'So you would sacrifice love, sacrifice happiness with another.'

'Yes. To avoid the pain you went through when you lost Nonna, to avoid the pain I went through losing our whole family, losing Luca. How can I take the risk? And what if something goes wrong, if fate steps in and causes tragedy? What if by being with him I cause that tragedy?'

'You can't think like that. You cannot let the ifs and buts take over your life. I will not make this decision for you, Amara, of course I cannot. But I will tell you this. Despite the pain of losing your *nonna*, I would never want to undo the love we had, and I know she would feel the same way if the situation had been reversed. I would always choose love, would always take the risk. Of course there are no guarantees that you will be lucky enough to live happily ever after into old age. But love, love brings you alive. It brings joy and I would never advise you to turn your back on it.'

Just as he hadn't. Amara thought about what Gio's family had done; they *had* elected to turn their backs on loving him. His mother had chosen her own lifestyle, his father had chosen bitterness and bullying. But her grandfather, despite losing so much, his wife, his only child, his grandson, his daughter-in-law, had found it in his heart to love Amara. To take that risk. To embrace joy.

'But even if you are right…' And she wasn't sure, was still trying to come to terms with the fact she loved Gio. The fact that she was capable of love, that somehow the switch had flipped to on, enabled her to feel, to care, to connect, to love. 'It doesn't matter. Gio doesn't love me. He needed to be married. He doesn't want love.' And she couldn't marry him knowing love was one-sided. So in truth this knowledge simply made everything worse.

'Doesn't want love?' Vittorio sounded perplexed. 'How can anyone not want love?'

Amara opened her mouth to answer, then closed it again. Perhaps Gio simply didn't believe he deserved love, didn't believe love was possible for him. And who could blame him? The closest he'd got was his grandparents, two people who Amara still felt ambivalent about. They had given Gio time, perhaps some form of affection, practical help because they owed him a moral duty of care. Where was the joy, the real love in that?

And Gio did deserve love. In the time they'd had together he'd held her, listened to her, really listened, made her laugh, made her happy. Shown her things about herself she'd never have known. Given her perspective. Given her joy. She wanted him to know that. However terrifying the idea was.

'Thank you,' she said to her grandfather. 'Truly. Thank you.'

She dropped a kiss on his cheek and left the room, for the first time in days the weight, the density of misery had diffused.

Milan. A café

Gio wondered if this was a good idea. Wondered if they would even come to meet him. Max and Antonio Romano, his half-siblings. Would he even recognise them if they did turn up? After all he hadn't seen them in ten years. He wished, really wished, that Amara was here. He'd been so close, so very close to calling her. To tell her his plan. Tell her he'd figured it all out. Possibly. Thank her for her input.

Those words she'd said. That his brothers had been brought up to be bullies. Taught that it was the right way to be, a way to win their parents' approval. That was wrong, and it was an aspect that had never occurred to Gio. That the real Romano family unit was a 'travesty'. Perhaps because to him real Romanos could do no wrong, or because maybe he craved his father's approval himself, or maybe because it had been so painful to endure his brother jibes, taunts and fists. But in the past days he had thought and he'd realised his brothers too had been manipulated just as much as Gio had been.

He looked up as the café door opened, saw a man walk in. A man who looked familiar, both from memory and from his own reflection. Gio rose as the man approached.

'Antonio?' he hazarded the guess, thought it was the younger of his brothers.

'Gio.' His brother hesitated and held out a hand, Gio hesitated and then took it.

'Is Max coming?'

Antonio shook his head. 'Papa told us both to ignore your invitation.'

'Yet you're here?'

'Yes.'

'Why?'

'Curiosity, but also…' Now suddenly Antonio looked very young, though Gio knew he must be twenty-five. 'I want to apologise.' The words stiff, jerky, yet they held sincerity as Antonio held his gaze, though Gio could see the effort it took. 'The way we treated you was wrong.' Antonio released a breath, and his jaw lost some tension.

'Thank you.' Gio wasn't sure what else to say, knew that everything couldn't be cancelled out with a few words; he still couldn't be sure Antonio didn't have an ulterior motive. But somehow, it felt like a start. And again, he wished so hard that Amara was here to share this event, this potential massive step forward. The hurt multiplying, deepening at the thought of never sharing anything with her again.

Boardroom of Gio's med-tech company

Three days after his meeting with Antonio, Gio looked across at his grandparents, could see the signs of strain, the lines of tiredness on Ava's face, the slight stoop to Aurelio's usually upright posture. He took a deep breath, knew he had to put aside his own sadness, a sadness that seemed to have seeped into his body and soul. Who knew muscles could ache from grief, feel heavy and uncoordinated. Who knew his very soul could feel so…so forlorn. Each day it seemed to get worse as if each further hour of life without Amara made the pain increase. All because she had exited his life. A woman he'd known a scant few days who had turned his world upside down, upended his beliefs and given him the courage to do this.

'Is this a good idea, Gio?' Aurelio asked.

'I think so.' In truth he didn't know. 'But if this doesn't work, I will find another way. I will not let your business go under.' And he meant it. 'But it is your business,' he said quietly. 'Yours and my father's and my brothers'. It was never mine.' Amara had been right to tell him that his love for his own company was worth something. He had built it up, he had plans for it, a passion and a drive to bring his technology to all corners of the globe, where it could do the most good. Had the ambition and the impetus to make new cutting-edge discoveries at the helm of his own company.

Aurelio opened his mouth and Gio raised a hand. 'It's okay,' he said gently.

'No, Gio. It isn't. I was wrong.' Gio stilled; they weren't words he had ever expected to hear from his grandfather. But he sensed they were important words, not only for him, but for Aurelio, and so he remained silent, let the older man continue. 'I want to say this now when it is just us, before the others get here. So you know I am not saying it as a ploy, or a move.'

'*We* were wrong, then and now,' Ava interjected. She glanced at Aurelio and then met Gio's gaze. 'We have talked a lot the past few days. Talked and reflected.' She took a deep breath. 'Salvatore was…he is our only child. I always wanted a large family, but it wasn't meant to be. So he became our world and we…or maybe I, could see no wrong in him. But that doesn't excuse what we did to you. Somehow it was only after my diagnosis, when I know I will lose so much it seems important to look back on my past with true eyes.'

'Our past,' Aurelio said. 'And you, Gio, you didn't deserve how we treated you. To exclude you like we did.'

'And then to snap our fingers twenty-eight years later and expect you to come to our rescue.' Ava looked at him 'To expect you to get married without love or even affection.'

Gio took a deep breath, emotions roller-coasting inside him and again how he wished Amara was here. 'Thank you, for what you have just said. It means more to me than I can tell you, but as for the getting married part...' Gio gave a sudden smile. 'It wasn't like that. I promise you. Amara and I...'

Now Aurelio frowned and he saw Ava's blue eyes spark. 'Amara and you...?'

'It doesn't matter.'

'Yes. It does.' Ava reached out and took her husband's hand and they exchanged a smile, so full of love and affection that Gio felt something twist inside him. He suddenly missed Amara with an intensity so fierce he had to brace himself against it, curl his hand around the edge of the boardroom table. 'Tell us about her,' his grandmother invited.

And suddenly the urge to talk about Amara, to paint a picture of her, to have an excuse to think about her overwhelmed him, even as he knew he should be focused on the meeting ahead.

'She is beautiful,' he said. 'I don't just mean on the outside, though she is—she is beautiful on the inside, as well. When I see her my breath catches, my heart leaps and I feel...happy.'

Ava frowned. 'I thought you told us you didn't want to marry her? That you didn't believe deception was the right way forward. That a false marriage was wrong. That there was a better way forward.'

'It is wrong and there is a better way forward for Romano Confectionery. And I don't want to marry her because marriage isn't for me. Not the real thing.'

'Why not?' Ava asked.

Gio shrugged. 'Why aren't I a real Romano? Sometimes things are just the way they are.'

'No.' Ava's voice was strong now, the lines of strain gone. 'Gio. Listen to me. My future doesn't look good. But right here, right now, I have full capacity and I want you to remember what I have to say. I want you to remember me for something good I have done for you.' She shook her head as he tried to speak. 'Firstly, you are a real Romano. No, you are actually better than that. We Romanos are hardly something to aspire to. You are a good person in your own right. You would have been justified in turning your back on us, but you haven't. You have gone on to make a massive success of your life. In your own right. You've made a difference. And I am proud of you, Gio. And the real thing is for you. You deserve to love and be loved. If you love Amara tell her. If you feel there is a chance she loves you back, then fight for her.'

Aurelio nodded. 'Your grandmother, as always, is right. Once, many years ago, I fell in love with the beautiful woman who came into my family bakery. But it took me a long while to convince her I was genuine. That I meant it. She thought I was after her recipe. Then she refused to believe I would defy my parents to marry her. It took me time to gain her trust. But I did. And I have never once regretted it. Love is a precious thing.

If you've found it, give it a chance. I don't know how Amara feels about you, but if you love her give that love a chance.'

Gio stared at them. If he loved Amara. The penny clanged down. Of course he loved her, loved her with every fibre of his being. Body and soul. The idea dizzied him even as his phone buzzed followed by his PA's voice. 'Your guests are here, Gio…'

His guests, his family. Salvatore and Max and Antonio Romano.

Gio wondered if this was the worst idea he could have had, reminded himself that he had thought it all through. Knew he had to focus, had to put this bedazzling, incredible revelation aside for now. He loved Amara…and maybe she didn't want that love, but dammit he wanted to fight, wanted to tell her, wanted to share this exhilaration with her. Even if it led to rejection, he wanted her to know the truth.

The boardroom door opened just as his phone pinged in his hand. He looked down, saw the message was from Amara. His heart somersaulted, even though he had no idea what the message said. But somehow, he felt as though she were here with him as he rose to his feet to greet the Romanos. One Romano to another.

CHAPTER THIRTEEN

AMARA COULD FEEL the butterflies ride the crest of nerves in her tummy, swooping and swirling with anxiety but also with anticipation. Because no matter what happened in the next few hours, she would be seeing Gio.

Clasping her phone, she reread their messages yet again. Tried to find any hidden meaning in them, but he'd been as careful as she to be matter of fact, prosaic.

She'd messaged and asked if they could meet. He'd agreed, asked for a time and place. She'd picked Modena, halfway between Milan and Tuscany, somewhere with no joint connotations. She'd also commandeered a small, cosy restaurant for privacy, had arrived ridiculously early to make sure everything looked right.

Perhaps it shouldn't matter, but no matter the outcome of this meeting she wanted Gio to be happy, to feel special and of value. She glanced at her watch and took one final look round. It was a restaurant she loved, owned by a friend and business colleague of her grandfather's, a man who also happened to be an award-winning chef. By a stroke of luck or perhaps fate the restaurant was closed for renovations and Enzo had been happy to allow Amara to use it.

The walls of the small, intimate dining area sported eclectic prints, a mix of local talent and famous patrons. Glorious abstracts provided splashes of colour on the white walls. The five tables all had plain white table-cloths of the most exquisite quality, four of them un-adorned and unlit, the fifth the one Amara had prepared.

A bottle of red, not from the Rossi estate this time because Amara wanted this to be about Gio and her-self. Two crystal glasses and a few fresh flower petals adorned the tablecloth. Simple and evocative, or at least that's what she hoped.

Her heart pounded her ribcage as the steel door swung open and there was Gio.

Amara's head whirled, and she rooted her feet to the ground, the urge to run towards him nigh on overwhelm-ing.

'Gio,' she said. 'Thank you for agreeing to meet me here.'

'No problem.' There was an uncharacteristic hesi-tancy about him as he stood in the doorway. His eyes rested on her and she could see the tension in his body, could see it matched her own. 'Thank you for asking me.'

There was a silence and then Amara said, 'Come in. Sit.'

His brown eyes met hers and Amara threw caution to the wind, before they started talking about the weather or the state of the roads or their method of travel.

'I have something I need to say. Something I want to say,' she amended.

'So do I.'

He entered and approached the table and they both sat down.

'Do you want to go first?' Amara asked. Perhaps it was craven of her to offer, but maybe Gio was here to announce he'd married someone else. The idea came from nowhere and nearly toppled her off her chair, caught her breath and sent the butterflies into a frenzied swirl. 'In fact, you go first,' she said.

Gio must have heard the panic in her voice and now she saw his jaw clench, his hands flex on top of the table. And then he looked at her, really looked at her almost as if he was etching her face onto his memory, imprinting this moment on his brain and Amara was caught in his gaze. Saw such seriousness of purpose in his brown eyes, saw sincerity and certainty.

Then he smiled, a smile that tugged at her heartstrings. 'It's quite simple really.' He took a deep breath. 'I love you Amara. I love you and I wanted you to know. I understand how much the idea of love scares you. I understand what a risk it is. And I understand that there's a good chance that you don't love me back. There's no reason why you should. But if there is any chance any possibility that I can win your love then I will do my hardest to try.'

Amara realised her whole body was shaking, her heart so full it could burst and she realised she had to say something, had to tell him her truth. And as the butterflies soared and flapped with disbelief, she allowed happiness to surge and she smiled at him.

'You stole my lines,' she said on a gulp and a hiccup as tears of sheer joy threatened.

Confusion touched his eyes and then his face broke into an answering smile.

'Because I love you. That's what I wanted to tell you, why I asked to meet. I love you and yes, it is terrifying, but it's also exhilarating and wonderful. And I missed you so much these past days, so much it hurts. And yes, I will probably always be scared of losing you, but I am far more scared of walking away from you. And being with you is worth the risk, you are worth any risk. I want to be with you, by your side.'

'And I want to be with you. I want to wake up beside you, I want to hold you, I want to love you and walk by your side for the rest of our days.' He reached into his pocket. 'Amara Rossi. Will you marry me. For real. A true marriage, a true fairy tale, a true happy ever after, together.'

'Yes, I will. With all my heart.'

He took the ring from his pocket, the same beautiful ring that glittered and glinted in the afternoon sun that slanted in from the windows and slipped it onto her finger. 'A perfect fit,' he said and she smiled at him.

'Just like us.'

He took her hands in his. 'And for the record, this marriage is strictly and solely for love.' His smile widened. 'So much love. I can't believe this is really happening, that it's true. That you love me.'

'Believe it.' Amara gave a soft laugh, held her hand out to show him the ring. 'It's you and me. Forever.'

'Forever,' he echoed.

Amara hesitated. 'But if our marriage helps with the board that would be fine with me. It wouldn't devalue our love in anyway.'

'I appreciate that, but I worked out another way.'

'What?' She moved round so now she was next to him on his side of the booth and it felt like coming home, sent further waves of happiness floating through her. 'How? What happened with your father, with the board?' Amara asked.

'I brokered a deal,' Gio said. 'I decided to stop being a chess piece. To stop trying to prove I am a real Romano. I contacted my brothers.'

Amara reached out, took his hand. 'That must have been difficult.'

'Only Antonio agreed to see me, but we did meet and…' Gio shrugged. 'And we'll see. I think, I think there is a chance, a real chance, we may forge some sort of relationship. Max…is still set against me and as for my father I don't think anything can change how he feels about me. But when we met, Antonio did admit he doesn't agree with what my father is doing. That he has tried to speak with him but to no avail.'

'So what did you do next?'

'I called a meeting. In my boardroom.' Gio gave a small smile. 'My territory. The company that I am proud of, passionate about. My grandparents were there and my father and brothers. And I confronted my father, called his bluff. I told him he could try to prove my grandmother lacks capacity but he would fail. I showed him letters from two top consultants. I told him he could keep the shares he has but he isn't getting any more. That my grandparents are hanging onto those. That I won't join the board. But the articles would be changed and then my brothers can join the board, be part of the decision-making, that after a while they would be given some shares, as well. But that my grandparents would retain control, and I would act as their proxy and if need be, I would be brought on board in the future. If everyone couldn't work together.' He squeezed her hand. 'Once I stopped worrying about being a real Romano everything became clear. You helped me see that, Amara. Helped me see that I am a good person in my own right. That I have nothing to prove to anyone. That Romano Confectionery isn't my holy grail. You changed me.'

'And you changed me. You switched on a switch I thought was locked shut. You showed me how to live, how to see life through a different filter. To see that solitude is safe, but there is so much more to life than safety. That I am more than just an heir to the Rossi estate. I have other skills and talents. Other ideas. You showed me that it is right to welcome Lorenzo and Daisy to the family, but that I need to do it out of more than a moral duty, that I need to do it with an open heart and mind. You have shown me that I am capable of letting people in, letting people close.' She blinked back tears. 'I love you, Gio.'

'And I love you, Amara.'

She reached out and poured them both a glass of the ruby-red wine. 'To us,' she said.

'To us,' he repeated.

She grinned at him. 'And I have food to go with it. The owner and chef here is a family friend and he has made us some amazing things. All fairy tale themed. There is something he has called The Glass Slipper, which is made of crystallised ginger and oh, so many ingredients, and he's made a Let's Change the Pumpkin and a Magic Wand. I can tell you all about them.'

'And I will love listening to every word. But first I bought you a present.' He reached down and handed her a bag.

She opened it and now her smile lit her face. Inside was a snow globe, a fairy tale castle nestled against a backdrop of mountains and as she shook it and watched the swirl of flakes, she knew that fate had brought them to this perfect precious moment, the start of their happy ever after.

EPILOGUE

AMARA LOOKED AROUND the living room at Alavario castle and felt her heart sing with joy and a near disbelief at how much life had changed in a few months. Knew it was all thanks to a chance encounter in the Bavarian Alps, brought about by so many random events, so many dominoes falling in different times and places, culminating in a mistake made by a hotel staff member, that had left one table for two single diners.

Gio and Amara, Amara and Gio. Yet as she looked across at Gio now, Amara knew with all her being that they were meant to be together, that if they hadn't met at that table then they would have met somewhere else. Somehow their paths would have crossed because they were meant to be.

And now here they were celebrating their engagement with family. That idea too was incredible. Filled her with happiness as she took a moment to watch the assembled guests. Aurelio and Ava were stood together and the protective way Aurelio stood by his wife, the obvious love between them brought a tear to her eye.

The past months had wrought such a change in their relationship with Gio, a change that Amara knew had made Gio happy, had laid some demons to rest. The older Romanos had stood by their apology for excluding Gio, had done all they could to remedy past wrongs. And Gio's surprise, Gio's happiness had made Amara happy, made her able to give Aurelio and Ava a chance. And as she had got to know them, to like them, she'd begun to see just how complex relationships could be. That people weren't black and white, that Gio was right. People could do something wrong, something inexcusable, but it didn't define the whole of them.

The same went for Antonio; Gio had been right to say that he thought there was potential there and again Amara felt admiration surge for the man she loved, for his capacity to forgive, his capacity to see good in people. And so slowly tentatively the half-brothers were forging a relationship. Enough so that Antonio had accepted the invitation to attend this family gathering, was stood chatting to Gio and Vittorio as she watched all three men laugh. And as Vittorio placed an affectionate hand on Gio's shoulder, Amara felt the familiar sense of happiness that the two men she loved so much had clicked, got on so well, so easily. Gio turned his head now and caught her eye and her heart swelled with a love that she knew he could see in her eyes, just like she could see the love in his.

But now as her gaze continued to sweep the room, she took in Lorenzo, her half-brother and for a moment she watched him, saw that he too was watching the group, and she wondered how it made him feel. She knew that Vittorio and Gio had both tried to engage with Lorenzo, suspected that her half-brother was standing aloof through his own choice.

In the past months, Lorenzo had visited the estate only the once. The initial planned meeting, once so dreaded

by Amara, had been part revelation and part surprise.
Seeing him had impacted both herself and Vittorio, because he was the spitting image of Roberto. Amara's
dad, Lorenzo's dad. Their dad. Now as she studied him,
of course she could see some differences, but overall the
hair, the aquiline jut of his nose, the unexpectedly dark
blue of his eyes was true Rossi.

But looks apart, Lorenzo had been at pains to state
that he expected nothing from the Rossis. Any idea
Amara had had of being displaced had been well and
truly erased. He'd said he simply wanted to meet them
out of curiosity, but he accepted he had no claim.

The rest of the meeting had been a little awkward
though Lorenzo had been perfectly civil, had been re-
spectful and courteous to both Vittorio and Amara and
had even agreed to return with his sister at some point.
A point that hadn't materialised.

Amara took a deep breath, suddenly aware of how
this tableau must feel to Lorenzo. All these people. All
this family. Talking and laughing, at ease with each
other. Yet he was stood looking on. Not that he looked
uncomfortable, or distressed. He looked… As though
he was perfectly content to observe.

But Amara felt a curiosity and more than that, she
wanted to include him. They were related and she knew
how much it would mean to her grandfather if Lorenzo
chose to became family.

She headed towards him and saw him tense slightly,
though his smile was perfectly civil.

'I just wanted to thank you for coming.'

He nodded acknowledgement. 'It was kind of you to
ask me.'

Yet she sensed the words were ambiguous and had some hidden meaning. 'We wanted you to be here. After all, we are family,' she said.

'Technically speaking,' he said, then shook his head. 'I apologise. That was rude. I simply meant to make it clear that Daisy and I know we have no claim on you.'

'I understand that and it goes both ways. We know we have no claim on you.' She knew that her grandfather had contacted Lorenzo a couple of times but had been scrupulous to exert no pressure, had told Amara and Gio he was simply keeping the door open. 'We know it must have been a massive shock to find out the truth. But I wish Daisy could have come today. We would very much like to meet her when or if she wants to.' She hesitated. 'So no pressure, but I wanted you to know that truly we would welcome you.'

He looked at her and as she met those dark blue eyes, Amara was hit by a punch of emotion, because somehow just for an instant she could see an echo of Luca in Lorenzo's eyes. Like her twin's—a slightly mischievous look, but also a look that seemed to read her.

'You sure?' her half-brother asked. 'After all, it must have been a shock to you, as well. I wouldn't blame you for feeling resentment.'

A penny dropped. 'Is that why Daisy hasn't come today? Is that why you haven't been back? Because you think I don't want you here?' She could hardly blame him if he did.

'That's not the only reason, but we would understand if you'd rather we faded into the background, disappeared into the woodwork.'

Amara took a deep breath. 'I wouldn't. We wouldn't.

Of course we feel a moral obligation to acknowledge the link, but I promise it is more than that. I want to welcome you into the family. I would like you and Daisy to become part of the family in the ways that count. Not just because we share a father but because we like each other.'

'Maybe we won't like each other,' he said, his words only half light.

'Then so be it.' After all, Amara was pretty sure that Max and Salvatore would never become part of their family circle. And she was good with that. 'But I'd like to try. If you want to?'

There was a pause as Lorenzo considered her words. 'I'll talk to Daisy,' he said in the end. 'Maybe next time we'll come together.'

Amara smiled. It wasn't a promise—it was tenuous—but she hoped it was a start.

'And of course I really hope you'll both come to our wedding.' She grinned at him, hoped to introduce a less emotional topic. 'Though it won't be as grand as Prince Ashan's, which I saw that you will be attending.' She'd been reading a lot of bridal magazines of late and had seen an article about the forthcoming nuptials of Prince Ashan, prince of a small but prosperous island principality in Indonesia. And in that article had been mention of Lorenzo, who was to be the prince's best man. Amara had stored the information away, hoped it would be a good conversational topic.

But now as she saw Lorenzo's expression she saw she'd thought wrong. For an instant she'd been sure she recognised a hint of panic in those blue eyes, the expression once again reminiscent of her brother when he was anticipating trouble. Then it was gone and Lorenzo's expression shuttered, his lips slightly set, his jaw set. But all he said was, 'Yes, I will be. I'm looking forward to it.'

But somehow Amara sensed that wasn't the case at all and it was with relief she saw Gio approach. A relief she sensed her half-brother shared.

She smiled up at Gio, 'I was just telling Lorenzo how glad we are he came today.' Not exactly true, they had just been discussing a royal wedding, but somehow she was sure Lorenzo appreciated her dropping that topic.

'Absolutely.' Gio nodded. 'In fact, whilst you're here I'd like to pick your brains. I read recently that you've floated your company on the stock exchange.'

Amara smiled as the conversation turned to business, knew Gio was doing his best to put Lorenzo completely at ease. Hoped anew that this truly was the start of a relationship.

Because now the idea of being a part of a family filled her with joy. She would never forget Luca or her parents or her grandmother, would always grieve them, but it would no longer stop her from living, from risking, from protecting herself from joy and closeness. To all the people in this room right now. And she hoped to one day include Daisy as well and perhaps one day children of her own would join in here.

An image of their children running round the room, playing hide-and-seek in the castle. Gio throwing them up in the air, family outings. Pictures of a true fairy tale coming to life. Her and Gio's happy ever after.

* * * * *

BRIDESMAID'S FAST-TRACK FLING

ELLE BROWN

MILLS & BOON

For my grandmother, Meme,
who said I would write books. So I did.

SUNDAY MORNING

"GOOD MORNING, FOLKS. This is your captain speaking. As we make our final approach into Nice, we've got some bad news…"

Olivia Keller picked her head up from her travel pillow and frowned.

Just in case they were about to attempt a water landing, she popped the AirPod out of her right ear to hear the rest of the pilot's announcement. She promptly dropped the earbud between the seats, likely never to be seen again. Money lost before she'd even landed.

"…unfortunately, the anticipated French transportation strike began this morning while we were in the air. This may cause a delay in reuniting you with your checked baggage. We apologize for the inconvenience. We'll be on the ground shortly. Welcome to France."

Despite the discouraging news, Olivia eagerly pushed her face against the window. Her first glimpse of the French Riviera was spectacular. She marveled at the gradients of teal-and-turquoise water encircling Côte d'Azur Airport as it came into view.

"Damn."

It wasn't as if she had never traveled or seen the sights. She'd spent a semester abroad and partied her way through some of the most beautiful cities in Europe. But her shenanigan days were done. At twenty-six, she was a professional analyst at an exclusive New York City firm. She was categorically too old and blasé to be awestruck.

That being said, this trip was a fresh start. A big, exciting reset button. She'd recently put an end to a situationship that had dragged on for far too long. It was absolutely the right choice; she wasn't heartbroken over Sebastian. At all. She'd simply decided that, realistically, he wasn't worth it. Like every man she'd ever known—starting with her father—he wasn't worth her time or energy. Certainly not her heart.

But now, looking out the plane's window, seeing the Mediterranean so vivid that it seemed unreal…it stole her breath. Instant magic. It gave her a tingly feeling, like a premonition that something incredible was about to happen. Maybe the protective shell hardened around her heart might have a tiny crack. Maybe she might be open to new and unimagined possibilities unattainable in her daily life in New York. Maybe once she landed…

Or not. If there was anything that could kill a magic buzz, it was navigating a French airport during a transportation strike.

After finally clearing customs, Olivia stood at the unmoving baggage carousel alongside fellow passengers who had been foolish enough to check a bag on the eight-hour flight. She waited. Nothing happened.

This situation required professional intervention. She approached a nearby glass-fronted office.

"Bonjour, Madame." Olivia knew the French valued politeness. "I was on the New York flight…there is no luggage yet at the baggage claim."

The perfectly coiffed woman behind the counter did not look up. She kept typing, her lacquered nails clickety-clacking over her keyboard.

"Non. It is not here." The woman shrugged. *"Très désolée. Je ne sais pas."*

She didn't know. Okay. Helpful.

With no clear answer, Olivia gave up on her checked bag

and set off through the terminal to determine if the economy bus she'd pre-booked to Monte Carlo was still running. She had a feeling that it wouldn't be.

Her fears were confirmed. Handwritten signs on the bus, tram, and taxi kiosks included three critical French words, written in bold: *Grève des Transports*. Transportation strike.

In her sleep-deprived state, she was definitely not coherent enough to figure out how to get herself from Nice to Monaco. A text popped up before she could devise a plausible solution.

Have you landed?

Her frustration vanished, if only temporarily.

YES!!!!!! I'm HERE!!!! But not sure how to get to Monte Carlo. Everyone on strike

Her phone buzzed.

"Oh my God, what is happening?" Olivia's favorite voice in the world bounced across the airwaves.

She spent the next five minutes explaining her travel woes to Maggie, her best friend since forever and the soon-to-be bride. During their European adventures, Mags had met her now fiancé, who happened to be a Swiss-banking genius. It was their wedding that drew Olivia across the pond to Monaco.

She heard someone murmuring to Maggie in the background.

"What about a helicopter? It's a quick seven-minute flight. Easiest way to get here," Mags suggested. "Stefano's Uncle Klaus and Aunt Kiki might still be at the heliport...you could hitch a ride with them on their helicopter...oh? No?" Maggie resumed a muffled conversation with the unseen third party.

"Klaus and Kiki?!" Olivia couldn't help laughing. "Those can't be real names."

"Those are indeed their real names, but it doesn't matter. Klaus and Kiki have already arrived in Monte Carlo," Maggie said. "I'm here with my wedding coordinator. She'll call the concierge at the Hotel Negresco in Nice and arrange to have someone give you a ride. The car can pick you up at the airport and take the scenic route along the coast. It's amazing. You'll love it."

"Okay," Olivia hated to ask, but… "Mags, any idea how much this will cost me…?"

"Stop," Maggie insisted. "I'll add it to the wedding tab. It's fine."

"You already covered the cost of my room!"

"Because I can't get married without you. Also…" Maggie's voice dropped to a whisper, presumably so the wedding coordinator wouldn't overhear. "…I have a job for you."

Two hours later, a black Mercedes limo rolled Olivia in style to an ornate Belle Époque palace, the iconic Hôtel de Paris Monte-Carlo. She had expected to doze during the ride, but the breathtaking scenery was enough to keep her wide awake, gaping out the window. Mags hadn't lied—the sea vista on one side and medieval French villages on the opposite cliffs were straight out of a fairy tale.

She had imagined strolling the glamorous Casino Square, but that would have to wait. Utter exhaustion washed over her. Climbing the stairs under the imposing alabaster sculpted entrance, she had one goal: hit the bed and get some sleep.

But she hesitated inside the glass-domed lobby. The magnificent space, with its marble floor, golden pillars, and gigantic floral arrangement, was opulent beyond anything she'd ever experienced, even in New York City. She watched four impeccable women walk through the lobby, each carrying a Birkin bag. Apparently, Monaco was one big Hermès meetup.

She'd planned to change out of her travel sweats before leaving the airport. Sweats were obviously too casual—plus her top was stained with a dollop of mustard from the hot dog she had eaten in the cab on the way to the airport. It wasn't her best look.

Unfortunately, her carefully curated outfits were all stashed in the missing suitcase. She had pajamas and a bathing suit in her backpack, but neither seemed a good option for her Monte Carlo debut.

Olivia nonchalantly tugged loose her travel bun to allow her recently highlighted hair to tumble over her shoulders. She hoped it would give her movie-star-sexy tumbled-out-of-bed vibes, although she suspected her look was more like a witch caught in a windstorm. But there was nothing to be done at this point. She just needed to escape the lobby as quickly as possible. She approached the front desk, ready to bluster through.

"Olivia!"

Olivia twirled toward the greeting, delighted that Mags didn't care that Europeans generally didn't shriek indoors unless they were watching soccer. Maggie tackled her in a crushing hug, and Olivia could barely keep upright against the aggressive greeting.

"It is so good to see you! I know we talk constantly, but it's not the same. You're here!" Maggie exclaimed. "You're *here*."

"I'm here," Olivia confirmed. "Just a little worse for the wear. It was a long trip. Long day. I've been up since yesterday morning, five o'clock."

"Your hair looks really good, though."

God, Olivia loved this girl. There was a reason they'd been friends since birth.

"Thanks. And look at you, the blushing bride!" Olivia choked up a little as she spoke.

Then she remembered Maggie's odd, secretive comment on the phone. "So, what's this job you need me to do? Tell me so I can go get some sleep."

As the room key was obtained, Maggie explained. "Céline, the wedding planner who arranged the car to get you here…

She's amazing at handling all the wedding details. She's Swiss, so she's totally on top of it. Like clockwork, as they say."

"But?"

Mags sighed deeply. "The cookie table."

"A cookie table? You are going to have a cookie table?!" Olivia questioned, linking her arm through her friend's elbow as they moved through the lobby.

"*Of course* I'm going to have a cookie table."

In Western Pennsylvania, where they had grown up, most weddings included a cookie table during the reception. But Monte Carlo wasn't Pittsburgh.

"So what's the problem?"

Mags shut her eyes and took a deep breath. "The hotel catering—which is fabulous, world class—doesn't really do cookies. They do cakes and pastries—amazing French things that I can't pronounce and taste divine. But that's not what I want. I want homemade cookies like my mom and grandma would have made if they were still with us. I have their recipes. I keep trying to explain to Céline. But she's being weird about it. She doesn't get it."

Her face turned wistful.

"Liv, ever since we were little girls and went to your aunt's wedding…"

"We planned our dresses and our honeymoons. And we planned out every variety of cookies we wanted on our cookie tables," Olivia remembered.

"Exactly!" Mags confirmed. "I still have the list."

"You do recall that we were supposed to have a double wedding…" Olivia teased. "I guess that part of the plan fell through. You didn't bother to wait for me."

"If I waited for you, I'd likely be waiting forever." Maggie raised an eyebrow. "Last I checked, you'd sworn off any possibility of happily-ever-after."

"Love 'em and leave 'em. And definitely don't trust 'em. Still true," Olivia confirmed.

As a friend, Maggie had helped Olivia survive every lie, betrayal, and rejection her father had dished out over the years. Through cycles of disappointing boyfriends and dead-end relationships, Maggie understood why Olivia had never been willing to fully open her heart, why she'd never let any guy get close enough to do any real damage. Olivia didn't need to reiterate why the likelihood of her traipsing down the aisle was slim.

Maggie shrugged. "Someday you might sing a different tune. For your sake, I hope so. But until then, I just need you to get me my cookies. Do that, and maybe I'll introduce you to some hot friends of Stefano's so you can fall in *L-O-V-E* love. You can have your wedding here next year. We can make an annual Mediterranean trip a thing."

The girl was a hopeless romantic. Why wouldn't she be? She'd found her own Prince Charming, complete with an alpine chalet.

Olivia hugged her best friend to her side. "Don't hold your breath. But before you set me up with a Euro stud, you need me to convince Céline to do a cookie table? You want me to channel an insistent, won't-take-no-for-an-answer New York attitude?"

"Yes." She smiled. "You go and be rude to Céline, so I don't have to be a bridezilla."

"Do I have to be rude right now, though?" Olivia wheedled. "I'm better at getting stuff done when I'm not exhausted."

"I know, babe," Maggie said. "But tomorrow is Céline's day off. The wedding is only a few days away, so I won't have my cookies if I don't get this nailed down. I need you to be on it."

Olivia made a face at her. "Got it. You're the bride. Point me in the right direction."

Mustard stains and all, Olivia marched off to deal with Céline. Sleep would have to wait.

Half an hour later, though, stuck in the hotel underbelly, Olivia was ready to topple over. The sophisticated wedding planner had apparently left her to rot. After graciously professing to understand the cookie table request, Céline explained that she would need to convey the information to the pastry chef. His station was deep inside the kitchen. Olivia was not permitted into that inner sanctum of sweetness, so she waited. And waited.

As Céline's absence stretched past fifteen minutes into infinity, Olivia wasn't sure if the woman was trying to outlast her fading ability to stay awake or if the pastry chef was just incredibly long-winded in his refusal to bake cookies.

After a couple of jarring, jerky head bobs toward oblivion, Olivia reached the desperate stage of exhaustion.

Finally, she heard a door opening and a group of people making their way down the hall. If the elusive Céline wasn't with them, perhaps one of the approaching employees would have access to the kitchen and could take a message.

Olivia careened out the office door and abruptly collided with someone who was definitely not the wedding coordinator.

Nikos Leonikaros jammed his sunglasses over his face and strode briskly out of the paddock team center. He ignored the spectators who yelled across the barrier, begging for his attention. Anyone appearing at the circuit a full week before the race bordered on obsessive. He didn't want to encourage that kind of fan fixation.

He slid into the back seat of the waiting courtesy car. Along with the driver, his security agent, Aleko, was in the front seat. The older man had been with Nikos his entire life, first to protect against kidnapping and ransom, now mostly to keep Nikos's frustrations at bay.

Bryson, Nikos's media director and sometime assistant, also huddled in the back seat, swiping across his ever-present iPad. He'd only been a part of the entourage for a few years. He regularly added to Nikos's frustrations.

"What's on for the rest of the day?" Nikos asked.

"Your lunch should be in the suite when we return to the hotel. Then, you've got an initial strategy and telemetry debrief this afternoon. A workout in the pool. You've got a massage before dinner. Dinner is with TAG Heuer in their hospitality suite—they want to discuss a limited-edition watch. And you've got a lifestyle shoot tonight with them, too. They want some photos by the harbor and some with the car in front of the casino. Clothes for the shoot will be sent up to your room. Pick what you like. We'll bring the rest along in case they want to switch it up."

"And tomorrow…" Nikos said resignedly.

His assistant paused. "Other than your morning workout, you've actually got a free day."

Nikos was stunned.

"Damn."

"I was thinking…" Bryson began.

"Don't think," Nikos interrupted. "You just said it was a free day."

"I know, but we are behind on social content creation."

Nikos groaned. "You know I despise social media."

"It makes the sponsors happy. And it brings new fans to Formula 1."

Nikos glared at him. "Winning races brings new fans to F1. I've been winning since I was seventeen years old. I'm a driver. Not an influencer."

"Well, you can complain all you like," Bryson insisted, "but it's in your contract. And right now, we are behind on the amount of content you're supposed to produce. I thought we could use tomorrow to catch up."

There was no point arguing.

"What do I have to do?" Nikos sighed.

Bryson swiped across the iPad. "The latest concept focuses on drivers' favorite foods. They want to get video of everyone baking their favorite desserts from childhood. There is a kitchen setup at catering we can use, or given that the yacht is here in Monaco, we could get footage in the galley. Give people an exclusive glimpse into the private life of Nikos Leonikaros. They love that."

"No one needs to see inside my yacht or any other aspect of my private life. You know how I feel about that. And a baker? Really? That's perfect," Nikos said sarcastically. "You want a video of me baking cookies I don't eat during the season. *Kourabiedes* aren't exactly on the prescribed diet."

"You just need to make them. Not eat them. And one cookie won't kill you," Bryson retorted. "They want the recipe, too."

Resistance was futile. Nikos shut his eyes.

"I'll call my grandmother for the recipe." He sighed. "So tomorrow, I'm going to be an influencer. And a baker. On my day off."

It never failed to amaze Nikos how his life was no longer his own. Money—even the billions he and his family were worth—didn't buy autonomy. And with fame came confinement.

It hadn't mattered when he was young and living in a glorious bubble. Back then, wealth made it possible to start gokart racing at the age of five. When he showed some aptitude for motorsports, the money helped him advance. His family could afford the best equipment, training, and travel. And then, when he began to build an enviable record as a driver, his growing fame helped him establish an independent identity from the Leonikaros name. He wasn't merely the son of a Greek shipping magnate but successful in his own right. It was perfect—until wealth and fame sabotaged his relationship with the first girl he'd ever loved and overshadowed every relationship since. As an unintentional celebrity, he had built a life he could barely call his own.

He wasn't sure exactly when, but even some of his joy in racing had dwindled. The heart-stopping thrill of pushing his body and car to unprecedented limits was too often eclipsed by the nonstop demands off track. Everyone wanted a piece of him. Unless he was driving the car, riding his motorcycle, or sailing the boat, he was constantly subject to someone else's agenda.

So, after a lifetime in motorsports, he needed a first-place podium one more time at Monaco to secure the record for most wins on that circuit and then finish the remainder of the season with another world championship. Retirement loomed at the ripe old age of twenty-seven.

The problem was that he had no idea what he was going to do next.

"Service entrance?" The driver asked as they turned onto Avenue des Spélugues.

"Yes," Nikos confirmed before Bryson could say otherwise.

There were drivers for whom being a celebrity was still a thrilling novelty. They would walk through the Hôtel de Paris front door and bask in the adulation of the admirers haunting the entrance and lobby. But because of the threats his father's wealth attracted, Nikos had been raised to be cautious in public. He always used back entrances and went incognito when and where he could. Now he wondered if true anonymity would ever be possible, if he could escape the frustrations of a lifestyle he'd never meant to pursue.

Aleko scanned the area and opened the car door for Nikos. The hotel security guard quickly waved them into the building.

Nikos removed his sunglasses and followed Aleko through the labyrinth of service corridors. Bryson strode ahead, still swiping. Nikos glanced down at his watch and eagerly anticipated taking the private elevator to his suite to enjoy his midday meal alone, free of his minders for at least a few hours. Maybe he could watch a movie.

Before he realized what was happening, a blur of motion sprang at him, bursting into the corridor from behind a partially closed office door. Nikos had quick reflexes and was nimble enough to avoid being knocked against the opposite wall, but only by catching hold of the human cannonball.

Bryson yelped; Aleko swung around, poised to neutralize any threat. The situation teetered on the edge of chaos.

Except there wasn't a threat. She wasn't a threat. Nikos wasn't sure how he knew, but there was no doubt in his mind that the lovely but rumpled girl staring up at him wide-eyed meant no harm.

Curiously, there wasn't a hint of recognition in her hazel eyes. She appeared to have no idea she'd nearly taken down the number one driver in the world.

"Oh my God, I am so sorry!"

She was American by her accent. That might explain it. The US fan base for Formula 1 racing was small but growing. Perhaps she didn't know who he was. That was a novelty.

She continued to hold fast to Nikos's forearms as he held hers. He tried to shift her to one side to step around, but she simultaneously shifted in the same direction. Once again, in an awkward parody of a dance, they bumped against one another, arms still clasped.

"Sorry—oh whoops—sorry...sorry," she apologized.

Nikos was used to having women throw themselves at him, dropping hints and shedding clothing. There had been women who had tried to accost him, sneaking into hotel suites, reserved paddock areas, and VIP enclosures in restaurants. He'd managed to dodge them all. Or at least the ones he wanted to dodge. This woman, however, had succeeded in blindsiding him, literally and figuratively.

She appeared genuinely mortified by their collision. Yet despite her discombobulated state, there was something appealing about her, coupled with an inexplicable sense of déjà vu. His body was humming. Was it the endorphins from his earlier workout? Or perhaps it was just the weird buzz of fluorescent lighting? The whole exchange was bizarre.

He was intrigued, to say the least.

Gently, almost unwillingly, he disentangled himself from her grasp, and she held up her palms apologetically.

"Again, I am so sorry. I just got to Monaco. I've been awake for thirty-six hours and am completely loopy."

Somehow, he didn't think she was here for the race.

"It's all right—it was an accident. No harm done."

She swiped her hand over her head, her fingers lifting her hair from the roots. The silken strands slid through her fingers, and he envisioned her illuminated by ocean sunlight, like a goddess risen from the sea.

The image took his breath away. Damn. Who was this girl? And why was he unable to look away? No one had caught his attention like this since…well, in a very long time.

In that instant, the exhilaration of anonymity was profound. Until this chance encounter, Nikos hadn't realized how badly he wanted someone to look at him like this girl was looking at him. To not presume any knowledge, but to see him as a stranger to discover. And to allow him the opportunity to discover her in return. Someone who would see him as Nikos—not Nikos Leonikaros, celebrity F1 driver—just Nikos.

Visceral desire flooded his senses.

He held his breath. She looked him over quizzically. Calculating. "Could I ask you a favor?"

The bubble burst; his heart sank. He knew that look. He knew it from every autograph seeker, his conniving ex-girlfriend, Athena, and every woman he'd since dated. They all wanted him primarily for his celebrity status and its benefits.

Despite this girl's initial innocent expression, she, too, had apparently recognized him and she wanted something. It was inescapable. No wonder he was suspicious of every person he met. No wonder he was ready to retire. Until he quit racing and stepped out of the public eye, the kind of connection he craved would remain elusive.

The sizzling flare of attraction had gone cold. He needed to wrap it up.

"Sure. What do you want?"

Bryson stepped up and held out a Sharpie for the anticipated autograph request.

She regarded Bryson perplexedly, then turned back to Nikos.

"I'm trying to find Céline, the wedding coordinator, and she disappeared into the kitchen about twenty minutes ago." She pointed to the stainless-steel door across the corridor. "I need someone who works here to take a message to her and tell her to forget it. I can't wait any longer… I'm going to pass out from exhaustion."

"Take a message?"

Hope surged back through his body. Nikos bit the insides of his cheeks to keep the hilarious disbelief from showing. Did this girl really think he was staff at the hotel?

"Are you maybe kitchen or hospitality? Front desk?"

Nikos couldn't help it; he gave her a wry grin. Bryson's jaw dropped. Aleko's eyes widened.

Nikos quirked an intentional eyebrow at his assistant and then somberly addressed the girl: "I'm a baker."

If she had surprised him by barreling into him, now her reaction astonished him.

"A baker?!" She gasped with all the enthusiasm of a rabid racing fan. "Are you kidding me? You are just who I need to talk to!"

"I am?"

"Yes." She exhaled dramatically. "Oh, this is perfect. Oh my God. Okay. My friend is getting married at the hotel and needs someone to bake. She needs American cookies, not French pastries."

"I'm Greek," he offered.

"Perfect!" She lifted her hands and gazed upward in emphasis. "Greeks own just about every diner in New York. And I've had some amazing cookies in those diners. You get what I'm trying to say. You understand what I need."

Nikos was speechless. Aleko looked like he might pass out. Bryson was fighting not to laugh.

"So you need cookies?"

"Yes." She glanced side to side as if she feared being overheard. "And no offense, I don't think the French pastry chef at the hotel is the right person to bake them."

"Definitely not," Nikos agreed. He had no idea how long he could keep up the farce, but he was willing to string it along indefinitely. This was the most entertainment he'd had in ages. And a persistent voice inside his head suggested that engaging with this captivating girl might be an extraordinary opportunity to discover what a woman might see in him beyond his money and fame.

"So what do you recommend? Can you bake the cookies in the hotel kitchen even if the pastry chef won't? Or would that be frowned upon?" She hesitated. "That is, I should first ask if you are willing to help me. Are you? I wouldn't want to get you in trouble."

"How about this…" Nikos was thinking fast. He typically spent some of his off-season in Monte Carlo. He knew the shops and the restaurants. If they went out early, before the city awoke and the streets got crowded…

"I can't bake cookies here at the hotel. So how about I take you around to all the pâtisseries early tomorrow? I know the city. I'm sure we can find someone who can bake the cookies you want."

He wasn't ready to invite her onto the yacht and have his staff bake whatever she needed. He wasn't crazy. And it would require too much of an explanation. He'd have to correct her misperceptions about who he was. But if the morning went well…

"Oh my God." Her eyes softened. "Thank you so much— that would be amazing. But…" She frowned. "How are we going to get around town? Just getting to the hotel was a nightmare. I guess there's a race coming up. They've got streets blocked for the course and grandstands."

Nikos swallowed a laugh.

"A race," he repeated. "Yes. A Grand Prix. You're not a racing fan, huh?"

She shrugged. "No. I'm not much of a sports fan in general. I'll go to a baseball game, but that's more for the vibes."

"I've never been to a baseball game. But Formula 1 racing has a lot of vibes," he suggested.

"I'm sure it does. I just have no particular interest."

A look of horrified comprehension washed over her face. "Oh, I see your shirt. I'm so sorry. I bet you're a big fan. I'm not trying to be rude. I'm sure it's a really cool sport. A great time. No offense."

"None taken." He smiled. "But back to your cookies. I've got a bike. We can get around the barricades."

"A bike, huh?" She tilted her head. She paused and scrutinized him. He couldn't blame her; she'd just been invited to accompany a total stranger around a foreign city. Did she have a sense of adventure?

Say yes, say yes, his heart thudded.

"Is this a bike, as in a vehicle you pedal? Or is it a Vespa? Or a motorcycle? What are we talking about?"

Fluttery, flirtatious bubbles rose in his chest.

He could get any kind of bike she liked, although he desperately wanted her on the back of his Ducati. Unbidden, he imagined her arms encircling his body…

She blushed as if she could read his thoughts. Or was she having similar thoughts of her own? Either way, she didn't appear to be put off, which was encouraging. But he still wasn't sure she would accept. There was uncertainty, and he wasn't used to uncertainty with women. This was a challenge. He liked challenges.

God, say yes.

"What kind of bike would you prefer?"

She grinned flirtatiously at him. "Oh, no you don't. I'm already exhausted and babbling, so don't ask me what I prefer. Just tell me what kind of bike to expect. I'm game."

He cracked an unfiltered grin. "Expect to have to hang on tight. It's a motorcycle. I'll meet you in the alley outside the back door at eight o'clock. The exit is down this corridor and to the right. Does that work?"

She bit her lip, looking adorably pleased, and nodded.

"Okay, then I'll see you tomorrow…" She laughed and ducked past Bryson and Aleko with a little wave.

Just as she was about to disappear around the corner into the next corridor, Nikos called out. "Hey!"

She twisted back toward him. He could see her cheeks flush even from a distance.

"What's your name?"

"Liv. Olivia. What's yours?"

"Nikos. Just Nikos."

MONDAY MORNING

OLIVIA STRETCHED DECADENTLY in the crisp white sheets and sighed with contentment. There was nothing better than waking up in a hotel bed, especially in such an exquisite, golden-hued room. She'd crashed hard the day before, forgetting to close the drapes in her single-minded focus on sleep. Now she was bathed in early-morning light, illuminating her room and the palm-fringed, crystalline harbor below. Yachts of every conceivable configuration bobbed in tidy rows. Buildings, tinged pink in sunlight, rose in layers against the cliffs. The scenery was utterly unreal.

A knock interrupted her reverie.

She padded to the door and peeked out. Mags, accompanied by a hotel employee, stood in the hall.

"Good morning, sunshine! Room service!" Maggie exclaimed as Olivia opened the door. Mags handed the attendant a few euros after the food trolley had been discreetly positioned.

"May I tempt you?" Maggie lifted the corner of a linen napkin to reveal a pile of pastries in a sterling-silver basket.

"Oh yes, please."

Olivia debated the impossible choice between a croissant and a *pain au chocolat*. She decided there could be no wrong selection. She chose the latter and groaned as the flaky dough and rich chocolate melted in her mouth.

"Yeah, I can see why you wouldn't want anything like this

at your wedding. This totally sucks." She took another emphatic bite.

"Shut up." Maggie grinned as she poured coffee into two porcelain cups. "So? I got your text yesterday about Plan B for Operation Cookie Table. Do tell."

"Okay…" Olivia finished the last scrumptious bite and washed it down with a swallow of fresh-squeezed orange juice. "I lost track of Céline, but I arranged a date with a Greek baker who works here at the hotel to visit every pastry shop in Monte Carlo this morning."

The look on Maggie's face was priceless. *"What?"*

Olivia started laughing and nearly choked on her first bite of croissant. "I know, right?"

"Damn, girl. You move fast. Say more."

"So, I ran into him…literally ran into him…in the corridor outside Céline's office. We got to talking…"

"Talking?" Maggie rolled her eyes.

"Yes. Maggie, I wasn't flirting. My focus was entirely on your need for cookies. Not how scrumptiously good-looking this guy was. I didn't even notice."

"Right. All cookie business. Tell me more about this guy. He's totally hot?"

Olivia raised an eyebrow in wicked confirmation. "Why, yes. Yes, he is. I don't even know how to describe it. There was…is…something about him. He isn't a very big guy. Not super tall. But he has an incredibly fit body. Not bulging muscles. Really lithe and lean. Like, not an ounce of fat."

"How would you know his fat ratio? I mean, the man was presumably wearing clothes, right?" Maggie demanded.

"I told you I physically ran into him. And then we did that awkward thing where you bump into someone, then you both go the same way and bump again."

"Two bumps and you could tell everything you needed to know?"

"Absolutely," Olivia insisted. "And it wasn't just his body…"

She gave Maggie an arched look. "He has really striking green-blue eyes. And silky, sun-kissed brown hair. It's short in the back but flops over his face in the front. It makes him look kind of shy."

"Shy? He asked you on a date after two bumps. That's not shy."

Olivia grinned and shrugged. "The sacrifices I make for you. If I have to hang on to the back of a hot guy on a motor-cycle to make your wedding dreams come true, I'll do it…"

"A motorcycle!" Maggie squealed. But then she frowned. "What are you going to wear? Did your suitcase arrive?"

Olivia pushed up off the bed. "No, not yet. I thought about it. I have a plan." She rummaged through her backpack and pulled out her carefully rolled pajamas. "I slept in my sweats, but I have these—they're new linen drawstring pajamas with a cropped shirt. I bought the set to double as a bathing suit cover-up if I needed one. So, these over my bikini…" She pulled out the bathing suit and dangled it for Maggie's assessment. "I thought it would be a good boho look."

"I like it," Maggie affirmed. "But you need some accessories. Come to my room, and we'll see what works. I've got a Prada mini crossbody you can use. And I bought you gold metallic Birkenstock sandals to say thanks for being my maid of honor and making this trip. Oh!"

"What?"

"I've got some vintage silk scarves from Stefano's mom. I think one is Hermès and the other is Pucci. I tie them onto my purses. But if you are going to be on a motorcycle, you could wear one tied over your hair."

"Like a bandana?"

"No, more like a fortune teller, if you know what I mean?"

Olivia cackled, waiving her hands over the coffee pot like a crystal ball. "In my future, I see a handsome blue-eyed stranger who tastes suspiciously like Greek sugar cookies…"

"Tastes?" Maggie hooted. "That escalated quickly. Behave,

Madame Boho, or you will have a hundred years of bad luck. Or not. Maybe you'll have a hot Greek for lunch."

Olivia batted her eyes and mocked her friend primly. "Thank you, Margaret. Without you and your bridezilla demands, I wouldn't have a date with Nikos."

"Nikos, Nikos—hot, hot Nikos," Mags chanted in a singsong accent. Olivia threw a pillow at her.

"I just hope he's not an exhaustion-induced fever dream…" Olivia admitted.

A half hour later, in the golden morning light, she watched Nikos take off his helmet and run his hand through his hair, the beads of his bracelets sliding along his wrist. Fitted white T-shirt. Faded jeans. Eyes as brilliant as the Mediterranean. He was no fever dream. He was gorgeously, gloriously real. A travel fling on her whirlwind trip to Monaco hadn't been on the itinerary; however, since the possibility so attractively presented itself and facilitated her bridesmaid responsibilities, who was she to refuse?

Grinning like a fool, she walked toward him. She knew that she was rocking her improvised outfit. Mags had done her makeup, giving Olivia a natural-looking glow. She was a far cry from the bedraggled waif she'd been the day before.

Olivia projected confidence, but inside, she acknowledged a certain amount of false bravado and tempered expectations. She had no idea who this guy was or what they were about to do. And no matter how strongly she was attracted to him—and holy moly, she was attracted to him—she was heading back to New York in five days. But perhaps a sizzling holiday romance was exactly what she needed. It wouldn't—couldn't—go anywhere, but damn, a Monte Carlo adventure with a hot guy might be the perfect morale boost before diving back into the eternally disappointing New York dating scene.

Nikos remained still, eyeing her approach. He wasn't blatantly gawping; he wasn't leering. But a subtle expression of pleasure passed over his face. The appreciative look warmed Olivia to the core, and she strolled with a bit more sway. Her bravado shifted into actual confidence. Whatever she was doing with Nikos, it felt inexplicably right.

"Good morning, Nikos," she called out.

"*Kaliméra*, Olivia."

She grinned. She didn't speak Greek, but the sentiment was clear. "I wasn't sure if you were going to show up. I thought I might have dreamed our whole conversation."

"But here I am," he replied. He flashed an endearing, sexy smile. He was pleased to see her, perhaps even eager. There was nothing cocky about him, which was surprising given the sleek beast of a motorcycle he straddled.

The bike looked fast. Really fast. And dangerous. Olivia should have been terrified at the thought of zooming through an unfamiliar city, hanging precariously on the back of a total stranger. Yet the butterflies in her stomach weren't from fear. Instead, she was almost giddy, as though embarking on a journey to some previously unknown but incredibly desirable destination.

Even so, she had to ask.

"Can you handle this bike with someone riding behind? Tell me the truth. Are you a good driver?"

He looked at her, perplexedly, like she had two heads, as if the answer was a foregone conclusion. Sure, it had been a silly question, a way to buy time before she fully committed to getting on the motorcycle. There was no way he would admit to being a lousy driver, even if he were. No guy would acknowledge that kind of shortcoming.

"I can handle the bike," he insisted.

"Look, it's just that I've never ridden a motorcycle before. By myself or with anyone else," she admitted.

"It's easy," he said. "You just have to hang on and let me do the rest."

"I can do that," she agreed. "I think."

He had an extra helmet attached to the back of the bike. He twisted his torso in a beautiful, fluid motion and unfastened the spare.

"Come here," he beckoned.

The sultry, quiet demand set Olivia's heart pounding. The butterflies in her stomach morphed into happy, back-flipping otters. Hoping she looked calmer than she felt, she moved closer, close enough to smell the spice of his cologne, mingled with the burnt scent of the bike's engine. It was an intoxicating combination. Oh yeah, she would enjoy getting to know him better.

"Lean forward. Let me help you with this."

With a deep breath, she complied. He settled the spare helmet on her head.

His attentiveness was surprisingly lovely. She'd never wanted or allowed a man to fuss over her, but she had to admit that the kindness in the simple gesture of helping with her helmet was appealing.

"Good idea to wear a scarf over your hair," he muttered while he adjusted the chin strap.

It was odd, Olivia thought. He was a stranger, yet he'd touched her both times they'd been face-to-face, and it felt perfectly natural. Yesterday he had clutched her to keep from falling, and now his fingers brushed against the sensitive skin where her neck met her jaw.

In each instance, his touch had been innocent. Usually, if a guy put his hand on her, no matter how casually, it was a precursor to something sexual. Which was fine—everybody knew the game. Except that Nikos's gentle, considerate contact somehow made her feel cared for, tended to, in a strange and unprecedented way that was even more irresistible.

"Okay." He nodded, satisfied with the helmet's fit. "Your seat is probably going to be a little uncomfortable. I hadn't planned to use this bike to ride with anyone else. This model is more for racing than a touring bike. It's not really designed for someone to ride pillion. In fact, I was going to remove the passenger pegs—I didn't think I'd need them. I just haven't gotten around to it."

He paused abruptly, and she realized she wasn't the only one prone to babbling. Despite his confident assurance that he could handle the bike, she wondered if he, too, might feel some eager butterflies at the prospect of their outing together. She smiled through the helmet's visor. He grinned back.

"Here, can you get on behind?"

He steadied himself so she might take hold of his shoulder. She clutched him and felt a little thrill at the bones and sinews in her grasp. She kicked her leg up over the bike and shifted onto it. The seat pitched her at an angle toward his body. He twisted back to look at her, and she nearly banged his face with her helmet.

"Hold on to me," he instructed. "Put both your feet up on the pegs. You'll feel more balanced, and it will be easier once we're moving."

In following his instructions, she tipped even further forward against his back. She placed her hands on his waist, trying to create space between their bodies and to position herself with some decorum. After all, no matter how tempting, it felt supremely bizarre to wrap her arms around someone she'd just met. He reached for his helmet. Touching him, she was hyper-aware of the stretch and pull of his muscles moving under his T-shirt. She tried not to think about the sensation of her inner thighs squeezing against him.

He leaned forward. "Ready?"

"Uh-huh." She gulped.

He flicked something, and the bike roared to life. Olivia panicked at the sudden power and unexpected thrust. Decorum be damned, she plastered herself to his torso and wrapped her arms around him tight as a Band-Aid. But slowly, as she acclimated to their forward movement, she began to breathe and slightly loosened her grip. She opened her eyes to make sense of the world blurring by in an incomprehensible rush. For a fleeting moment, she thought she might get the hang of riding pillion.

Suddenly, Nikos leaned low and sideways, pulling the bike and their bodies almost parallel to the ground. They swung around a corner. Terrified, Olivia squashed tightly against him once more, anticipating imminent death. Then, Nikos straightened back up, and they swung in the opposite direction. And back. Again and again through the twisting streets. It was too much.

Riding pillion was like the roiling sensation of being on a carnival ride that had been allowed to run too fast and for too long. She wanted the ride to end but feared it would end badly. Painfully. She dizzily squeezed her eyes shut and fervently prayed to any friendly deity who might be sympathetic to the pleas of a girl so easily enticed by an attractive man on a bike. The gods just laughed. The motorcycle thundered on.

No sooner had she surrendered all hope of survival than the bike growled to a stop, the engine cut, and Nikos dropped his legs. Olivia was too paralyzed to move.

"You can let go now," he hinted. "We're here. Rue Grimaldi."

Shaking, Olivia peeled her arms from his warm body. Clutching his shoulders, she placed one foot on terra firma and awkwardly hauled her leg over the bike.

With trembling fingers, she unfastened the now claustrophobic helmet and tugged it off.

He turned to her, his face unreadable behind his tinted visor. "Too much?" he asked.

"Um, no, yeah. Wow. Yeah. Give me a minute."

She sensed he was laughing—actually laughing. Was he nuts? Was she the only one who felt like they had cheated death a thousand times in under ten minutes?

"Sorry." He shrugged with a chuckle. "I tried to take it easy."

"Oh, my dear God," she muttered. "That was taking it easy? I can't even…"

"Anyhow," he continued while she attempted to breathe normally. "The first pâtisserie is across the street. There isn't any place to park, so I'll circle around while you talk to them about the cookies. I'll be back to pick you up." He paused and cocked his head. "That is, if you want me to come back for you?"

She steeled herself and shook off her jitters. As unbelievable as it was…they had survived.

"Despite my deeply held conviction that you nearly killed me, um, yeah…" she said shakily. "Please do come back for me. Thanks."

He nodded. She crossed the street on unsteady legs. She heard the roar of the bike as he sped off.

Now it was time to do her assigned job and focus on procuring cookies. She needed to ignore the whiff of his cologne still clinging to her linen shirt. Focus. She needed to focus.

But she had no luck in the pastry shop. Everything looked mouth-wateringly delicious, and the woman behind the counter was exceedingly polite. But before Olivia could describe exactly what she needed, the woman apologetically explained that they were at capacity for special orders because of the upcoming Grand Prix. Apparently, lots of fans meant a high demand for baked goods. It made sense, but it was discouraging.

Olivia crossed to where Nikos had returned, the bike's engine still running.

"No." She shook her head. "They can't do it."

"That was just the first shop," he said reassuringly. "I'm sure we can find what you need somewhere else. We can keep going."

Once again, he helped her with her helmet while she mentally repeated the old adage about getting back in the saddle. Of course, the saying referred to a horse, not a bike capable of breaking the sound barrier. She inhaled a deep breath for courage and flung herself onto the bike. Had she lost her mind? It was a distinct possibility.

Like a python, she twined her arms around Nikos and propped her feet onto the pegs. As they sped off, before fear and adrenaline consumed her, Olivia realized she'd wrapped herself around him without a second thought. It was as if holding him close was the most natural thing in the world. As they leaned into another turn, she wondered how it would feel to be so intimate if they weren't riding a two-wheeled rocket. Holding him, she concluded, was very, very appealing. If they survived their motorcycle adventure, she definitely wanted to get close to him when they were on steady, unmoving ground.

Over the following hours, they visited countless other pastry shops, each with a similar response: *Sorry, not sorry, we can't help you this week. All special orders are for Grand Prix parties.*

It was frustrating.

Nikos patiently suggested each successive stop—after all, Olivia had no idea how many pastry shops were in Monte Carlo—but she noticed a subtle transformation in him as the sun rose higher and the streets became more crowded. His words were polite, but his tone grew terse. And because of their forced proximity, she could feel the increasing tension in his body.

After another negative response from a pastry shop in a particularly crowded area, she had barely settled onto the bike before he shot off, weaving precariously through throngs of people, some of whom stopped and stared.

Once loose and fluid, his body now felt like he'd been wrapped in steel coils, emanating stress. Clearly, he was losing patience. Whether with her or with the errand…she wasn't sure, but she didn't want to continue if he was unwilling and reckless. She'd spent her childhood hyperaware of her father's body language, learning to recognize any pending eruption. She knew what male frustration looked like.

"Hey!" she yelled and poked him as they accelerated to an alarming speed on a long straightaway. He abruptly banked into a turn, and they halted in a deserted alleyway.

"I don't think this is going to work, and I don't want to

take up any more of your time," she blurted over the still-loud engine.

She felt his body sag in apparent relief.

Okay, she thought. It was fun while it lasted. Who knew traveling at death-defying speeds could be enjoyable? Hanging on to a ridiculously attractive guy wasn't the worst way to have spent the morning. The outing wasn't a total loss.

He cut the engine so they could speak at a normal volume.

"I apologize. I feel awful. I truly thought this would be easy," he said with obvious frustration.

Was that it? Was Nikos a man who became irritable at any perceived challenge or, God forbid, failure? She'd known plenty of guys like that, starting with her father. He had been one for grand dramatic gestures…so long as they suited his purposes or fed his ego. But when complications arose or it was no longer convenient for him to accommodate a wife or a daughter, he'd lie, make excuses, or punish them for his failures, withholding affection and financial support. So, she'd learned to take care of herself, thank you very much. She had no tolerance for men who got angry at the first sign of complication, men who twisted the narrative to bolster their own self-image.

"It's not your fault." She sighed. "We can head back to the hotel. Thank you. I appreciate the effort."

Which was true. But she wouldn't stroke his ego and gush about how wonderful he was just for trying, even though his offer to help had been rather remarkable. When they'd started out that morning, she'd been intrigued and enticed by his seemingly selfless act. What guy gave up his morning for a stranger? But if he couldn't handle a less-than-optimal outcome without getting upset, she had no further interest.

Unfortunately, it also meant that Olivia might as well accept that she wouldn't be able to provide the one thing her best friend wanted, something money alone couldn't buy, something that celebrated their shared history.

Nikos paused before firing up the bike again. He looked like he was about to speak. Olivia waited for the inevitable defensiveness.

"Would you want to get lunch?"

The question took her by surprise. Was it possible that Nikos wasn't bothered by the morning's failure? Was he able to simply move on without pouting? That was unusual for a guy.

A renewed tingling of curiosity and attraction replaced her skepticism.

Nikos had offered to help the American girl on a wild whim. He was rarely spontaneous, but the novelty of being unrecognized had been too appealing to refuse. Nor could he deny Olivia's inexplicable allure.

He had expected a brief but amusing outing. Afterward, he assumed he'd return her to the hotel and spend his afternoon at the gym.

But as the morning progressed, after each disappointing stop, she'd gamely climbed back onto the bike despite her obvious nervousness. She'd twined her arms trustingly around his waist. And no matter what his rational mind cautioned, his body thrilled to her touch. But more than his blatant physical response, their time together piqued a long-suppressed desire for genuine connection. He'd felt it the first moment they'd met.

He had time to think as he circled Monte Carlo, waiting for her to emerge from each shop. He decided it was worth skipping his workout to enjoy her company a little longer.

But why? What exactly were they doing? Had their excursion morphed into a date? Was that what he wanted all along? Ever since the explosive breakup with Athena that almost derailed his career ten years earlier, Nikos had largely avoided dating during the season. And when he did date...

There were objectively stunning women in his past. Finding a woman to appreciate the fit body he spent so much time cultivating was easy. And sex with a gorgeous woman was, theoretically, more entertaining than watching movies, playing video games, or playing padel. And yet…these increasingly infrequent encounters left him dissatisfied. He felt no emotional involvement, depth, or passion with anyone he dated. And he was sick of being nothing more than passing entertainment, a means of bolstering a woman's status, or a way for her to access the perks of wealth and fame. Yes, everyone understood the game and what was being bartered and traded. It was purely transactional. Nothing more. Lately, the effort of dating simply wasn't worth it.

Today, however, he reveled in the unprecedented opportunity to slip his tiresome identity and experience the enchantment of a mysterious woman who knew as little about him as he knew of her.

It was incredibly freeing. It threw him back to being an anonymous sixteen-year-old consumed with the angst and ecstasy of his first real crush, when he'd first met Athena, before they were caught up in fame and all its temptations. Before Athena sacrificed his heart to the altar of her own greed and ego. Before she'd cheated on him while burning through an obscene percentage of his early winnings. After their breakup, he'd sworn never to let anyone get close enough to eviscerate him again. He had easily kept that vow.

But now his surprising attraction to this girl triggered an intoxication and foolhardy rush he'd not felt in a long time. Her sense of adventure and loyalty to her friend intrigued him.

He didn't want their adventure to end, but unfortunately, the likelihood of being recognized had increased every time they stopped. So, while Olivia visited yet another pâtisserie, Nikos optimistically contacted Bryson to reserve the discreet terrace at his favorite café. For a price, they'd cordon off the entire space. Nikos and Olivia could slip in the back. He made it clear that no one was to hint at his identity. He needed to explore the freedom of anonymity a little longer. He refused to risk the crushing disappointment of seeing greed take the place of curiosity in the eyes of a girl who appeared to be as attracted to him as he was to her. Perhaps their fledgling connection might increase over the intimacy of a meal together. He desperately wanted to find out.

When Olivia suggested they give up on the cookie quest, Nikos twisted around to gauge her mood. Hopefully, her obvious irritation wasn't directed at him. Was she too annoyed to accept an invitation to continue their day together?

"Would you want to get lunch?"

He could tell he had surprised her. Nikos's stomach dropped at the thought of being refused. The last time he worried about being turned down was a decade earlier, before he'd gotten behind the wheel of an F1 car. But more importantly, he wasn't used to caring that a woman might reject him.

"Sure, that would be great."

Inordinately pleased, he fired up the bike and reminded himself to take it at a reasonable pace, no matter how eager he was to go somewhere to get to know her better.

At the café, they were seated in a tranquil garden bordered with clay pots of fresh herbs—rosemary, mint, and thyme. Their mingled scent reminded Nikos of home, his parents contentedly puttering about on the patio with a view of the sea, tending their fragrant plants. He'd always assumed he might do the same with his wife someday. Based on his grandparents' and parents' loving marriages, he'd taken it for granted that he would find a woman with whom he could build a family, share a home, and enjoy life's simple pleasures. But that assumption had shattered with Athena, and he'd found no one with whom to resurrect that dream. But now he couldn't quash the tiny but defiant spark that wondered if the girl sitting across from him might represent that possibility.

"It's strange that no one else is here," Olivia commented. "It's such a gorgeous day."

Nikos shrugged. "I think this café gets crowded for dinner."

Olivia eyed the menu, periodically glancing at him with subtle but encouraging scrutiny.

The server kept his gaze averted, granting Nikos the anonymity he'd paid for.

"Une bouteille d'eau, s'il vous plait..." Nikos requested. He might've been willing to skip the gym, but he didn't want to go so far as to order wine. He hoped Olivia wouldn't find that odd.

"...plate ou gazeuse?" the server replied.

Before he could respond, Olivia answered confidently in passable French that she preferred sparkling water.

Interesting.

She was American but had possibly spent some time in Europe. His curiosity piqued.

"We don't know each other, but I think I would like to get to know you, Olivia… Olivia… Olivia…?" Nikos realized a critical gap in his knowledge.

"Keller?" she prompted helpfully.

He grinned and tried it out, "Olivia Keller."

"What do you want to know about me, Nikos… Nikos…?" she mimicked.

"Nikolaes Giorgos Alexandros Christos Michális Leonikaros." The syllables rolled off his tongue at lightning speed. Hopefully, she'd not extract *Nikos Leonikaros*, much less associate the name with an F1 driver.

"I'm afraid I got lost in that mouthful," she teased. "I'm going to need you to repeat your name one more time for me. And maybe spell it out."

"Not a chance." He shook his head. "Just stick with Nikos."

"Okay, just Nikos. You can call me Liv. What do you want to know about me?"

"You are American. What part of the US are you from?"

"I currently work in New York City but grew up in Pittsburgh."

He blanked, so she clarified. "It's in Pennsylvania, which

is a big state. Pittsburgh is about eight hours from New York City. Have you ever been to New York?"

"When I was a child," he replied, smiling at the memory. "My family went to New York City. I was young—all I remember is eating a hot dog from a cart on the street. Have you ever been to Greece?"

She shook her head. "No, but I'd love to visit. What part of the country are you from?"

"A tiny island called Kallitheira, in the southern Cyclades. The island has belonged to my family for centuries. I am related to everyone there."

"And I thought New York was a tough dating pool. It's got to be rough trying to find a girlfriend on a family island," she joked.

She was fishing for information about his relationship status. So maybe this was a date? His heart gave a happy thump.

"It is tough. I had no choice but to come to Monte Carlo to find a beautiful American girl."

She laughed out loud.

"Yikes. That is a pretty cheesy pickup line." She looked flattered nonetheless. "Do girls in Monaco fall for it?"

How would he know? He'd never tried to pick up a girl in Monaco or anywhere else with a pickup line. He didn't need to.

"Probably not. This is the first time I've said it."

"Well, that's okay, then. I'm susceptible to flattery, especially because you are honest about its effectiveness."

Honest.

He tried not to cringe. If she only knew. She'd probably be appalled if he explained how he met prospective romantic partners.

Nikos and the women he dated had support staff. Publicists contacted assistants, and media managers chatted at celebrity galas. Overtures and introductions were made. VIP areas at clubs and restaurants were secured. Rooms were booked on the same floor of the same hotel. The F1 driver was photographed with the supermodel. Or singer. Or actress. When the season got intense, the pop tour launched, or movie production began, then both parties went their separate ways. What passed for a relationship often played out on social media, which he despised. The whole unappetizing process was soul-wearying and precisely why Nikos wasn't currently dating...and why pickup lines weren't his strong suit.

But facing retirement, perhaps it was time to try a new approach to dating. One that might result in a genuine relationship. For that, he had to get to know her better.

"Tell me about what you do in New York City..."

He couldn't venture a guess.

"The short answer is that I help large multinational corporations with risk assessment."

"Wow." He whistled. "That's quite impressive."

"Tell it to my boss." She shrugged. "Maybe I'll get a raise. What's it like being a baker in Monte Carlo?"

He replied with a noncommittal "meh." He wanted to discourage her from questioning him too closely. His ruse would unravel if she discovered he knew next to nothing about baking.

"So, you are here for a wedding?"

This time, her smile was broad and unfiltered. It dazzled him. What would it be like to be the reason for a smile like that?

"Yes! Until Saturday. My best friend is getting married to a guy from Zurich. She met him when we did a study abroad. Maggie and I have known each other since birth. We're like sisters."

"Do you have other siblings?"

"Nope. Basically, it's just me and my mom." She pursed her lips, clearly unwilling to say more.

Her response was ambiguous, but he didn't think he should push her. It was odd talking to a stranger for whom he had no preconceived idea of their life. Getting to know someone freed from the usual celebrity image and status-related presumptions was fascinating.

"And you? What is your family like?" she turned the conversation.

At least he didn't have to lie. He just needed to be selective about the details.

"Where to begin?" He shook his head in amusement. "There are a lot of us. Not only my two older sisters and parents, but a host of grandparents, aunts, uncles, and cousins. Lots of random spouses and second cousins. And everyone is very lovingly but aggressively in each other's business, all the time."

"And they all live on this island? Together?"

"Mostly, although many of us spend time in different parts of Europe for various reasons. Jobs. School. But home is Kallitheira."

"That sounds incredible." She nodded. "Very insular, so probably intimidating for anyone who visits, but to have that many people in your family to rely on must be really comforting. You're lucky. I bet it's beautiful there."

The accuracy of Olivia's insight knocked the breath out of him. Few comprehended or appreciated the unique dynamics of his family and their home. Certainly Athena hadn't. She'd tolerated his family so that she might access their wealth to cultivate a flashy public image. She'd sensationalized her relationship with Nikos—including her poisonous affair with a rival driver—to titillate an insatiable social media audience. Her obsession with creating a buzz for herself had betrayed everything Nikos's family valued. After their relationship exploded, Nikos had never introduced another woman to his family's distinctive way of life. It was safer to separate his private and public personas.

Now it astounded him that a girl from such a different background could be so astute in her understanding. And talking with someone oblivious to his fame, he could instead share stories of his childhood and the people he loved.

As they ate, he told her about racing bicycles with his cousins on his island's infrequently used airstrip. She responded with tales of the ice rink where she learned how to skate as a child and how she now loved to skate at the iconic rink under the Christmas tree in Rockefeller Plaza. He'd seen the place in movies and could imagine her spinning on the ice, her hair twirling around her face.

Their conversation prompted memories he'd almost forgotten. It was an incredible feeling, and he realized he definitely wanted this unanticipated connection to continue. The girl enthralled him. One more meetup couldn't hurt. But how far should he carry his false identity? Was it worth confessing now? How should he explain it?

Despite an undeniable attraction, he also had to be realistic. During race week, his time wasn't his own. They'd both be gone in a few short days. He didn't want to overcommit. He didn't want to give her the wrong idea, even if he wasn't sure what the wrong idea might be.

So what did he want with Olivia Keller? He wasn't sure, but fortunately, the cookies were a perfect excuse to see her again.

After their charming lunch, Olivia walked beside Nikos back to his bike. During the meal, he'd never once bragged about himself, as guys were apt to do on first dates. Instead, he'd asked questions about her life and actually listened to what she had to say. It was bizarre. It was appealing.

"I've been thinking about your cookies, and I have a backup plan," Nikos said. "But I need to make some arrangements. Can I get in touch later?"

Olivia hesitated. He sounded sincere, but she simply couldn't wrap her head around a guy who would help her when it didn't benefit him. Hell, her ex-boyfriend Sebastian pitched a fit when she asked him to go around the block to pick up takeout rather than wait on delivery for his own dinner!

And how many false promises had she heard? Her dad had

always promised the moon. Countless times he said he'd take her clothes shopping or pay for new skates and lessons. He had insisted he would cover the cost of her tuition. But inevitably, he failed to deliver anything other than pathetic excuses. Olivia and her mom were left scrambling. On those rare occasions when the man did produce some unexpected, extravagant gift or grand gesture, it always came with strings attached. Olivia had learned to always look a gift horse in the mouth.

Seriously, what guy was generous without expecting something in return? What did Nikos want? His offer seemed too complicated to simply be a ploy to hook up. Which, in all honesty, she might agree to regardless. Was he just an incredibly thoughtful guy?

She couldn't fathom it, but perhaps she was too quick to assume the worst. And she still needed cookies. The clock was ticking. If Nikos had an idea, she was willing to reconnect. It didn't hurt that he was so lusciously attractive.

"Sure, you can get in touch," she agreed.

"What's your room number?"

Okay. Maybe he was hoping to hook up after all. Was he planning to show up at her room unannounced? Was that the price of cookies? She wasn't ready to give him that level of access. Whatever might happen between them, Olivia wanted to control the pace.

"My room number?" she questioned. "Just take my cell— I'm unlikely to spend much time sitting in my room. I've got a wedding to help prepare for."

"Oh. Right."

There was definite reluctance in his response. Why wouldn't they just exchange phone numbers? Presumably he wanted contact information. Something was odd.

He unzipped the black pouch slung across his body and pulled out two phones, then hesitated again, apparently struggling to choose between them. Was one a work phone? If so, why the struggle?

Weird.

"Okay, go ahead and type your info." He held out a phone.

"Why don't you just tell me your number and I'll text you, so you have mine?" she countered. Two could play at this game.

He took a deep breath as if the suggestion wasn't one he liked. Did he have a girlfriend? She decided to give him a chance to be honest.

"Don't want your girlfriend to catch you with someone else's number?"

The question appeared to take him by surprise.

"No. I don't have a girlfriend," he insisted. "That's not it."

As if to prove the point, he committedly rattled off a series of digits. She sent a text with her name. The message popped up—but not on the phone he'd first offered. What was the difference between his two phones? She couldn't let it go.

"So I made the cut?" she guessed.

"It's complicated." He sighed. "But yes. I don't typically... well... I mean... Please don't share my number with anyone, okay?"

"Okay..." she said, still baffled. "I'm not sure who would be asking me for your number, but I'll keep it to myself."

"Thank you."

She was so distracted by the question of why he would have such privacy concerns that she didn't once contemplate death on the motorcycle ride back to the hotel.

When they pulled up in the alley behind the hotel, Olivia dismounted the bike, suspecting her inner thighs might feel it the next day. They both removed their helmets, and Nikos resecured hers to the back of the bike.

He faced her, and the moment became awkward with the ambiguity of their outing. Nikos paid for lunch—did that make it a date? She still wasn't sure.

"Thanks again..."

"So I guess I'll..."

They both spoke at the same time, then laughed.

"Go ahead…" he insisted.

"I just want to thank you for everything today. It's been great…"

"Don't thank me yet. Wait until we get your cookies."

We? Was there going to be a *we*? Or was it just a language thing?

"Yeah, that would be awesome," she said. He sounded serious. Maybe it wasn't a false promise, maybe there was hope for cookies yet. Was there hope for anything more with him?

"Nikos, I will understand if you can't get any cookies."

"Trust me," he said. "I'll take care of them. I'll text you later with the details."

Okay, she thought. Obviously, he meant well, which was more than she would expect from a guy. Give him an A for effort. And appearance.

Nikos was still on the bike. Olivia would need to step closer if their outing was indeed a date and a goodbye kiss was warranted. But if it wasn't a date? She'd be embarrassingly up in his face.

With split-second courage, she decided to kiss him.

She took a step closer, and his cologne teased her senses again.

"Like I said, um, thank you. I had a really good time today," she murmured, hoping he'd take a hint. "I appreciate your help."

He didn't pull away.

God, his eyes were intense. They widened and held her gaze. He clearly recognized what she intended, and a slow, encouraging grin spread across his face. Okay. He wanted it, too.

She licked her upper lip. Bit her lower lip. Delicious anticipatory tension flared between them, and she nearly giggled at the nervous delight of it. What was it about this guy that made her act like an idiot?

"Yeah, today was…" His voice trailed off with a deep inhalation. He lifted his hand and brushed her cheek with the back of his fingers. She slightly leaned into his caress. Damn. If she were a cat, she'd be purring.

Did he feel all fluttery, too? Or as a gorgeous guy on a sexy bike, was this just what he expected from a girl? Was it just what he did? Even if he wasn't great at pickup lines, surely he had frequent opportunities to kiss plenty of girls. Was this a typical encounter?

He cradled the nape of her neck and leaned infinitesimally closer, their foreheads nearly touching, his breath warm on her lips. He was showing incredible restraint, not greedily taking the kiss so clearly offered. Perhaps he didn't take it for granted at all. The pause was torturous. It was maddening. It was totally hot.

Olivia slid an encouraging hand along the smooth skin of his bicep. Although she'd innocently clutched his waist all day, this touch was an invitation. He accepted.

His mouth took hers, and she nearly groaned. He tasted heavenly; his lips were divine, moving in perfect harmony with hers, his tongue teasing deeper. In their sensuous exchange, there was no awkwardness or first-time weirdness. Instead, it was an indulgent, lazy, utterly perfect kiss. An open-mouthed, soul-stirring, time-stopping kiss. One with no demands but a tantalizing promise of future pleasures. Dear God, had there ever been such a first kiss? Not in her experience.

It should have scared her to death, experiencing such a profound kiss with someone she barely knew. But she wasn't scared. In fact, she realized it was the kind of kiss she could get very used to.

When they finally separated, Olivia opened her eyes, dazed and dazzled. A distinct look of satisfaction spread across Nikos's face, too. She wasn't sure if it was her imagination, but he appeared to be equally awestruck.

"I will see you again soon," he promised.

It was definitely a date.

MONDAY EVENING

AFTER AN ABBREVIATED WORKOUT, Nikos, still full of adrenaline, ricocheted around his hotel suite. Reliving the unexpectedly vulnerable kiss was amazing…but agitating. He vacillated between euphoria at the intense suspicion that Olivia Keller was someone he would like to kiss forever and alarm at what those feelings implied. Since Athena, he had refused anything beyond a superficial relationship. Now he was losing his mind over the most perfect kiss he'd ever experienced… The possibilities whirled.

He needed energy-absorbent racetrack barriers. Not that he made a habit of crashing his car into the walls, but barriers were there, just in case. They kept a driver safe when he got too rash. And right now, Nikos felt as though he'd careened well past safety, through the gravel, and was headed toward a wall. He knew precisely how to straddle the line between recklessness and victory in a race car, but a true romantic relationship was a different story. He'd played it safe for so many years; now he felt a crazy, impulsive desire for a girl he'd only known for twenty-four hours! Who would leave in less than a week!

Was it wise to take such a risk?

He reminded himself that normal people do this every day. They meet someone who surprises and intrigues them. They flirt. They kiss. They exchange contact information. They text. Normal people did not have their staff arrange their romantic affairs. Normal people gambled and opened their hearts, sometimes trusting strangers on nothing more than an instinctual attraction.

Was he ready for that? At least the cookie situation gave him an excuse. But who would have thought securing baked goods would be so difficult? Did people deal with this kind of annoyance all the time? Apparently so. He felt foolish, realizing how far he'd disassociated from life beyond the track. If he genuinely wanted a real relationship that mirrored that of his parents, he needed to learn how to live in a world that didn't cater to his every whim. True, his parents had enough money to make things happen. But as a couple, they were grounded by family. His parents were humble, hardworking, and wholly committed to one another. Not that he wasn't hardworking, but he'd forged a solitary path for so long, eager to build an individual identity distinct from his family, that he'd almost convinced himself he was fine alone. But now, meeting Olivia Keller reminded him of what he was missing in his life.

For the first time in years, the power of a kiss and the electrifying high-speed sensation of two bodies pressed against one another tempted Nikos to recklessly imagine a relationship with a woman who wasn't a celebrity orbiting him in a publicity-driven universe. A woman with whom he could share a home. A life. Far from fans. Away from the spotlight.

Was it possible? Could this fledgling relationship be something special? Something personal? Private.

And for that matter, how did he go about it? He needed a strategy.

During their first encounter, he'd imagined Olivia with ocean sunlight glinting off her hair. Now Nikos had an idea, even though he knew he should keep his expectations in check. Likely, once she discovered his true identity, their connection would sour no matter how unaffected he imagined her to be. But for the time being, he needed to be her Greek baker for at least another day. He wanted to live the fantastic dream of getting to know a woman who liked him simply for himself.

He texted Bryson.

I'll bake cookies on yacht if you clear tomorrow—don't argue just do it

Why? don't forget VIP event in an hour, so let's make cookies after that...

...and ok, I will cancel everything tomorrow

Nikos couldn't quite answer the initial question; he simply trusted Bryson to make it happen without explanation.

He debated his next move—call or text? Okay, maybe call. He needed to hear the tone of her voice. Texts were too ambiguous, too hard to read.

He found her number—not hard to do as there were so few others on his private phone.

Deep breath. He tapped the Call icon. His heart rate accelerated with each unanswered ring.

"Hello, this is Olivia..." He grinned at her American accent and breezy tone on the recording. *"Clearly, I don't want to talk to you right now...just kidding... But don't leave a message. I never check my inbox. Please call back later or text me..."*

How did people do this? Okay, text.

Hi this is Nikos

He was an idiot. He backspaced over his name and sent it. She knew who the text was from; he was already in her phone.

He waited, anticipatory energy building as if waiting for lights out to cue the start of a race.

Hi—sorry I didn't answer—meeting w/ wedding florist

Whew. Quick breath. Okay.

Can you txt me the cookies you need? recipes?

If I told you, I'd have to kill you. grandma recipes = top secret

Then no cookies for you

JK—I'll take pics and send—recipes are all handwritten. good luck with that

How many cookies do you need?

60 guests… 5 or 6 per guest…so 360 cookies? 30 doz?

!! that's a lot of cookies

Too many? I'll take less—whatever you can do

I can do 30 doz

The conversation paused.

Seriously?!!!! you are AWESOME

A torrent of happiness ran through his body. Now to the most crucial question.

Want to go on a boat w me tomorrow?

A long pause. Had he overplayed his hand? The uncertainty of waiting for her answer was exhilarating.

Speedboat? will I need a helmet?! pls say no

He laughed.

No speedboat no helmet just bathing suit…sea + sun = good
vibes

That got a thumbs-up.

Omg, perfect, no bridesmaid duties tomorrow. I'd love to

Nikos grinned like an idiot. This was not his typical race-week preparation, and there would be hell to pay with Bryson, Aleko, the Segno Rosso team, and sponsors, but he couldn't have cared less. He'd never invited a woman to spend the whole day alone with him on his boat, but he suspected Olivia Keller was like no other woman he'd ever met.

Meet at same time/place as this morning, if that works

Sounds good. I like sea + sun vibes—see you tomorrow :-)

Nikos texted Aleko, hoping the old man would refrain from asking questions. He would disapprove of anything or anyone that distracted Nikos from racing.

Get day boat ready to take out tomorrow AM—include wine
& food

Okay why? What are you doing?

Nikos had absolutely no idea what he was doing, but it was the most excitement he'd had off the track for as long as he could remember.

* * *

As the evening sun set over Port Hercules, Olivia graciously accepted another glass of champagne from one of countless black-clad servers circulating on the immense luxury superyacht owned by Stefano's firm. The only larger boat in the harbor was a behemoth that occupied the next slip. It was so big it blocked her view of the sea, which was annoying. *Wealthy men must suffer from yacht envy*, Olivia thought.

She snagged another *barbagiuan*, a ridiculously good cheese-and-spinach pastry that was evidently a Monegasque specialty.

She was brushing the crumbs from her cleavage when Maggs sidled up to her. "My dress looks good on you."

Olivia rolled her eyes. "If by *good* you mean *showcases my chest because it's too tight…*"

"At least you have boobs." Maggie shrugged. "And now, because I am your friend, I will introduce you to Stefano's friends. Unless you've made an undying vow to your Greek-motorcycle-baker boy and aren't interested."

Her sarcasm was obvious, as Maggie had never known Olivia to express a genuine commitment to any guy. But now, Olivia felt an uncharacteristic urge to defend Nikos rather than respond with the usual smart-aleck retort.

"Not undying vows yet…but Maggie, it's bizarre, because there is something there. Something different. We chatted all through lunch, and the way he listened to me… I felt like I'd known him forever. Like I could trust him."

"What?" Maggie demanded. "Who are you and what have you done with Olivia?!"

"I know," Olivia admitted. "Here's what's crazy…after Nikos shuttled me all over to look for cookies, I suddenly realized that my dad would never do anything like that for me. Nor would Sebastian. Or anyone else I've ever dated. Until Nikos, it hadn't occurred to me that a guy would be willing to do something nice without making me feel obligated. I mean, you would do anything for me. I would do anything for you. But that kind of gracious selflessness and generosity from a man? Never. Until today. It was an aha moment. It snuck up on me, and then I was like, *Oh, okay. This is how it should be. This is how a decent man should behave.* Who knew?"

"You aren't wrong. That is absolutely how a man should behave. Not that you would know, given your history with your dad. But Liv, don't swing too far the other way, gush over a guy, and get your heart broken just because someone is nice. You don't know this guy Nikos. Be careful. Spending the whole day on a boat? I'm not saying don't do it…" She paused. "Liv, you've had some travel flings, but this sounds different. I love you, and I don't want to see you hurt."

"I appreciate your concern, Mags, but believe me," Olivia insisted, "after that kiss, I'm ready for whatever happens on the boat…"

Maggie raised her eyebrows knowingly.

"Yes, if *that* happens, it will be good. I'm sure of it. And seriously, Nikos is nothing like my father or Sebastian. He's different. I can feel it. I trust him. I mean, that kiss. A kiss like that doesn't lie."

That got another look.

"Even so"—Maggie rolled her eyes—"let me introduce you to Stefano's friends. Just in case."

They approached a group of handsome men in exquisitely tailored linen suits coupled with sockless suede loafers. They were hotly debating the upcoming race.

"I'm telling you, Leonikaros is done…"

"No, he desperately wants this last win in Monaco…"

"He may want it, but Mancinelli is hot on his tail—and both teams are tied for points…and Leonikaros's seat will be up for grabs next year."

"Gentlemen," Maggie interrupted. "As much as I'd love to discuss F1 drama with you, I want to introduce you to my best friend, Olivia Keller…"

Twenty minutes later, Olivia had concluded that European bros were just as annoying as American bros, albeit these ones had more money and were thus more obnoxious than the guys she usually met over drinks. Admittedly, she had herself to blame as she typically gravitated toward guys who shared her aversion to forever commitments, wedding bells, and white picket fences.

The contrast to Nikos was striking. She marveled at the miracle of meeting the only guy in Monaco who wasn't so wealthy that he couldn't get past his own self-importance.

She quickly extricated herself from the racing-obsessed bro-fest and engaged in a far more interesting conversation with Stefano's aunt and uncle. As Uncle Klaus was a longtime racing aficionado, the couple planned to stay in Monaco after the wedding for the Grand Prix. Aunt Kiki asked Olivia questions about her life in New York City before the charming older couple excused themselves to return to the hotel.

As the other guests also said good-night, Olivia contentedly stood near the deck railing, waiting for Maggie and Stefano to make the rounds. The tranquil ocean under the moonlight was magical. How amazing it would be to spend the night on the sea, under the infinite sky. The planned daytime outing with Nikos was exciting—she was uncharacteristically giddy imagining it. And that kiss? What might it lead to? This wedding trip was proving to be far more exciting than expected. She had no complaints.

As Olivia waited, she watched with mild curiosity as a few men appeared on the deck of the neighboring superyacht. It took a moment, but then she looked more closely, and her interest piqued. One guy moved in a smooth, familiar way. He had a recognizable silhouette.

But what was he doing on the gigantic boat? She whipped out her phone and texted.

Look to your left

* * *

The phone in Nikos's back pocket buzzed. His private phone. He knew it was her before he looked and felt a surge of inexplicable happiness.

But then he read the text, and his heart thudded against his ribcage. Slowly, he turned.

Across the dark water gap, she stood on the deck of a nearby yacht, her hair dancing in the breeze and her body beautifully illuminated by moonlight. The gorgeous image sucked the air right out of his lungs. Why did she have this effect on him?

As much as he wanted to simply enjoy the sight, he found himself mentally scrambling once again for an explanation. He took a few of the calming breaths he so often practiced with his trainer.

Okay. If he could maintain his wits at two hundred miles per hour, he could bluff through this.

She'd clearly recognized him, so he couldn't just disappear. He gamely waved. She returned the gesture. Now, how to explain his presence on the most expensive boat in the harbor? She'd mentioned she was headed to a cocktail party that evening, but it never occurred to him that it would be on the neighboring yacht.

Hi gorgeous

Lame, but that would at least buy a moment to think up a story…any story…an excuse.

What's with the big boat? moving up in the world?

Part-time 2nd job, don't tell my boss

Damn I thought NYC was expensive but Monaco must be crazy—side gigs suck

Relieved that she seemed to accept—and even sympathize—with his explanation, further inspiration took him.

Hold on

He pulled out his phone, saved a cut-down version of the cookie-baking content Bryson had just produced, and sent it to her.

Making your cookies in boat's galley—decided to add another variety...

...Greek cookies are the best

He waited. He could tell from her silhouette that she was watching the video. He trusted she wouldn't realize the Segno Rosso shirt he wore in the video was an exclusive driver jersey.

Then she looked up.

Even across the water, he knew she was smiling. It was as if she were only millimeters away, and he could feel the pleasure and warmth in her gaze. It undid him.

Love the video you are too cute

Until she'd exploded into his life, he'd had no idea he wanted someone to look at him with such fondness. He was used to awe. To adulation and greed, as though he were a gilded prize rather than a living, breathing person with feelings. But her gaze was completely different, unlike anything he'd felt in a long time, if ever. Now, for a crazy second, it was as if he would prefer her affectionate expression over standing on a podium before thousands of cheering spectators and millions of rapt TV viewers. Those people didn't celebrate him with their idolization. They merely affirmed the curated image he represented. The fans saw the F1 driver. Olivia saw Nikos. And, incredibly, she liked what she saw. Could this connection become something more?

He suspected he would know when they spent time alone on the sea. No phones, no interruptions. Just the two of them. It was a miracle that she had agreed to go on the boat. She didn't know him; he never let anyone get so close on such short acquaintance. But something about her made him willing to drop his usual caution.

All cookies will be ready on thursday AM

Incredible! You seriously are the best!! see you tomorrow— can't wait! :)

Maybe it was the night air or the full moon, but he couldn't help himself.

I really liked kissing you

Even as he sent it, he panicked. Too honest?

Me, too. Maybe we should do it again?

Oh hell yes.

That can be arranged…

…are you headed back to the hotel? Want an escort?

…protection from the mean streets of Monte Carlo

He heard her laughter echo across the water.

Another stellar pickup attempt...

...I'm going to wait for my friends and walk back with them

...but maybe more kisses tomorrow ;-)

I'm gonna hold you to that

Even as he thrilled at the exchange, an irritating little voice in his head reminded him that sooner or later, he would have to tell her the truth. And when he did, would she still see him the same way, still want to kiss him? Or would it all explode in his face?

TUESDAY MORNING

FOR THE SECOND MORNING, Nikos waited for Olivia outside the service entrance, eager to be on their way. He hoped she'd be prompt; he didn't like sitting exposed outside the hotel. Fortunately, right on time, the back door opened and she appeared, radiant in the early light. As she sashayed down the alley, smiling that glorious smile, she suddenly paused and pulled out her buzzing phone.

"Oh! Oh my gosh! My suitcase has finally arrived!" She looked up. "It was delayed because of the strike. Do you mind if I go back up to my hotel room for a second? I can get my sunblock and a few other things…"

Nikos wavered. He could ride around while waiting for her. Would she think that was strange? Impatient? Rude?

"You can come up, if you want," she offered. "I'll only be a minute or two."

Nikos dismounted and parked the bike near the door. Out of habit, he put on his sunglasses and pulled his hood up.

"Keep an eye on the bike," he murmured to the security guard, who nodded in agreement.

He followed Olivia down the service corridor. As expected, she headed directly for the public elevator, chatting about the outfits she'd had to make do without. He wondered why she hadn't simply purchased replacement clothing. And he wondered if she was so talkative because she was as excited as he was for their planned outing.

The elevator doors closed, and Olivia hit the appropriate floor button. Nikos stood behind her, head down, praying no one else would get on.

No such luck. As Olivia mentioned something about peanut butter, which he understood to be an American delicacy, the elevator stopped in the hotel lobby. Two men and a young boy got on. Olivia greeted them with a polite "Good morning." Nikos hoped the distraction of a beautiful woman would hold their attention. Eyes glued to the floor, he held his breath. *Keep looking forward*, he willed them. *Keep looking forward.*

When the elevator arrived at her floor, Olivia exited, and Nikos made to follow. As he hastily trailed her down the hall, he heard the child's excited voice in French: *"Papa! Vois-tu qui c'est..."*

Did Olivia know enough French to realize the little boy had recognized him? Thankfully, the elevator doors closed before his cover was blown.

They entered Olivia's hotel room. Nikos hung back, not wanting to invade her privacy. Even so, he was mesmerized by the intimacy of the turned-back bed covers, the cosmetic jumble spilled across the credenza, and the towel tossed over the chair back. In the small room, her presence hung in the air like perfume. He suspected the spaces he occupied weren't as revealing of his personality, merely his identity.

"Oh, thank God," she exclaimed as she hoisted the suitcase onto the bench at the foot of the bed and unzipped it. It was filled with tidy pouches. Nikos watched, curious, as she rifled through the bag. He never packed his own gear. The crew was responsible for the enormously complicated task of packing the car, the tools, the electronics, the building structures, and all of the garage components. Bryson arranged for someone to handle Nikos's clothing and the few belongings he required when traveling from race to race. The most Nikos ever personally carried was a backpack with the bare minimum of what he needed to tune out the accompanying circus.

"You are going to need this." Olivia turned and held out a plastic tub.

"And this is…?"

"The peanut butter!" she exclaimed. "Maggie asked me to bring it. I didn't know it was for cookies. You'll need it for the Peanut Butter Blossoms—the cookies that have chocolate drops in the middle. You should use Hershey Kisses, but you may have to make do with Swiss chocolate."

"A hardship, to be sure." He laughed. She smirked at him.

"Is peanut butter used only for cookies?" he asked.

"No." She shook her head. "It's like Nutella. You put it on toast or bagels. It's amazing on ice cream. I'm not going to lie—I've been known to eat peanut butter straight from the jar."

He envisioned her life, her days and nights in her apartment in New York City. He quirked an eyebrow. "I need to taste this peanut butter."

"Oh, you do, do you?" she replied. Her voice dropped to a sultry hint.

He wasn't exactly sure what she was proposing…but he would gladly agree to whatever it was.

She dipped her chin and opened the jar. She swiped her finger and extended it to him without breaking eye contact.

His mouth went dry. Was she really inviting him to…

He leaned forward, eyes still locked. He closed his lips and curled his tongue around her proffered finger. As he sucked on it, she slowly, suggestively drew it out of his mouth. She lightly touched his lip, traces of unreadable emotions playing across her face. He forgot how to breathe. The world stopped.

Until the taste hit him. It was awful.

Furthermore, he couldn't say anything profound because his tongue was stuck to the roof of his mouth. He frowned and tried to swallow the stuff while she dissolved into laughter, breaking the moment's intensity.

"Oh my God, you should see your face," she hooted. "I'm sorry—I had to do it."

"That is clearly an acquired taste," he admitted, making inelegant but necessary movements to reclaim use of his mouth and jaw.

"Don't be insulted, but the funniest thing in the world is feeding a dog peanut butter and watching them try to slurp it down," she admitted. "I had to see how a person who had never tried it would react."

"I'm not going to ask who is more amusing, me or the dog," he said.

She laughed harder. Humor was so cultural. Was she teasing him for fun? Was this a good sign? He'd down a whole jar of the vile goo if it endeared him to her.

"I love dogs," she said with a smile. "They are loyal and authentic in their enthusiasm. They live in the moment. If people were more like dogs, we'd all be much happier."

"I love dogs, too. We always had them when I was growing up." He then fixed her with a stern look. "But you took advantage of my innocence by feeding me that nasty stuff. You'll be sorry when my family serves you lamb's head for Easter. And as a special guest, I will make sure you are honored with the eyeballs."

She grimaced, laughing, then caught his gaze.

They both froze, wary of the moment's intimacy and all that the prospect of spending a holiday together implied.

Later that morning, after a motorcycle ride at a nerve-wracking speed along the spectacular coast, they arrived at the charming French town of Beaulieu-sur-Mer. Olivia would have loved to explore, but Nikos was focused on their excursion. She followed him briskly down the long wooden dock in Porte de Fourmis. It was a tiny harbor compared to the superyacht parking lot in Monte Carlo and felt more down-to-earth. As they approached the boat, several people called out enthusiastic greetings in rapid French. Everyone seemed to know Nikos.

"I've been in New York too long," Olivia admitted. "People

in Pittsburgh are more like the people here. Everyone talks to everyone else, including strangers. It's nice."

"Very friendly," Nikos agreed, although Olivia noticed he didn't respond to everyone's greetings. Perhaps he was generally reserved, although he hadn't been shy with her. And now she had an entire day to get to know him better. How much better remained to be seen.

The boat was gorgeous—a gleaming forty-foot Cranchi cabin cruiser. Nikos explained the small yacht was perfect for a day trip or a weekend on the water. Olivia took his word for it. The only boating she'd ever done was on a pontoon on her hometown's three rivers or taking the Staten Island Ferry.

At Nikos's invitation, Olivia lounged on a rear bench and watched him bustle about, casting off the lines connecting them to the dock. Sure-footed, he moved back and forth effortlessly, confidently from dock to boat. The sun gleamed in his hair and bounced brilliantly off his sunglasses.

"How do you know how to do all this?" she wondered.

"I'm Greek," he explained. "I've got saltwater in my veins."

"Whose boat is this?"

"Umm…" He hesitated. "The same person who owns the superyacht."

Olivia figured it was up to Nikos to determine whether taking out the boat was permitted. She was happy to go along for the ride as long as she didn't miss the wedding because she was in a French jail for stealing a yacht. Her budget wouldn't cover bail.

Nikos took up the helm as the engines below shuddered to life. They backed away from the dock, and he detached the final line. With a broad smile at Olivia, he steered toward the open sea, utterly in command and clearly in his natural element. Olivia was delightfully out of her element but loving every minute. One could get used to this life, she mused. One could get used to spending time with this man.

Keeping his eyes on the horizon, Nikos nudged off his burgundy Adidas. Olivia had always felt there was something particularly intimate and vulnerable about a guy in bare feet. Seeing Nikos without his shoes confirmed it.

His T-shirt was the next piece of clothing to be shed.

Olivia gawked. Holy Lord.

His skin was tinted with an olive-bronze undertone, a blessing of his Mediterranean heritage. A tangle of gold chain, leather cording, and beads draped around his neck. A tapestry of tattoos accentuated and glorified the sculpted musculature on his back. Did he realize how alluring he was?

"That's some serious artwork you've got," she commented.

He stiffened almost infinitesimally, and she wondered if she'd embarrassed him. But then he shot a curious glance over his shoulder.

"Do you like it?"

"I do," she said. She'd never dated a guy with such extensive tattoos. Then again, she'd also not gone sailing off the coast of France. She could adapt to both. Easily. Happily.

"Will you tell me about them?"

"Greek cross on this arm. Greek key design here," he explained, pointing at each bicep in turn. "The big tattoo on my upper back shows the Resurrection based on an ancient Greek mosaic called the Anastasis. My mother disapproved of me getting tattoos but couldn't say no because of the subject matter."

"I see." She laughed, itching to trace the intricate design with her finger. "I've been to Greek churches for food festivals and seen icons in that style. Very cool. What are the squiggly tattoos along your waist?" It was another area of his body that invited her touch.

He paused before he answered. "Racing circuit maps."

"Racing circuits like the upcoming one in Monte Carlo?"

He nodded and made a noncommittal noise. "Mm-hmm."

"Why the dates?"

Another pause. "I was at those races on those dates."

Okay. The man was a major fan but hesitant to admit it.

Olivia didn't care one way or another and was impressed he didn't blab on and on like most guys would about their sports obsessions.

"You must really be into racing. Where is each particular tattoo from?"

Reaching behind his back, he touched each image with his thumb and rattled off cities on every continent except Antarctica. Monte Carlo was above his right hip.

While ambivalent about racing, Olivia was impressed at the extent of his globe-hopping. She loved to travel, and Nikos had evidently seen the world. She wasn't sure how a baker could afford such travel, but then again, he worked two jobs. Maybe he traveled inexpensively as part of the superyacht's crew.

"None from the United States?"

"Nope. But there are a few races there. I hope to add one or two of them soon."

"I see. So, do you generally enjoy traveling, or is it all about the races?"

"Both." He stretched, rolling his shoulders and twisting his neck. Olivia was fascinated by the way the movement rippled through the images on his back. From the captain's seat, he turned toward her, lightly keeping one hand on the helm. The motion accentuated his abs, which were every bit as mouth-watering as his back.

Not wanting to be caught blatantly staring, she turned toward the water and smoothed back the hair that blew free from her braid. Without a word, Nikos opened a storage compartment and produced a cap with a Segno Rosso racing logo. He handed it to her.

Somehow, that simple, thoughtful gesture appealed to her even more than the tantalizing glimpse of his body or their sweet kiss the day before. It would be all too easy to fall for a man who anticipated and responded to her needs before she even asked. One who was willing to run her all over the city to find baked goods for a wedding he wasn't attending, for a couple he had never met. As she'd explained to Maggie, his graciousness and attentiveness were unprecedented…and incredibly sexy.

"What do you think of Monte Carlo?" he asked, drawing her attention back to their travel conversation.

Olivia paused, then decided to be honest. "Monaco is an odd place," she said. "It's beautiful, but it's so unreal. That cocktail party I was at last night? It was insane. Superyachts, private helicopters, couture, sports cars? I mean, who lives like that? In real life?"

An odd look passed over Nikos's face.

"Maybe you don't notice how bizarre it is. You must see that kind of opulence all the time, at the hotel and on the yacht where you work. How do you deal with the crazy wealth? If you grew up on a small Greek island, it's got to be strange, right?" she persisted.

He turned to the horizon, reflecting. "Money doesn't make a difference to me. I think life is what you experience. And there are many different ways to live in the world."

Olivia considered this. "True. And in New York, I see it all. Wealthy people, poor people. Mostly, people like you and me, just scrambling to get by. Even though I don't travel as much as I would like, I am surrounded by people from every corner of the globe, which is cool. I think you're right. There are many different ways to live in the world."

He nodded, seemingly lost in thought.

After a comfortable, companionable silence, Nikos steered them into a cove of translucent, calm, turquoise water. He cut the engine on the boat and gestured to the ocean.

"Do you want to swim?"

"Absolutely!" Olivia agreed.

He dropped anchor and then pulled two foam rafts from a storage compartment. He tossed them into the water and lowered a ladder from the back platform.

Olivia pulled off her cover-up. Although he wasn't blatant

about it, she knew Nikos appreciated the sight of her in a bathing suit. And she, in turn, enjoyed his appreciation. She also knew some women in the Mediterranean went topless at the beach. She would if they were on a crowded beach with a thousand other people. But alone, with just Nikos? Going topless would escalate whatever might happen between them. Perhaps she was only postponing the inevitable, but she wasn't quite ready to take the next step. Although she did have every intention of repeating that kiss.

"Best way to get in the water? Should I go down the ladder or...?" she asked.

Nikos flashed a wicked grin, took two steps, and effortlessly executed a perfect flip over the side of the boat. She peered into the water to watch him surface, sleek as a seal, and sluice water over his head to slick back his hair. His performance made her flush with appreciation...and a few other heated emotions. Damn, he was gorgeous.

"Okay, well, that's not going to happen."

She moved to the edge of the platform, squeezed her arms over her chest, covered her face, pinched her nose, and jumped. She came up from the water, sputtering. "Not as graceful as you, but wow, this water feels good."

They circled each other, grinning like idiots, treading water, lolling in the gentle ebb and flow.

"Do you want a raft?" Nikos pushed one toward her. He hoisted himself easily onto his; Olivia floundered. Nikos laughed. It was at her expense, but it was a delightful sound.

"This is payback for the peanut butter, isn't it?" she panted, finally coming to rest on her stomach after a few failed attempts. "Unlike you, I'm not part dolphin. I grew up inland."

Their rafts bobbed in the undulating current. Nikos, his eyes shut, held loosely to a line tied to the boat, his other hand dangling in the crystalline water.

"Give me your hand," he murmured lazily, extending his. "So if we fall asleep, you don't drift away."

Keeping one arm as a pillow, she stretched out and hooked her fingers around his. As they touched, he opened his eyes, their hue mirroring the azure sea. His expression was fathomless. Then, without letting go of her hand, he shut his eyes and tipped his face back toward the sun.

"So tell me more about your job…" he prompted.

Olivia moaned. "I'm drifting in a Mediterranean paradise, and you ask about my job. That's kind of a buzzkill, you know?"

"Sorry." He grinned. "I'm curious. Did you go to school to learn how to do it?"

Olivia laughed. "Nope. I fell into it. I studied philosophy. Love the ancient Greeks."

He opened his eyes and quirked a curious eyebrow. "I think you must be a very smart person, Olivia Keller."

"What about you?"

"Me?"

"Do you see anyone else out here on a raft? Yes, Nikos, you. Did you go to culinary school?"

He took a deep breath and exhaled. She waited for his story while admiring how the light illuminated his profile and seductive lips. Oh, she wanted to taste those lips again.

"I didn't go to culinary school. I've known what I've wanted to do since I was a kid. You could say I learned by doing. I trained all over Europe."

"I could tell you love baking when you made me that video. There was a lot of joy in it. It must be nice to know exactly what you want to be. Unlike me. No kid says they want to go into insurance when they grow up."

"I suppose not," he said. "But now I find myself facing a serious question, and I don't have your philosophical background to help me decide what to do next."

"What do you mean?" she asked.

"My contract is up in December. It's time to make a major career change and do something different with my life. I've always been goal-driven, but I don't know what to do next. My father would love me to be part of the family shipping business along with my sisters. I'm not sure that's what I want, though."

"Goals aren't everything. I've always been a fly-by-the-seat-of-my-pants kind of girl, but I've made it work," Olivia offered.

"'Fly by the seat of my pants'..." he repeated slowly. "I'm not so familiar with that phrase. Not sure I follow what you mean."

"It means you don't have a plan or a long-term goal. You rely on instinct. You just make the best decision possible at each critical junction and keep moving forward."

"I see." He raised an eyebrow. "I hoped it meant someone who would enjoy going fast on a motorcycle."

"Nice try." She laughed.

"Hmm," he pondered. "So, is that your particular approach, or is it an American thing?"

Olivia sighed. How much should she explain?

"I'd say it's my circumstance. I grew up with a lot of uncertainty. My dad was selfish and unpredictable—a total narcissist and only around when he wanted to play at being the perfect family. We couldn't rely on him. He lied about everything. Made promises and broke them. Did whatever suited him, with no consideration for how it might impact us. For example, he signed a lease with my mom, then defaulted. She and I had to move, and I bounced around to different schools. He'd reappear, apologetic and charming, and she'd take him back. The cycle would repeat.

"Don't get me wrong—my mom is an amazing woman. She did her best to protect me, and I appreciate all her sacrifices. But our life wasn't one in which we could plan ahead. We couldn't rely on my dad. We had to figure it out as we went along. Not surprisingly, I didn't know what I wanted to be when I grew up. I just knew I never wanted to be dependent on anyone else. I wanted to be able to take care of myself, but I wasn't sure how. Then in high school, I wrote an essay on

Socrates and got a full scholarship. Great! I didn't have to depend on my dad for tuition. But when I graduated, I discovered nobody hires philosophy majors to sit around and ponder, so I had to talk my way into a job I wasn't technically qualified for. But that's what New York City is all about, right? Making something from nothing, reinventing yourself."

He opened one eye. "Maybe that's what I need to do—reinvent myself in New York City."

Her heart hiccupped. "Then you'll have to look me up when you're in town."

Nikos was dropping hints all over the place that whatever they were doing, he didn't view it as a quick fling. Olivia didn't think his words were sheer flattery—he appeared sincere. But should she encourage him? Could she believe him? And why did it matter? Could she honestly imagine a relationship with someone who lived half a world away? Incredibly, every instinct said yes, for the first time in her life, this was someone she might trust. Someone who wouldn't flatter her with convenient lies, someone she could rely on.

"I am still really jet-lagged," Olivia murmured, shifting the conversation before it stretched into scary territory. "The travel is catching up with me. Tell me something else, so I don't fall asleep. Tell me a story…"

She waited to see how he would respond to that request. If he told her a story about racing or any other sport, she'd tip him right off his raft.

"A story…" His voice turned thoughtful. "I know some Greek myths. How about Eros and Psyche?"

That was a surprising and delightful offer.

"Perfect. I forget how that one goes."

Olivia basked in the warmth of the sun and the warmth of his voice as he told her the tale of the beautiful god sneaking incognito to pay conjugal visits to his doubting mortal wife and the punishment she endured for exposing him.

"I don't know if I like that story. I think she got a bad rap,"

Olivia argued when he reached the end of the tale. It reminded her of how her father punished her mom for his own failings. "Eros's expectations were unfair. I have no patience for people who need to test love to prove it exists. And what was she supposed to do when her lover wasn't truthful about who he was? Just forgive and trust him? Not a chance."

Nikos squeezed her hand. "At least the story has a happy ending. Try to keep that in mind." Olivia snorted but didn't argue.

After another extended silence, dozing and floating in the warm sunlight, Olivia sighed. "I think my back is burning. I should probably get into some shade."

They rolled off their rafts, Nikos with far more grace. As Olivia struggled to hoist herself out of the water and up the ladder onto the swaying boat, Nikos placed a hand on her rear and gave her a boost.

Once safely on the deck, she turned to where he floated below.

"Was that you being helpful or a poorly disguised excuse to grab my ass?" She raised a flirtatious eyebrow.

"Absolutely."

He smiled broadly from the water, and her heart turned upside down.

Sailing once again, Olivia relaxed, and Nikos steered the boat to another spectacular and seemingly unpopulated section of the coast.

"This is a good place to stop for a while. If you are hungry, I brought food."

"Fantastic. I'm starved," Olivia agreed. "Hey, but first, do you think you could get my back?"

She held out the sunblock. She wanted to ask before he was busy with the food…and before she lost her nerve. She'd spent the previous day wrapped around him. Sunblock assistance shouldn't be a big deal. But…

He took the tube, and she turned to face the ocean. Anticipating his touch, her stomach started crazy flip-flopping again. *It's just sunblock*, she silently repeated.

However, as soon as his palms settled warmly on her shoulders, she knew she was lying to herself.

Good heavens, the man had good hands. His touch was mesmerizing. He squeezed her shoulders like a deep-tissue massage. He worked the lotion into her skin, rubbing slow, sensuous circles over her entire back, inch by inch. He rested his hands on her hips, his thumbs tenderly working above the edge of her bikini bottom. Throughout, his warm breath caressed her neck.

His touch aroused every part of her body, and her entire being yearned for the same pleasured treatment he was bestowing on her back. She knew her quickened breathing revealed her feelings. It would be impossible for him not to realize the effect he was having. But what would he do about it? What should she do?

Just when she thought he would step away, he nestled his face in the spot where her neck met her shoulder. She held her breath. He nuzzled her skin and squeezed her hips. That did it; she was all in.

Encouragingly, Olivia twined her arms up and back around his neck. He brought his lips to her shoulder.

"About that kiss…" he murmured.

She twisted back, turning toward him, and discovered his mouth searching for hers. There was no hesitancy when they connected, just a devouring kiss of incredible longing, intensity, and passion. How could a kiss contain such richness? Such depth? It confirmed what she'd suspected after their first kiss—she'd never experienced this kind of physical passion with anyone. A kiss wasn't enough.

As their mouths moved in perfect cadence, she leaned back into Nikos and felt the irrefutable evidence of how badly he wanted her. Ridiculously pleased, she smiled against his lips. Growing bolder, his hands roved over her body, exploring the landscape of her figure. Enflamed by the increasing intimacy of his touch, she moaned softly. He moved to untie the back of her bikini top; she loosened the tie at her neck. The garment fell to the ground. Their encounter was escalating, and she had no intention of slowing down.

Now his hands could cradle her freely. She needed more. She needed all of him.

Too tormented to hold on to their kiss, she shut her eyes and relaxed her head back onto his chest, her arms still wrapped behind his head. The world was spinning. It was as if she were deliriously drunk on the intoxicating scent of salty air, sunblock, and the lingering hint of cologne.

He kept one hand on her breast, the other hand slid down her side, in answer to her silent plea. He lightly teased the top edge of her bikini bottom, and she involuntarily lifted her hips, urging him on.

With a decisive motion, his hand dropped lower. Even through the barrier of her bathing suit, the contact was electrifying. One direct caress and she would shatter. Desperately, she arched her back, silently begging. Finally, finally, he slipped his hand under the fabric. She clutched his neck as he simultaneously touched her and nipped at her shoulder with his teeth.

It was all she needed to peak. With his free arm, he held her tight, safe against his chest, until she caught her breath and came back to rational consciousness. Flush against his body, she felt a disconcerting bond she had never experienced with any other guy.

Was this what it felt like to fall in love?

The thought sent her spiraling into a blind panic.

What was happening?

It was too much. The experience…the feelings were too big. Yes, she'd fooled around with guys before. No harm, no foul. It happened. Sometimes it was fun. Sometimes it was awkward. Sometimes it led to something more. She had suspected her feelings for Nikos were adding up to something different. Something unprecedented. But never—never—had she been touched in a way that rocked her very soul.

Her body stilled, and Nikos sensed it. He carefully placed both hands on her hips. Olivia swallowed and drew her arms over her chest. She was too exposed. How in the hell was she going to get her bikini top back on…

"Here," he murmured.

He reached for his discarded T-shirt but stayed behind her as she accepted it, allowing her some privacy. Relieved, confused…she pulled the shirt over her head.

"Hey." He brushed her upper arm lightly as he turned to face her. "I'm sorry. We shouldn't have… I shouldn't have…"

He looked a little dazed as well.

"No, no…" She squeezed her eyes shut, frustrated. What was wrong with her? Their interaction should not have been upsetting. At all. They'd both wanted it. After the delightful two days they'd spent together, it wasn't a surprise. She'd predicted it to Maggie. She'd eagerly imagined his hands all over her. Furthermore, their physical connection was incredible. She should be begging for more, not doing…whatever awkward thing she was doing.

She grabbed a beach towel and tossed it around her shoulders. She sank into the corner of the bench and crossed her legs tightly. Foot jangling nervously, she stared out over the water, embarrassed to look at him, trying to pull herself together.

She wasn't a prude. She'd had boyfriends. Situations. She'd had some flings and illicit encounters with pretty faces and successful flirts. She'd enjoyed travel romances and one-night stands. Her panic wasn't about the physical act. She'd had plenty of hot encounters with hot guys.

But the feelings Nikos provoked were beyond anything she'd known before. Even more disconcerting, she suspected those emotions might be reciprocated. He, too, might be feeling something profound. Was she ready to consider that? Had her

life turned upside down before she'd realized it? With someone she'd leave behind in a few short days?

Intimacy with Nikos had unexpectedly opened a whole new
realm, like they'd ignited something deeper, a truth that had
always been theirs, simply waiting to be discovered. They'd
clicked together like two missing puzzle pieces. It was perfect
but overwhelming. She was both tempted and terrified. None
of her exes ever made her feel this way. She'd intentionally
chosen guys who wanted to keep their distance as much as
she did. Now she was sailing into uncharted waters. And she
didn't mean the Mediterranean.

She chanced a glimpse at Nikos. Not surprisingly, he looked
confused.

"Nikos. Just give me a minute," she pleaded. "It's me—I
am being stupid. I don't know why I'm reacting so… I don't
know. Like this."

She heard him take a deep breath.

"Should I make us something to eat?" he offered. "My
grandmother says that no matter what upsets you, you will
always feel better if you eat something."

Olivia choked on a burst of nervous laughter. "My grandmother says the same thing. It's universal grandma wisdom.
Food would be wonderful. Please. I'd like something to eat.
That's probably it—I'm hungry and tired. I got a little over-
wrought. I'm sorry."

"Don't apologize," he said, squeezing her shoulder lightly,
then descended the few steps to the lower deck.

As he disappeared, the tension drained from her body. Okay.
A Mediterranean fling was one thing. That she could easily
enjoy.

But feeling as though she had met her soulmate? That hadn't
been on the bingo card for this trip, this month, this year…
this lifetime. Soulmates didn't exist. Love was a fantasy and a
trap that nearly destroyed her mother. And love at first sight—
or first touch?—absolutely didn't exist. That was a fairytale,

and she'd never been a sucker for make-believe…until she met Nikos. How had this happened? And what should she do about it?

She heard him coming back up the steps. She took a deep breath. Which way did she want this to go?

He hovered, carrying a tray of something that looked and smelled delicious. Clearly, his Greek grandma knew her business.

Olivia tried to smile. "Thanks for the T-shirt. More racing gear, huh?"

"I have too much of it," he admitted. He unfolded a clever little table from a cabinet under the bench and set the tray on it.

"Salade Niçoise," he said. "Fresh bread. And wine. Berry galette for dessert."

"God, that looks divine." Olivia nodded as he offered wine and poured.

She took a bite. "Oh wow. You are an artist."

"Glad you like it. After we eat, we can head back to the harbor."

Olivia paused mid-bite and put down her fork. She looked out over the horizon, the sun well past its midpoint. It was a glorious view, a glorious day, with a glorious man.

Her day with Nikos was literally the stuff epic romances were made of. Was she brave enough to consider a romance? Not just a fling?

She'd overreacted. Now, was it too late to salvage the situation? Or should she shrug and acknowledge the chance had passed?

She realized she desperately didn't want their first attempt at intimacy to be their last.

They could hook up. If it was fantastic—and she had no doubt it would be—she would head home with some scintillating Monte Carlo memories. Or…if she really was in mortal danger of falling for this guy…well. She had never permitted herself that kind of surrender, but she wasn't a coward. She needed to understand what was happening, and there was only one way to find out.

"When you take out the boat, how long do you usually stay out?"

"That depends." He shrugged. "However long I want."

"You said you sometimes stay overnight?"

He stilled. "Yes, but I wasn't presuming we would…"

"I know. Do you have to be back tonight?"

"No…" he said slowly.

She knew she was bewildering him, even though it wasn't her intent to mess around or play games. She decided to be honest. She owed him that much.

"Nikos. The reason I pulled back isn't because I didn't want to be with you. I pulled back because I do want you. Badly. And that scared me. Terrified me. I don't really know you. But I think I'm starting to really like you."

His eyes widened. She suspected she had shocked him with her honesty. He looked at her intently. "So, what are you saying?"

"I want to stay out all night. Here. On the boat. With you."

He caught his breath sharply, as if carefully weighing her words and proposition. Finally, he nodded and flashed that devastatingly sexy smile. "Okay. No matter what happens, I really like being with you, too. I want you to know that."

He reached across the table, pausing before he touched her face, giving her plenty of time to pull back. When she didn't, he caressed her cheek with a butterfly touch.

"Olivia Keller, how did you come crashing into my life? And what am I going to do with you?" He gently brushed the hair back from her temple. "But I'm glad we're here. We can do whatever you like."

TUESDAY EVENING

NIKOS FELT LIKE he'd flipped into a rollover. He'd only rolled a car twice in all his years as a driver. But when he had, it was a completely disorienting and terrifying experience. And like those hair-raising situations, he now suspected he might not emerge intact. Especially after encountering Olivia's whiplash emotions, he knew the safest move would be to chart a course back to Monte Carlo immediately.

But he'd never been one to stick to a conservative strategy behind the wheel. Why start now? Olivia said she wanted to stay out all night with him. Great. But what exactly did this girl want? Did she even know? What did he want? His desire for her was different from whatever he felt—or didn't feel— for the women he typically dated. But how deep was his desire? Did it extend to something more profound?

On top of his uncertainty, he also heard Bryson's nagging voice inside his head insisting that if they stayed out, Nikos would never get back in time for Media Day and all the other escalating pre-race commitments. It was a valid concern, but Nikos had no answer. Right now, his priority was seeing how the evening would unfold. He couldn't deny that he hoped it would include making love to Olivia Keller.

After they finished their meal, he opened another bottle of wine, grateful that there was more than one. Nikos never drank during the season, and after a day in the sun, on the water, and in the company of this unpredictable woman, he suspected the wine affected him more than usual, made him a bit more emotional. Perhaps more honest. Which was fine. The team nutritionist might kill him, and this was not how he should prepare for a race, but in the moment, he didn't regret a thing.

He refilled their glasses and studied Olivia over the rim of his wineglass as she untangled her hair with her fingers and loosely re-braided it. The unconscious gesture, arms lifted and stretching to reach the back of her head, mimicked the way she'd anchored her arms around his neck earlier, accelerating his body's instinctual need faster than his conscious mind could comprehend.

He was a driver. On the track, he made split-second decisions and took decisive action. But he also knew that his best split-second decisions were grounded in calculated, intentional planning.

But how could he have planned for this? His recent futile attempts at romance had been planned and pursued based mainly on a woman's image and appearance. All had been sadly dissatisfying.

Olivia appeared to have little interest in glamour.

Not that he was unaffected by her appearance. Far from it. The golden glow of a Mediterranean sunset illuminated her face and made her eyes shine. Tiny sun-dappled freckles danced across her nose. The outline of her breasts pushing against the thin fabric of his shirt was even more erotic than seeing her in a bikini top. She'd pulled her linen pants back on but wore them low on her hips. The still-visible strings of her bikini bottoms teased him to distraction, just begging to be untied. She wore no makeup, no jewelry, and despite her efforts to keep it contained, her hair waved riotously in the ocean breeze. She took his breath away.

Unlike the other women he'd dated, her appearance didn't seem to be the cornerstone of her identity. He liked that. Her essence enthralled him. She was resilient, confident, and intelligent. A philosophy major! She was kind, clearly a loyal friend. Not to mention, she was funny. She made him laugh, even at himself. He'd spent a lifetime taking himself too seriously. Plus, she seemed to intuitively grasp the nature of his family...without criticism.

He shifted in his seat, unsure of what was happening but suspecting he was falling fast. But what was her relationship status? Was there someone in her life? Could that be why she was upset after their earlier encounter?

"So Olivia Keller...do you have a boyfriend in New York or Pittsburgh or some other American city that I probably can't find on a map?"

She smirked. It was not quite a denial. His gut clenched.

"Define 'boyfriend'..." she began. "I thought I had something with a guy. We were in an odd relationship..."

Okay, she referred to the situation in past tense and with a comforting ambivalence. That was good.

"I was seeing him... Sebastian Alexander...doesn't that sound like it should be a fake name? That alone should have been a hint. Anyhow, we'd been on and off, and recently it became more off than on. The final straw was when he decided to go on a Las Vegas boys' trip rather than accompany me to my best friend's wedding. And honestly, my heart checked out long before my head, if my heart was ever involved at all. You know how sometimes you get into something because it's convenient and becomes a habit, but then you set an arbitrary endpoint? That was me getting on the plane to Monaco. I knew the relationship was done."

Nikos understood more than he wanted to admit, especially regarding dead-end relationships. He wished he could explain his life to her. But then he'd have to reveal too much. It wasn't the time. Yet.

"And you?" She eyed him directly. "You aren't seeing anyone?"

"No, no one. Like I told you yesterday, I'm currently quite single." At least that wasn't a lie.

Ironically, in the two days he'd spent with Olivia, she'd seen more of the real Nikos Leonikaros than he shared with anyone. Could she possibly understand that he wasn't trying to be dishonest but was intrigued by the novel sensation of a woman liking him for himself? Not for his money or image?

And when, not if, he confessed all, and if they were somehow to become a couple, could he guarantee Olivia wouldn't take advantage of him? His blood ran cold at the thought. It wasn't an idle fear. Athena had shamelessly milked their relationship for her own profit. Then she'd cheated on him and left him to pay her bills. It was not an experience he ever wanted to repeat, and since then, he'd not let anyone close enough to cause that kind of emotional damage. But now, an urgent voice inside his head insisted that he couldn't let that past drag him down. He had to trust that this American girl might be different.

And hopefully, when he did reveal his true identity, Olivia would recognize his confession as one of those critical junctions she mentioned. Could she appreciate his wealth and the opportunities it represented as another example of her stumbling unintentionally into good fortune? Or would she, too, become blinded by the proximity to status and fame?

"Here's a question…if money were no object, what would you do? Would you still work at your current job?" he asked.

"Oh, *let's pretend* is always an interesting game…" she said, swirling the wine slowly around her glass. "Would I continue to live in a studio apartment smaller than a Monaco hotel room? No, definitely not. Would I stay in New York City? Uncertain. Would I stop working? I probably wouldn't stay at my current job, but I couldn't stand not doing anything. I mean, I may not have a long-term goal, but everyone needs a purpose, right?"

She lifted a brow. "Are you thinking about what you might do next? You said you were facing a big career change."

"I am," he agreed, "but it's more that I want to learn what's important to you. You asked me earlier about traveling. Is that something you would do?"

"Absolutely, yes," she said. "When Maggie and I graduated, we took a ten-day cruise. I think the most magical thing in the world is waking up somewhere you've never been. We splurged and got a room with a balcony. Looking out over the landscape as you arrive at a port in someplace new is the best."

"And what would you do when you got off the boat?" he wondered. "Again, if money were no object."

"Oh, that's easy," she insisted. "I'd visit every museum in the world. Art, history. Cultural sites. I'd see live performances—theater, music, dance, whatever. Explore. The seven wonders of the world. UNESCO heritage sites."

"Not much of a shopper?" he prompted. Athena had maxed out several of his credit cards despite their exorbitant limits.

"It depends," she replied. "I'd hit Paris flea markets hard and buy vintage clothes and antiques to decorate my money-is-no-object mountain chalet. But I don't think I'd splurge on designer clothes."

"A mountain chalet," he repeated. "So, you are a mountain person? Not an ocean person."

"Where I grew up is hilly, so yes, I love the mountains, but I'm sure I could be swayed to favor the sea. You're doing a great job today convincing me. I could adapt." She tilted her head. "And what about you? You obviously like to travel, if the ink on your back is any indication. If money were no object, what would you do differently? Other than expand your already extensive collection of racing paraphernalia."

Oh God, if she had any idea that money really was no object. But her question interrupted the ever-present narrative that most women would exploit his wealth. He turned his thoughts back inward.

What could he be doing that he wasn't already? If he weren't racing, what might he do differently? How would he travel if he could be anonymous in the places he visited?

And what would it be like to travel with Olivia, to roam freely? Explore anonymously? Drink coffee at sidewalk cafés uninterrupted. Take the subway. Sit among the fans at sporting events. Go to a baseball game and see what the American sport was all about.

"I'd eat different foods in all the places I visited. Try all the famous restaurants. Sample all the local specialties. Taste everything. Take cooking classes."

Over-indulging in international cuisine was a plan his nutritionist discouraged.

"Oh, I support that." She smiled. "The food has been the best part of my visit to Monte Carlo so far…" She caught herself and hesitated before she amended her statement. "Other than spending time with you…" She faltered, eyeing him to gauge his reaction. "That's actually been the best and completely unanticipated aspect of my trip."

"Do you mean that?" he asked. His heart skipped an erratic beat.

"I do," she said after the briefest pause. She looked at him intently. "I just don't know what to do about it."

Indeed. They could pretend time would stand still, and they could float along on the brilliant blue sea forever. But in reality, she had a job and a life awaiting her in New York City. He had five more months on his contract. Ten more races. However, after that…could a future exist for them based on a precious few days' worth of encounters? Or did she assume he'd be just a fond memory, a sweet souvenir of Monte Carlo?

Did he want to build a relationship? Was he finally ready to try for something real?

Judging by how his heart leapt at the thought, it was a distinct possibility.

He hesitantly considered certain daydreams that he hadn't allowed himself to imagine for a very long time. What would it be like to sail home to Kallitheira with Olivia at his side?

Oddly, he could see it. She said she liked waking up in unexplored locations. He could make that happen. They could spend the night making love on his favorite secluded island beach and then greet the Aegean dawn. He could imagine her discussing art with his mother or debating business strategy with his father and sisters.

But for the moment, he had more pressing concerns.

The sun spilled molten fire over the edge of the horizon. It was getting late.

"If we are going to stay out all night, I need to move the boat."

She nodded, although it wasn't an unequivocal answer.

"Do you want to stay out?"

"Yes," she said. "I do. I do want to."

Okay. The adventure continued.

He wouldn't assume she was saying yes to resuming their earlier passions. Still uncertain but willing to see how the night might progress, he steered the boat to a sheltered spot a good distance away from their previous anchor spot. He wanted to give her plenty of time to tell him to change course.

She didn't.

He prompted her to tell him more about her childhood. She unselfconsciously complied, painting a place he'd never considered but was now curious about. He noticed she focused on stories of her and her best friend rather than any further mention of her family. He chose not to push her. Apparently, her past was complicated.

When they arrived at his intended destination, he dropped anchor in the rapidly growing dark and set the mandatory night lights.

What next?

"I've got blankets and pillows. Do you want to sleep in the bed on the lower deck or up on the sun pad?" he asked. "Both are comfortable. I could sleep in one place and you in the other…"

"Sleep in different places?" She raised a provocative eyebrow. "What fun would that be? It would defeat the purpose of staying out. Right?"

His mouth went dry. "Would it?"

"Yeah." She stood and moved toward him, her intentions

clear. His heart thudded. When the girl made up her mind, apparently, she made up her mind. He admired decisiveness.

"I told you—I think spending time with you is the best thing I've experienced in Monaco so far. But I'm hoping the trip is about to get even better," she murmured.

Okay. The way she said it left little doubt that she was interested in taking their relationship to the next level very soon, if not immediately. He was glad he had optimistically stashed a few condoms. Even so...

What if they did make love? Would she regret it? This time, he wouldn't make any assumptions.

"Are you saying we should continue where we left off this afternoon?"

"Yeah," she murmured. "I behaved weirdly then, but that was my mistake. A mistake I'd like to rectify."

"I don't know if it was a mistake. Maybe just a little uncertainty. But I would like to try again. See what happens between us. I would like that very much. Because I find myself very, very attracted to you."

She took a deep breath and pulled the shirt up over her head.

"Damn." He caught his breath.

She stood, waiting. Not with uncertainty, but it seemed she was simply allowing him the pleasure of looking at her. She unconsciously ran her tongue over her upper lip, not in planned seduction but perhaps in anticipation. He wanted her badly.

"Come here," he gently beckoned.

She stepped closer to where he sat. She stood between his legs and grasped his shoulders. He reached for her hips. They were perfectly designed to fit between his hands. He inhaled the intoxicating scent of skin, sunblock, and salt.

He reverently traced her faded tan lines. As her chest rose and fell, the muscles of her abdomen constricted and jumped. Was it with pleasure? Anticipation? He held her gaze and leaned forward to take her breast into his mouth.

Would her reaction reflect desire or...?

There was no hesitancy. Her eyes grew dark with need. She twisted her fingers through his hair encouragingly.

"Do you know," she whispered, "I've never had sex outdoors."

He grinned against her skin, allowing wicked thoughts to run wild as he rubbed his cheek in the silken valley of her chest.

"First time on a motorcycle. First time to make love outdoors. I think I am good for you, Olivia Keller," he suggested.

"And how am I good for you, Nikos?" she prompted.

"Oh, you are very good," he growled. "Maybe even perfect."

He nipped her ever so lightly. Her breath caught, and he felt her hips rock beneath his hands.

"Am I the first American girl you've been with?" she asked.

"Yes, but that's the least of it," he admitted distractedly. "I think it might be more than that. Maybe you make me remember things I'd forgotten that I wanted."

"What do you mean?"

He couldn't answer. Wouldn't answer. He was not ready to voice his feelings; they were too raw, made him too vulnerable. Could he trust this intensity? This fervor? Could their unprecedented connection evolve into the kind of relationship he'd longed for but refused to attempt since Athena?

He hooked a finger in one knot of her bikini bottom side strings. "May I?"

She nodded, and he slowly loosened each tie. He spanned her hips and began to ease her clothing down. It slid slowly over the curve of her hips, then dropped rapidly to the floor. She stepped free and stood before him, his own Venus on a half shell, surrounded by gentle waves.

Looking at her, his raw need was demanding and blatant. He made no effort to conceal it; she had to be aware. Olivia coaxed him to stand, then fussed with the drawstring at his waist. He couldn't wait. He shoved his still-tied trunks down and off and kicked them aside.

The moment hung, infinite and incredible. He reveled in the

extraordinary sensation of being together, their naked bodies caressed by the salty air, under the darkening sky. He carefully wrapped her in his arms. As her smooth belly brushed against him, he covered her warm mouth with his own, desperate to resume the earth-shattering kisses they shared earlier. His fingers worked through her braided hair. Some loosened and danced around them like a halo.

They stood, kissing, hands stroking, bodies undulating, for as long as he could endure. But she was melting into his arms. He needed to have her, be one with her.

"Do you want to go below deck or stay outside?" he asked.

"Mmm, outside. Under the sky," she purred.

He maneuvered them toward the boat's bow without breaking contact or ceasing his foray of kisses. They stumbled backward onto the sun pad. As they lay down together, he leaned over her, carefully aligning his body alongside hers. He didn't want her to feel trapped, even though he yearned to feel her moving beneath him. Desire flared acute and insistent; he was hard as a marble statue. But he didn't want to rush her; he wanted her invitation. Dear God, she was so beautiful. He could only hold off for so long. He ached for her but wanted her to find pleasure first. He intensified his kisses as he traced his hands over her body. It didn't take long to coax her to peak. He had barely touched her before her face crumpled, and she jammed her fist into her mouth to tamp her cry.

"Olivia," he whispered, nudging his face into her hair. "You don't need to be quiet. There's no one out here but us."

Her eyes stayed closed, but the side of her mouth quirked up in half a smile.

"I'm used to thin apartment walls," she admitted. "You make me feel so good."

"We're not done yet," he said.

"I know." She opened her eyes and lazily rolled toward him. She cradled his cheek. "Just give me a minute and I'll return the favor."

"That's not what I meant," he insisted. If she touched him, the encounter would end in a hot second. "I'm not finished with you yet. Making you feel good."

He demonstrated exactly what he meant.

She gasped and quivered.

"Damn. What did I do to get so lucky?" she managed to ask before he made her moan again.

He chuckled and increased the intensity of his efforts, watching her face and waiting for the delicious moment she lost control.

"I want to hear you cry out," he cajoled as she approached another glorious peak.

As he felt her begin to shudder, to tip over the edge, she called his name.

"Nikos," she insisted. She tugged at him. "Now, I need you now."

Ready to explode at the sound of his name in her mouth, the pleading tone of her voice, and the intensity in her eyes, he reached for the condom packet he'd tucked in the compartment by the sunbed. Once it was secure, he shifted on top of her pliant and receptive body.

"Please, Nikos…"

She snaked her arms around his neck and strained upward to kiss him. Her desire destroyed any shred of restraint or sanity, and he enthusiastically met her demand.

The rhythm of their bodies surged, accentuated by the motion of the boat. Nikos fought valiantly to remain in control but utterly lost himself in the glory of the act. Ensconced in her heat, cocooned in her arms and legs, her gasps ringing in his ears…emotion poured out of him. Words of lust and love spilled out, whispered in Greek. The sensations he experienced were simply too profound to express in anything other than his native language. It didn't matter. He intuitively trusted that she would somehow, miraculously, understand what he meant, how he felt, and how he'd never experienced anything like this before.

His release was immense and encompassed by hers. Even before the last throbbing shudders had subsided, he dropped heavily atop her. She instinctively stroked his back until consciousness returned. He realized he was probably crushing her, so although he didn't want to move, he rolled beside her. She nestled snugly against his chest, and he pulled a blanket over their flushed bodies.

He took a huge gulping breath. What to say after a possibly life-altering experience? Had it been the same for her? Where to even begin?

"That was…" He faltered.

"It was," she whispered, affirming perfectly the indescribable pleasure they'd shared. He grinned and cuddled her a little closer to kiss her shoulder.

"I didn't mean to rush, but it was intense…" he apologized. "Sorry if I went too fast."

Her body started shaking. Was she crying again? Laughing?

"What?"

"That's not what you said about the motorcycle…" She rolled toward him, definitely laughing. "You know I'm joking, right?" She paused. "It wasn't too fast—it was perfect."

He grinned against her hair. He loved that she teased him. She wasn't stupefied in awe of Nikos Leonikaros, celebrity driver. She was affectionately amused by Nikos, just Nikos, and his tendency to go too fast, even when experiences might be better savored.

"It's exactly what I told you about riding the motorcycle…" he insisted. "Hang on tight and let me do the rest."

"I'll keep that in mind for next time."

Next time. She wanted there to be a next time.

Whatever was happening between them, it was accelerating. Rapidly. Should he go flat out or hit the brakes? He'd made mistakes before and paid the price. But being too cautious was also a mistake. He had no idea which way to go. At the moment, he was driving blind.

WEDNESDAY MORNING

OLIVIA BLINKED AS the unflinching Mediterranean morning sun forced her awake. She'd slept like the dead under the infinite sky, in the warm shelter of Nikos's body. He was still unconscious, breathing heavily next to her. She turned over onto her belly and picked up his leaden arm to look at his watch.

"Oh no, no, no, no, no… It's late! I'm going to be so late!" she yelped. She scrambled off the sun pad and snatched up her discarded clothing.

Murmuring in Greek, Nikos rolled into a groggy, half-awake state.

"Damn, damn, damn," Olivia muttered, hopping on one leg to get into her linen pants, giving up on the missing bikini bottoms in the name of dressing expediently. "I'm supposed to be at a gown fitting in less than an hour."

"What time is it…?" Nikos muttered and then groaned. "Oh damn, I'm in trouble."

Apparently, Nikos also had commitments that morning. She had precious little time to relish the sight of his sculpted body in full light as they both hustled to put on the bare minimum of clothing.

Fortunately, there was also no time for any morning-after awkwardness. Always attentive, Nikos offered, and Olivia gratefully accepted, another race-themed garment. As he started the boat and raised the anchor, she pulled on his sweatshirt and tamed her hair under the cap he'd given her the day before.

"Full speed?" he confirmed.

She dropped onto the bench and braced herself. "Full speed."

It wasn't a long trip back to Porte de Fourmis. When they pulled into the slip, Nikos gave precise instructions, and Olivia helped him secure the boat efficiently.

"What about the leftovers from dinner?"

"Leave them."

That was going to be gross, but it wasn't her problem. Hopefully, it wouldn't get him in trouble with the boat's owner.

Nikos set a fast pace. They sprinted up the long dock toward the lot where he'd left his bike the morning before. So much had happened since then; it felt like her entire life had transformed. But she had no time to reflect on it.

Before they donned their helmets, she eyed him squarely. "Nikos."

He looked up, and she thought she saw a hint of wariness at her abrupt tone.

"I can't believe I'm saying this, but I cannot be late for this appointment. We need to get back to Monte Carlo as quickly as possible. We need to go as fast as you can."

His guarded expression turned into a brilliant smile. "That sounds like my favorite kind of challenge. Are you sure? Because I can go very fast."

"I'm trusting you, but let me tell you, if you get me killed... who is the mythical Greek guy who has to push the boulder up the hill forever?"

"Sisyphus."

"And the guy who gets his liver plucked out by an eagle every day?"

"Prometheus."

"Okay. If you get me killed, I am going to spend eternity haunting your ass so hard that it's going to seem like Sisyphus and Prometheus have it easy in the afterlife."

Undeterred, he took up her hand and kissed it. "Get on. Hang on tight. Let me do the rest."

"Where have I heard that before?" she murmured from the rear seat, giving him an affectionate and trusting squeeze.

Thirty death-defying minutes later, they came to an abrupt stop at the hotel's service entrance. Olivia jerked her helmet off. Nikos removed his as well.

As she started to bolt for the door, he grabbed her arm. "Olivia."

"Yes?" She spun back toward him. "Nikos, I have to go…"

Before she could finish the statement, he pulled her close and kissed her. Hard.

"Olivia. My next few days are complicated. I want to see you again, but we need to talk."

Olivia's stomach instinctively lurched. Those were always dangerous and confusing words. When her father used them—and he had used them a lot—it inevitably meant something bad was going to happen. But she didn't have time to hear what Nikos wanted to discuss. She fought down a flare of panic. Had he not been as profoundly moved by their night together as she had? It was hard to tell during their mad scramble to get back to the hotel.

"Okay, you have my number. Last night was amazing. Text and we'll meet. I still have to get the cookies from you, so I assume I'll see you tomorrow. Right?"

He nodded. Okay, well, that was a good sign.

Olivia glanced up and noticed her reflection in a nearby window. It was rough. "Heh, can I borrow your sunglasses? I'm a hot mess."

"No, you're not. You're gorgeous."

He was still tossing out cheesy lines, which was also good.

"Nikos, please. Just let me borrow your sunglasses. I will give them back…"

"Here, take them. Keep them. And yes, I'll have the cookies for you tomorrow morning."

"You're the best. Really. Thank you for everything."

She crammed the sunglasses onto her face and recklessly kissed him once more before sprinting into the hotel. Whatever he wanted to talk about, a lingering kiss couldn't hurt.

There was no time to stop by her room and pull herself together. As she entered the private wedding salon, she assured herself she could own the superstar-celebrity-sunglasses look. And everybody in Monte Carlo was wearing racing gear. No one could fault her for that.

Maggie and Céline, perfectly attired, waited in the elegant space. It was mortifying.

Céline's eyes widened. Maggie flashed an ornery grin that hadn't changed since she was two years old. Olivia knew she was totally busted.

"Oh, hey, Liv!" Maggie said brightly.

"Mags, I'm so sorry I was running late this morning," Olivia apologized. "Something, er…came up. It took me longer than I thought to get here."

Mags raised her eyebrows knowingly, and Olivia could read every double entendre and innuendo unsaid.

"No problem. Of course we waited for you. Céline, you remember my friend Olivia? My maid of honor?"

Maggie's lips were twitching, and Olivia knew her best friend was suppressing a fit of laughter.

Céline nodded graciously. It was to her credit that she betrayed no disapproving looks. This was the second time she'd seen Olivia in utter disarray.

"Bonjour." The wedding planner poured a cup of coffee, which Olivia accepted gratefully. Unfortunately, no *pain au chocolat* accompanied it.

Céline turned to Maggie. "Margot, I will go get the gown and the seamstress now that Olivia has arrived."

Olivia could almost hear the silent countdown as the wedding coordinator left the room. The instant the door shut, Maggie pounced.

"Olivia. Keller. Tell me everything, *right now*. When I searched your location this morning, your dot was in the Mediterranean. I guessed you either had a *hot* night with a hot Greek…*or* the guy was psycho and dumped your body at sea. Given that you are not dead *and* you are wearing an interesting mix of purloined race-wear with the clothes you wore yesterday, am I correct in assuming you just did a Monte Carlo walk of shame?"

Maggie should have been a trial lawyer. She knew how to badger a suspect. So many words before Olivia had managed to finish her coffee.

Olivia tried to look innocent. And failed. She couldn't suppress the insanely satisfied grin of a woman who had just crawled back from an earth-shattering night. On a boat. With the sexiest man ever.

"Oh my God, you *did* do a Monte Carlo walk of shame. That is *epic*!" Maggie shrieked. "Liv, I want to be you when I grow up."

"Oh, because Stefano and the Swiss chateau isn't a fairy tale enough?" Olivia retorted good-naturedly. "Margot."

"Margot is my European alter ego," said Maggie primly. "And true, Stefano is too cute to give up. But! Forget my fairy tale. You need to tell all right now. What happened on your magical Mediterranean cruise? You spent the night on the boat with Nikos?"

Olivia could only nod, the color in her cheeks rising.

"So, I'm getting my cookies, and from the way you are blushing, you got a little something sweet, too?" Maggie suggested euphemistically.

Olivia collapsed forward and buried her face in her hands. "Oh my God, Mags, that man made me feel like I have never felt before."

Maggie persisted. "And? Say more. Will you see him again? Is there a possibility for a repeat performance? Damn, Liv, do you even know his last name?"

"Oh Lord, he told me, but he's got about sixteen Greek middle names, so I'm not exactly sure where one name ends and the other begins. Does it matter? And yes, I absolutely need to see him again."

Maggie went wide-eyed. "Seriously?! Do you think it's for real? Like, not a travel fling?"

"I don't know," Olivia moaned. "How can it be for real? He lives here. I live in New York City and I'm leaving on Saturday. And remember, please don't say anything in front of Céline. He works here, and I don't want to get him in trouble."

"Oh, right, right," Maggie agreed. She assumed a mask of innocence as Céline, accompanied by the seamstress, returned with the dress. Momentarily suppressing thoughts of Nikos, Olivia gave her full attention to the maid-of-honor gown. It looked small. Way too small.

In the dressing room, Olivia tried to wriggle her way into the dress. It wasn't going past her hips. She imagined frighteningly large dollar signs to cover the cost of alterations.

"Heh, Liv…these are some serious sunglasses you have here. Expensive ones. Stefano just bought a pair," Maggie commented from beyond the curtain.

"I borrowed them from Nikos," Olivia said. "My boy likes some bling. You should see his watch. I've got to tell him if you're going to wear dupes, at least go for something a little more subtle."

"You aren't going to change his mind on the sunglasses. Every guy in Monaco is wearing this style—real ones and dupes—because one of the F1 drivers always wears them. I don't remember which one. I can't keep up with all the racing divas."

"And people say women are trendy." Olivia snorted.

She tried to ignore a disconcerting ripping noise as she forced her shoulders through the dress.

"I'm struggling. Can you try to zip me?" Olivia poked her head out.

As she'd done with every formal gown Olivia had ever tried on, Maggie joined her in the dressing room and fought with the zipper. Olivia assessed her reflection.

"I may be a hot mess this morning, Mags, but clean hair and makeup will not fix this."

Maggie frowned. "I know, babe. It won't zip. This is not going to work. And by the way, nice hickey on your shoulder. Haven't seen one like that since you were sixteen."

"Shut it, Margaret. But I have an idea," Olivia suggested, seizing on a money-saving possibility. "My suitcase finally arrived. I have a bronze satin Ralph Lauren that I was going to wear for the yacht cocktail party. I got it at a vintage store in Brooklyn for sixty bucks. It's the most gorgeous dress I've ever put on my body. I could wear that. And the dress will conceal the um…yeah, the mark on my shoulder."

Maggie turned decisively to the wedding coordinator. "Céline, can you work bronze into the color scheme?"

Maggie wasn't worried about the expense.

"Oui." The wedding planner made a note. "We will add bronze elements to the flower arrangements and use bronze napkin rings. It will be very elegant."

"I'm going to inspire napkin rings?" Olivia whispered.

Maggie kicked her in the shins. "That sounds perfect. Thank you, Céline."

"That woman has got to hate me," Olivia admitted as the wedding planner left, presumably to round up napkin rings. "Hey Mags…you know how my wedding invitation originally included a plus-one?"

Maggie grinned broadly. "I know what you're about to ask. I should make you beg."

"Nikos is baking a billion cookies for you. I would like to bring him as my date."

Maggie pretended to hesitate, then surrendered to excitement. "Of course! I am dying to meet this guy."

Olivia hugged the incredibly accommodating bride-to-be.

"You are the best. I don't know exactly when I'll talk to him next. He had to rush back this morning, so I assume he is working today. And he said those four terrifying words—'We need to talk.' I want to hear what that's all about before I invite him."

"Scary," Maggie agreed. "Honestly, Liv, you can decide at the last minute. It's all good. Céline can squeeze in an extra place setting."

"I'll let you know as soon as I get an answer."

She hugged Maggie again, and then Olivia headed to her hotel room for a long shower and an even longer nap. And to mentally revisit every glorious moment with Nikos.

But as she got onto the elevator, a niggling anxiety rose in her throat. How could she fully enjoy reliving their passionate night when she knew she was boarding a plane for New York in three days?

And since when had she felt any remorse about leaving a travel fling behind? She shivered, afraid to acknowledge the uncharted territory she'd stumbled into.

After being waylaid by a succession of fans who easily recognized him without his sunglasses, Nikos finally made it back to the team suite.

The troops were marshaled.

"Ya," Nikos met them with a casual Greek greeting.

"Where have you been?" Aleko demanded, responding in Greek.

Nikos ignored him.

"You are late. Really late." Bryson picked up the conversation in English. "You skipped training, which you will regret when that shoulder flares up midway through the race. You have a press conference in fifteen minutes, and there is no way you are going to be on time."

"Then they'll wait," Nikos growled. "Let me get my kit on—give me ten seconds."

Within minutes, they were hustling down the hall. Bryson handed Nikos a bottle of water.

"Your parents and sisters arrive Saturday. I've put them in Hôtel Hermitage…" Bryson commented as they entered the elevator. "You've got the press conference in ten minutes. After that, you've got the pit walk. Then the crew needs you in the garage to check the seat fitting." He swiped his iPad. "The Monaco commemorative helmet and suit will be unveiled this afternoon. They want photos. And Eero wants an extra strategy session to make sure it's a Segno Rosso double podium. I can try to work in another massage for the shoulder."

"Eero's strategy better involve Juan-Carlos keeping his head and doing his job," Nikos muttered, referring to the team principal and Nikos's rookie teammate. Mentoring the kid made Nikos feel like an old man. He'd once been that raw, that talented, and that undisciplined. But racing had been exhilarating back then. Now the exhilaration he felt resulted not from the possibility of a podium but the possibility of spending more time with an incredible woman. What an unbelievable night it had been. But could it become an ongoing thing? Could he handle a true relationship? What if it went all south? Last time, relationship trauma had nearly ended his career. Now, when he was so close to achieving his final major racing goal, was it wise to allow himself to become distracted?

He didn't bother protesting as they took Bryson's preferred exit route through the main lobby, but Nikos ignored all autograph requests. He usually wasn't blatantly rude to fans, but the clock was ticking. It was bad enough facing the scrum of reporters at the mandatory press conference, let alone arriving late.

A courtesy car waited outside the hotel. Aleko cut through the gathered crowd. As he opened the door for Nikos, he turned to Bryson. "I need a word with him. Get in the front."

Nikos was definitely in for it. Then again, how much grief could the old man heap on him in the five-minute drive to the media center?

Aleko eyed Nikos. "What the hell are you doing?" he demanded in Greek.

"What do you mean?" Nikos answered in English.

"With this girl. What are you doing?"

Nikos was getting irritated. He switched over to Greek. "None of your damn business."

"Nikolaes, it is my business." When Aleko used his full name, Nikos knew the man was about to get heavy. But Nikos wasn't a child. He wasn't a shy first-year driver overwhelmed by newfound celebrity. He didn't need a babysitter. He had no patience for lectures from his long-time minder.

"What is my job? What has always been my job?"

"Don't be vague, Aleko," Nikos ground out. "Say what you're going to say. Better yet, just shut the hell up."

"What is my job?" he repeated.

"Damn it, Aleko. I don't know."

"You do know!" the old man exploded. "It's to keep you safe! It's always been to keep you safe. That's it. That's my job." He paused for effect. "And right now, you aren't safe. Think about how things went with...with you know who."

Aleko wouldn't even say Athena's name.

"For God's sake..."

But Aleko wasn't done.

"You're distracted. You're not focused on the race, and you know it. This is how drivers get hurt. Think, Nikolaes! This is why you don't date during the season. You need a woman? Bryson has plenty of women who want to meet you. You have dinner. You take her back to your room. Easy. Done."

"Stop. You need to stop right there. It's offensive."

"You don't go sailing off and spend the night on the damn boat! You don't get moony over a nobody American girl and walk around with your head up your ass! This will not end well, Nikolaes. You are living dangerously. And I can't let you do that."

"How are you going to stop me?" Nikos opened the car

door and prepared to brave the gauntlet of photographers surrounding the media center. He turned back to Aleko. "I don't know how you think you can stop me, but I'm telling you right now—do not cross me on this, Aleko. Do. Not."

With that, Nikos kicked the door shut and steeled himself for a day of forced conviviality. He would endure it so he could win one more time at Monaco.

Late that night, after the rehearsal dinner, Olivia lay drowsily in bed, staring at her phone's wan glow. Monte Carlo was blanketed in serene silence, but a raging mental debate kept her awake.

Should she text? It had been exactly twenty-four hours since they'd made love. Less time since she'd kissed him goodbye in the alleyway. By her usual timeline, it was way too soon to text. In New York, she'd give a guy she'd hooked up with at least a week. She was no clinging vine. And when she did check in, she always kept the tone light and the expectations low. But now she didn't have unlimited time to see how things would play out. Nikos was a craving she couldn't ignore, like knowing she had peanut butter–chip ice cream in the freezer. She couldn't hold off for twenty-four hours, let alone a week. But would her eagerness scare him? She was used to pushing guys away, not reeling them in!

As she deliberated, her phone lit up; it was a text from Nikos.

Olivia let out a massive sigh of relief. Okay, she could still steer this boat. She didn't have to act like she'd lost her mind. Even if maybe, she had.

I've been thinking about you all day

Oh yeah? What have you been thinking?

Can't say—phone would explode, thoughts are too hot…

She blushed from head to toe with pleasure. His next text appeared before she could respond.

…was that cheesy?

Absolutely. But very appreciated and reciprocated

Any chance I might see you again? Not just for hot stuff

Olivia shrieked out loud, thankful she was alone.

I'd like that—and hot stuff would be fun—just saying

Anything you want. When?

Was asking him to be her plus-one for the wedding be too much? She wavered. Maybe he wasn't available; she didn't know his work schedule. Olivia didn't want to take a big, vulnerable risk if his attendance wasn't even possible.

Maybe see you tomorrow? What's your schedule?

I'll check and text you in the AM

Okay. She'd hold off on the big ask until then.
Apparently, she wasn't the only one eager for this, whatever it was, to continue.

Sounds good…

…Good night Nikos

Kalinixta, Olivia

THURSDAY MORNING—WEDDING DAY

OLIVIA BASKED IN another glorious Mediterranean sunrise. She had awoken in a state of euphoria. It was going to be a fantastic day. Her best friend was getting married. And Olivia was head over heels for her own guy, who was surely evidence that magic existed in the world. Life was good. So good. Maybe it would only last for another day or two…maybe once the pixie dust cleared, she'd be back to her ho-hum reality, but in the beautiful sun-drenched morning, she didn't care. She'd enjoy it while it lasted.

While simultaneously drying her hair and dancing around with pent-up joy, there was a knock on her hotel room door. She paused her music and pulled on the hotel bathrobe, thinking there was nothing so luxurious as a plush, complimentary robe.

In the hall, a uniformed attendant revealed a cart piled high with wide, shallow cardboard bakery boxes.

"Madame." He nodded. "I am to deliver these to you."

Olivia waited while he stacked the boxes on the credenza. Nikos was such a gem. A keeper. What man would bake wedding cookies for someone who had been a perfect stranger only thirty-six hours earlier?

Well. They certainly weren't strangers anymore. An infusion of heat stirred Olivia's entire body, remembering their time on the boat. Damn, her knees literally went weak. How soon could she see him again? Would he agree to be her last-

minute date for the wedding? She pictured his appreciative look when he saw her in the bronze gown. Her fantasy
morphed to imagining them dancing together at the reception...and then returning to her hotel room where he could
take off her dress and treat her to another round of indulgent
lovemaking. It was almost too much to contemplate. She felt
like she might explode out of her skin.

She had no sooner picked up her hair dryer again than her
phone buzzed. Speak of the devil.

Did cookies arrive?

YES so amazing! they look delicious thank you...

...I can't even tell you how happy you've made me

She didn't care. She was utterly shameless at this point,
rapid-fire texting. She wanted him again. Badly.

I'd rather show you my appreciation—you around?

There was a longer pause than Olivia would have liked.

Finishing up at the gym—could stop briefly before work

How briefly? you like to go fast. just saying

Be there in 5

When he knocked approximately three minutes later, Olivia
threw the door open to discover Nikos, glistening with sweat,
his hair damp under his hoodie. The evidence of his workout
only made him more appealing as he flashed that devastat-

ing smile she'd been dreaming of. Good Lord, she wanted to devour him.

"Did you run all the way here?"

"Figured I'd extend the workout."

Olivia bit her tongue. Oh, she had plans to extend his workout. "Come on in…"

He noticed the towering boxes and lifted the lid of the top one. "Are the cookies good?"

Why would he doubt it?

"The cookies are exactly what I needed, what Maggie wanted. You don't even understand how important this is."

He smiled again with such sweetness that it made her ache. "It wasn't a big deal."

Olivia had to correct that perception. "Nikos, it is a big deal. Like me, Maggie was raised by a single mom. Her mom and grandma died before she graduated. They never got to celebrate her international internship. They never got to meet her fiancé. They couldn't imagine her living this crazy, glamorous life." Olivia paused, taking a moment to compose her emotions. "The cookies are the connection to people from her childhood, like me. That's important to me. I can't afford to give Maggie an expensive gift, but this means so much more. It's what is truly important. Does that make sense? You made this possible."

He swallowed. "I had no idea," he admitted. "And I admit I did it for selfish reasons. You see, this incredible girl knocked me off my feet, and I had to convince her to get to know me…"

She rolled her eyes.

"Too cheesy again?"

"Cheesy but effective." Olivia smiled, moved closer, and placed her hands on his warm chest.

His eyes darkened with desire. "I don't know if you want to get too close—I just came from the gym…" He made an unconvincing attempt to warn her off.

She ignored his warning and pulled him into a demanding kiss.

While their previous physical encounter had been framed in uncertainty, this time it was obvious that they both agreed exactly where they wanted to go, even if they didn't have much time to get there.

The belt came undone, and her robe gaped open.

"Oh my God," Nikos murmured, sliding his hands under the garment in appreciation of her naked body. "You smell so good."

"Fancy hotel shampoo," she admitted.

He buried his face in her neck, his hands roving, pulling her closer.

She peeled the damp sweatshirt over his head. He nudged off his running shoes as she backed him toward her still-unmade bed.

"I should maybe put the Do Not Disturb on the door…" she murmured as he slid the robe off her shoulders.

"They'll knock…"

He dropped his running shorts and collapsed like a fallen angel onto the bed.

She waited, wanting to hear his sultry voice issue an invitation once again.

"Come here," he whispered. God, she loved those words when he said them.

Tossing her hair over her shoulder, Olivia settled astride his gloriously chiseled body. Eyes locked with his, she leaned forward and snagged a condom she'd strategically placed on the nightstand.

"Looks like I've got you right where I want you," she murmured. "Maybe it's your turn to hang on and let me drive."

From the fervent look on his face, he required no convincing. "I yield."

She rubbed against him, watching the tremors of pleasure play across his face. Finally, sensing that she'd tormented him enough, she ripped the foil packet open and rolled the condom over him. Holding his smoldering gaze, she sank down and reveled in his groan of pleasure.

Moving her hips ever so slightly, she leaned forward, her hair a curtain around his face. She touched her forehead to his. As he brought his mouth onto her skin, she whispered, "Is this going to be a fast or slow ride?"

She felt him smile against her chest. "Whatever you like—you're the driver..."

But despite her intent to prolong their encounter, her body had other ideas. His hands gripped and squeezed as she picked up the pace. Gasping for breath, just when she thought they both were at the point of no return, he abruptly lifted her off his body. She was momentarily confused until she felt him slide down beneath her. Every nerve ending in her body tingled in anticipation. Gripping her hips, he pulled her onto his scalding mouth. If she had thought he was masterful at pleasing her with his fingers, it was nothing compared to what he did with his tongue.

Relentless, he teased her until she absolutely combusted. But before she could collapse boneless onto the bed, he knelt behind her. With her head cradled in her arms on the pillow, she was too raw to do anything but open herself to him. He drove home, the connection pushing her beyond any pleasure she'd ever known. She was coherent of nothing but the sensation of his body filling hers.

"Nikos."

Between gasps, she pleadingly whispered his name. She wasn't sure she could withstand the building crescendo. But she did. And when she shattered for a second time, he exploded with her. He clutched her tightly, and together, they trembled.

As the sensation faded, he collapsed, depleted, along her back and with unintelligible murmurs of satisfaction, dropped sideways, taking her with him. Nikos held her, spooned from nape to thighs. He sighed.

"This wasn't… I mean… I know my text…and your text said…" he murmured.

"What?" she wondered. "What are you trying to say?"

"I wanted to make sure you liked the cookies. I wanted to see you. I didn't come to your room just for this."

"I hope you still managed to enjoy it."

He snorted into her hair. "That's putting it mildly. Good God."

They lay in silence, facing the window, the sparkling vista of Monte Carlo sprawled below them. Olivia swallowed hard. Their lovemaking, whatever physical magic was happening between them, was extraordinary. Unprecedented. Normally, she'd be content with that alone, thrilled by it. But now, wrapped in Nikos's arms, she had a sudden gut-clenching epiphany. She, Olivia Keller, wanted more from him. His sweet words delighted rather than horrified her. Now her biggest terror was knowing her involvement with Nikos would come to a crashing end the moment she stepped on the plane to New York. How was she going to bear it?

Somehow, without realizing it, she'd let this beautiful, kind, and glorious man slip under her well-honed defenses. She suspected this was how people fell in love. Unbelievably, she realized she might be ready for it.

"Yesterday morning, you said we needed to talk," Olivia prompted. She now felt confident enough to ask. Unlike her father, she couldn't believe Nikos would let her down. "Should I ask what you wanted to talk about?"

Before he could reply, Nikos heard his phone buzz. He rolled away from Olivia's delectable body and leaned precariously over the edge of the bed, trying to reach his discarded shorts. No luck. He swung his legs to the floor and rooted through their clothing to locate the phone. It was Bryson.

"Ya."

"Where are you? You said you'd be back from the gym

thirty minutes ago. Eero wants you on the portable driving SIM to review the team's final adjustments to the car before you do the track walk. And I've got new content assignments. And we've got the sponsor reception this afternoon. You've got to get over here. Aleko is losing it."

"Good to know," Nikos murmured, standing naked in front of the window. He'd briefly slipped his handlers, but three days before a race, every movement he made was part of a carefully orchestrated and scheduled preparation. On the streets below, he could see the temporary race structures swarming with people, a hive of industrious bees, all doing their part. He should feel guilty for shrugging off his responsibilities, but somehow, he didn't.

"I'll be there shortly. Tell Aleko to relax."

This was likely one of the few times he'd be able to steal a few moments with Olivia before she left. He'd already concluded he wanted to pursue a relationship that went beyond their sizzling physical encounters. Her impassioned explanation of why the cookies were so important only confirmed his decision.

Unfortunately, there simply wasn't enough time to confess and explain his identity.

She appeared to have absolutely no clue that he wasn't a hotel employee. However, pre-race hoopla was escalating to the point that it would be impossible to ignore. Would she connect the dots? Or would she remain oblivious until he had sufficient time to explain? When she called him to her room, he had planned to tell her the truth. But then her robe gaped open…and coherent thought had flown out of his head.

Now his obligations demanded him. He didn't have time to drop any bombshells. He could only hope the wedding would keep Olivia distracted until he could carve out another hour with her to come clean. But when might that occur?

He turned to her, her skin elegant against the stark white sheets.

"About what I said yesterday, that we needed to talk…"

She rolled over and gave him a questioning look. Frustration gripped him. An insistent voice in his head argued that he just tell her, timing be damned. But it would be messy.

He concentrated on reclaiming his clothing and dressing, not looking at her until he was ready to speak. But what exactly should he say?

She interrupted his thoughts. "Would you want to come to Maggie's wedding with me this afternoon?"

The invitation surprised him.

"It's just that…" he began. "You need to understand…the next few days…"

He looked up, trying to mask his bittersweet disappointment. But when he saw her stricken look, he realized she misunderstood.

Her innocent invitation was so far beyond the realm of possibility—and exactly why it was time for him to be done with racing. He needed to reclaim his life so that when a charming woman asked him to accompany her to an important event, he could do so. And maybe someday he could attend without anyone staring or interrupting to ask for an autograph. His refusal was not about her.

"I'd love to. Really. I'd love to go with you. It would be great to meet your friend and see the cookie display…"

"But?" She sighed. "This is obviously a no."

"I can't," he said, willing her to believe he truly regretted refusing. "I have to work. The next few days are insane."

She sighed while he tied his shoes. "Yeah, I get it. I'm sure with the race coming up, you're slammed."

For a moment, he panicked, but then it made sense. Right. She thought he worked at the hotel. Indeed, the Grand Prix did increase demands on the hotel staff.

But he wasn't on the staff. He was an F1 driver with contractual obligations. He had to be realistic. Before the race, there was no way he could carve out time to do justice to the conversation they needed to have. It was ridiculous to imagine it. His hands were tied. All he could do was hope she didn't stumble onto the truth. But maybe she might stick around a little longer. Was that too much to ask?

"Any chance you might delay your departure for a day?" he suggested. "I will be free Sunday night. It will be late, but we could have dinner. Maybe decide when we might see each other again. If you want to see me again. Because I definitely want to keep seeing you."

There. He'd said it.

Her face fell. "Nikos, by Sunday night, I will be back in New York to go to work on Monday. I'm leaving Saturday."

His gut clenched. "There is no way you might…"

He caught himself. Reality hit hard. What was he asking her to do? Reorder her life? For what? To share one more night so he could confess…and then fly to Spain for the next race? And onto the Segno Rosso headquarters in Italy? Then Montreal. Followed by a tour of cities across the world. He wouldn't be free until mid-December. How could he ask her to do what he could not?

"Olivia…"

She got up, retrieved the discarded bathrobe, and sank into the chair in front of the window. She crossed her legs, ankle hooked behind her calf, and folded her arms protectively.

"I guess this is the problem with travel flings, huh?" Glancing out the window, she looked like she was trying to play it cool and nonchalant, but he suspected it was a facade.

That nearly broke him. He couldn't leave her with the wrong impression. "I don't think of this as a fling. Whatever is happening between us, this isn't a fling."

His phone buzzed again. He ignored it, but she noticed.

"Okay, okay. I understand you need to go. People want you."

"Yeah."

"Nikos…" she blurted. "I am here until Saturday. If you have any time at all, I'd love the chance to get together again."

Okay. Somehow, despite the inconvenience, he had to make it happen. Even if he had to track her down in the wee hours after the wedding, when he probably should be sleeping. He couldn't just let it go. Couldn't just let her go.

"I would love to see you again, too. And it doesn't have to involve sex," he said.

She grinned slyly. "I don't know. The sex is pretty great, so why not take advantage of it while we can? As for long distance, we can figure it out as we go along. If that's what you want."

Long distance? As they went along? She also wanted this to continue?

"I do want to. I really do. What did you call it? Fly by the seat of our pants?"

She smiled brilliantly. "Exactly."

Desire flared once again. He was still savoring the taste of her. God, if he had even another half an hour to spare, he would take her right back to that disheveled bed and prove that his interest would last beyond the weekend, beyond the end of the season. If they could just figure out how to make it work until then.

"I would be thrilled to spend more time with you while you're here. Doing whatever you'd like to do. I'll see what I can work out."

She flashed him an endearing grin.

But he had dallied long enough. He didn't want to say goodbye, so he hovered, leaning over her chair, capturing her between his arms. Her gold-flecked gaze held his, straightforward and clear. How would those luminous eyes regard him when she knew the truth?

"I meant what I said about my contract being up in December. I could come to New York."

Her body softened, and she blushed, almost shyly. She was many things, this woman, but he didn't think shy was part of her equation.

"You do understand that I live in a tiny studio apartment.

Smaller than this hotel room. You'd have to stay very, very close to me." She turned her obvious embarrassment about her small apartment into a flirtatious invitation.

"I would be delighted," he murmured before kissing her, sweet and tender. He made a mental note to tell Bryson to look at property in New York City.

He allowed himself one more kiss and then left her, the door clicking softly behind him.

He showered, dressed, and then endured Bryson and Aleko's directives. But all the while, his thoughts were full of Olivia, the sun catching her hair when they were out on the water. The noises she made when he moved in her body. The frank appreciation she'd shown for their physical encounters. The implication that she might want their relationship to extend beyond a short-term fling.

Something had changed in him the moment he met her. Some switch had flipped. Her appreciation for his help in procuring the cookies had clinched it. It wasn't about his money. He'd help her create something that, by her own admission, money couldn't buy.

Now, for the first time in a very long time, he was tempted to build a relationship that wasn't about convenience or proximity because a relationship with Olivia Keller offered neither. But it might be something real.

However, as the courtesy car transported him through the crowded streets, his confidence began to unravel. He should have found the time to tell her the truth. Could they sustain a relationship once she knew the truth? And would it be worth the effort? For that matter, was there something truly special about Olivia, or was he reacting so powerfully to her merely because the end of his career loomed? Had she simply shown up at a vulnerable moment? He didn't think so. Intuitively, he recognized something unique about her and what they might share. But how could he be sure? He'd misjudged a woman before and been nearly destroyed in the process. The transition out of racing was going to be difficult enough—would it help or hurt trying to simultaneously build a relationship?

As he walked toward the paddock, he wondered, could a relationship ever be more important than racing?

That astounding thought stopped him dead in his tracks. Literally.

Reality kicked in. What the hell was he thinking?

By standing still, he encouraged the fans who called his name and held their phones to record his approach. He needed to keep moving. At the moment, he was still a driver. He was still very much a part of the show.

The situation with Olivia was a lot to consider. He wanted it—damn, he wanted it—but maybe it was all too much, too soon? He ran his hand through his hair without thinking. The female fans staring at him gave a collective sigh, a thousand camera lenses clicked, and he knew his mindless gesture would be featured on a million social media accounts within moments.

Could he balance the current realities of his very public life on the racing circuit with building a private long-term, long-distance relationship? And what would Olivia make of all this anyhow? Could she handle it?

Almost without realizing it, he had arrived at the Segno Rosso headquarters. He took a deep breath. The familiar, managed chaos of the garage and team center, where everyone was intent on their pre-race preparations, immediately consoled him and brought him back into focus. His spiraling thoughts slammed to a halt as abruptly as a race coming under a red flag.

What was he doing? Why was he focused on five months in the future? Nothing good happened when he got too far ahead of himself. He'd always raced one segment, one turn, one straightaway at a time. Not getting sidetracked had served him well.

Nikos took a deep breath. Maybe Aleko was right. Tying

himself in knots before a race, being so distracted...this was dangerous. It wasn't smart. It wasn't fair to his team. People relied on him. Eero, Juan-Carlos. The Segno Rosso engineers and mechanics. The pit crew. His trainers and nutritionists. The marketing team. The sponsors. The fans. Bryson and Aleko, for all that they put up with him. All these people, right here, right now, weighed against a nebulous possibility with a girl who intrigued him but whom he barely knew.

She was leaving on Saturday. She'd mentioned staying connected long-distance, but that might be unrealistically well-intentioned. She might get back home and rekindle with her New York boyfriend, flick the off switch back on. There was no way to predict the future. His best approach would be to give his all to winning the Monaco race and nailing the remainder of the season. Until then, he had to hold off thinking about Olivia Keller, no matter how earth-shattering their connection. Come December, if she was still interested, he could refocus on how a potential relationship could fit into his new life. Whatever that was.

Willing himself to jam his emotions into a tight mental box, Nikos drew upon the discipline he'd cultivated over his long career. He had a job to do, in this moment, in this race. Fantasizing about the next chapter would get him nowhere. Olivia, enticing as she was, would have to wait. He had Media Day and a race to prepare for.

Maggie and Stefano's afternoon wedding was stunningly elegant. It was everything Olivia wanted for her dearest friend. And while having Nikos at her side would have been a pleasure, focusing exclusively on Maggie was also a gift. Still, Olivia hoped there would be at least one more chance to see Nikos before she got on the plane for New York. And after that? Who knew? Their conversation that morning hinted at an unanticipated and tempting future.

When the ceremony concluded, the guests mingled in the

ornate gilt ballroom. Olivia joined Maggie, Stefano, and his family for photos as the ever-organized Céline moved them from one spectacular hotel setting to another.

"We need to go to the patio right now," the wedding co-ordinator insisted. "There is a Formula 1 reception that will take place there shortly. We only have a few minutes before the patio is closed off."

Olivia trotted after the bride, carrying both of their bouquets. Céline, working from her notebook, directed the photographer in rapid French. Maggie and Stefano were instructed to pose for a series of shots by the palms with Monte Carlo as the photogenic background. The newlyweds didn't seem to notice the scenery, however. They were in post-nuptial bliss, positively glowing with love. It was adorable.

Olivia stood with Uncle Klaus and Aunt Kiki, waiting patiently to be summoned for their assigned photos.

"The cookies were such a fabulous touch!" Aunt Kiki whispered to Olivia. "Such a unique tradition. Margot was so appreciative that you would go to such lengths."

"I love Maggie. I'd do anything for her. And I had help with the cookies," Olivia admitted.

Olivia found herself unexpectedly emotional at the heartfelt compliment and the thought of the person who had made the cookie table possible. Weddings made one sentimental, she supposed. It was astounding to recognize that her overflowing feelings weren't only because Nikos physically set her aflame. He also tempted her to rethink longstanding doubts about walking down the aisle. It was hard to believe a whirlwind connection could provoke such desires, but there she was, contemplating a real relationship. Falling in love. Being vulnerable. Trusting someone with her whole heart. She'd never imagined any of these things for herself.

Although she and Maggie had planned their nuptial celebrations from the time they were little girls, those childish plans had focused on the accoutrements of the day—the gowns, the menus, the decor. Their prospective grooms had been vague: tuxedo-clad mysteries overshadowed by other more vividly imagined details. But now, watching Maggie and her husband—husband!—kiss and laugh, Olivia felt an aching sense of nostalgia. Somehow, meeting Nikos and witnessing Maggie and Stefano's wedding resurrected those innocent and long-buried girlhood dreams.

When had Olivia stopped dreaming of a happily-ever-after? That was easy. Probably the umpteenth time her father let her down. Left her and her mother to their own devices; left them to muddle through, terrified they couldn't keep their heads above water. Claimed he couldn't afford to support either of them when, in fact, he was lavishing gifts on a steady stream of mistresses. Olivia had learned to assume that every word out of the man's mouth was likely a lie. Because it was. You couldn't lie your way into a happily-ever-after, so Olivia had been convinced that happily-ever-after didn't exist.

Not surprisingly, she'd had been forced to rely on herself. Not expect help from anyone. And she'd done fine. Not quite happily-ever-after, but fine. Sufficient.

Until Nikos.

Olivia had never met a guy who would selflessly care for her like he did. Her relationships had been with guys who, by mutual agreement, stayed at arm's length. They respected her independence…but they couldn't be bothered to go out of their way for her. Everyone assumed that both parties would benefit from firm boundaries. They were very cognizant of the danger of becoming too reliant on one another. That was how relationships went, right?

Olivia certainly had never expected a guy to show the same kind of reciprocal selflessness she and Maggie shared in their longstanding friendship. She had never met a guy she could imagine capable of a similar unwavering commitment.

Until Nikos.

As a perfect stranger, he had patiently escorted her all over town and asked nothing in return except a tolerance for high speed. He had stayed up all night baking cookies for people he'd never met. He had asked questions and then listened—really listened!—to her answers. He responded to her cues as their physical relationship unfolded. As a lover, he proved generous and passionate…no, he was downright extraordinary. In the whirlwind days they'd spent together, Nikos embodied the kind of man she hadn't known existed. Unbelievably, she might even be falling in love with him.

But she had to leave in thirty-six hours. Was she crazy to get on the plane?

What if she didn't leave? Would she be crazy to stay?

He'd ask if she might delay her departure. Changing her flight based on a guy she'd only met would be a major leap of faith. Not to mention insanely expensive. But December was a long time to wait to see him again. A lot could happen before December. He could forget all about her.

Olivia grappled with her churning, conflicting instincts. Should she go all in or keep her guard up and expectations low?

"We're going to have to wrap this up. We can finish pictures in the ballroom," Céline said, interrupting Olivia's thoughts. Maintenance workers had arrived with a cherry picker, which they maneuvered next to one of the light poles. As they worked to secure a rolled-up banner, Olivia noticed other people entering the patio.

She took Maggie's bouquet and followed the wedding coordinator toward the oncoming group.

Olivia glanced up…and did a double take. Nikos was one of the people walking toward her. It was as if her fond thoughts had conjured him. She felt a rush of warmth. She really might be falling in love with him. She'd never felt so energized by a mere glimpse of someone. He was unique.

"Nikos!" she called, smiling and waving the flowers jubilantly overhead.

He looked up at the sound of her voice. Even though his

eyes were hidden by sunglasses, she was sure she saw pleasure on his face. It delighted her. Perhaps she could take a quick moment and introduce him to Maggie. Would it be premature to introduce him as her boyfriend? She flushed at the thought of it.

But as she opened her mouth to call the bride, Nikos's expression changed. Now his face reflected some other emotion Olivia couldn't quite decode…

"My goodness!" exclaimed Uncle Klaus. "That's Nikos Leonikaros! And I thought you weren't a racing fan!"

"What?" Olivia asked stupidly. "Who?"

Three things happened at once.

One: A gaggle of women—racing fans, based on their apparel—burst forth from a side door and sprinted toward Nikos, two security guards in pursuit.

Two: The men who had been in the service corridor where she first met Nikos—the burly old man and the smooth talker—flanked Nikos protectively on either side, shielding him from the women headed his way.

Three: The workers on the cherry picker unfurled a gigantic banner. Astoundingly, it depicted… Nikos. But in the picture, he was wearing a red Segno Rosso racing suit and holding a helmet. Number 19.

It made no sense. None of it made any sense.

Olivia stood frozen, dumbly, trying to process what she was seeing.

The security guards intercepted the rowdy fans and steered them back toward the hotel.

Céline murmured apologetically and gestured for the wedding party to make themselves scarce. Quickly. The family complied, even though Uncle Klaus kept sneaking curious glances.

Olivia remained rooted to the spot, her eyes locked on Nikos's inscrutable face. He, too, seemed incapable of movement.

What the hell was going on?

The workers unrolled more banners featuring different F1 drivers. Why was Nikos depicted as one of them?

What. The. Hell?

Olivia's mind turned slowly, replaying her interactions with him over the past few days. The vagueness about his job. The high-speed bike ride. The avoidance of crowds. The expensive sunglasses. She'd been so focused on their intense connection, she hadn't noticed that his story didn't quite add up. Some profound realization nibbled at the edge of her consciousness.

She heard someone else calling his name, demanding an autograph.

Who would want the autograph of a hotel baker?

Surely he hadn't been misrepresenting himself the whole time…surely not. He said he was a baker, not an F1 driver. Right?

The thirty-foot banner strongly suggested otherwise.

Olivia gasped with sudden comprehension.

With picture-perfect slow-motion clarity, in her mind's eye, she saw him on the boat, stripping off his shirt. His beautiful back with its many tattoos. So many racetrack tattoos. Every single one with a date.

The date he won each race.

Everything clicked into place.

Good God.

The utterly unbelievable truth could not be denied. She'd been a total idiot. How had she not seen it?

She clutched her fists against her gut. It was good that she'd eaten very little that day; otherwise, she would have puked on the spot. She could barely breathe. She could barely see. But she'd be damned before she keeled over, damned before she let him drift away in his sea of lies. Blindly, Olivia stormed in his direction.

"Olivia!" Céline cried out. "Please, come this way…"

She ignored the wedding coordinator. "Get out of my way."

"No, no, not here, you cannot talk to him here…" said the burly man in a heavy Greek accent.

The bodyguard moved to block her. She scowled, determined to come face-to-face with Nikos, who had obviously prevaricated from the moment they'd met. He was as big a liar as her father. Maybe bigger. The biggest liar she'd ever met. And that was saying something.

Damn it, how had she been so stupid, stupid, stupid? She knew better than to trust a man. Any man. Especially one who had appeared too good to be true.

"Give us a minute…" she heard Nikos insist as he turned in her direction.

He grimaced in either guilt or shock; Olivia wasn't sure which. But she had no sympathy for whatever he was feeling. Liars never wanted to deal with the consequences of their lies. She'd learned that the hard way, and she wasn't going to let him off the hook. Her father had tried to worm his way back into her good graces, only to lie again. Lies begat more lies. Not a chance she'd allow Nikos to lie to her again. Ever.

The older man refused to budge, so Olivia tried to circumvent him. He placed a restraining hand on her arm. It was a mistake.

"Aleko!" Nikos warned.

Olivia lived in New York City. No one touched her without her permission.

"Get. Your. Hand. Off. Me. *Now*," she growled. Loudly.

"Aleko!" Nikos repeated. He felt utterly helpless as the situation devolved into chaos. "Let her *go*!"

Aleko relented. Olivia thrust her face close to Nikos's. She was frighteningly, blisteringly angry. Rage emanated from her entire body. He could see it in every pore.

"I can explain. Please let me explain." He tried to forestall whatever she was about to say. Of course, her accusations would all be true. He couldn't deny any of it. His gut roiled with guilt.

"Nikos! I do not understand!" Olivia hissed. "Who the hell are you?"

"It doesn't matter. It changes nothing between us. Nothing changes," he desperately pleaded. "I wanted to tell you. Let's take this someplace else…"

"What are you talking about? It changes everything!"

Nikos foolishly attempted to touch Olivia's arm. She shrugged him off as violently as she'd shaken off Aleko.

Yet another group of fans managed to get past the overwhelmed security guards and surged toward them, but Olivia stubbornly held her ground.

He broke into a sickening, ice-cold sweat. Dear God, he needed her to move, to take this conversation somewhere, anywhere, else. Why wouldn't she move? Didn't she understand they could not have this confrontation publicly? He knew the social media storm that would ensue. He'd been forced to weather that kind of grotesque exposure before and would not do it again. Ever. For anyone.

"What the hell is going on?" she ground out through gritted teeth. "Tell me who you really are!"

The answer was as blatant as the gigantic banner and the Segno Rosso faithful clamoring for his attention. Calling his name. Demanding autographs.

Nikos's stomach clenched as he leaned closer to Olivia. He dropped his voice so only she could hear. Her breath was heartbreakingly warm, but he felt like he'd taken a knife to the chest. How had it come to this?

The answer was obvious. He'd been a fool. He should have found the time to explain. He never should have let the ruse go so far. How had he imagined he could fly under the radar in Monaco, of all places? On a race weekend? There had to be a trophy for that kind of wishful thinking, that kind of hubris.

"Please let me explain."

"You lied to me," she seethed. "I cannot, will not deal with men who lie."

"Olivia…"

"A hotel baker?"

He froze, guilty as charged. What was there to say?

"Simple question—is that you on that banner? Yes or no?"

"Yes."

"So, you lied to me. Say it to my face. Say it. Take off your sunglasses, look me in the eyes, and say, 'I am a liar.'"

Keenly aware of the fans closing in, Nikos felt a molten core of anger building at her demand. Why? Why was this happening? Again. With Olivia, he'd hoped to avoid the ravenous public consumption of his most intimate experiences. Yet here was an explosive confrontation. Like Athena all over again. He was blindsided by shame and frustration, spilling out for everyone to witness. Was privacy too much to ask? Of anyone? Ever? And why couldn't Olivia listen to him for two seconds? Could she not grasp that his ruse wasn't intended to hurt her? It was a white lie that, if anything, had allowed them to get to know each other better. If they could just get off the damn patio, he could explain. Or was she reveling in this public smackdown, just like Athena?

He squeezed his eyes shut, trying to find some internal peace and sanity. But for that, he needed to escape the tumult. The intrusiveness of the fans, the incessant video recording and photo taking, Aleko's shouts, the fury in Olivia's face, the hovering sponsors… Nikos wanted to wrap his arms over his head and howl.

He was at the end of his rope. He had to get off the patio immediately, away from salacious onlookers. Away from the rabid audience. Even if Olivia refused.

He made one last attempt. "Olivia, please. We cannot have this conversation here. There are too many fans around."

She inhaled a sharp breath, and a wave of pronounced pain washed over her face. "Why? Are you embarrassed by me?"

"What?" The question caught him off guard. It was so unexpectedly ridiculous that it was baffling.

"Are. You. Embarrassed. By. Me?" she repeated in a strangled voice, slowly emphasizing each word.

He didn't know how to answer.

"Is that why you didn't tell me who you are? Why you wanted me alone on the boat? So no one would discover you were hooking up with someone like me? Some random American girl. Am I not good enough for you, Mr. Celebrity Formula 1 Driver?"

"What?" he repeated, dumbfounded. Good Lord, this was one argument he'd never anticipated. "No, no! What are you talking about? Why would I be embarrassed by you? Far from it! I didn't...don't want you to be the focus of attention. To be surrounded by all this. To have to deal with the intrusiveness. Wherever I go, people want a piece of me. They follow me. I just wanted some space for us to get to know each other without complications. Privately. Away from this circus. To make it easier on you."

"Oh, get over yourself," Olivia snapped. "You lied to me, *lied*, and now you are suggesting that you only lied to protect me. Stop it. That is some total narcissistic crap right there. And believe me, I know narcissism when I see it. All that flattery, all those cheesy compliments and pickup lines. All lies, right?"

"No, *no*! Don't you understand?!" Niko begged, trying to modulate his voice. "People will record this...our conversation. Every word. You don't get it. You don't want that to happen. Trust me. By tomorrow, we will be all over social media!"

"So what?" Olivia retorted loudly, throwing her arms in the air as an invitation to all onlookers. "What do I care what people record and post on social media? I'm not ashamed of what I'm doing! Are you?"

That did it. The agony of every piece of mortifying content Athena had ever posted with the sole intent to hurt him rose like bile in his throat. Never again.

"I will not do this," Nikos hissed at Olivia. "Not here, not now. I will not."

"Well, that's too bad," Olivia countered. "It's now or never, buddy. Because after this moment, I never want to see you again. Ever."

Her words were a visceral blow.

"Nikolaes!" Aleko warned.

"Now!" Bryson demanded.

"Olivia!" the wedding coordinator pleaded.

Olivia whirled on her heel before Nikos could reply.

Five hours, one wedding reception, and at least two entire bottles of champagne later, Olivia still hadn't reconciled Nikos's betrayal or recovered from the ugly argument. The whole situation made no sense. Why had he lied about being a baker in the first place? That was just strange. A simple *I don't work at the hotel* would have sufficed. And then, when they spent the day together chasing down pastries, why hadn't he come clean at some appropriate moment? And why had he perpetuated his lie when they were together all day on the boat? In addition to getting to know one another quite intimately, they had talked about everything under the sun. She asked about his tattoos. That would have been a perfect opportunity to confess his real identity.

Not only had he been dishonest, but he'd also gone all in with the deception, made the big splashy gesture, just like her father. Where had the cookies come from? The suspiciously well-produced video of him baking cookies? What was that all about? Was he just a pathological liar?

Or was it a celebrity thing? He'd taken serious pains to keep her in the dark and hidden from his adoring public. Was it a way to keep his female fan base engaged, encourage them to fantasize that they, too, might have a chance with him? Lies to flatter other women? That, too, was straight out of her father's playbook.

Olivia had no clue.

Worst of all, she couldn't talk to Maggie about it. The bride had other important things on her mind, namely enjoying her wedding reception. Olivia kept a brittle smile pasted on her face. She wasn't going to ruin the most important day of her best friend's life with relationship drama.

So, Olivia drank champagne and ate appetizers. She drank champagne and chatted up her dinner-table companions. She drank champagne and ate cake, purposefully avoiding the cookie table. She drank champagne and hit the dance floor. But when one of the Euro bros got a little too handsy and tried to kiss her while they were dancing, Olivia broke. Summoning her last shred of dignity, she retreated from the ballroom.

Maggie found her fifteen minutes later, in the restroom, splashing cold water onto her face. "You're going to ruin your makeup, Liv."

"I think I'm beyond caring about that, Mags."

Maggie enfolded Olivia in a consoling hug and then handed Olivia a Peanut Butter Blossom cookie. "Are you going to tell me about it or spend the rest of the night pretending everything is fine?"

That did it. The emotions Olivia had repressed all evening poured forth in a wave of big, gasping, ugly sobs. Maggie made shushing noises and rubbed her back.

"Oh my God, I'm getting mascara on your dress. I'm so sorry. I'm ruining your reception."

"Olivia Keller." Maggie held her at arm's length. "How long have we known each other? And for that matter, how many middle and high school dances did we spend in the bathroom crying over some boy? Why should my wedding be any different?"

Olivia snuffled and broke off the Hershey Kiss. She ate it, then took a bite of cookie. "But I shouldn't do this to you during your wedding reception. I'm so sorry. I did not want to be a distraction. I just wanted you to have your cookies and have the perfect wedding."

Olivia shoved the rest of the cookie into her mouth to keep from crying again. She hoped to keep the cookie and the champagne down. She'd had a lot of champagne.

"Olivia, it might be my wedding, but you are my best friend. You tripped the boy who made fun of my braces at the ice rink. You held my hair when I threw up at that awful fraternity formal. You told off the guy on the cruise who wouldn't take no for an answer. Do you think I'm going to leave you to deal with this all by yourself?"

"I don't even know what this is, what just happened. I don't understand any of it," Olivia wailed.

"Oh, Liv. Only you could accidentally hook up with the most famous driver in Europe and not know it."

Olivia moaned in embarrassment.

Maggie shook her head in awed disbelief. "Your fight with Nikos gave the wedding guests way more entertainment than they expected. Uncle Klaus is really impressed, by the way. He's a big Segno Rosso fan."

"Then tell Uncle Klaus to hook up with Nikos," Olivia grumbled. "Mags, I feel so stupid. How could I be so stupid? You won't believe it, but for a hot moment, I thought Nikos was for real. After all these years of assuming every guy was as big a liar as my dad, for once, I thought maybe I'd been wrong. Maybe a trustworthy man wasn't some mythical creature and I'd found a unicorn in Monte Carlo. Maggie, I felt it. I thought he was my Meant-to-Be, my M2B."

Maggie smiled fondly at the shorthand code they'd written all over their notebooks when they were twelve years old and agonizing over celebrity crushes.

"Does Harry Styles know you've thrown him over for a Greek F1 driver?" Maggie asked.

Olivia snorted.

"But Olivia, the real question is what are you going to do about Nikos?"

Olivia had no idea.

FRIDAY MORNING

It was remarkable the difference twenty-four hours could make. And not for the better.

Yesterday she'd leapt from the bed and danced around the room, basking in the Monaco sunlight. She'd indulged in incredibly passionate lovemaking with a delicious man.

Now the sky was gray, and rain dulled the city below. Her hotel sheets were stale and sweaty, the goddess-like bronze gown crumpled in a ball on the floor, an unfortunate casualty. She'd worn the dress with Nikos in mind. He was still infuriatingly sexy—but not who he claimed to be. Why were guys such rats? Liars, liars, liars, every last one of them.

She turned on the TV. The weather forecast showed increasing rain and thunderstorms. That squashed her plan to spend this final day in Monaco basking on the beach. Then again, she left her bikini bottoms on the boat. She didn't even want to think about why she took them off. So much for meeting the perfect guy. So much for sunbathing on the Mediterranean shore. The whole trip had gone from debacle to devastation.

Olivia dragged herself to the bathroom, thinking that at this point, like a vampire, she couldn't withstand direct sunlight anyhow.

A shower and a few aspirin marginally improved her physical state. She bundled herself in the snuggly comfort of the hotel robe and contemplated whether her stomach could withstand food. Did she have the energy to get dressed and leave the room, or should she shamelessly splurge and order room service?

She decided the situation warranted a splurge.

However, before she could place the overpriced order, there was a knock at the door. Olivia blessed her best friend as the breakfast trolley was wheeled in.

Who but Mags would even think about anyone else's needs the morning after her own wedding? Who but someone who truly loved Olivia would recognize that breakfast pastries and strong coffee were potent antidotes to hangovers and emotional chaos? Eating away her sorrow was a solid strategy.

As she eyed the pastry selection, another employee entered, bearing a gigantic bouquet. Olivia's gut lurched, which she told herself was entirely caused by her hangover.

There was a card on the flowers.

Maggie wouldn't send flowers. Olivia opened the card with shaky fingers.

I'm sorry. About everything. Please. Will you let me explain?

Grandma wisdom: always eat breakfast.

—Nikos

Damn the man and his *pain au chocolat*. Damn his grandma, too.

Olivia flopped back onto the bed with the pastry and licked her fingers. She suspected she had chocolate smeared across her face. She didn't care.

Fine. She could eat the pastries he provided, but beyond that…what next? What did she want? What did he want?

But first, who the hell was he?

Olivia picked up her phone and googled his name.

It was a mistake. Her mouth went dry, and her gut roiled.

Dear God, nine zillion hits popped up.

He was the subject of a lengthy Wikipedia page.

There were countless images of him spraying champagne on podiums. Blurring around corners in a low-slung red car.

Passing under a checkered flag, fist in the air. Close-up shots of his unmistakable azure eyes staring intensely through the narrow slit of a helmet before the start of a race.

She opened Instagram. Oddly, he had no account of his own, but then again, he didn't need one. His name was tagged in pictures, posts, fan accounts, Segno Rosso accounts, F1 accounts, motorsports updates, and product ads. TikTok was even worse.

As he had warned, snippets of their argument were posted on fan accounts, with horrid comments directed at the unknown girl who dared provoke their favorite crush. Olivia hoped another driver would quickly do something outrageous and supersede her drama with Nikos before it went completely viral.

Even so, she reminded herself that he was the one who would bear the brunt. She was headed back to New York, where literally no one cared about Nikos Leonikaros or any other celebrity.

But until then… Olivia felt nauseous. How incredibly oblivious had she been?

Meanwhile, Nikos must've been laughing his ass off. He couldn't have felt anything for her. Right? The flowers and breakfast were a meaningless grand gesture to assuage his guilt. She'd watched her mother fall for those kinds of gestures, which were inevitably followed by more lies. It was an ugly game. Instead of her dad, now Nikos was playing. Their whole connection must have been a game to see how long he could string along a clueless American girl before she uncovered his true identity.

Could he speed her all over Monaco on his bike? Yes. Could he tempt her to join him on a private yacht for the day? Yes. Could he have sex with her repeatedly? Yes, yes, yes. Damn it, yes. And she'd wanted it. She'd asked for it. Thrown herself at him.

It was mortifying. No wonder he was embarrassed by her.

So much for her New York City street smarts; she had been a total sucker. Totally played.

And at least now she knew how he'd gotten to be so good in bed—plenty of practice. Online there were pictures of him two steps behind every It Girl in Europe. Dodging paparazzi. Attending galas and awards shows. And in each image, he looked achingly, hauntingly, painfully luscious. He rarely posed, but in every candid photo, he was beyond sexy in well-tailored designer clothes and expensive sunglasses, his sun-kissed hair sliding over his face. Like a Greek god.

Should she be grateful that she, a mere mortal, had been touched by a god? Okay, more than a touch. She'd been seduced and seared.

She tried to remember her mythology. Didn't Zeus conceal his identity when seducing mortal women? To her recollection, he did. And sneaky Eros. She should have known something was up when Nikos chose that story.

Damn the Greek gods. All of them.

To hell with it. To hell with Nikos.

But it hurt. It hurt so badly.

No wonder he had hesitated to give her his mobile number.

But she couldn't quite bring herself to block him or delete his texts. Somewhere, in a small, stupid corner of her heart, she held on to a splinter of pathetic hope. She wasn't sure what exactly she hoped for, but damn it, it was there. Hope was an awful thing.

She slammed her phone decisively on the nightstand.

If it was going to rain all day, there was nothing to do but hole up in the hotel room and watch movies. In fact, that was precisely what she needed: watch some cheesy romances, order room service, and have herself a good cathartic cry. And then, tomorrow, she would get on the plane and fly back to New York City. *My night with Nikos Leonikaros* would be a crazy, risqué story she could tell at parties.

She picked up the clicker and tried to navigate the hotel TV.

Much to her disappointment, she discovered that European hotel TVs were not designed to provide soothing American rom-com content to the lovelorn. There were French programs, news, and more weather graphics showing incessant rain. And joy of joys, there were sports channels, including multiple ones dedicated to motorsports.

As she frustratedly clicked through her limited options, she became aware of a high-pitched whine emanating from outside. Good grief, was Monte Carlo under attack? It probably was, given her luck and how the trip had gone. The sound grew louder. Olivia pulled back the curtains and watched as a series of race cars screamed past the hotel. Apparently, the Grand Prix festivities had begun despite the gloomy weather.

She peeked out the window again. Was Nikos driving one of the cars she'd just seen? She couldn't help but wonder. She told herself she didn't care if he was.

One of the cars had been red. Wasn't his car red?

Perhaps she could find out. She knew she shouldn't care, but… She clicked back to one of the motorsports channels with English-speaking commentators. Two men wearing rain gear were blathering on in pronouncedly British accents about practice laps, the impact of the weather, and a series of speculations about car configurations, tire strategies, team standings, and racing personalities. It was foreign to Olivia. They might as well have been speaking Greek.

"But our biggest story this Monaco race weekend is Nikos Leonikaros…"

Well, she could relate to that. He had been the big story of her entire trip. She turned up the volume, trying to drown out the noise from the streets below.

She listened as the commentators expounded on the significance of this particular race to Nikos's career. Apparently, he'd won a lot of races. Now he was only one win away from a record-breaking number of Monaco podiums. Olivia swallowed uncomfortably, remembering the Monaco track schematic tattooed on his right hip. She couldn't suppress the memory of how incredible it felt to grip those narrow hips between her legs.

Damn the man.

The coverage cut to commercial. A series of vignettes with a voiceover in French showed Nikos living the glamorous life, flashing a big, blingy watch. Olivia ruefully concluded that the watch she'd seen him wear was, in fact, not a dupe. Her mistake. Who would have thought it? She didn't want to imagine the price tag.

She couldn't stop watching.

When the racing program resumed, the commentators explained they were cutting away from live coverage to present *Nikos Leonikaros: The Enigma*, a thirty-minute feature on the man they described as one of Formula 1's most successful but mysterious drivers.

Olivia snorted and helped herself to another *pain au chocolat*. At least he was consistent. Knowing she wasn't the only one who struggled to figure him out was validating. She opened a leftover bottle of wedding champagne and added it to the fresh orange juice to make herself a mimosa. It was probably a bad idea, but watching a retrospective on Nikos required fortification.

However, as the program progressed, Olivia became confused. And it wasn't the alcohol. Nikos was described as a voracious and brilliant competitor of iron-willed discipline but with an unfathomably aloof personality. Fellow drivers and members of the Segno Rosso racing team offered awed but perplexed depictions of a man who rarely engaged with anyone in the paddock other than when it was time to race. Media clips depicted awkward press conferences, his reticence leaving seasoned interviewers fumbling to fill the gaps in his monosyllabic responses. Even his nickname, "The Enigma," alluded to the mystique surrounding the son of a notoriously reclusive family—a family of eye-popping, staggering wealth.

In fact, his net worth meant that he didn't have to trade on his image for additional income. He was said to loathe the social media promotions the team and its sponsors required.

Try as she might, Olivia struggled to align the overall portrayal with the warm, affectionate, thoughtful, down-to-earth person she'd spent two days with. She continued watching, trying to understand, trying to connect the dots. And trying to remember how angry she was at him for lying. It was hard to sustain animosity toward a man who had tempted her to think foolish happily-ever-after thoughts. And baked her cookies. And sent her room service. And never once acted like he had enough money to buy the Taj Mahal three times over.

Damn. She fought to keep the edge on her anger, but it was wavering. Had she misread him? Could there be a legitimate explanation for the lie? Could a lie ever be justified? Experience said no. Every time her dad had cajoled her mother into letting a falsehood slide, a part of Olivia's trusting young heart had died. Their family dynamic had been toxic. But what about Nikos's idyllic descriptions of his family life?

As part of the documentary, historic footage of an impossibly young Nikos zipping around a track as a kart racer included another familiar face. The protective thug who had tried to keep Olivia from confronting Nikos was omnipresent. Who was that guy? What was his role? He'd been with Nikos for a long time. Considering Nikos's upbringing, Olivia wondered if perhaps Nikos had been raised with the idea that a lie was sometimes acceptable or necessary. Maybe he'd known situations in which a lie was warranted? A kindness, even?

As the program concluded, Olivia mixed herself another mimosa. She had a lot to think about.

Thunder sounded overhead, and the chatty Brits returned to the screen, announcing that practice had been suspended because of the weather and would hopefully resume in a few hours.

On cue, there was a knock on her hotel room door.

* * *

Nikos stood, dripping wet, in the hotel corridor. But it wasn't the rain that caused him to break into a cold sweat. Yesterday he'd resolved to focus on the upcoming race and relegate Olivia Keller to an appealing possibility for when the season concluded.

That seemingly reasonable decision had lasted until their confrontation. Finding himself on the receiving end of Olivia's fury, he acknowledged he'd been dishonest; he couldn't deny it. But being called out in public, along with her flippant disregard for privacy, had put him absolutely over the edge. It touched raw wounds he thought had healed.

Now, for better or worse, at least everything was out in the open. No more secrets.

Did the truth matter? They would both soon depart Monte Carlo, and the chance conditions that brought them together would no longer exist. In another twenty-four hours, she'd be on a plane to New York, and shortly thereafter, he'd fly to Spain.

He would likely never see Olivia Keller again, so there was little point in making amends and no reason to answer the painful questions she must be asking.

Even so, something in him couldn't allow her to leave, believing he'd been callous or that he'd been embarrassed by her company. Far from it. For a brief, tantalizing moment, he'd actually imagined building a life with her, beyond his career in racing. That shocking realization was easier to admit now that he knew it was impossible.

He owed her an explanation beyond apologies or flowers.

When he knocked, there was a long pause. He knew she was in the room. Would she ignore him? If so, that would be the end of it.

Thankfully, the door opened.

"Was any of it true?"

He admired her tactics. He, too, preferred to take an aggressive approach, assuming control directly from the start.

"I never meant to lie to you. The joke about being a baker was directed at Bryson, my media manager. Then it got awkward because we were spending time together. I tried to stick as close to the truth as possible but didn't know how to tell you. I wanted us to have a chance to get to know each other without the complications and craziness of my life."

She looked like she might slam the door in his face. "That's nonsense, and you know it. All that flattery. Why?"

"I meant every compliment I gave you. Those cheesy lines? They were honest. Every one of them."

He heard the elevator ding. He'd left Bryson and Aleko at the ends of the hall to ward off any fans. He didn't want to give anyone else a chance to overhear this conversation.

"Olivia…"

She glared, offended at his familiarity with her name.

"Can I please come in?"

"What, dodging admirers?"

"Actually, yes. It's why I was using the back entrance when I first met you."

She rolled her eyes but opened the door. He gestured to the chair and she shrugged, so he sat.

Silently, she double-knotted her robe's belt. Remembering how easily the robe had slid from her shoulders the day before and the torrid interlude that followed…he swallowed the lump in his throat.

"First off, please believe I was never embarrassed by you. I think you're incredible. I just wanted to keep everything between us private. That's why I suggested we go on the boat. Not because I was ashamed of you. Far from it."

"That's your boat, isn't it?"

"Yes."

"But you told me someone else owned it. That's a lie."

"No, I said it had the same owner as…"

"You own the monster yacht, too?! Oh my God, that hadn't even occurred to me."

She dropped down onto the bed, gobsmacked.

It appeared they were going to rehash the past few days, picking apart assumptions, lies, and omissions. His heart sank. This was not how he wanted the conversation to go.

"You told me you wanted to be a baker since you were a kid. That was a lie."

He shut his eyes, ashamed to admit how carefully he'd chosen words to mislead her. "No, I told you I've trained across Europe since I was young. That's true. I started kart racing at age five."

She glared. "Yeah, I saw that on TV this morning. I watched a feature on you. Who knew you were such a big deal? I certainly wouldn't have guessed you warranted a thirty-minute special."

"It was produced by the motorsports network. I honestly had nothing to do with it."

Honestly. He winced at the inadvertent word choice.

"Olivia, I hate that everyone sees my life as content to consume."

She shrugged. "It comes with the territory, doesn't it?"

"It shouldn't. People forget that I'm not some character on TV. I'm a real person. You saw more of the real me than I've shared with just about anyone."

"Do you even know how to make cookies?" she demanded. "I know that video wasn't for me. I saw the full version on the F1 Instagram. Don't tell me that was real."

He shut his eyes and ran his hands through his hair. "I know you won't believe me, but it was for you. Yes, I had to make the video for F1 media. But I despise making social content. Despise it. So, when I was recording, I imagined myself baking cookies for you. You said I appeared to be joyful? It's because I was doing something for you. Sharing something of my family, my grandmother's recipe, with you. You make me feel joy. I feel like myself, not some made-up character, when I'm with you. You have no idea how long since I've felt that."

She paused, considering. He pressed the advantage.

"Yesterday part of the reason I lost my temper was because I knew our argument would be all over social media. I saw fans recording every word. I lost control. I didn't mean to take it out on you. You have every right to be angry. About all of it."

"I mean, okay. Thank you for saying that, but why is social media such a big deal? I get that it sucks, but can't you just ignore it?"

Might as well tell her.

"It's hard to ignore when that's how I found out my previous girlfriend was screwing another driver…"

Her eyes widened. He'd kept the experience bottled up for so long, but now it poured out.

"Athena was my first girlfriend. We started dating as teenagers when I was coming up through the racing ranks. When I made it to F1 and started to be recognized, she took advantage of our relationship to build her own brand, became a celebrity influencer. Then she started a jewelry line…with money I invested. She maxed out my credit cards. All the while, she was cheating on me with…him. Now they have a kid." He shrugged.

"Shit. Okay, that's horrible…" Olivia acknowledged.

Nikos didn't want pity. "Yeah, well, at least I beat him on the track, right? He dropped out of racing, and I won five world championships, partially because I felt I had to prove myself. Prove I wasn't pathetic for letting a woman use me like that. So, screw her. Screw him. Screw them both."

Olivia gave him a long look. He suspected she saw through his posturing.

"It took me a long time to get over it. Maybe I never really did."

"Look, you have every right to be bitter. She sounds awful,

but Nikos, I'm not her. The only thing I've posted from this trip is the food I've eaten."

"No, you aren't her. I know that."

"Nikos, the bottom line is that you lied to me. Do you have any idea…the lies I've heard over the years? Every guy I've ever met, including my own father…"

Olivia got up and paced the small room, struggling to continue.

"He promised to always be there for me. He wasn't. He promised to provide for my mom and me financially. He didn't. If I hadn't gotten a scholarship, I wouldn't have been able to afford school. He didn't bother showing up for my graduation. What did it matter to him? What did I matter to him?" She paused to let her words sink in. "You were similarly hurt by your girlfriend cheating and stealing from you, right? Nikos, that's just another way of saying Athena lied. She lied to you… so you know exactly how devastating it is to be lied to. You should understand why I'm so hurt. Why I cannot tolerate lies. Why I never trusted anyone enough to allow them to get close to me. Until you."

She wasn't wrong, but equating his behavior to Athena's gutted him.

"Olivia, I'm not like your father," he insisted. "Nor Athena."

It made him nauseated even to consider he might be anything like his ex.

Olivia pinned him with a look. "Nikos. That's an unconvincing argument, considering you did, in fact, lie to me."

Her words shut him down. There was nothing he could say. It felt disingenuous to reiterate that this was merely a situation that spiraled out of control and that he hadn't confessed because he couldn't bear to complicate the joy he'd found with her, even in their short time together. Even if that was the truth.

He tried to catch her gaze. "Olivia. I am so sorry…not just for claiming to be a baker, but for everything… You're right. I lied. I shouldn't have. I have no excuse."

Instead of reassuring her, his words appeared to have the opposite effect. He tried again.

"But I want you to know the time I spent with you was real. Going from pastry shop to pastry shop with you on the bike with me…was amazing. And then I wanted to see you again so badly that I didn't want to risk it by telling the truth. So much of my life doesn't feel real anymore, but every time we were together, I tried to show you what I couldn't explain. You make me feel something I've never felt before. And our time on the boat…"

"Don't even mention what we did on the boat!" She looked away, pain evident on her face. "I cannot discuss that right now. And I'm just curious, did you pay someone to make the rest of the cookies? All thirty dozen?"

He paused before answering because he realized she was fighting hard not to cry. Did it mean she cared or that she hated him? Maybe a little of both?

"Yes. I had my staff on the big yacht make them."

She let out a disappointed groan.

"So what if someone else baked them?" he argued. "Yes. I paid someone to make cookies. But you were prepared to pay for them. I helped you. I made the cookies happen, even if I didn't actually bake them. You wanted cookies, I delivered them. For you. Why can't that be good enough?"

She sagged back down onto the bed and covered her face in her hands. "I liked you better when you were a hotel baker."

Now it was Nikos's turn to get up in pace in frustration. "So do I—is that what you want me to say? Because in some ways it's true. Because if I'm a hotel baker, then I know your interest in me isn't about the money and it isn't about racing. It's about me, who I am as a person. I needed to be sure of that. To trust you."

"Trust me? You let me think you had to work two gigs to afford living here. Did you want me to feel bad for you?"

"No! That's not it. I just didn't want you to know I was a

driver. But here's the important thing," he insisted, taking a new tack, "I'm done being a driver when the season ends. I told you my contract is ending. That is true. Who knows what my next gig will be? Whatever it is, I can be just Nikos."

"Wrong. Even when you quit racing, this is who you've been since you were a child. Being a driver is as much a part of you as being Greek. You can't erase your history. That was the whole point of the cookie table you helped me with—it's part of my friend's history, even though it's not how she lives now. Don't you see that?"

Her words cut him to the core. He didn't want to admit it, but she had a point. But where did that leave them? Where did it leave him? What next?

Olivia challenged him. "Seriously. How far would you go to erase your history? Your back is covered in racing circuits—would you have the tattoos removed? I doubt it."

"No… I…but…" He switched gears again. "Back to the money…what I spent on the cookies. I meant what I said when I told you money doesn't make any difference."

She scoffed. "Spoken like someone who has never had to worry about money."

"What does it matter?" he snapped. "Your friend…from what you told me about her, I guess she now has a lot of money by your standards. Does it make you think differently about her?"

"She never lied to me about it. That's the point, Nikos. You lied to me. About everything."

They were right back where they had started, at a discouraging impasse. Olivia retook control of the conversation.

"What I want to know is why me?" Olivia asked. She didn't give him a chance to answer. "I'm just a girl who hustles at a job I don't really care about. I live in a three-hundred-square-foot studio apartment, smaller than this hotel room, with a single window looking over a trash dumpster. It isn't glamorous. It isn't Monaco. What could you possibly want with me?

Or is this just what you do? Have a thing with a random girl wherever you race?"

"Oh my God, have you heard nothing I said?" he snapped. "It's not like that. I'm not like that. During the season, I focus on my job. Believe me when I tell you that I'm not dating anyone and not looking for quick flings. I've never taken a woman out on my boat for the day, much less overnight. Have I spent time with different women? Yes. Sure. But there's been no one serious. Nothing long-term. I met you and had a glimpse of a possibility between us. I wanted to see where it might go. I thought we had potential. Maybe that's pathetic. I don't know."

He shut his eyes in anguish. "And anyhow, why do you care?"

He felt her grow quiet. He turned toward the window, so as not to see the expression in her eyes. Maybe she didn't care at all.

"Because, because…" she muttered, "I also thought this could be something. I felt like there was something special between us. We could be something."

Why were they having this conversation now, when it was too late?

Yesterday he'd almost convinced himself that as intensely as he had fallen for Olivia, it wasn't the right time; he couldn't get involved with her until the season ended.

So maybe this argument simply confirmed that he couldn't concentrate on a real relationship, especially one that made him feel like he was being ripped open and turned inside out. Perhaps he should cut his losses and move on.

"This has all been really fast," he murmured, testing that theory. But as soon as the words left his mouth, he knew they were cowardly.

"Yeah, well." She threw his words back at him before he could correct himself. "You were the one who said you liked to go fast."

Her sarcastic reference confirmed a harsh reality. There was no way they could make this, whatever it was, work. There just wasn't enough time to make up for his mistakes.

"Olivia, I don't know what to tell you. I came to apologize. I was wrong. I admit it. I told you I wanted to explain and try to make it up to you. I'm not sure you're willing to accept what I'm saying or accept me. I can't argue with you any longer. This is who I am. You see it all now. Take it or leave it."

He'd never escape her hotel room if he stayed any longer. Emotionally, he was wiped out.

"I have to go drive. I had time to stop by because practice was delayed, but now I need to go."

So, would this be the final word? Would his last glimpse of Olivia Keller be of her standing before him in doubt and disappointment?

He was damned either way.

"If…" He was about to say something utterly foolish, but he couldn't stop himself. "If there is any chance of you staying until Sunday, I can send you a VIP pass for Qualifying tomorrow and the race on Sunday. Come. See what my life is like. Then, after the race, we will have time to talk. I can arrange for you to fly home on Monday. Or Tuesday. Or whenever you want. I have a plane. But…but that's all I can do. The rest is up to you. Just let me know what you want to do. Text me. Please."

He stepped closer, silently willing her to accept his offer on the spot. She stood still as a statue, her breathing erratic, hinting at the depth of her emotions. He leaned closer. She didn't flinch, so he kissed her at the edge of her lips and tasted a hint of chocolate.

"Olivia…"

She didn't return his kiss.

With a final sigh of frustration, Nikos slipped out of the hotel room and let the door slam behind him.

SATURDAY MORNING

As he approached the circuit for the final practice session, Nikos appreciated that the entire team worked methodically. He'd spent his entire ten-year career with this team. Their preparations provided a framework to function with some normalcy despite his churning emotions. He'd had a rough night. Usually, he got his best sleep during race weekends.

The garage and Segno Rosso headquarters were a world where everyone knew their precise role and function. Eero, Juan-Carlos, and the engineers were analyzing the information displayed on various monitors as they waited for Nikos. They needed to make calculated decisions to form a strategy to successfully perform in the ongoing rain. They could precisely game out possible scenarios and predict outcomes. It was intense, but it was comforting. Familiar. Clear. Unlike his failed romance with Olivia Keller.

The crew was hard at work, readying the car and other necessary equipment. Nikos trusted his car. While in the car, he shared a communication shorthand with his engineer that bordered on telepathic. The mechanics knew how to tweak the car to be maximally responsive to his driving style. And Nikos knew the contours of the Monaco circuit as intimately as the curves of a lover's body. In some ways, the circuit had been his first true love. He had been a seventeen-year-old virgin when he earned his maiden win on this podium. He and Athena became lovers shortly thereafter, and he conquered the race eight more times over the next ten years. One more win and he'd hold the record.

His connection to the circuit was the real long-term relationship. But that was cold comfort in the moment. It was not a relationship that would carry him into the future.

He realized he had precious little time, if any, for a final attempt to talk with Olivia. He looked at his watch. What time was her flight? Usually, transatlantic flights departed in the late afternoon. Was she still at the hotel? Had she left for the airport? Was it too late?

He checked his phone, hoping against hope she'd messaged him to accept his offer of a VIP pass. She hadn't. Should he text her? That felt too pathetic. He wouldn't beg her to stay. At least not yet.

Nikos changed into his kit: the fireproof undergarments, his boots, the balaclava, the racing jumpsuit. Instead of leaving his phone with his street clothes in his private driver's room, he went looking for Bryson.

"Ya." He found the media manager talking to reporters at the edge of the paddock. Camera lenses clicked. Nikos coaxed Bryson far enough away that their conversation wouldn't be overheard. "I need you to do me a favor."

Bryson pulled out his iPad, poised for instructions.

"Get a VIP pass for today and tomorrow. See if you can get some rain gear, too. Here is my private phone. If Olivia texts that she wants to come for Quali or the race tomorrow, then answer and take the stuff to her. Accompany her to the paddock so she isn't by herself."

To Bryson's credit, he took the instructions in stride. "Okay, got it. Olivia texts, go get her. Provide some weather gear. Keep her happy. What if she texts but doesn't plan to attend? What do I tell her? And do you want to know if she isn't coming?"

Nikos winced. "No, no. That would probably be a bad idea. I'll check in with you when I can. Now I've got to get over to engineering. Just use your best judgment, Bryson. I trust you."

"And if I see Aleko?"

Nikos paused. Aleko vocally disapproved of Nikos's interest in Olivia. It wasn't Bryson's job to run errands and carry messages, but he was at least amenable. The old man might take it on himself to give Olivia some off-base advice. Things were messy enough. Nikos didn't need Aleko stirring the pot.

"Nah, don't say anything to him. I don't want to involve Aleko. Thanks, Bryson."

The screaming whine from cars on the track below provided a headache-inducing soundtrack as Olivia haphazardly stuffed clothing into her suitcase. It was a different approach from the painstakingly organized packing process. There were no fashion decisions to make, no cute outfits to plan. Just dirty laundry and disappointment. It was symbolic of the whole stupid trip.

And she was irritated that she'd lost half of her bikini. With the opportunity to hit a Mediterranean beach, she had justified the expense of buying a nice bathing suit. Now she would have to spend money on a new one if she wanted to do any more beach going this summer. And for what? A poor decision on a boat? She should have kept her bikini bottoms on.

Damn the man.

It was far easier to stay angry at him than to entertain what-ifs. But deep down, those what-ifs still tantalized. If only she had a little more time to maybe, possibly, sort things out.

There was an expected knock on the hotel room door.

"Hi, Mags…"

Olivia did a double take. It wasn't Maggie.

The smooth-talking man who often accompanied Nikos stood in the hallway. Olivia wedged her foot behind the door in case he thought he could barge in.

"Can I help you?" She ensured her tone made it clear that she did not welcome his presence.

"We've not been properly introduced. I'm Bryson Samuelson, Nikos's PR and media manager."

Olivia stood silently, waiting. Why would Nikos send an underling? Let him state his piece and leave.

"I brought you these." Bryson held out a pile of Segno Rosso racing gear.

"And what is this?"

She already had Nikos's sweatshirt, hat, and sunglasses. She didn't need any more mementos. Her gut clenched—did this guy think souvenirs would buy her off? She wondered what the going rate was for discouraging celebrity girlfriend wannabes. If she had no integrity, she could probably recoup the cost of the entire trip.

"VIP passes for today. And rain gear because it's going to be wet. Practice is happening right now—Qualifying will be at four o'clock. The race is at three o'clock tomorrow, but there will be a Drivers' Parade beforehand."

"I won't need any of it because I'm leaving for New York today."

The media manager hesitated. "Maybe just take it, in case you change your mind."

"Did Nikos send you?"

Bryson shifted his weight. "Not exactly."

Olivia raised her eyebrows.

"He told me to have the passes and the gear ready in case you texted that you want to come to the race. He hoped you would contact him, but he's in the middle of practice. I'm supposed to be watching his phone for your message."

The image of Nikos waiting for a text thawed some of the ice around her heart. But not entirely.

"I didn't text him. That should have been a sign."

"No, you didn't." Bryson shook his head. "But I have to go pick up his family. They're coming in for the race. I thought I'd drop this stuff off with you before I left. In case you decided to see what his life is all about."

Bryson shoved the stuff at her. "Look, just think about it. Whatever is happening with you two, it is good for him."

And me? Olivia snorted. *Is it good for me?*

"I'm sure he is acquainted with plenty of women who might be good for him. I looked him up. He apparently doesn't lack for female companionship. I'm sure he'll have plenty of fan girlies to cheer him on."

Bryson sighed. "Don't believe everything you see."

"Or everything I hear from him? He lied to me. He didn't tell me about any of this." She waved her hands vaguely to encompass the enormity of it.

Bryson frowned. "He omitted a lot. Yes. But he found time for you during a race week. That doesn't happen. Ever. And forget about anything you see online or in the media. Look, it's my job to shape how the public perceives Nikos Leonikaros. It's not easy. When someone is as private as he is, it gets interpreted as being mysterious. And people love nothing more than a good mystery. So, the fans become even more fixated on everything he does. If he is seated next to someone at an event, inevitably there's a photograph. Then speculation that they're dating, whether they are or not. Photographers are always present to take pictures—he's eager to be done with that. He loves racing but has achieved almost everything he wants to as a driver. Soon, it will be time to move on, get out of the spotlight. But he's not quite sure how. Or what comes next. And I think you might be the person he needs to help him figure it out."

"Whatever." Olivia shrugged. "I can take the gear and the passes, but don't take it as a sign. Don't tell him I'll be there, unless you want him to be disappointed. I am getting on a plane this afternoon. Maybe I'll check the race results when I get back to New York. I'm sure I can find out anything I need to know."

Bryson persisted. "Yeah, well. Just think about it."

Olivia heard the elevator ding, and thankfully, Maggie appeared in the hallway.

Bryson nodded and excused himself.

"Who was that?" Maggie asked.

"Nikos's PR guy."

"What did he want?"

"For me to forgive Nikos for lying and show up at the race to cheer my favorite driver on to victory. Rah, rah. Because it would be good for Nikos. Forget about what might be good for me."

Maggie followed Olivia into the room. Olivia flopped face down onto the bed.

"God, Liv, I hate saying goodbye to you like this."

Parting from her best friend was always awful, but it felt a thousand times worse than usual. Olivia wasn't ready to say goodbye or leave the cocoon of the hotel and its plush robes.

Maggie sat down and hugged her. "Admit it—you are a lovesick fool, aren't you?"

"Oh my God, don't be sympathetic. It will just irritate me," Olivia insisted.

She'd maintained a cool attitude with Bryson but wasn't sure she could sustain such nonchalance with her best friend. But she had to try. "And I'm not in love. I've been had by a duplicitous man. And I know all about that, so don't try to tell me otherwise."

"Okay, babe, let's see if I can restate your situation," Maggie paused. "Olivia, I am so sorry you came to Monaco, stayed in one of the most glamorous hotels in Europe, ate *pain au chocolat* twice daily, and enthusiastically slept with a hot F1 driver who's one of the wealthiest people in the world. You scored a ridiculous amount of racing swag and a pair of expensive sunglasses. This trip must've been awful for you. My heart breaks. Oh, and you spent quality time with me, your best friend. That counts for something, right?"

The irreverence made Olivia feel a little better, and she managed half a smile. "Well, since you put it that way..."

Maggie looked at her sympathetically. "So, have you spoken to him? I'm sorry I couldn't fully check on you in person yesterday. I had to spend the day with Stefano's family."

"I understand. And yes, I did talk to Nikos. He showed up at my room unannounced," Olivia admitted.

"And?"

"He tried to explain, tried to apologize. He says he only claimed to be a baker as a joke, but then it got out of control. I didn't question it at the time because I was tired and trying to obtain your cookies..."

"Which he provided," Maggie interrupted.

"Yes, but he lied. It was all a lie. Just like my dad."

"Is he really like your dad?" Maggie asked. "Your dad lied to serve his own selfish purposes. From what you've said, Nikos wasn't selfish. Far from it."

"Okay, maybe he's not selfish," Olivia admitted. "But even so, I googled him and blew through all my international cellular data. Total mistake. You are right—he's famous. Like *famous* famous. I watched a thirty-minute documentary on him yesterday. And Mags, the celebrities he's dated? All over Instagram. Oh my God. It's completely intimidating."

Olivia collapsed back onto the bed. It was all so ridiculous. Maggie snuggled up beside her, and they stared at the ceiling together.

Olivia sighed. "Okay, true confessions. I'm head over heels for this guy. I'm desperately hurt and confused and don't know what to do. My head and life experience say to forget him. He lied. And a celebrity wouldn't want anything authentic with someone like me anyhow. It would all be lies. But...my heart says otherwise. I just can't help it. But I am getting on an airplane in—" she paused to check the time "—five hours."

"First of all, you don't give yourself enough credit, Liv. You never do. Why wouldn't he be attracted to you and want to be with you? You're wonderful. And seriously, social media? You can't trust what you see there. You know that."

"Okay," Olivia admitted. "Let's say you are correct. There is more to him than what shows up on TikTok. Great. Agreed. But Mags, it doesn't change the fact that he lives this crazy life that is so far from anything I could ever imagine. How can I possibly believe I might have a place in his world?"

Maggie was silent for a long moment, her head on Olivia's shoulder. She took a deep breath and let it out in a long sigh. "Are you forgetting where we grew up? We thought being a high school cheerleader was the pinnacle of existence. Back then, Switzerland was not on my radar. But we did our semester abroad. I met Stefano. Do you remember?"

Olivia nodded. "At the bar in Spain. Tapas, Rioja, and destiny."

"Right," Maggie continued. "And before the sun came up the next morning, I knew he was the guy I wanted. Meant-to-Be. M2B, baby."

Olivia sighed. "I hear you, but I'm not sure I can be like you. Becoming a part of Nikos's life might be too big a hurdle. It's all part of the lie. Did you see the monster yacht the other night? That's his. I wouldn't know how to live like that…"

"Oh, come on." Maggie snorted. "I mean, Nikos must have a pretty nice lifestyle, to say the least. Most people would find a way to adapt. You moved to New York City and learned to live completely differently from how you grew up. What's to say you can't make a change again? The question isn't about money, although money makes a lot of nice things possible. The question is whether you want to go for it with him. Is he worth it? But don't refuse because you are insecure or your pride is hurt or you're still suffering from your dad's failings."

Olivia swallowed down that accusation without comment. She suspected it might be entirely too accurate.

She glanced at the time. "Oh my God, Maggie, I've got to call for the car right now or I'm going to miss my flight."

As Olivia picked up the hotel phone to arrange transportation, her cell phone buzzed from the credenza where she'd dropped it. She and Maggie stared at the device. Was it Nikos? Once again, she felt that pathetic glimmer of hope. She hung up the hotel phone.

She looked at the text message. And moaned. "I can't believe this is happening. I don't need to call for a car because my flight has been canceled. Forecasted thunderstorms. Not delayed, canceled."

Maggie gaped, wide-eyed. "You are either exceedingly unlucky…or maybe it's a sign?" she suggested.

Olivia frowned. "A sign of what? A sign that I hate French transportation? A sign that, other than your wedding, this whole trip has been a debacle? And don't try to convince me otherwise."

Maggie's lips twitched. "If you say so. But now you have a flight to rebook, and I have an appointment with Céline to review the wedding account. Tonight we're meeting Uncle Klaus and Aunt Kiki for dinner at Alain Ducasse. Come to dinner. I'll add you to the reservation. Good food always helps."

Olivia moaned. She'd heard that before.

"Okay, thank you. I guess I'm staying in Monte Carlo whether I want to or not."

"So it's a good thing I booked some of the rooms through race day. I'll let Céline know you're staying. Love you! See you at dinner! Think about what I said."

Apparently, Olivia would have at least one more day to consider the situation with Nikos. She wasn't sure if it was a curse or a gift.

SATURDAY AFTERNOON—QUALIFYING

THAT MORNING'S FINAL practice had been wet but largely un-eventful. Nikos kept his focus and took the circuit confidently. He secured one of the fastest practice lap times, which was what he needed. Now he just had to push a little harder in Qualifying to ensure he kept the lead. Quali laps were critical. They determined pole. In the precise, tight corners of the Monaco circuit, if he started the grid in first position, it would be unlikely that anyone could prevent him from staying out front and winning the race.

"We need to get you out before the weather worsens," Eero confirmed. "I wish we had more time, but we don't."

The forecast called for the rain to increase, with a high probability of a thunderstorm. Nikos usually wasn't part of the scrum of drivers who took to the track during the congested first minutes of Q1. He didn't need to be. But today strategy called for him to accomplish a fast lap as early as possible.

When it was time, shielded by a crew member holding an umbrella, Nikos positioned himself at the car. He plugged in his earphones and put on his neck collar support, helmet, and gloves. A mechanic removed the car cover and extracted the steering wheel from the car. Nikos lowered himself into the tight cockpit. His supportive safety devices and harness were connected. The steering wheel was locked back into the car.

"Radio check—confirm you can hear me."

He confirmed. It was time.

With a sharp bark and a jolt, the engine snapped on. Idling, the car whined, metallic and shrill. The chassis trembled, vibrating through every molecule in his body. During these moments, his breathing and heart rate pulsated with the engine, and he felt almost one with the car. All external thoughts and consciousness gave way to utter focus. The anticipation, this adrenaline, this was why he raced. Waiting. Waiting.

"Q1 Started—Pit Exit Light Green."

The tire blankets were whipped away; the jacks dropped the car. With a signal from his team, he was off.

Minutes later, the lap concluded, and he was back in the pit lane. It was a decent lap. Good by anyone else's standards. But not his best. Would it be enough? He hated going out early. Better to wait and know what he was up against.

The clock counted down to zero, and the checkered flag waved, signaling the end of Q1. The slowest drivers would be eliminated and start from the back of the grid on race day. Fortunately, Nikos's lap sufficed. Both he and his teammate advanced to Q2. So far, so good.

The rain had picked up, although the track now held more rubber, which made it easier for the tires to grip. Over the radio, the team debated tire choice for the next round, and Nikos's risky opinion prevailed. He was vindicated when he put down the day's fastest Quali lap. Juan-Carlos did his part with a quick enough time to also advance to Q3. Everything was going according to plan for the Segno Rosso team. At least something was going right in his life.

It was in Q3 that disaster struck.

Olivia headed toward her room later that evening, full and sleepy after another exceptional meal. That in and of itself made the extra day in Monte Carlo almost worth it. She told herself that when she returned to her room, however, it was time to rebook the flight. She had to get back to New York. Right?

She meandered into the room. Without bothering to put down her purse or take off her shoes, she fumbled with the clicker to turn on the TV. Might as well check the motorsports channel for updates.

The chatty Brits were back like old friends. It came as no surprise that they were talking about Nikos. Apparently, he was always the big story. She hated to admit it, but that had to get old, always being the focus of such unwavering attention. He had a valid complaint.

"What do we make of Nikos Leonikaros today?" the first commentator asked.

"Woo-hoo, he had a doozy of a day!" his partner replied gleefully. "Quite a scare for Segno Rosso!"

Scare? Her curiosity piqued, Olivia dropped her purse, kicked off her shoes, and anxiously turned up the volume.

"After the crash today, Segno Rosso must be questioning their decision to send Leonikaros out on intermediate tires!"

Crash?! Olivia felt like she'd been punched in the gut. *There was a crash?!* The commentators appeared to be matter-of-factly discussing whatever mishap had occurred. Surely if Nikos were injured, they'd be talking in less gleeful tones. Surely.

"So was it the tires? I think we can attribute this mistake directly to Leonikaros. We've not seen this kind of reckless performance since he got in a bad situation in Barcelona three years ago!"

Okay. Whatever happened to Nikos, it didn't sound life-threatening. Hopefully, it was just a minor incident. Racing drama. Which was, admittedly, his whole life.

But was he okay? Couldn't the commentators talk about that instead of tires?

Olivia felt queasy, desperate for reassurance, and horribly suspecting their argument had impacted Nikos's driving.

"The question is why? This is not the Nikos Leonikaros we've come to expect. He's dominated every Monaco race since his Formula 1 arrival. He is a ferocious and laser-focused competitor, which makes this kind of hotheaded performance so strange. He doesn't make mistakes. So what went wrong?"

Olivia hated that she might have contributed to the answer, whether the commentators knew it or not. The internet girlies would be sure to cast blame.

"Let's look at the replay…"

Olivia watched Nikos's red car slice through the impossibly tight, winding Monte Carlo streets. Traversing those streets on the back of a motorcycle had been terrifying enough. How could a car manage at high speeds? And in the rain?

"He dominated Q2. Fastest lap of the day! But then, his Q3 lap attempt is like he's an entirely different driver! Look at how he deviates from the best line. He's skimming curbs, brushing too close to barriers. Some courses might forgive, but not Monaco. He is flirting with disaster from the moment he leaves the pit. Watch!"

Olivia held her breath as the second commentator picked up the narrative. She didn't want to watch but couldn't look away.

"Let's see exactly where the problem occurs. Here's Leonikaros through the second-to-last turn. He's coming in at a high speed… We see that he's already too hot…"

"As he makes the turn and enters the blind apex, coming out…here! We've got O'Sullivan and Yakimoto in a kerfuffle! Yokimoto has spun out in the rain, blocking Leonikaros. And here…"

Olivia gasped in horror as Nikos's car plowed into the stalled race car, sandwiching it into the already wrecked third car. Those vehicles seemed to disintegrate on impact, but somehow, Nikos's car remained intact and moved with enough momentum to tilt sideways onto two wheels, teeter, and then ride grotesquely along the length of a side barrier, shedding parts, until it flipped entirely over—on top of Nikos.

Olivia nearly puked.

"Quite a scare, that! Let's look at the replay again and have a listen…"

A static-filled audio recording with subtitles popped up on the screen.

"What the…?" She heard the split-second surprise and a string of Greek curses.

Crashing, crunching, crushing sounds followed. Then silence.

"Nikos—mate, are you okay?" crackled across the line.

There was a heart-stopping pause.

"Yes, yes… I'm okay. Just give me a minute. Mick and Haruto—are they okay?"

Nikos sounded dazed. But alive. Thank God, alive.

"They're fine. Everyone is fine."

"Good. Good. Can someone get me out…?" His voice was shaky, but he was coherent.

Trembling, Olivia watched footage of a bevy of track workers shifting pieces, righting his cockpit, detaching his steering wheel, and supporting him as he climbed out. Similar groups were helping the other two drivers while race officials waved red flags. Nikos stumbled for a few steps, assisted by a hovering medic. He turned back to reconnect his steering wheel, even though the car was in no shape to go anywhere. Only one tire remained. The wings and rear tail lay in tatters.

"So now, instead of taking the first slot on the grid as expected, Segno Rosso must contend with Leonikaros having no set time from Q3. At least his fast lap in Q2 secured him tenth position on the starting grid. But will he be able to race at all? This is not the victorious, career-defining Monaco race we expected from Nikos Leonikaros!"

The commentary was overwhelming; Olivia snapped off the TV. She couldn't listen to or watch any more of it. She couldn't shake the image of Nikos's car tumbling over and over, crushing him beneath. She couldn't unhear the hideous sounds of impact. How horrific must it have been for him, trapped in what could have been a death box?

Had their argument contributed to his wreck? Had it distracted him? Did it cause him to lose focus?

She might've been upset with him, but if he had been hurt or, worse, killed… Olivia couldn't even admit to that blood-chilling possibility. He was alive. That was all that mattered.

She reconsidered their situation in a different light. She'd been so stubbornly angry at his deception that she never stopped to consider what it meant to drive a Formula 1 car, the risk he took every time he took to the circuit. Racing changed the whole context of their conversation. She'd been too furious to see it.

Yes, he'd lied. He'd kept an essential part of his life hidden. But admittedly, if she had first known him as an F1 driver, it might have changed her entire perception. Exactly what he wished to avoid.

And…if she was being truly honest, well, she'd lied, too. She wasn't sincere enough with him—or herself—to admit how her past made it almost impossible for her to trust a man. She'd blithely pursued Nikos as a meaningless fling merely because he offered to help her and was incredibly attractive. She had realized her mistake, but it didn't change the fact that when they first met, she never would have considered the possibility of a genuine relationship. Maybe it was time for both of them to face the truth.

Without giving herself time to reconsider, she picked up her phone.

Nikos gingerly rolled over. Of the crashes he'd experienced, the day's unexpected mishap wasn't the worst wreck in terms of how battered he felt, but he was still banged up. After a thorough medical examination, he'd been cleared to race. Of course, that assumed the team could repair the car in time.

Even though they could work miracles, he should not have put his team in this position.

He winced as he eased onto his already problematic shoulder.

The whole situation was entirely his fault. Q1 and Q2 had gone precisely according to plan. There had been time after his successful Q2 lap to get out of the car. But rather than staying close and concentrating on Quali, he had gone to the paddock looking for Bryson. It was a poor decision, but he'd needed to know—had Olivia texted? Was there any possibility of her staying in Monte Carlo a little longer? Attending the race? But Bryson was nowhere to be found, which meant Nikos's phone and any communication from her were also inaccessible.

Aleko had spotted Nikos. The nosy old man had handed him Olivia's bikini bottoms, which she'd left on the boat, and then wheedled it out of Nikos that he was desperate to hear from her. Predictably, Aleko berated him for thinking about anything other than the task at hand, specifically a fast lap in Q3. Even though Aleko was right, Nikos had pushed back. Hard.

The start of Q3 had interrupted their argument. If there was one thing Nikos knew, it was that getting into the car in the heat of emotion was a mistake. But that was exactly what he had done. And paid the price.

Well. He'd have to make it up tomorrow.

P10 put him at a disadvantage, but he'd taken other unlikely podiums.

There would be a million media questions. Rampant speculation on social media.

He had no answer, but everybody would want a sound bite. They didn't care what he thought or said; they merely wanted him to support their narrative.

At least Olivia hadn't wanted a sound bite, an easy answer. Although his final conversation with her had been frustrating, at some level, he was relieved she finally understood him.

But could he convince her to give him a second chance?

He didn't deserve it. And she'd already departed. They were an ocean apart. Was it worth the attempt?

He wondered if during the long flight, she felt any regret that they parted on bad terms. Would it be possible to repair their fledgling relationship? There was a Canadian race in a few weeks. How far was Montreal from New York City? Close enough for her to easily attend? Or could he schedule a stopover in New York? Or maybe she could come to Austin in the fall. Or Las Vegas. He'd put Bryson in charge of the logistics. He simply wasn't willing to give up on Olivia Keller yet. Not a chance.

He knew he needed sleep, but a comfortable position remained elusive. Racing while injured and exhausted would be disastrous.

Rest. Rest. He had to rest.

Thirty minutes later, still tormented by thoughts of Olivia, he gave up on sleep and rechecked his phone. He opened her text thread to reread it, hoping to glean some encouragement.

Shockingly, three dots flickered—was she texting him?! Right at this moment?! From the plane?

He jerked upward too quickly, which hurt. He sank back onto his pillow, staring anxiously at the screen.

The dots disappeared…and reappeared. His pulse accelerated every time she restarted but didn't complete the message. *Come on, come on*, he mentally urged. *Send me something. Talk to me*.

Finally, a text came through.

Hey, are you ok? I saw the wreck

He was surprised she'd seen footage and embarrassed that the crash was her introduction to his abilities as a driver, but it pleased him that she cared enough to reach out. That had to be a good sign, right?

I'm ok. A little sore

It looked awful. Terrifying. What happened?

Stupid mistake

Maybe this is dumb, but did our argument have anything to do with it?

Oh Lord, he couldn't let her feel guilty. Not for one second. There was no one to blame other than himself.

No, no. Not your fault. Really. I was careless

…but I'm so glad to hear from you. Did you land in NYC yet?

Nope. What will you do now?

Was she talking about the race? Or in general?

Try not to dwell on past mistakes. Fly by the seat of my pants. Make it work

Will you race tomorrow?

Probably, but I'm not talking about racing

There was a long pause. The dots flickered, again disappearing and reappearing. Did she not want to get into it by text? Was texting too impersonal? Should he call and try to catch her when her flight landed?

Her reply came through.

I get it

She made no promises, but her simple, compassionate words brought to the surface every experience and emotion from the previous week. His body flooded with the tantalizing and un-anticipated joy of meeting her, the profound and intimate connection they'd shared on the boat, the anguished frustration at his lie's impact, and, finally, the wreck's concussive jolt. He'd always kept strong feelings to himself, tightly regulated. Repressed, even. But in the darkness of his hotel room, bruised in body and soul, he couldn't exert his usual iron will. Couldn't regulate his emotions or keep them zipped up. Couldn't contain his desperate yearning for her. Didn't want to.

I wish you were still here. I'm sorry about everything. I want to make it right

He knew he'd have to wait for a response to that declaration. It was probably too honest. He hoped she'd be receptive to his apology someday, but he suspected it was too soon for her to forgive him. But he had to keep trying. It would be challenging. But he liked challenges.

She answered more quickly than expected.

You should get some sleep so you can race tomorrow

Okay. She didn't acknowledge his apology but still expressed concern for him. That was fine. It was enough for the time being. He could work with it.

Ok. You too—try to get some rest…not always easy on a plane

I'm glad you are okay

Olivia?

What?

God, how to condense the breadth of his feelings into believable texts. No more lies.

I don't want things to end between us

…I could never be ashamed of you

…whatever it takes, can we start again?

…don't answer now, just think about it

He didn't want an immediate response because he was too afraid she'd say no. He needed to live in hope at least until after the race.

I'll think about it

…Good night Nikos

Kalinixta, Olivia

Finally, he dropped off to sleep.

SUNDAY—RACE DAY

OLIVIA PAUSED IN the hotel hallway, poised to knock. Did she really want to do this? There were still seats available on the afternoon flight to New York. If she booked and left Monte Carlo immediately, she would still make it to the airport on time. She could…

No.

She'd made up her mind to see this thing through. The horror she'd felt watching footage of the wreck and Nikos's sincere late-night texts convinced her that, despite everything, she still cared for him. Deeply. As she'd never cared for any man before. Might even be falling in love with him.

He had been untruthful, yes. But unlike her father, she acknowledged the lie hadn't been at her expense. Far from it. In fact, she couldn't find fault with a single moment they'd spent together up until the confrontation on the patio. And given everything she'd come to understand about him, in a strange way, he had been honest with her about who he really was— just not about his job.

But if she gave him another chance, it would be on her terms.

She rapped sharply.

Aunt Kiki, wearing a plush hotel bathrobe, opened the door to a large suite. She beamed at Olivia. "Hello, my dear! I am so glad you accepted our offer! Come in, come in. Have some breakfast."

Olivia followed Kiki and settled near the breakfast trolley. "Help yourself! Klaus is still getting dressed."

"Are you sure you don't want to go to the race?" Olivia asked as she served herself some eggs.

"Oh my goodness, no! I've seen enough Grand Prix races to last me for a lifetime."

"I appreciate it," Olivia said. "I have the VIP pass, but I'd feel strange showing up alone. I don't know anyone or anything about racing."

"Klaus will be happy to provide any explanation you need. He will be so tickled to attend the race with a lovely young lady, he'll talk your ear off. And you'll be sitting directly across from the pit lane, so if you take advantage of that VIP pass, it will be easy to find your friend Nikos."

She had a knowing twinkle in her eye. Aunt Kiki might be ambivalent about racing but apparently enjoyed matchmaking.

Uncle Klaus emerged from the bedroom. Olivia's eyes widened. Gone was the urbane Swiss banker. In his place was a superfan.

The older man wore a shirt circa 1980, judging from its style, coupled with a pair of extraordinary leather lederhosen with the Segno Rosso logo and racing motifs embroidered on the suspenders and pockets. He topped off this notable ensemble with a Segno Rosso newsboy cap.

Aunt Kiki caught Olivia's eye with the universal expression of a woman questioning her partner's sartorial choices. "Klaus was quite the fan of an Austrian driver who raced in the early seventies," she explained with a wink before turning to her husband. "Klaus, dear, you really must wear a raincoat. It's going to be wet." She held up a blinding neon-yellow slicker.

"But won't that hide my clothes?"

Olivia suspected this might be Kiki's ulterior motive.

"We could trade so you could use my raincoat," Olivia suggested. "It's an official team jacket."

"Well! That's a different story!" Uncle Klaus accepted the

coat gleefully. In exchange, Olivia took his yellow slicker. She hadn't known what to wear to a Grand Prix race, so she'd opted for a short linen romper. She wore Nikos's cap, with her hair in two long braids. If she had to sit in the rain, at least it would keep some water out of her eyes. No matter what, she was going to look like a drowned rat before the day was done. Might as well wrap up her time in Monte Carlo as bedraggled as when she began.

She and Uncle Klaus made quite the pair.

At dinner the night before, the older gentleman had asked Olivia how she met his current favorite driver. Aunt Kiki quickly discerned that Olivia's interest in Nikos had nothing to do with racing and diplomatically turned the conversation. But after dinner, Kiki quietly offered to surrender her ticket, should Olivia wish to attend the race. Before Olivia could refuse, Maggie enthusiastically accepted on Olivia's behalf.

Olivia wanted to strangle her.

But as they said their final teary goodbye before the happy couple left for their honeymoon, Maggie whispered into Olivia's ear, "Go to the race. If you don't, you'll always wonder what could have been with Nikos."

Especially after seeing the awful wreck, Olivia knew her best friend was right.

So now Olivia was prepared to go to her first F1 race in unceasing rain, to watch her potential lover try to achieve his lifelong goal, accompanied by a grandfatherly man dressed like a mad elf. To say this was just another one of the trip's unexpected hijinks was the understatement of the decade.

Accessing the grandstand was a hike. As they walked, carried along by the crowd, Uncle Klaus kept up an incessant narration of circuit features and turns, histories, and suggested strategies. Olivia's head swam.

Since her arrival, the streets of Monte Carlo had been overrun with racing fans, the hype, the energy, the events, and the crowds increasing daily. Now the excitement had reached a fevered pitch. Every bunting-decorated balcony on every circuit-lining building groaned with people and free-flowing celebration. For the truly well-heeled fan, the harbor contained a flotilla of party yachts.

In the human wave that swarmed toward the circuit, tribal alliances to various teams were evident by each person's apparel. In addition to colorful T-shirts, Olivia witnessed painted faces, signs, and gigantic hats molded in the shape of race cars.

It was bonkers. She saw Nikos's image everywhere—on banners, posters, T-shirts, signs, and video monitors. One devoted woman wore a bikini top with his face on each breast. No wonder he fled to the sanctuary of the sea. Olivia remembered the look of sheer panic when they'd argued in public. Given the level of public fixation she now witnessed, his insistence on privacy was justified. His attitude made perfect sense.

When they finally reached their top-row seats, Uncle Klaus handed Olivia binoculars and pointed. "There you go! Take a look! I like being up high so we can see pit lane. You can see the Segno Rosso garages from here…"

"Is Nikos there now?"

Could she see him? Might he somehow spot her in the crowd? It wasn't very likely. She was one of roughly one zillion spectators.

"Right now, he will be at team headquarters, warming up, meeting with his engineers, preparing…"

"Okay. Is this where the race starts?"

"The starting grid is here, yes. You'll be able to see the beginning and end of the race. You'll love the podium ceremony…a member of the Monaco royal family presents the trophy!"

It was impossible not to get caught up in the excitement.

However, there was a maddening amount of time to kill before the Drivers' Parade. Olivia thought she might lose all sanity, anticipating the opportunity to witness Niko in his natural habitat.

"Tell me more about driving for Segno Rosso," she prompted Uncle Klaus. The man could talk. He would be an informative diversion. "Why are you a fan?"

"Well," the old man began, "your friend Nikos has incredible intuition. He makes his moves quickly—one minute, a competitor has the lead, the next moment, they are in his rearview mirror. In the blink of an eye!"

Incredible intuition. She'd experienced that.

"Is he truly a great driver compared to all the others?"

It was what the commentators on TV had implied. She never would have guessed it from his humble behavior.

"Yes, absolutely…" Uncle Klaus confirmed. "But that's just one reason I like him. My company is involved with asset management for the Segno Rosso Foundation. Without betraying confidentiality, Nikos Leonikaros does a lot of charitable work in the cities where he races. But at his insistence, there is no publicity around his initiatives."

"He didn't mention that."

Nor had these philanthropic initiatives appeared in any online media. Olivia had no idea how he had hidden something so significant, but she was beginning to understand why.

"His family is equally generous with their wealth," Klaus continued. "Did he tell you anything about them?"

Olivia shook her head. "Just that they live on a tiny private island. I assumed it was rustic, but now I'm guessing that's not the case."

Uncle Klaus had a good laugh.

"Quite the opposite!" He chuckled. "The Leonikaros family has spent immense amounts of money preserving the cultural heritage of Greece. Restoring architecture and artwork. Purchasing antiquities from private collections and donating them to the national museums. Incredible work. But all of it is done utterly behind the scenes. You'll never find the Leonikaros name on the wing of a building."

Damn. It was exactly what Olivia would do if she had that kind of money.

"They are an incredibly private family. No one visits their island unless by special invitation."

Nikos had mentioned joining his family for Easter dinner. Did he see her as someone special? Each new bit of information about Nikos sent her reeling, rethinking every conversation.

He had lied. True. But the picture of him that emerged was more complex. Based on everything she'd learned, Nikos was an incredibly private person from an equally private family. Yet he had decided to share some of himself with her. He wasn't ashamed of her after all.

But she had to keep Klaus talking. Otherwise she'd go out of her mind waiting for the race to start.

"Tell me how you and Kiki met…"

While Klaus waxed nostalgic on clandestine rendezvous at a Swiss boarding school, Olivia recalled her own grandparents. They met at a bar the night before her grandfather shipped out to Vietnam. They'd shared a few too many beers and a hot make-out session in the parking lot. Olivia suspected that it had gone beyond a few kisses. Three years' worth of letters and fifty-three years of marriage followed. Was that kind of love story possible? By focusing entirely on her parents' failed marriage, was she selling herself short, denying a beautiful possibility for her and Nikos? Maybe her parents hadn't managed an epic love story, but her grandparents had.

Abruptly, she realized she had a decision to make. What was the point of attending this race if Nikos didn't know she was still in Monaco? Should she text him? Would he look at his phone this close to race time? Would a text distract him? She couldn't live with herself if she contributed to another crash.

Nikos groaned as his trainer worked his recalcitrant shoulder. It felt like the woman was trying to detach his arm from its socket. He was still stiff from the wreck and would pay for it during the race. He took another long sip of water and fought to concentrate on the music pulsing in his AirPods, trying to lose himself in a laser-focused pre-race mindset.

All things considered, his headspace was good. That morning he'd been so keyed up, he was afraid he might puke. That hadn't happened since he was a nervous rookie. He couldn't risk dehydration. But now his agitation had coalesced into a good energy, an excited tension he hadn't felt in a long time. Starting from P10, this race would pose a significant challenge. He thrived on challenges.

When the punishing massage was done, it was time to make his way through the drizzle to the flatbed float used for the Drivers' Parade. He was thankful that all he had to do was stand with the others like a herd of cattle on a truck. Assuming he could lift his arm above his head, he'd wave. He hated the media circus, but the thousands of fans braving the crappy weather deserved acknowledgment. Hopefully, he'd put on a real show during the race and give the Segno Rosso faithful a treat. But until then... Nikos flipped up the hood of his sweatshirt, trying to remain incognito before he got onto the float.

Once it began, the parade's speed—or lack thereof—was torturous. As the float passed the last grandstand, Nikos gratefully lowered his arm and took one final glance at the appreciative crowd. And then, not quite trusting his eyes, he whipped around and leaned over the safety rail to see more clearly. His view was blocked, so he had to step and squeeze past the other drivers to get to the back of the truck. He squinted at the sea of faces receding into the distance...

He was seeing ghosts. How crazy was it that he imagined seeing Olivia's face in the crowd? He shook his head, annoyed at himself. He was being sloppy. How could he race when every unguarded thought strayed in her direction?

After donning his layers of racing gear, he had a few spare moments in his private room before going down to the garage.

He debated for a second, then picked up his phone. By sending her message, maybe he could exorcise his thoughts at least until the race was over.

Race starts soon. Wish me luck. Wish you were here

What time was it in New York? For someone who traveled the globe as much as he did, one would think he could keep time zones straight. He guessed Olivia was at least six hours behind. So, it was still early morning in the US. She probably wasn't awake yet, especially after a long day of travel. He imagined her sleeping in bed in her tiny apartment and, hopefully, dreaming of their time together. She'd see his text first thing when she awoke.

Look across pit lane

Shocked to receive a response, he nearly dropped the phone. It took him a long moment to process the message's implications. And then he thought his heart might stop. Completely cease beating.

Still, just to make sure he understood correctly…

Why? What will I see across pit lane?

A very wet American girl wearing a Segno Rosso hat

ARE YOU HERE????

His entire life balanced on her answer.

I am. Couldn't leave without seeing you again

He sprinted down the stairs and wove through the garage, navigating tools, tires, the car, and the crew.

"Hey, Nikos…" Someone started a question.

"Not now…"

He grabbed an open umbrella from one of the crew and burst out onto pit lane. All nonessential visitors had been cleared from the area in anticipation of the race's start. Nikos had an unobstructed view of the grandstand, but it contained a multitude of people.

He fumbled, trying to hold the stupid umbrella and text simultaneously.

Where are you?

Top row. Grandstand to your left. Look for neon yellow. Can't miss me

He scanned the scene wildly… *There!* It had to be her, top row, waving her arms in the air. She was standing on her seat; she stood higher than the rest of the crowd.

He dropped the umbrella and raised both arms above his head, forgetting all about the rain and the achy shoulder. Nikos signaled wildly, making no effort to hide the enormous grin on his face.

Seeing this atypical display of emotion from their favorite driver, the crowd roared, assuming it was for their benefit. Lenses clicked, countless phones popped up. But for once, he didn't care. All that mattered was that she was here.

Nikos lost sight of her in a sea of flailing arms. But she was at the race. For him. She hadn't left Monte Carlo. It changed everything.

This was a girl who, even when justifiably hurt and upset, had still decided that he was worth showing up for. No girlfriend had ever shown up for him like this.

I have to go now, but Olivia…

What?

He paused. He had so many emotions, so many big emotions. He had to articulate his feelings. Let them loose. Only then would he be able to concentrate on winning the race. One didn't win races or relationships by hesitating or being cautious. At least Nikos Leonikaros didn't.

I might be falling in love with you

His breath hitched, waiting.

Me, too. It happened fast. You like to go fast

…Good luck on your race

In that moment, Olivia was thankful for the rain. It disguised the tears that spilled over seeing Nikos, whole and unharmed. And she couldn't even begin to process his message. Was love possible? Her heart said yes.

He was sexy as hell, even in the rain. For once, he wasn't wearing sunglasses, and she imagined she could see the azure intensity of his eyes, even from so far away. As he waved his arms, the top half of his unzipped jumpsuit hung low, accentuating those narrow hips. He was so beautiful; he drew everyone's attention. But today it seemed he didn't care who watched. The crowd ate him up, but Olivia knew his greeting was entirely for her and her alone.

He disappeared back into the Segno Rosso garage. God, how soon could she see him, talk to him, touch him again? Somehow, they had to make things right between them. He was worth it.

The race preparations were moving at molasses speed. Would the event never start?

Finally, the grid cleared.

Uncle Klaus tapped her on the arm and pointed. "The cars are being released!"

Olivia used the binoculars to track Nikos as he slowly exited the garage and negotiated the narrow pit lane before steering his car to his designated spot on the grid. There were a lot of cars positioned in front of him, which did not bode well for his chances. Olivia wondered if Nikos didn't win, would he want to continue his racing career for another season? Did the prospect of a relationship with her change his perspective? She had no idea. But for today, for his sake, she hoped for a miraculous win.

Once the grid was set, the start was imminent. Olivia began anxiety-sweating in the borrowed rain slicker. What must Nikos be experiencing at this moment? Was he calm? Focused? Determined? Anxious? Or was he thinking about her? She did not want to be a distraction.

"They're calling for a safety car start because of the rain!"

Like baby ducks in a row, cars began to creep forward on the straightaway, carefully trailing the flashing lights.

At Klaus's suggestion, Olivia listened to the live feed between Nikos and his team.

After four laps parading behind the safety car, an announcement crackled through the airwaves: "Safety car, in this lap."

This was the signal they'd all been waiting for. When the safety car peeled off, the shrill pitch of twenty engines ratcheted. The tidy configuration of cars instantly scrambled. The race was on.

Watching the sheer speed of the vehicles and aggressiveness of the drivers was unlike anything she'd ever witnessed before. Olivia couldn't ignore the hypnotic energy that mesmerized her and pulled her in. With one eye on the stretch of pavement in front of her and one eye on a gigantic monitor, she realized that no video footage could do justice. No wonder Nikos considered their motorcycle adventures to be tame.

One had to admire how the drivers pushed their cars and each other, the hairsbreadth control when overtaking at blistering speeds, the exhilaration of watching cars jostle on impossible turns, and the heartbreak when a car spun out of contention.

As the laps progressed, Olivia couldn't visually follow his car as it made its way around and around the entire city circuit. The monitor showed the leader, cutting to video of other drivers when they experienced mishaps. Three drivers ahead of Nikos had already wrecked out of contention. The loudspeaker commentary switched between various languages. Listening to Nikos's somewhat cryptic messages with his engineer on the team audio feed was only marginally better.

"A lot of water for these tires."

"Copy that. Rain is expected to lighten up. Stay out."

Suddenly, the video monitor switched to an interior view of the famous curving Monte Carlo tunnel, with the camera focused on Nikos's car. Olivia's stomach dropped, unsure if this foretold a disastrous outcome.

"Watch!" Uncle Klaus yelped. "He might overtake!"

Sure enough, Nikos crept dangerously alongside another car in the eerie yellow light, the sounds of their engines amplified in the enclosed space. Maybe it was better that Olivia hadn't seen every risky move he made. It was terrifying.

"Now! Send it!" Uncle Klaus cried.

Olivia gripped the old man's arm and held her breath. Exiting the tunnel, Nikos prevailed and darted deep into the exit curve, forcing the other car out. Segno Rosso fans screamed their approval of the daring move.

Five cars remained in front of him. Olivia willed Nikos on, willed him to use every ounce of his considerable talent to seize a victory. Just, please, God, not to wreck while doing it. Her heart couldn't take it.

Lap after lap, the race progressed. The conversation between Nikos and his engineer remained calm. Despite Olivia's anxiety, he apparently took it all in stride. This was the driver the motorsports commentators had described. She was thrilled to see him in action.

Across from the grandstand, drivers took turns boxing in pit lane with incomprehensible speed. They zipped in and out, seemingly without stopping. Suddenly, one car was delayed. The monitor cut to coverage of a crew unexpectedly struggling to remove a stuck front tire. Nikos was approaching the entrance, having been instructed to make his stop.

"Nikos. P5 is delayed in the box. Possibility to overtake."

"Keep me posted. Approaching pit lane entrance."

"P5 is still delayed. Do not box. You are cleared to overtake if you can pick up the pace. Push it. You can overtake, but it's going to be close."

"Copy. Accelerating."

Nikos's car ran parallel to the delayed car as it attempted to exit pit lane before he could catch up. If he could just gain a bit more speed…

Nikos surged ahead, narrowly cutting in front of the other car as it reentered the course. The crowd roared. Nikos had gained another position.

Four cars were between him and a win. Was there enough time remaining in the race? Was the impossible possible? Olivia was all in, pulling for him to succeed.

One of the leaders sustained damage to a front wing and limped through the tunnel, sparks flying. Three more places to grab the win.

"Nikos. Juan-Carlos in P3 is working to overtake Yakimoto in P2, with a two-second gap. You have a five-second gap."

"Copy."

With only seven laps to go, Nikos's teammate pinched the P2 car and then snuck by with a risky move that sent it swerving over a painted crosswalk. The car spun and bounced roughly over a curb, damaging the front wing. White smoke shot out of the back, and the car stalled. Nikos negotiated the immobile car and accelerated out of the turn. Now only his teammate and one other car—driven by his rival, Mancinelli—were ahead.

"If the Segno Rosso cars can hold out, your young man and his teammate will be on the podium!" Uncle Klaus exclaimed. "That would be a strong team finish!"

But would it be enough? Olivia guessed Nikos wouldn't be content to take second or third place. He needed to win. But as much as she wanted a victory, she dreaded a reckless attempt.

"Nikos. Juan-Carlos will drop back for you to overtake. You are at a two-second gap."

"Hold back? No, I don't want him to cede me a position. What is his gap?"

"Three seconds."

"Tell him to go for it. I'll pick up my pace, and we'll see who wins."

"That's an interesting approach," Uncle Klaus worried. "They are as likely to take each other out and not finish the race at all. Teams should work together."

"I don't think Nikos will want to set a record because his teammate allowed him to pass. He'll want to earn it himself."

Could he do it?

Nikos pushed hard, gaining on the two cars in front of him. His teammate moved erratically, slowing both vehicles ahead of Nikos.

"Nikos. A half second back. Push to overtake."

"Copy that. It's time."

The video monitor remained locked on the three cars vying for the lead. The commentators went bananas, crying out in multiple languages as they narrated the action.

And then, as if in slow motion, Olivia's worst fears were realized. The two lead cars slowed into a tight turn. On the twisting exit, while fighting for position, one car clipped the rear tire of the other. The seemingly insignificant contact triggered a split-second chain reaction. Nikos's teammate's car shot into the air, rolled, and came to rest in a million pieces against the barrier. From the driver's angry gestures, he had obviously survived the wreck. Meanwhile, Mancinelli's car was forced to jerk sideways to avoid the debris. Unaware and in hot pursuit, Nikos roared around the blind corner just as his slowed rival smashed against a barrier. Swerving to avoid the stopped car, Nikos spun with almost balletic grace, his car pirouetting past his damaged competitor and coming to rest facing the wrong direction, one back wheel on the raised curb.

Olivia stopped breathing. Was this how Nikos's Monaco dream would die? Would another car come around the turn and slam into him? Dear God, she couldn't witness another crash.

Fortunately, the announcers stated that a virtual safety car had been declared. Flashing yellow lights warned approaching drivers of the wreckage field.

"There's no passing under a yellow flag," Uncle Kraus exclaimed. "He'll be in first position if he can get straightened out!"

In the narrow corner, with barriers, curbs, and detritus from the other cars, Olivia assumed there was no way for Nikos to turn around in time—if even his vehicle was drivable. There was simply no room to maneuver on the narrowest part of the circuit.

Nikos's car jerked in reverse and then forward. It was functional. He desperately attempted to rotate in the right direction.

Back and forth, back and forth. It was worse than watching a new driver learn to parallel park. Just as the remainder of the field bore down on the corner, Nikos's car leapt forward, headed in the right direction. Nikos took command and eased around the next curve. He had established himself in first position.

"He did it!" Olivia screamed, along with every other Segno Rosso fan.

The crowd collectively held its breath as the field drove two more laps under the yellow flag. Then, for the final two laps, the flag was lifted. Nikos shot forward decisively.

No one knew the Monaco circuit like Nikos Leonikaros. With a considerable lead, smoothly, effortlessly, he coaxed his car through every chicane with a lover's touch. He was in a world of his own, the other cars far behind. His final, flawless laps clinched the victory, icing on the cake.

The checkered flag appeared. As Nikos sailed down the final straightaway, Olivia's pulse raced as fast as the speedometer.

When he shot over the finish line, the crowd's roar was so deafening that it drowned out the shrieking engines of the trailing cars. Olivia leapt up and down, ecstatically hugging Uncle Klaus and anyone else in the immediate vicinity. The entire grandstand rocked and swayed with uncontained rapture.

Over the team audio, she could hear Nikos's jubilant "Yes! Yes!" The gigantic image on the video monitor zoomed in on him in the cockpit of his car. He pumped his fist in the air, his visor flipped up to reveal his brilliant eyes.

The sun came out and bathed the scene in gold. It was a fairy tale. A storybook ending. And she was a part of it.

Olivia was crying. She couldn't help it. She heaved gigantic sobs of relief. Uncle Klaus was not as incoherent.

"Your VIP pass!" Uncle Klaus hollered into her ear. "We need to get you down there! Right now! Go! Go!"

He grabbed her by the hand and, with surprising strength and nimbleness, steered them down through the rows of seats toward the grandstand exit. Where crowds blocked the steps, he hauled himself and Olivia up and over the seats. Clearly, life in the Swiss Alps had rendered the old man part mountain goat.

Trying not to stumble as she was tugged along, Olivia watched on the monitor as Nikos concluded his celebratory lap with a spectacular three-hundred-sixty-degree wheel-shred-ding, smoke-inducing doughnut spin at the end of the straight-away. The crowd, already euphoric, lost all control. She was engulfed in a pulsating human wave. People surged toward the track, determined to share their hero's glory.

On the screen, Nikos cruised into the special *parc fermé* area next to a signboard showing a large number one with his name. He climbed out, replaced the wheel, removed his helmet, and stood jubilant atop his car. Someone in the seats above tossed him a Greek flag. He snatched it out of the air and waved it over his head, triumphant. He was like a Greek god come to life. Olivia could hardly bear it; she was so damn proud of him.

"Come on, come on!" Uncle Klaus urged.

The entire Segno Rosso team mobbed the circuit fence, chanting Nikos's name.

When they reached the security entrance, Olivia yanked her pass from beneath the neckline of her linen romper. Cleared to enter, she was about to shove her way into the crowd…but first, she turned and gave Uncle Klaus a grateful hug.

"Thank you! For everything," she murmured. "Kiki is a lucky lady."

The old man blushed and nudged Olivia forward. "Go get him, girl!"

She turned toward the fence that separated everyone from Nikos. A sea of people stood between her and the barrier. How was she going to get through and avoid being crushed? But she told herself if she could handle a NYC subway platform at rush hour, she could handle a scrum of race fans. Nikos was worth it.

She placed a hand on a random shoulder and, using it for support, jumped up, trying to see over the heads in front of her.

Not surprisingly, Nikos's bodyguard, Aleko, stood at the front fence. He faced the crowd, scanning faces. Would he help?

She jumped again. This time, the old man spotted her.

Like a bull elephant, he began to muscle his way to her. She wriggled and squirmed between bodies, popping up every few steps to make sure their paths would intersect. Finally, the man thrust a meat-hook hand toward her, and she seized it. Her progress through the crowd became much easier with a human plow.

Near the front of the fence, Nikos had thrown his arms wide and, with absolute trust, dropped backward into celebratory hands. Borne aloft by his ecstatic team, they passed him overhead.

"Nikos!" Olivia vainly screamed his name. How could he hear her? How would he discern her voice from all the others? How could she get his attention? Yes, she would definitely see him later, but she wanted to be with him *now*, now in his moment of triumph.

"Nikos!"

Beside her, Aleko dropped down and patted his knee. Understanding the invitation, Olivia placed a hand on the old man's shoulder for balance and stood tall on his thigh. She screamed Nikos's name again. He twisted around at the sound of her voice.

He surveyed the crowd, searching.

Finally, their eyes locked, and to her, everything else—the chaos, the crowd, the noise—fell instantly silent.

Nikos's face split into a gigantic smile; Olivia beamed approvingly back at him.

Laughing, Nikos coached the crowd to surf him in Olivia's direction. When they dropped him next to her, no force in the world could have kept them apart. Jostled by the multitude, their bodies collided hard.

Everyone was so loud that he had to place his mouth to her ear to be heard. She could feel his breath, hot and quick.

"You're here," he gasped. "I can't believe you're here. God, Olivia, I was afraid I'd never see you again. I'm sorry—I'm sorry for everything. I've been selfish. I've been stupid."

"Stop. Don't apologize," she reassured him, her arms around his neck, pulling him closer so he might hear her reply. "I understand. And I'm sorry, too. I've been afraid. Afraid I wasn't good enough for you. Afraid to trust you, that you would be there for me."

"Please believe me," he insisted. "I'll always be there for you."

"Only if I can be there for you, too. I'm so proud of you. I liked you as a baker, I like you even more as an F1 driver. But it's all about who you are, Nikos, just yourself. That's what matters to me."

He replied with a devouring kiss.

God, the taste of her. He'd been so afraid he'd never kiss her like this again. The force of their encounter knocked his hat from her head—no doubt someone would grab it as a souvenir. Nikos didn't care. He couldn't get close enough; he needed to feel the sensation of her entire body pressed against his. He felt almost feral. Beyond words. Sheer adrenaline-fueled desire.

Cupping his hands just under the fluttery edges of her shorts, on that delectable stretch of bare skin where her ass met the tops of her thighs, he hoisted her up, bearing her weight. She wrapped those gorgeous legs around his hips, locked her ankles, and twisted her fingers through his hair. She consumed his whole being. Could she feel how hard he was for her underneath his racing jumpsuit? He wanted to escape the crowd and have her up against the nearest wall, to be inside of her, to cause her to moan, and to hear the sound of his name in her mouth. Damn, he never wanted to stop kissing her.

Everyone around them roared at their favorite driver, so typically emotionless, now passionately embracing a beautiful woman. A zillion camera lenses clicked. He didn't care. He was vaguely aware of Aleko trying to hold back the crowd. Someone soaked them with a spray of celebratory champagne, which brought Nikos back to some semblance of consciousness and control.

"Champagne and cookies?" He pulled back from the kiss just enough to catch her hazel gaze. He needed to memorize every freckle, every eyelash.

"The perfect combination," she murmured, kissing him again. "So sweet together."

Soon, he would have to join the imminent podium celebration and accept a trophy from the prince of Monaco, as his family watched nearby. He would have to answer a thousand questions in the mandatory post-race press conference. There would be a race debrief. He couldn't escape those obligations, and honestly, after his success, he didn't mind. It was all part of savoring the victory.

But he'd come so close to losing Olivia. Right now, he needed just a few more moments to indulge in her, indulge in the fact that she had chosen to stay in Monte Carlo for him, even though he didn't deserve it. He needed to convey what her trust meant to him, how he suspected she had become as essential to him as the air he breathed. An idea began to form.

He placed her solidly back on the ground. She looked at him expectantly. Fondly. He always wanted to be the focus of that gaze.

"Come on."

He compelled them both through the crush.

"Where are we going?" She laughingly kept pace, clinging tightly. He loved the sensation of her hand in his; he wanted her at his side, grasping his hand, hanging on to him, forever.

"Trust me," he called over his shoulder. Curious race fans let them pass, eager to witness the unexpected spectacle of a joyful Nikos Leonikaros in their midst.

Finally, the unmistakable blue of the harbor yawned ahead.

Olivia paused, guessing his plan when they arrived at the very end of the pavement. The water lapped enticingly below, and people on the nearby yachts whooped encouragingly.

Nikos smiled wickedly at her.

"Oh my God, Nikos, you don't mean to…"

"I do." He turned, catching both her hands in his and explaining, "It's a tradition in Monte Carlo whenever there is something truly worth celebrating…"

"You go ahead and celebrate, then." She smiled. "This is your victory. I'm proud of you. You won. You got your record."

"I'm not celebrating any racing wins." He leaned closer to whisper in her ear. He felt the quick, warm intake of her breath. He kissed her on her delicious neck. "I'm celebrating that you came back, that you forgave me. I'm celebrating us. What I think we can be together."

He dipped his chin and raised one eyebrow in invitation. "Are you with me?"

She tilted her head but smiled gamely at him. "I am already soaking wet…"

He winked before catapulting himself airborne off the edge, doing a full flip and splashing into the sea. He bobbed to the surface and shook the water out of his hair. Olivia stepped, laughing, to the edge.

Thousands of voices spontaneously chanted in unison, "Jump! Jump! Jump!"

"Are you sure about this?" she asked.

He was. And she needed to know it.

"I love you, Olivia Keller!" he yelled loudly enough for all of Monaco to hear.

She beamed at him.

"You're crazy, but I love you, too, Nikos Leonikaros! So, I guess that means…" She took a running start, covered her face, and leapt, plunging into the water at his side.

The fans on land and the spectators on the yachts screamed their approval.

She came up sputtering. Awkwardly paddling, legs tangling, gulping sea water, he kissed her again.

The water around Olivia and Nikos churned. They were

in full view of countless other people, but no one else could hear him.

"Olivia, I want you. So badly. Please. We can stay on the big yacht tonight and be in Spain tomorrow morning to see the sun come up. And I have the plane. I can fly you back to New York whenever you need to go, but promise me we'll be together again soon. After Spain, I'll be at team headquarters in Italy. I'm going to Montreal soon…and then a bunch of other races. I'll be in the US for Austin and Las Vegas in the fall. I'll get you a schedule. I can fly you to any of them. Whatever you need. Whenever you want. When I have a break, I'll come to New York. And when my contract is up, we can go anywhere you want. Just please say we can be together."

He was babbling, loopy tired from the race.

Olivia paddled closer and shushed him with a gentle finger on his lips. "Nikos. We'll figure it out as we go along. Fly by the seat of our pants. All that matters is that we trust each other and will be together. I promise we will be."

That was all he needed to hear.

Now they just needed to figure out how to get out of the harbor.

EPILOGUE—ONE YEAR LATER

OLIVIA STEPPED OUT of the shower and brushed back her wet hair. She pulled on a thick white robe that Nikos had sent her from one of the hotels he'd stayed in over the past year on the few occasions they'd been apart.

Not surprisingly, she found him relaxing in his usual spot on the comfy sectional sofa on the superyacht's main bedroom balcony overlooking the ocean, watching one of his favorite movies. Their puppy, Eros, lay curled up beside him. Olivia settled down between Nikos's legs and leaned back.

"I'll bet the red car wins," she commented. "Or at least it did the last ten times you watched this movie."

He nipped her earlobe. "Shush. I like seeing all the old-school cars in this movie."

She leaned back, contentedly, and closed her eyes. "What time will we dock in Monte Carlo tomorrow?"

"In time to see the sun come up."

Olivia smiled. "Perfect. That will be spectacular. While we are there, I want to take Mags and Stefano out from Beaulieu-sur-Mer on the small boat."

"That's fine," Nikos agreed. He interlaced his fingers with hers. "But I also want the two of us to go out alone."

"Oh, absolutely." Olivia grinned, remembering the intimate Mediterranean adventure that started it all. "I like that plan."

She lifted his hand, kissed it, then inspected it closely. "I can't believe you already got a wedding band with my first initial tattooed on your finger. We aren't getting married until October. You've got three more months yet."

"I was in Italy at the tattoo shop to add my Austin podium, so I thought I'd get the ring tattoo while I was there…"

Olivia laughed, but his unwavering commitment warmed her to the core. "You'll be back in Italy before the wedding. You could have waited."

He shrugged. "Yeah, I'll probably go back twice more before October. But I'm not going to change my mind about getting married. Not going to change my mind about the girl. So, I got the tattoo while I was there."

Nikos had accepted a consulting position with Segno Rosso. He regularly visited their Italian headquarters and test track to refine developments on the prototype cars and work with younger drivers. After she'd resigned from her old job, Olivia was free to travel with him and to visit Maggie in Switzerland to work on a project close to all their hearts.

"I must admit, this tattoo is my favorite…" Olivia turned his hand over to reveal the small *M2B* tattooed on the inside of his wrist. For their first Christmas together, he had given Olivia a gold necklace with the same code in diamonds. "You are the embodiment of my middle school–notebook doodles. I heart Nikos."

Nikos nuzzled his face in her damp hair. "I heart Olivia. I heart how she smells. I heart her wearing a bathrobe."

She couldn't help it. Olivia cracked up. "You weirdo. Most guys would think their fiancée looks hot in a bathing suit…"

"You do."

"…or sexy lingerie."

"Absolutely sexy."

"…or a gorgeous dress."

"Stunning."

"But a bathrobe? I look like the Stay Puft Marshmallow Man's girlfriend."

"Hey, I've kept up my training, so don't call me a marshmallow. And it isn't how you look in a bathrobe, you goof," he explained as his hand slid underneath the garment in question. "It's the ease of access that I appreciate."

"Ah," Olivia murmured. "I begin to understand."

He proceeded to do something very intriguing with his fingers that further confirmed his point.

Just when things were really getting interesting, Nikos's phone buzzed. His private phone.

"Ugh," Olivia moaned. "Bad timing. Bad, bad timing."

"Hold that thought," Nikos muttered into her ear, then turned his attention to the phone. "Ya?"

It was Bryson.

"It's ready? Great, can't wait to see it. Yeah, we'll watch it right now."

He put the phone down, and Olivia turned to Nikos curiously.

"He's got the first cut done?"

"Yes…let me find the clicker…"

They clambered over one another, shifting around, digging under the cushions for the always elusive device.

Nikos found it and eagerly navigated to the new content Bryson had produced.

The video opened with a shot of a low-slung race car speeding along a road twisting through rugged mountains, along a coastal vista. The scene cut to the car screaming past the iconic Hollywood sign, the letters illuminating one at a time as it passed.

"Oh, that's a nice touch," Olivia murmured.

The camera angle changed to capture the car zooming under a blue-sky canopy lined with palms. Finally, it stopped in front of the Santa Monica Pier.

The words *Welcome to the Los Angeles Grand Prix* appeared, accompanied by a voiceover Nikos had recorded a month earlier. He invited investors to participate in an exciting new project, with seed money from Leonikaros Racing, that would expand Formula 1 in the United States. In addition to an LA circuit, the initiative would create driving academies in three other US cities where races were held. Scholarships would be available to encourage both boys and girls to take up the sport.

"This is really good," Nikos confirmed. "I think the investors are going to be impressed."

"It's so exciting to see it coming together," Olivia agreed.

"It is happening because you and my sister are a formidable management team, plus our Swiss gurus on financials…"

"And what about you?" Olivia teased. "Do you think you are just the pretty face of Leonikaros Racing…?"

"Everybody has a role." Nikos laughed.

"Seriously, though," Olivia said, "Nikos, this is awesome. I'm so proud of you for pushing for this dream. It was your idea and your drive that pulled it all together. It's incredible."

He didn't respond, but she could tell her compliment pleased him. She knew the transition from being a driver hadn't been as difficult as he'd feared, but there were still times he missed the sheer adrenaline of competing at the highest level. But their new project would keep him connected and allow him to expand the sport he loved. And if he needed speed-driven adrenaline, he always had the motorcycle.

"Did you set the date for the initial investors meeting in New York?" Nikos asked.

"Yep, it will be in early October, then we can fly back to Pittsburgh for the wedding. My mother has a full itinerary planned. We are going to be busy every day through Thanksgiving. Then we can head over to Europe for Christmas with Mags and Stefano. Spend New Year's in Greece with your family. And then…"

"Our honeymoon at last." He squeezed her enthusiastically.

"Someplace on the beach…" Olivia sighed. Nikos was in charge of planning the honeymoon. He was keeping the details a surprise, but Olivia knew it included sun and salt water. "Give me a hint."

"Nope." He kissed her. His hand drifted back under her robe.

"Please…"

"Okay, just a few little hints," he conceded as his fingers traced lazy circles over her skin. "It will involve complete privacy and a warm ocean. We won't have to wear bathing suits when we swim or do anything else we like to do outside…"

"I do enjoy activities outside without bathing suits…" Olivia teased.

"I wonder what you have in mind…?"

"Use your imagination."

Nikos's grin left little doubt that he knew exactly what she liked to do outside.

Thinking of their wedding and honeymoon plans, Olivia sighed contentedly. "Nikos, do you know your mom already has everyone in your family baking cookies for the reception? They will ship them to my mom for the cookie table. There will be a billion cookies."

"I did hear about that. I'm making the *kourabiedes*."

He had taken up baking with a passion. The man did nothing halfway.

Olivia laughed. "You know, traditionally it isn't the groom who does the baking."

"I need to make sure there are cookies at our wedding that don't contain peanut butter," he insisted. "Also, if it hadn't been for cookies, we wouldn't be together now."

And that was the last thing he said to Olivia for quite some time because he was too busy proving to her how sweet life could be.

* * * * *

Bridesmaid's Fast-Track Fling
is Elle Brown's debut title for Harlequin.
Look out for more books from Elle Brown,
coming soon!

MILLS & BOON ®

Coming next month

FOR BUSINESS... OR PLEASURE
Joss Wood

'Everybody loses their breath when they first walk onto the veranda.'

Instant recognition stiffened her spine and caused her heart to flutter, then shudder. That voice...deeper, darker, more compelling, it was the same one that painted compliments on her skin, whispered dirty, delightful suggestions against her lips. Calla felt her knees weaken and clenched her fists, telling herself she couldn't pass out, couldn't gasp or sway or act like a fool.

What was she supposed to do? Say?

Biting down hard on her lip, she half turned and, as casually as possible, slipped her Audrey Hepburn glasses onto her face, hoping the gesture would give her a couple of seconds to gather her composure. But how was it that her sexy bartender was standing on the terrace of Judah Reyes's luxury St Croix house...

Unless...no! Unless he was the owner, the CEO...

No. Way.

Continue reading

FOR BUSINESS... OR PLEASURE
Joss Wood

Available next month
millsandboon.co.uk

COMING SOON!

We really hope you enjoyed reading this book.
If you're looking for more romance
be sure to head to the shops when
new books are available on

Thursday 26th February

To see which titles are coming soon, please visit

millsandboon.co.uk/nextmonth

MILLS & BOON

LET'S TALK

Romance

For exclusive extracts, competitions and special offers, find us online:

f MillsandBoon

X @MillsandBoon

o @MillsandBoonUK

d @MillsandBoonUK

Get in touch on 01413 063 232